Emma Cooper is a former teaching assistant, who lives in Shropshire with her partner and four children. She spends her spare time writing novels, drinking wine and watching box-sets with her partner of twenty-four years, who still makes her smile every day.

Emma has always wanted to be a writer – ever since childhood, she's been inventing characters (her favourite being her imaginary friend 'Boot') and is thrilled that she now gets to use this imagination to bring to life all of her creations.

Praise for *The Songs of Us*

'Quirky, clever and original, this will break your heart, but put it back together again' Katie Fforde

'A warm and touching novel about love and loss, and the healing power of family' *Woman and Home*

'Poignant and beautifully written' *Woman*

'[A] sweet, moving debut' *Good Housekeeping*

'This is a very special book indeed: funny, powerful, heart-wrenching and so poignant. I have laughed and cried and cried . . . it reminded me to hold my family close and tell each of them how much I love them' Jo Thomas

'*The Songs of Us* is an emotional rollercoaster of a book that made me laugh and cry in equal measures. A tragically beautiful story of love and loss, family and hope. Emma Cooper has been swiftly added to my list of authors to read'

Fiona Harper

Also by Emma Cooper

The Songs of Us

EMMA COOPER

First published in Ebook in 2019 by Headline Review
An imprint of HEADLINE PUBLISHING GROUP

First published in paperback in 2020 by Headline Review
An imprint of HEADLINE PUBLISHING GROUP

1

Cataloguing in Publication Data is available from the British Library

ISBN 978 1 4722 6502 9

Typeset in Garamond MT by Palimpsest Book Production Limited,
Falkirk, Stirlingshire

Printed and bound in Great Britain by Clays Ltd, Elcograf S.p.A.

Headline's policy is to use papers that are natural, renewable and recyclable products and made from wood grown in sustainable forests. The logging and manufacturing processes are expected to conform to the environmental regulations of the country of origin.

HEADLINE PUBLISHING GROUP
An Hachette UK Company
Carmelite House
50 Victoria Embankment
London EC4Y 0DZ

www.headline.co.uk
www.hachette.co.uk

For Russell . . .
who always shows me there
is light at the end of the tunnel

'Life is not about what you get, but what is taken from you. It's in the things we lose that we discover what we most treasure.'

– Adriana Trigiani – *The Shoemaker's Wife*

AUTUMN

Chapter One

Sophie

At the beginning of our life, we see things differently. As a small child, I would look at the world and it was innocent. I could see the smile on my mother's face as she sang to me, see the creases in her skin as she smiled, see the love in her eyes as she kissed me goodnight. The scene before me had been clear and pure, but as we get older the image changes: like a hologram, you tilt the scene one way and you see a woman smiling; tilt it the other way and she is crying.

My damp feet pad into the hotel bedroom; the reflection in the mirror catches my attention and my mum stares back at me. It's happening a lot lately – the older I get, the more I look like her. I trace the shape of my face with my finger: the same shaped face, the same point at the tip of the chin, the same dimples either side of my mouth.

I know how I must have seemed to everyone when she died. Cold and indifferent. Someone at the trial said that my heart must have been made of stone; after all, how can someone not attend their mother's funeral? How could I not scream and shout, or cheer and whoop when her killer was put behind bars? I did cry, though. I did scream and shout, but then, after I hit the darkest waters in the deepest depths of grief, I suddenly realised that he was winning: he was still hurting us. So, I stopped. I closed the door on the what-ifs and the whys and instead just accepted that it was: that's how I am still so close to Helen; that's how I still call her my sister.

My back turns on the mirror; I don't have time for this today. I have to be the woman that I have worked so hard to become, who no longer speaks with the Welsh accent of her childhood, who can walk into a company and exploit its faults; who lives a life without close friends because they take up too much time.

I slip into my underwear, the silk camisole sliding over my pale skin: the first layer of the armour. The white blouse eases off the hanger, expensive material eradicating my memories of cheap, supermarket-bought school shirts, sharp creases protecting my bare shoulders from the images of being teased at school; the buttons fastening firmly across my chest, enclosing my heart. The stockings glide over my legs: legs that walked me into the school that I hated, legs that were grazed as I tried to pull him off her. I step into the winter-white pencil skirt – zipping myself in – before sliding my feet into shoes that my mother would only have ever dreamed of, the heels like daggers, their soles the colour of blood.

I cover my freckles with concealer, cover my eyelashes with heavy mascara and apply a deep crimson lipstick. With each subtle layer, my armour becomes tougher; the natural waves of my hair are straightened and sprayed, my natural scent covered in a mist of perfume that I haven't acquired by rubbing my wrist on the inside of a magazine advertisement.

Before I leave the room, I reach for my calf-length yellow coat – a coat my teenage self would have shied away from; the colour too bold, the style too confrontational. I shrug on this final piece of my defence and turn back towards the mirror: my mother's reflection is gone.

My heels clip along Pennsylvania Avenue just west of the White House, my reflection in the towering buildings showing a confident woman in charge of her destiny. I stop and look up at the Greenlight regional office, but I don't enter the building. I'm here just to get a feel for the city, to visit Greenlight's competitors and to see what we're up against.

I never set out to do this job; I just fell into it. Funny phrase, 'fell into it'. How do we just fall into something? We don't fall: we don't tumble like a gymnast with a CV in our hands; we don't jump off the end of a cliff and land in the cradled arms of an interviewer. We don't 'fall' in love; we just find ourselves part of something that we didn't know we were missing from in the first place.

My job found me, I suppose. I have always been good at maths, always been able to analyse problems and see a solution. It was a natural path for me to go into accounting. It suited me; I liked the solitary, irrefutable answers it gave me, until the small company that I worked for after university gave me the wrong answers. Answers that revealed money being hidden in the private accounts of my employer. After I exposed this, I was approached by the agency – Sandwell Incorporated. It felt strange to be sought after, to have somebody asking me to work for them, and at first, I didn't think I could do it, but I soon found out that I could. I could work up to eighteen hours a day, analyse their data and find a gap, a thread; a hook to make it easy for us to help them – or if not, for us to make them an offer they couldn't refuse.

The afternoon is spent in meetings with other small loan firms. I ask difficult questions, find holes in their processes, manipulate conversations with smiles and understanding nods.

My throat is dry and my work for the day is done, so I find a café and take a seat outside, grateful to be breathing in the fresh air after an afternoon in stuffy offices. I'm confident our new software is a strong enough tool for us to merge with Greenlight. It will put them head and shoulders above their competitors, and if they fight us, I know we will win.

Unfamiliar accents and unfamiliar smells surround me. I watch the couple on the opposite table; they aren't speaking a word to each other. She slurps her soup as he sits, devouring a giant pretzel, which he intermittently dips into sauce. They look past each other, that place just above the shoulder where life carries on even if you can't quite see it. How odd that they should both be watching life pass them by, but from opposing views. The man begins to cough – a rogue piece of pretzel, lodged where it shouldn't be. His companion is out of her chair, passing him water, rubbing his back, wiping away the tears that have formed around his eyes. The coughing stops: he pats her hand; she strokes his face and then sits back down, the world beyond their shoulders continuing.

I watch the concern on her face; the gratitude and love on his.

Nobody knows where I am.

This thought startles me. I haven't spoken to Helen for weeks; I've told work that I'm having an informal visit to our next project – the details of which are, at this moment, still very much under wraps. A few people know I'm in DC, but other than that, nobody knows that I'm here, sitting outside a restaurant; invisible to the lives around me just as I am invisible to the lives back home.

What if a photographer were to pass by this café today and take a photo – the scene frozen: not a sound, not a blink, not a breath? The woman leaning towards her soup; the man with the pretzel halfway to his face; a waitress looking out of the corner of her eyes at a blond businessman drinking beer and laughing loudly; the group of women on the pavement, smart shopping bags in mid-swing, their heads thrown back in laughter . . . and me. A thirty-year-old English woman in a stylish white suit, sitting still with an almost cold cup of coffee in front of her. A click, a close of the shutter, the image captured as an advert for the café, perhaps? Perhaps the photographer would see the English woman in the centre of the frame and decide to take her out of it; she doesn't quite fit there. He crops the photo, cutting the scene in two, then drags the halves back together: the woman is gone. He sips his coffee, smiles at the screen at a job well done, pleased with the result: it's as if she was never there at all.

It is starting to rain. The colours that surround me are drenched in grey, as though the photographer decided on a black-and-white filter. People scurry away, their plates are discarded, their chairs scrape back, their glasses are carried inside; but I remain still, watching the chaos. I pull on my yellow raincoat and open my green umbrella. If the photographer had stayed, he would have seen the English woman sitting in the middle of the scene . . . the yellow of her coat and the green of her umbrella no longer invisible. Because across the road, through the black-and-white filter, a man is looking straight at me.

Chapter Two

Samuel

'Ah, feck it!' I've had the day from hell already and now, to top it off, the heavens have just opened. The rain here is different from home – the rain in Northern Ireland doesn't hold the dust and chemicals like the rain in the city; the rain here almost feels toxic.

From the corner of my eye, I see a flash of yellow. There is a woman sitting outside a café in a yellow coat. My feet stop moving and I find myself staring at her. All around her there is movement – people holding newspapers above their heads, pushing back chairs and heading inside for shelter – but the woman is motionless, the yellow of her raincoat refusing to be muted, no matter how much the grey rain sweeps across the city.

'Move it!' An angry man, whose voice seems double the size of his frail body, yells at me. I blink, apologise, and begin to take another step, but then a burst of Irish green flickers in my peripheral vision as the woman outside the café opens her umbrella, stopping my feet again. I stand still while people saturated in the greys and blacks of the storm rush around me as they try to escape the sudden downpour, hoods hastily covering new highlights and hair gel.

She tilts the green umbrella and she is covered from my view; it twirls from one side to another, like a scene from a musical, her actions obscured behind it. She stands. Fat raindrops slide down from the umbrella and on to her white high-heels. Thunder rumbles – dark and threatening – before lightning slices open the sky: a battle of good and evil, of dark and light, of fate and serendipity. The traffic pauses, and I dash between the headlights as furious windscreen wipers clear the view and lull the angry horns. I don't know the woman behind the umbrella, don't really know why I'm crossing the road – one of those moments when you end up at a destination and can't remember how you got there – but here I am, and so is she.

Beneath the umbrella I can see that her heel is trapped in a crack in the pavement. That is the first thing I really see of this woman: a slim leg and a high heel. The heel twists just as I begin to offer my help, then snaps itself free, the point of the shoe connecting with a sharp kick towards my leg. I barely flinch; I'm an ex rugby player so I'm used to worse things than a stiletto to the ankle.

'I'm so sorry! Are you OK?' I register the English accent as she crouches down, the green umbrella discarded as her white skirt rides up her thigh – all business, peeking out from beneath the girlish coat. The rain drips from her blond hair as she hovers, unsure what to do now she is faced with my suited and booted trouser leg. She is stuck between what I think had been an automatic response, like the way you would attend to a child's grazed knee, but instead, is left with the uncomfortable situation of how to deal with a strange man's trouser leg. Her eyes look up at me, these golden eyes that are the strangest colour, somewhere between gold and deep brown, I guess, almost fluid, but it's not the colour that is the most striking: it is the emptiness behind them; she looks so . . . lost.

I crouch down, knee to knee, and it takes everything in me not to reach out and touch her hand.

'I didn't see you there,' she gasps.

'You were all I could see,' I reply, inwardly wincing, worried that my words sound cheesy. But she smiles, two small dimples forming – a finger space apart from her mouth – her eyes losing that lost look because I, me, some stupid, tactless Irishman, have found her.

Chapter Three

Sophie

My heel is caught in a crack in the paving. I twist my foot to the left, to the right, the grainy sound of my actions blunted by the rain which is pummelling clenched fists on the outside of my umbrella. I twist my heel again before pulling it upwards with as much force as I can. Lightning flashes on to the street as the heel snaps. I expect to hear the deep rumble of thunder, but instead, I hear the high-pitched wail of a little girl, coming from the mouth of an exceptionally tall man. My decapitated shoe, connecting with his ankle.

'I'm so sorry! Are you OK?' I ask as I crouch down, instantly regretting my descent. What exactly am I going to do? Roll up his trouser leg? Apply a plaster? I sigh and look up. He has the stature of someone who is confident in his body. His frame is relaxed but solid; his shoulders are broad but his chest isn't puffed out; his shoulders aren't squared. He crouches down, scanning my face and his eyebrows lift, the creases in his face relax; the same expression you might have after you have been frantically searching for something but then find it in the last place you look. His face is relieved: he's found it.

'I didn't see you there,' I say, my words tumbling from my mouth.

'You were all I could see,' he replies. He stands and takes

a step back, as though his words have pushed him away, and I find myself smiling at him, offering him reassurance as he reaches his hand towards me.

I decline it with a 'thank you but I'm fine' expression, but as I try to stand, the missing heel throws my balance. I haven't even got halfway to standing when I feel my whole body sliding slowly to the left. He reaches out his hand again, but again, I decline: I'm used to doing things by myself. My hand reaches for the edge of the table, slick with rain, but it glances off and I topple, landing in a foetal curl on the quickly formed puddle.

Embarrassment seeps through my body as quickly as the puddle is seeping into my clothes. I can already see a brown stain stretching across the white of my skirt as I straighten myself into a sitting position. My eyes are drawn upwards to where the man is still standing, amusement playing at the corners of his mouth. He offers his hand to me for the third time, but this time, I don't hesitate; I don't overthink his gesture; I don't ignore him; instead, I slip my palm inside his. Mine feels tiny inside the warmth of his, and I yield to the gentle pressure he applies as he helps me stand.

'Thank you,' I say. He lets my hand drop once I'm standing. Thunder cracks loudly as he crouches down and retrieves my broken heel and umbrella. Around us, the storm shrouds the chaos of the city and its inhabitants. He passes the heel back to me with a grin and I clutch it towards my chest, giving him a quick nod of gratitude, and then turn my back, my green umbrella and I walking away, salvaging what little dignity I have left . . . but my dignity is dissolving with every ungainly, lopsided step I take. Up and down, up and down, my body goes, rain dripping from my eyelashes, brown stains covering my white skirt as I hobble away.

Footsteps splash towards me and he stands in my path.

'Ah look, you're drenched and in no shape to walk—' His

accent is Northern Irish, I think. His tone rises at the end of each sentence but snaps back down – a bit like a helium balloon in a child's chubby hands – always trying to rise. 'Why don't we head inside and call a cab?'

I find myself nodding, if only to stop myself from taking another ridiculous step.

He takes the umbrella from my hand and offers me his arm. My automatic response is to refuse his gesture, but at this stage of the game, I think my dignity ship has already sailed.

As our feet step through the rain, my world is being not just tipped upside down but shook, like a snow-globe: my life – my perfect image with clean lines and neat edges – has been protected from the outside world until now. Now it feels like it has been shaken.

He pulls his hand free of mine as we step into the warmth of the building and I feel the world tilt. How is it that I have been able to stay upright without this stranger holding my hand? I shake my head, raindrops scattering from my hair, and pull off my coat. He takes it from me and I let him.

'Your eyes are the colour of tea,' he smiles.

'Tea?' I ask. My voice sounds hoarse and I clear my throat as I process his description. I picture the colour of murky builders' tea.

'Yes, they look like tea through a glass cup, almost gold, really.'

'Huh,' I reply. He looks away, and I miss my moment to return the compliment. I shiver. My arms are bare; the fair hairs are rising, running along my skin in a wave, exposed and free of their armour. I take off my broken shoes, dropping them into my oversized bag, and pull myself to my full height, stretching out my hand formally. I need to take control of this . . . this thing that is happening. Maybe I have flu.

'I'm Sophie.' My voice is clear, crisp, controlled. He looks down at my hand, an embryonic smile on his full mouth, like I have said something endearing. His front tooth has a small chip at the edge. Instead of shaking my hand, he slaps the back of his hand against mine, then claps our palms together and does this strange fist-bump action.

'Ah, never mind—' he says the word 'mind' like 'moind'. 'We'll work on that. I'm Samuel, shall we get a bite? I'm starving.' He strides towards a waitress and I watch the damp line that runs down the back of his shirt cling to the curve of his spine as he negotiates a table.

I look around the restaurant, seeking a way to escape this situation I have found myself in, but I find that my stockinged feet are following him and my hands, which should be reaching for my phone and calling a cab, are pulling back a chair.

Samuel is already grabbing a menu and has begun to talk. My knees bend, and I find myself sitting down without making the decision to stay.

He talks passionately about everything, drawing me into his train of thought. I have to hold on to his words as they fly past our surroundings, the outside world blurring around me as the conversation twists and turns to new places, but the journey is never a one-way street: he questions, he listens, he laughs.

'What is it you do, Samuel? Here in DC?' I ask.

'I work in IT. I'm a stereotypical computer geek. What about you?'

'I'm an analyst. I work out how to streamline companies, help them work better. I spend weeks, sometimes months working out how to improve a business, then I fix it . . . or we make them an offer they can't refuse and take over the business.'

'That straightforward?'

'In a nutshell.'

'So you're a bit like Richard Gere in *Pretty Woman* but without the penchant for hookers?'

I laugh at this.

'Like a super accountant, then? You fly in, fix everything and then disappear until the next financial disaster.'

I laugh again. 'I suppose . . . Super Sophie, that's me.'

We order dinner, we order wine, his face lighting up as he talks about his family in Derry, about how he used to play rugby, about how he loves to run.

Afternoon bleeds into dusk, dusk into twilight; twilight begins to fade until night consumes the view outside. My brain is telling me to be on my guard, but I ignore it. I'm leaving in two days, anyway. I won't see him again.

'Excuse me while I nip to the little boys' room.' He pushes his chair back and rises; the space he filled is suddenly barren. Loneliness creeps up on me. I have been alone for so long that I don't often feel its presence, but I feel it now . . . how have I become accustomed to the sting? The chatter around me becomes louder; I notice the surroundings which, with him next to me, have been invisible. Samuel sits back down; the noises quieten, my senses instead filled with him.

'Poor man,' I say as I look towards a man in his early thirties, with his tie askew, as he begs into his phone: 'Please,' he is saying, 'I'll change. Please don't break up with me.'

'Ah, I remember feeling like that. I was twenty-four, her name was Isabella.' He gestures to the man who is staring blankly at the table top, seemingly oblivious to his surroundings. 'So how about you?' He leans forward and smells his food, his eyelids closing, and I can't help but smile as I get a quick glimpse of him as a child in front of home-cooked meals after a busy day at school.

'What about me?' I avoid his gaze.

'You ever been that heartbroken?'

I shake my head.

'Never?'

I shake my head again and twist the tagliatelle around my fork. How can I tell this man so full of life that I've never been hurt like that because I've never been in love? I lost my virginity in the first week at university to a boy called Harry who always smelt vaguely of sweat even after a shower. I always viewed virginity as something I needed to get rid of, a rite of passage so I could get on with my life at uni. I endured a relationship with him for two weeks and I was glad when it ended. I loved university because I had nobody to answer to. Nobody knew about my past. I saw university as my way into the life I wanted. I didn't want to have to depend on anyone. And so, after my brief relationship with Harry, I had stayed away from the parties, the one-night stands, the late arrivals to lectures still half-drunk. That's not to say that I didn't make friends – I did. I was the mum of the group. I was the one who made sure we had toilet roll. I was the one who made early morning trips for Diet Coke and paracetamol and I was the one who made the doctor's appointments for the morning-after pill. I came out with a First, I kissed and hugged them goodbye on graduation day and then I didn't see much of them after that. I wonder now if they even remember me.

'What's the longest relationship you've had?' he asks, bringing me back to the present, before filling his mouth with another forkful of food.

'Five years,' I answer, wiping the corners of my mouth with the napkin. My heart begins to pound. I haven't talked about my past relationships with anyone other than Helen, and I don't like how my mouth seems to be opening up to him, but on it goes. 'You?'

'Ah, now, there's a question. I've had a few girlfriends that have stayed for the long haul. There was Carol when I was sixteen, sweet girl, she used to blink all the time when I was around but then she started blinking at someone else, then there was Hattie.' He tears off a piece of bread and dips it in his cassoulet. 'She dumped me, I think, then there was Evie. I was with Evie for three years but we just grew apart; it wasn't a bad break-up, we just kind of called it a day . . . then there was Isabella, she was the one who did that to me.' He nods towards the heartbroken man who is making his way through a bottle of red at an alarming rate. 'Two and a half years of fighting and making up, it was a shit-storm of a relationship, but I was a mess when she left. 'So tell me about Mr Five Years.' He pours more wine into his glass.

'His name was Stephen with a p-h,' I begin. 'We met at a finance meeting. He always stood his shoes against the wall in a pair, it used to drive me mad.'

'Five years and that's all you've got to say about the fella?'

'It was more of a . . . business relationship. We met up on alternate weekends, maybe once or twice in the week if we were free, went to the cinema together, that sort of thing, then he met someone else, decided he wanted two-point-four kids and a family home, so that was it. I was relieved when it was over, to be honest. I heard he proposed to her with some wild romantic gesture . . . had "Will you Marry Me?" written in the sky by some Red Arrows or something. Funny. He didn't even pay for a meal with me, we always split it.'

'So, what's the most romantic thing anyone has ever done for you?'

I falter. His dark hair falls forward as he slices his way through some meat, waiting for my answer, seemingly confident that there will be one.

'I've never had anything romantic done for me.' The answer is out before I can stop myself. I straighten my posture. I've had too much wine; that's why I'm talking so freely. I pour water into my glass. He answers me after he swallows his mouthful of food.

'What, like ever?'

I shake my head and fold my napkin, looking around the restaurant so I can gain the attention of the waitress and ask for the bill. I need to leave this place.

'You've never had a bunch of flowers?'

I shake my head, folding the napkin into a triangle.

'Chocolates?'

'I'm not a romance type of girl.' I give him a tight smile and hate the way that I feel when I look at him, this stranger.

'Well, that's settled then.' He pushes his plate away. 'How long are you in DC for?'

'I'm leaving soon, I'm only here on business.' I can hear my voice losing some of its clarity.

'Are you here tomorrow?'

'Well, yes, but—'

He signals for the bill. 'All day?'

I nod and try to protest as he pays for the meal, ignoring me with a flap of his hand.

'Grand. I'll be outside . . . where are you staying?' He shrugs on his coat before I can gather my thoughts and my things.

'The White Square Hotel, but—'

I am still sitting as he bends down, his lips brushing me on the cheek before whispering into my ear, 'Tomorrow at ten.' The minute his lips touch my cheek and I feel his breath on my neck, I know I am lost.

Chapter Four

Samuel

The ends of her hair are still damp and they flick up at the ends, perfect arcs of gold that rest along her shoulders. She is beautiful; I've never felt an attraction towards anyone the way I do for her. It's as if I have spent my entire life looking for something precious, something fragile, and I finally have it in my palm. I'm petrified of losing it, of losing her.

With each hour that passes, with each glass of wine and mouthful of food, I feel as though I'm getting closer to her.

The next morning, I'm late, hurrying up the wrong side of the street. Traffic is busy and I can't find a gap to make my way over to her. She strides down the steps outside the hotel wearing a heavy white jacket with a grey fur trim around the collar; slim white trousers rest above high-heeled white shoes. It's strange that I should notice these things but something about the way that she is dressed demands attention. She doesn't see me at first, glancing up and down the street. My heart thuds against my ribs, just as it would when I'd try to kick goal from a penalty, the hush and apprehension of the crowd, the expectations of the fans, making my eyes narrow in concentration. My palms are sweating, and I rub them along my jeans as I watch her flick her wrist, her hair covering the side of her cheek as she inspects her watch-face. I quicken my pace; she has placed one heel on the step behind her, as though she is going to go back into the hotel. Her name leaves my mouth; the softness of it hangs in the air above me but doesn't reach her, so I begin to wave, not the discreet wave that I intended, but a great swooping archway with both my hands. Her head turns towards me; my arms are continuing to wave as I grin. She pulls at her earlobe, her foot remaining on the step. I begin to panic. I watch the hesitation in her footsteps; my hands stop waving and I stand there, my arms still raised to the sky. My breath hovers tightly as I inhale; it lies inside my lungs, taut and expectant. Her foot steps down, one step, two steps until she is crossing the road, her stride exuding confidence and certainty in contrast to the fragility I saw last night. She approaches me.

'Hello.' Her strange amber-coloured eyes stare up at me, that lost look I had first seen hiding in them eradicated with a blink.

'Hello,' I reply. It's hard to explain the way Sophie looks at me as we walk around the city: the way her eyes not only follow where I'm pointing, but follow my whole arm, from my shoulder to the tips of my fingers as I draw her attention to the Thomas Jefferson Memorial; the way her eyes linger over every part of my face as I talk about the White House and its secret tunnels; the way her hand brushes against mine as we approach the Lincoln Memorial. It is in the way that she listens to me speak, the way she watches my mouth, the way she lets me brush her hair away from those strange-coloured eyes.

'Tell me something you like,' I ask her as we sit down on a bench.

'Marmite,' she answers. I wrinkle my nose. 'And singing in the shower,' she adds, the last part coming out of her mouth like a hiccup – like something she is trying to control but can't. 'Tell me more about your family,' she asks as she shields her eyes from the autumn sun.

'My sister calls me Mule because she couldn't say Samuel when we were little.'

'Mule . . .' Her mouth tries to contain a smile.

'What's so funny?'

'Well, isn't a mule a bit close to an ass?'

I sit back. 'I hadn't thought of that.'

She laughs and looks across to where the light is hitting the top of the tall, pencil-like peak of the Washington Monument.

'It does sound like her, though. We've got a competitive relationship,' I explain, thinking of Sarah.

'I'd say she's won if she's been calling you an ass all your life and you didn't notice.'

'You're probably right.'

'Is that where Forrest Gump wades into the water?' She grabs my arm and shifts her body so she can crane her neck.

'Yeah, I think so. It's not my type of film. I'm more of a, you know . . .' I do some manly pow-pow noises and point my fingers into a gun shape. 'Action film fan. *Die Hard* is my favourite.'

'Is that so?' She smiles at me as if she already knows that my favourite film is really *Love Actually*, but it's not like I'm going to admit that on a first date, even though there are lots of reasons why this is as much a man's film as a woman's – just take that dorky Colin character. He flies off to America and ends up with a gaggle of women swooning at his feet.

She leans her head back and gazes into the sky above. 'This time tomorrow I'll be up there somewhere, on my way back home.' Her eyes close, the sun catching tiny bits of glitter in her eyeshadow.

Her whole demeanour changes when we arrive back outside her hotel. She smooths down her trousers and shrugs her hair back from her face.

‘It’s been a pleasure meeting you, Samuel.’ Her hand reaches out and I attempt to re-enact my fist bump from the day before. It isn’t a success.

‘Sophie, could we . . . grab a coffee? Tomorrow morning? Before you leave?’ Her mouth begins to open but then shuts, like she has taken a gulp of air that has filled her mouth and she can’t swallow it, but she nods and looks at me in a way that tells me what I need to know. She likes me, she wants to see me again, but it is such a cautious nod, so quickly executed that it’s as though her body has answered before she could keep it in check.

‘Shall-I-give-you-my-number?’ I ask. The words running into each other like a string of notes, not a melody with breaks and changes in tempo.

‘OK.’

‘Do you want to write it down?’ She shakes her head.

‘I’m good with numbers, I’ll remember it.’

I give her my number; her eyes look up to the sky as I say it. I hope that the numbers are clinging to her, not floating away into clouds.

She’s not going to call. My mouth is dry. I’ll never see her again. But then she leans forward and kisses me on the cheek.

‘Thank you, Samuel. It’s been a wonderful day.’ Her voice stays with me even though she is already running up the steps and out of my sight.

I’m just beginning to walk away when my phone vibrates against my leg.

How can you not like Marmite?

I wait until the clock says 22:30 until I ring her.

I don’t say hello and I don’t tell her it’s me; I don’t want to give her the chance for her head to rule her heart. ‘Meet me in the lobby at midnight . . . I have a surprise.’ Her reply isn't sleepy or confused, it isn't wary or suspicious; instead, she simply says, 'OK.'

The taxi drops us at the park and we walk hand in hand along the path. I simply reach for hers and there it is, cold inside my palm, feeling like it has been there a thousand times before. The trees yawn and arch their backs, pulling the cover of night over their weary bodies. I pause opposite a fountain – a tower in the middle layered with ascending stones lit up with hidden bulbs – the sound of the water making me wish I'd gone to the toilet before I left the hotel.

'This spot is perfect,' I say, taking off my backpack and retrieving the blanket, which I shake out and lay on the grass; then I begin placing battery-operated tea-lights around it.

'Ah shite,' I say, moving the small switch at the base of the candles back and forth, but the flame refuses to light. She takes it from my hand and pulls out a little tag from its base, the fake flame dancing in her palm. Her shoes, another pair of heels, are discarded. It's strange to see her feet bare; they are so small, so perfectly formed that I can't stop looking at them as she continues switching the candles on, her lips curving into a smile, her dimples deepening. I tear my gaze away from her feet in case she thinks I have some kind of foot fetish.

We sit on the blanket; her back is straight, her legs crossed like a child on the carpet in school. I empty the contents of my bag: a bottle of champagne, Tupperware boxes of sandwiches, plastic flutes.

'So tell me a bit more about your family,' she asks.

'They're loud.'

'I can imagine,' she answers with a sly smile. 'And your sister . . . do you look like each other?'

I pop the champagne and pour her a glass. 'My sister looks like a Celt. Have you seen that Disney film? *Brave*?' Her forehead furrows as if I've just asked her if she watches hard-core porn. 'Ah well, she looks like that, tall, red hair, green eyes. She's a walking cliché. What about your family?'

She takes a long sip of her drink. 'There's nothing to tell you, really, we're not close. We don't look like Disney characters, that's for sure. I have a step-sister, Helen, but I don't see her very often. She lives in Shropshire. Is your mum a redhead, then, or just your sister?'

'Nah, Mam has my colour hair and thinks she can save the world with a cup of tea and a custard cream.' I turn to the Tupperware and pass her a smoked salmon sandwich which she takes from me, nibbling the edge with a slightly repulsed look.

'What's the matter?' I ask, watching the struggle of the sandwich being forced down her throat, her hand reaching for the plastic flute and gulping the contents down.

'I'm sorry.' She places the triangle away from her. 'I'm sorry after you've gone to so much trouble, but I don't like salmon, it's too . . . slimy.'

She shudders, but I delve back into my bag and produce a Marmite sandwich. Her face changes into a grin. Not the demure smiles she has controlled so far, but a big, open-mouthed beam. There is nothing dainty about the way she eats this time – the sandwich is devoured in two bites. This shocks me a little. This woman wearing a suit jacket for a midnight picnic can eat like a teenage boy. The sky hangs darkly above us as we lie down side by side. Sophie asks me about my childhood, about the things I got up to when me and my friend Connor used to say we were staying at each other's houses.

'What about your childhood? What did you used to get up to?' I ask, topping up our glasses.

'My childhood was dull really . . .'

'What did you want to be when you grew up?'

'Oh, I don't know. I was just always good at maths, so . . . accounting.'

'That was your childhood dream job? An accountant?'

'You don't have to say it like a dirty word,' she answers, but I can hear the smile in her voice. 'Anyway, I'm not an accountant any more . . .'

It's past two in the morning before I pluck up the courage to do what I need to. I take her hands and pull her up and then sink down on one knee. She twists her blond hair around her finger as I produce a small box; from the amusement on her face I know she's not expecting me to propose marriage.

'You know my flight home is tomorrow, Samuel?' she says, scooping her hair into a ponytail before letting it drop back down over her shoulder.

'I know, that's why I need to ask you. Sophie Williams, will you do me the honour of being my house guest for a week instead?' I open the box and inside gleams my front door key. It's my only key, actually, as I haven't had time to get another one cut just yet.

'I never take time off work, Samuel. I have to go back.'

'Never?' She shakes her head and begins chewing the inside of her thumbnail. I can tell she is considering it. 'You analyse data, right?' She nods. 'Will that data have dramatically changed in a week's time?' She gives a little shake of her head. 'So what you're saying is . . .' I begin ticking things off on my fingers, 'you never take time off, which means your job isn't at risk because you're not taking the piss and having extra holidays.' I tick off another finger. 'Your work will still be there when you get back; the world isn't going to end if you don't analyse that oh-so-important data.' Another finger is counted. 'And you have a handsome, fun Irishman giving you free accommodation for a week in one of the most exciting cities in the world. Now would you just say yes already because my knee is killing me?' I can see what I'm asking her is more than she is used to giving. She seems to be battling silent warnings against the idea and I hold my breath, hoping I've done enough to convince her that I am a good man.

'No.' The word erupts from her, seeming to take her by surprise. She covers her mouth, responding to the look of desolation that I can feel falling across my face. 'But—' I raise my eyebrows hopefully, 'I will stay here, in DC, for a week. You can be my . . . tour guide.' Her smile lights up her face and she begins to laugh. 'I'll ring them in the morning and tell them . . . I'm taking a holiday.'

As the taxi takes us back to her hotel, she falls asleep on my shoulder. The weight of her head against me feels familiar, feels right. Her hair smells of something expensive, something citrusy, and I let my fingers twirl the ends of it as I listen to the little noises she makes, the silent breath in and the slight gasp of sound as she breathes out.

The brakes squeal as we pull up, and her eyes open with a confused, almost alarmed look, but it's ironed away as she sees me. Her eyebrows relax and her lips tilt into a shy smile as she straightens herself, opens the door and puts a foot on to the pavement before turning her head over her shoulder towards me.

'Thank you, Samuel . . . today has been perfect.'

Chapter Five

Sophie

I stretch and shift myself up the bed, rearranging my new pyjamas, pulling my feet up and rolling over to face him. Last night, I'd fallen asleep watching *Die Hard*. He doesn't have a DVD player downstairs so we'd brought popcorn and drinks up here. I don't remember Samuel turning the TV off, but I do remember not wanting to move from his bed.

Inside my shopping bags are the clothes I bought yesterday, the types of clothes that I haven't worn for a long time. Flat boots instead of heels, jeans instead of trouser suits, jumpers and blouses that hang loosely around my frame, letting me breathe, letting me relax.

Yesterday, he took me out on paddle boats. From the people who watched us it would seem like a nice thing to do for someone. *Look at that couple having a romantic trip across the water, look at how they are laughing, look at how they are so involved with each other that they barely even notice the beautiful scenery.* They can't see that the handsome man is afraid of the water, that that man with the broad shoulders and loud voice suffers from seasickness even on a paddle boat, that he is suffering this, bearing his own fear, for her.

With each day that passes, he gives something of himself to me, and I allow myself to accept these gifts, these parts of him that are filling the spaces inside me. I've been living my adult life filling my hunger with a career, snacking on snippets of success, not aware that I was starving, until I allowed myself a taste of this . . . fairy tale. I know that it won't last, that this is just a fragile dream that I'm not strong enough to hold on to. My career is what is real and my life in London is what will keep me alive, but that didn't stop me from agreeing to stay the night.

I study his face, his eyelids hiding the dreams beneath. Samuel sighs gently and reaches his arm around my waist. His skin is always warm, my skin always cold against his.

He hasn't kissed me yet. It's like our intimacies have started from the end of a relationship and are moving backwards against time. We started at the retirement end of the spectrum: holding hands and finishing each other's sentences. Yesterday we moved into our middle ages: he has kissed my cheek, the top of my head; quick, snatched moments where his movement seemed to burst from him, the action controlling him rather than the other way around.

Tentatively, I reach for his hair which is resting on his eyebrow. It's coarse and soft all at the same time and flicks back to the exact same position as it was before I touched it. I lean forward, stepping into adolescence. I ignore the voice inside that is telling me this will hurt even more when I leave, and let my lips brush his. His eyes flick open and we stare at each other. We don't smile, we just stare. I kiss him again, his hand reaching for the back of my neck, our bodies seeking each other's: there you are, how have I lived this long without you?

Our lovemaking is gentle, exquisite: love made.

Chapter Six

Samuel

We haven't left the house since the paddle boats. I don't think that we've spent more than a few minutes not touching each other. I ran her a bath and sprinkled rose petals in; we laughed as we tried to get down to it in the bath, but the petals kept getting in the way.

She made us cheese toasties in the middle of the night, wearing just her underwear, and I watched every muscle in her body flex, listened to the way she hummed while she moved around the kitchen. I had planned to take her to watch the sunset, but we were too wrapped up in each other to leave the house. We took it in turns reading *Anna Karenina* to each other (she was so pleased when she found it in my bathroom that I didn't have the heart to tell her it was Sarah's).

'Tolstoy?' she asked, as she came back downstairs holding it in her hands. We lay naked and wrapped up in each other's limbs until she fell asleep with the book in her hands; I don't think she ever looked more beautiful than she did right then.

Today, we are venturing out into the world. Her hair smells like my shampoo; my clothes smell of her perfume. I'm taking her to an old renovated cinema that still has intervals and ushers and shows the old classics like *Gone with the Wind.* It is a two-hour journey and I have borrowed Bret's convertible.

'What is that?' she asks, her eyebrows arched, her teeth sinking into her bottom lip.

'What?' I ask, rearranging the yellow woolly hat that Ma sent me in my most recent parcel. 'My mam bought it for me.' She reaches for the edge and helps shift it into position and drops a kiss on to my nose. My hands twist her red scarf around her neck. 'The forecast is sunny,' I say, pulling up her collar, 'but cold, so we need to wrap up warm, even if it means me wearing a hat the colour of baby poo.' Her nose wrinkles in disgust.

I turn on my playlist – 'Belters', I call it: Guns N' Roses, Whitesnake, Def Leppard, and sing along at the top of my voice even though she keeps putting her fingers in her ears.

The journey passes and I ignore the feeling in the pit of my stomach, the nagging that warns me of the pain to come, that I won't be able to see her soon, that she will be gone and that I may never see her again. We haven't talked about what will happen when the week is over, when she returns to that job that seems to mean so much. Instead, I watch her as much as I can, remember every smile that she gives me, and try my hardest to make her want to stay.

My playlist finishes and switches to my 'Tunes'. She bursts out laughing when 'You're the One That I Want' explodes from the speakers swiftly followed by 'Jesus Christ Superstar'.

'What?' I ask. 'You can't tell me that you didn't want to sing along.' She rolls her eyes but her leg is bouncing up and down as 'All That Jazz' starts.

I pull into the car park and we climb out. Her cheeks are pink and the tip of her nose is red, and I find myself kissing the end of it.

'It's like kissing the tip of an ice cube,' I say, my voice muffled. She's always cold, I notice, and I add it to the list of things that I'm trying to store in my memory. Her hands sneak beneath my shirt and I shriek.

'You scream like a girl,' she whispers into my ear, slipping her hand in mine, leaning against me as we walk into the cinema.

I balance an overflowing box of popcorn against my chest as I fumble with the tickets. Sophie walks ahead into the small auditorium, which must only seat about sixty people, making her way towards the front, but I stop her.

'We have to sit at the back.' I nod with my head towards the back row.

'But the seats in the middle are better.' She frowns.

'It's not romantic to sit in the middle. We have to snog on the back seats.' Two elderly women on the seats in front turn their heads to look in our direction. I grin at them and they chuckle back as Sophie hesitates, rolls her eyes and then follows me to the red-velvet covered seats.

I hate *Gone with the Wind*, but I knew she would love it. I don't watch the screen anyway; I watch her and I list the things I need to remember: her fingers can craft a sugar packet into a flower without her eyes leaving the screen; she always puts popcorn in her mouth one kernel at a time, pop, pop, pop, pop, pop; she crosses her right leg over her left and taps her foot twice before she settles; she always covers her mouth with her hand when she laughs so much that she snorts; she pulls at her earlobe when she's thinking . . . and she sometimes looks at me like she's afraid of me.

Chapter Seven

Sophie

Our hands swing in time to our steps, our fingers entwined as we walk around the edge of the lake. The trees are bowing majestically around it, their burnt oranges and reds reflecting perfectly in the water, like the poster-paint butterflies that I used to make as a child – blobs of autumn stretching out and folding into the water: a perfect print.

Nights spent in bed but without sleep, and my approaching departure, are making us both edgy. He stops walking as a russet leaf falls into my hair, his green eyes narrowing in concentration as he delicately plucks it from beneath my scarlet hat, his strong fingers opening my palm and placing the leaf inside, closing my hands gently around it.

'To take with you,' he says quietly, dancing around the subject of me leaving. I've been pushing it away, putting it in a locked cabinet, filing it away to be dealt with at a later date, but the drawer keeps sliding open: the woman in white, the woman in heels whose armour protects her from the girl she once was, keeps opening it. The time we are spending together is a fantasy; it isn't real. My life in London is real. 'Stay,' he says, smiling at me and tucking a stray piece of hair behind my ears.

'I can't stay . . . my job—'

'Ah yes. The job,' he replies sadly. 'Couldn't you, you know, do that for another company?'

'No,' I say with finality. 'I've worked my ass off to get where I am, Samuel.'

'But—'

'Don't you feel that way about your job? You left home to work over here, didn't you? To work in your, what do you call it? Emerald City?'

'Yeah, but—'

'Can we not talk about work? I'm on holiday, remember?' I turn to him and kiss him, looking deep into his eyes, trying to convey that the subject is too hard for me to talk about.

I'm lying on his bare chest as it rises up and down, the duvet pushed to the end of the bed, the curtains still open even though it's dark outside.

'You smell like strawberries,' he says, kissing the top of my head. I look at my nails running through the dark hair on his chest; they're stained pink beneath.

'You should have let me finish getting dessert ready,' I yawn. 'The meringues will be all mushy.'

'Mushy meringues are my favourite.' He runs his fingers up and down my spine. 'Soph . . . maybe, maybe I could come to London? Maybe I could get a job in the UK? I've got an interview next week for a promotion. I'm going to pitch an idea to the board next week, and if they like it, it could really get me noticed; if I left as head of IT I bet I could easily get a decent job over there.'

'What's your idea?' My eyes begin to close, sleep deprivation catching up with me.

He shifts further up the bed. 'OK, so, you know how search engines work, how they find recommendations for your next purchase, shite like that?' His voice changes, the excitement making me open my eyes and my body turn so I can look up at him. 'Well, what about if a piece of software was developed that could use this data, real-time data, to show how products are selling. What if—' Heat courses through my body as he speaks, my blood rushing in my ears and my hands beginning to shake. 'What if they use this information in a bank, if we could use it at Greenlight—'

Greenlight. He works for Greenlight.

'—we could streamline our loan applications, make the whole process faster. It could cut our losses on bad investments, we could see what is trending right at the moment of application. Just think of it, it could put us ahead in the market.'

How could I be so reckless?

I try to stop listening. I try to ignore his words as they sink their teeth into my skin, as they claw at my insides.

I have to leave. I have to get as far away from him as possible.

This could destroy my career; this could destroy me. If they find out I'm sleeping with a man from the company we're about to take over – if they find out he knows about the software that we're about to develop – I'll be finished. They would never believe that his idea is just a coincidence, and why would they? I hardly believe it myself. Panic fills me as I sort through our conversations.

'Let's not talk about work any more, Samuel.' I try to control the tremor in my voice, hoping that he can't hear it. 'I'm tired.' I enact a dramatic yawn. 'Let's just enjoy . . . this.' He catches my yawn as I concentrate on calming my breathing, making my body sink into his, fighting the tears beneath my eyelids and trying not to think that the last part of myself that I will give to Samuel is a yawn.

WINTER

Week One

Sophie

I close my eyes and rub my temple, a sigh escaping my lips. My eyelids open and blink at the laptop screen, my manicured fingers fluttering and kicking across the keyboard, describing the new strategy that will get me that promotion: work, work, work. I pause for a moment, tuck my hair behind my ear, then glance at the television which has been entertaining the walls of my house with grey and blue flashes. The movie has grabbed my attention – a forties musical. My hair whispers past my ear, and my mouth smiles. The laptop screen glares at me but I'm distracted; something about the way the leading male is delivering his line has reminded me of Samuel.

'*Your eyes are the colour of tea.*'

I shake my head, grab the controller and turn the television off. No time for distractions.

It's past one in the morning when I finally go to bed. A suit hangs inside my white, high-gloss wardrobe and a pair of black, five-inched heels await my stockinged feet. With numbers and flight details rushing around my head, I close my eyes, giving a small smile as I drift off to sleep: the image of the glass teacup swirling its amber liquid, drowning out financial reports.

A mere five hours later, my hand reaches for the alarm. I

stretch, smooth down my white vest over the flat stomach that my recent stomach bug has created and open my eyes. The memory of Samuel took over my dreams last night, just as it has every night since I left him. Familiar feelings of apprehension gurgle and skip at the thought of seeing him this week, and I'm nervous about how he will be around me after so long, and rightly so.

Samuel's phone calls and texts came relentlessly that first week. I tried to ignore him, but they just kept coming. In the end he left me no choice. I sent him one reply:

> Thanks for a wonderful week, Samuel, but it's over now. I wish you all the best, goodbye. Sophie.

And then I blocked his number . . . and cried for a week.

I shake the memories of him; I have to forget the woman I was during my time with Samuel, the woman who fell in love with a man only to leave him without an explanation in the middle of the night.

The taxi purrs patiently by the roadside as my handbag clicks shut: lipstick, passport, tickets, purse, tampons, hidden from view. I close the front door firmly behind me, pulling along my suitcase past the snowdrops, their heads braving the edges of winter.

'Mornin', Sophie. Airport again, is it?'

'Good morning, Bert. Yes, please.'

'Where are you off to, then?'

'Washington DC,' I reply. Bert gives a whistle and I can't help but meet his impressed expression in the rear-view mirror.

'Haven't you been there before? Last year, wasn't it?'

'Yes, in the autumn.' The memory of him hits me, as it does so often; his green eyes narrowed in concentration as he delicately plucked the leaf from beneath my scarlet hat.

'To take with you.'

'Business, is it?' I'm brought back to the present.

'Yes,' I reply, dismissing the memory. 'Business.'

Once in flight, I open my laptop and go through my notes again, double-checking figures, familiarising myself with the staff at Greenlight. His name sits there now: Samuel McLaughlin – Head of Information Technology. He got the promotion.

Hours pass, and I close my eyes as I try to ignore the child behind me talking incessantly, but every time I do, I see Samuel's face.

A stewardess approaches and I order a cup of coffee. She passes it to me with a smile; I take a sip and close my eyes again. Turbulence bounces the plane and the seat belt sign pings on. I drain the last of my cup, reach for my compact, and re-apply my make-up, pushing my memories to the back of my mind as the plane makes its descent.

I'm checked into the hotel by a petite girl with thick, orange eyebrows which look like furry orange peelings, and an hour later, I'm looking up at the Greenlight regional office. I take a deep breath and walk through the rotating doors.

'Sophie Williams to see Edward Johnson, please.' I hold my briefcase firmly in my hands, my palms dry despite the adrenaline pumping through me.

'Twenty-fifth floor.'

'Thank you.'

I step into the lift and with every floor that passes, my nerves bubble in my stomach. The doors open, and I'm surrounded by the hum of computers sliced with the sharp sounds of phones ringing, the mechanics softened by the warm smell of coffee and perfume. I'm greeted by an Amazonian brunette who takes my hand, giving it a firm shake.

'Ms Williams? I'm Katherine Day, Kat for short. Welcome to DC. Did you have a good journey?'

'I did, thank you.'

'Mr Johnson and the board are through here.' The door is pushed aside to reveal a huge oval-shaped conference table. I ignore the fact that there are possibly thirty to forty people sitting around it, most of whom are engrossed in heated arguments. I ignore that my hand is shaking and that I have just sat in the wrong seat and have had to get back up and move to another; I ignore that my boss isn't yet sitting at the table. I ignore all of this because he is here. From the corner of my eyes I see him agitatedly run his hands through his dark hair, his accent becoming thicker as his voice rises; but I can't let this happen again, can't let my feelings for him get the better of me. I'm here to make a proposal: that the company I work for 'acquires' his.

'Ah, Ms Williams, glad you could join us.' The conversations drop, like the end of an echo. My voice feels thick, but when I speak it is clear and steady.

'It's a pleasure, Mr Johnson. If we could just wait a few moments for my colleague to arrive?'

'Unfortunately, Mr Swift had to leave after an emergency call. He said that the proposal is your baby anyway?'

I try to curb the frustration I am feeling towards Bob Swift; his wife is in the last month of her pregnancy and I have no doubt that is the reason for his swift departure.

'Of course. If you could all turn to page two of the proposal?' I take a sip of water and begin to make my way to the computer at the front of the room. I smile as I open the presentation.

'Greenlight Finance has long been one of the champions

of small businesses; indeed, up until recently, it has been one of the leading lenders in its field.' I take a deep breath and meet the conflicting stares around the table. 'However, in the last two years there has been a considerable decline in profits.' I take another sip of water. The remnants of the Welsh accent I have tried so hard to lose have slipped in: 'prof-ets', I've said.

'This is not new news . . .' a mole of a man squints at me, clicking his pen repetitively, 'what with the recession and—'

'Your figures show a distinct decline before that, if I could continue?' There, much better.

'After a thorough evaluation of your financial reports, we can see that this coincides with the increase in small business loans realised by the bigger banking groups of the Washington DC financial district. We believe that this is due to a new piece of software that was implemented and sold exclusively to these three institutions.'

The faces are shadowed by the purple light shining from the screen; for a moment, I'm reminded of a punnet of blueberries.

'This is old news,' the mole digs at me. 'That software is tied into a watertight agreement with those companies – how does it help us?' I meet his poky eyes and I'm reminded of Danger Mouse's sidekick, but then I remember he was a hamster, not a mole.

'We at Sandwell Incorporated have had a breakthrough with one of our programmers in our tech department. He has designed a new piece of software that is faster and superior to any other systems of its kind.' I pause for a moment to allow the mutterings to subside. 'Our software uses real-time data from the most popular search engines to the biggest on-line shopping sites, which would streamline any small loan applications, making the process smoother, more transparent and – more importantly – faster. We own the patent for this software.'

‘And what is it that you want for this software?’ The Northern Irish voice stings my skin and for a moment I’m paralysed.

‘In a nutshell?’ I meet his eyes. ‘Greenlight Finance.’ My words cause an eruption of voices and movement. I take a sip of water and calm myself. We had expected this reaction, but it was supposed to be Bob dealing with the fallout, not me. He has a much softer way of approaching these things, using flowery language and humour to make the proceedings more pliable.

‘Ms Williams?’ Samuel’s accent masks the anger behind the statement. ‘Can I ask how long your programmer has been working on this software?’

‘I don’t see how that is relevant at this point.’ I turn away from his look of disgust and instead answer the barrage of questions being thrown my way. He doesn’t say another word to me for the next two hours.

Week One

Samuel

Sweet Jesus, would you look at her? My hair feels too heavy for my head and the room too full of, well . . . her. She's thinner than I remember, and her haircut is more severe, I notice as she speaks to Ed. She's annoyed about something, that's for sure, because she's tapping her hand against her thigh quickly, like the day we argued about women drivers.

'If you could all turn to page two of the proposal?' she instructs. As if she hadn't just left in the middle of the night without a word, without any explanation. She stands there as cool as you like: grey suit, sharp creases, heels . . . it's hard to imagine her in her jeans and one of my shirts.

When I saw her name on the email about the proposed 'merger' with Sandwell the week after she left, I was sure it must be somebody else. I mean, there must be a million Sophie Williamses, right? But when I saw her picture next to her bio . . . well, it all became clear. The girl who hiccups when she laughs too much, who made me origami roses out of sugar packets, is really this woman: the woman who could send me a message after the week we had together wishing me 'all the best'.

I watch her stride towards the front of the room, confident and sure – not slightly awkward and shy at all – and I hate myself for being played. How long had she taken over the decision of who to betray? Did she look at all the men in power and choose me because I looked weak, or did she already know about my idea?

Tim Smith is clicking his pen irritatingly and I turn to him as he squints towards her. I've always thought that he looks like a shrew, or a vole. What was the character in *Danger Mouse*? Somebody once said he was a hamster, but I'm sure it was a mole.

'We at Sandwell Incorporated have had a breakthrough with one of our programmers in our tech department. He has designed a new piece of software that is faster and superior to any other systems of its kind.'

As she says this, my whole body feels hot and shaky; anger bubbles up inside as I watch her, not a tremor in her hand, not an embarrassed flush of her cheeks, while she stands there and pitches my idea as if it's her fecking own.

'We own the patent for this software.'

She is unbelievable.

My mouth is dry, and I take a sip of water as I watch her.

'Ms Williams?' I ask, my voice thick and stilted. I meet her eyes, which are hard and cold like amber. 'Can I ask how long your programmer has been working on this software?'

'I don't see how that is relevant at this point.' She looks at me as if she doesn't know me at all. Maybe she has forgotten me? Perhaps I'm not the only one she has gleaned information from.

I can't bring myself to ask her any more questions for the rest of the meeting, so I watch her, this stranger. I try to forget how she laughed at my jokes, and instead think about the way she would avoid telling me about her past, about her family. I try to forget how I had felt when she had fallen asleep with a book in her hand and how I had taken it from her, closed it and kissed her on her cheek; the way she had smiled even though she was asleep. I wonder now if she really had been asleep or if that had been part of her plan, to look vulnerable . . . It can't all have been a lie, can it? But I push this tiny bit of doubt aside.

It's late by the time I return home.

The phone is ringing. I ignore it; it's Mam. I love her to bits, but I can't face hearing about Da's bowel movements or about how my sister, Sarah, and brother-in-law have angels flying out of their arses. I grab a beer and a packet of crisps and turn on the rugby: Ireland v. Italy. I wince at a particularly hard tackle and roll the beer between my palms. I miss the feel of the game: the primal instinct that pushes you forward; the smell of grass and mud; the burning in your legs and the euphoria as you slam down the ball and score a try. My beer is finished before the scrum is reset for the fourth time, so I grab a refill from the kitchen.

I'm trying to stay focused on the game, shouting at the referee for allowing so much extra time to the Italians, but my mind keeps wandering to her.

Nobody knows much about our relationship, at least I don't think they do, but the day I saw her name on the email, I had spoken to Bret about it. We've been mates for a while now; he joined the company not long after me. But I don't think he would have said anything. I mean, it's not like I did anything wrong. I told Sophie about an idea, that was all. Just an idea. I didn't know she worked for Sandwell.

Week Two

Sophie

I have been staying in this hotel for almost two weeks, not that I'm here very often. It seems that every waking minute of my day is spent hunched over a computer or talking into a phone. Samuel has not spoken to me, will not take my calls, has not seen me as I've locked myself away with only my colleagues – who have finally arrived to help me with the merger – and the legal team from Greenlight. His silence is gnawing away at me even as I submerge myself in my work, barely eating and drinking far too much coffee.

I kick off my heels and slump on to the bed. I'm exhausted but pleased with the way the business side of things has gone. The board members, although they're not going to ask me out for drinks anytime soon, can at least now see how the company will benefit; understanding that – although there may be some restructuring – the majority of the staff will remain. I flick on the TV, my room a festival of stages. I pick up the room service menu and order a chicken sandwich. My attention is pulled towards the ashen greys of a bygone era – my comfort food in television form. The credits are proclaimed across the screen in big billboard letters: 'Paramount Pictures Presents', swathed in Hollywood lights and accompanied by dramatic music that must have been recorded in a room full of musicians. I smile as the shot pans towards a man with his head bent, a trilby hat dipping in that casual yet strangely formal way. He speaks through the corner of his mouth, and the woman who replies pronounces the word 'back' like 'beck'. She explains she needs to find a 'forgotten man'. A forgotten man . . . is that what he is to me? Or is he a man who wants to forget?

'You needn't be fresh,' she announces piously. I like that phrase and mimic it at my reflection.

The stresses of the week are starting to slide away just as my phone vibrates. I turn the volume down and look at the phone screen. I don't recognise the number.

'Hello?' I answer.

'Pleased with yourself, are you? Pleased that all of your hard work has turned out well for you?' His words are slurred.

'Samuel, I—'

'What? What can you possibly have to say to me that will make this right?'

I consider telling him that he needn't be fresh, but I don't think it would strike the right tone. 'I, look, I'd rather talk to you about this in person. I need to explain why I—'

'Why you stole my idea and passed it off as your own? No thanks, I'm grand.'

'That's not what happened. If I could come and see you, I could explain?'

He laughs loudly – an ugly, forced laugh – not the one that I remember; that laugh was so infectious that it made you smile every time you heard it, even when his jokes were terrible. 'What, and be seen out with you? Consorting with the enemy? No thanks.'

'Then why did you call?' I ask, my voice quiet and unsure. I look at the screen and at the way the actress is looking down with a sultry smile at the man, and wish for a second that I had a cigarette holder and a glass of champagne too.

'To thank you!' I can hear the background noise of a bar, almost see him raising his pint glass theatrically. 'To thank you for leaving like you did! You almost had me fooled, I almost . . . well, anyway, cheers! To the biggest bitch I've ever met!' And with that he hangs up.

The black phone screen reflects my stricken face. I pace around the room, grab the controller and watch the sloping smile of the hero downing the rest of his whiskey disappearing into darkness. I throw a cushion across the room before taking a few deep breaths, reaching for my laptop, and submerging myself in work.

I am due to return home the day after tomorrow. The day after tomorrow everything will change; my life will not be the same, because I know that the promotion is mine. I knew that it would be; they have as much as said it. I will be partner.

The last few people leave the office and cleaning staff begin to clear away the debris of the working day. Tentatively, a young girl reaches over and takes the coffee cup from my desk and smiles at me. I nod my thanks, stretch and then close down my laptop.

The deal is done but I need to speak to him. I must make him understand why I had no other choice than to leave him.

Later, as I lie in the bath, softly scented bubbles quivering and gossiping while I sip my cold glass of prosecco, I pick up *Great Expectations* again. I have been trying to read this book on and off for a year, and each time I do, I get distracted. When I was younger, Helen and I used to love reading. We used to spend our pocket money in bookshops, hiding beneath the covers with a torch: disappearing into someone else's world. It would block out the sound of the fighting, of the slamming doors and the suffocating sobs from Mum as she locked the bathroom door.

Even though I'm yet to find out who jilted Miss Havisham

at the altar, I close the battered cover again. Sinking lower into the bath, I close my eyes and think of the way he spoke to me, the way he looked at me. He needs to know the truth.

I watch as the lights of the city glide past the taxi window. Will he just slam the door in my face? I try to quell the feeling of nausea in my stomach – I shouldn't have drunk so much prosecco.

The taxi pulls up outside his modest gable-fronted house, which hunches behind a cluster of budding trees. His silver car is gleaming in the driveway in front of a double garage and the lights in the kitchen are glowing amber. The car door thuds behind me, my hand remaining on the handle until an impatient revving of the engine reminds me to let go.

I knock on the door. Inside I can hear music, something upbeat, and I smile briefly as I remember what awful taste in music he has: dreadful eighties rock music along with a deeply rooted affection for show tunes.

The bottom of my heel twists into the gravel, and I step back to look up at the house. He's definitely in there. I peer through the lounge window, trying to stop myself from laughing out loud as I watch him dancing, badly, with a ridiculous expression on his face – somewhere between having a bowel movement and sneezing. I take in his height; I'd forgotten how tall he is – six foot-twoish – and the way his dark hair flicks up on the right-hand side no matter how hard he tries to tame it. The song, which has him enraptured, is some sort of power ballad. Dramatically, he fills his lungs for the climax, exhaling it with a heartfelt screech; simultaneously playing a strangely shaped air-guitar and gyrating his hips. I crouch down and sneak back to the front door, giving it another sharp knock before the playlist continues.

The door opens and in an instant, the man I fell in love

with is gone, and in his place is a man with cold, calculating eyes and a tight line where his smile should be.

'What do you want?' he asks, his voice deep and serious; no hint of the high-pitched yelp I had first heard from him, as if his leg had been sliced by an axe, not kicked in the ankle by a Louboutin.

'To explain,' I reply. 'May I come in? Unless you're, um, busy?' I smile.

'I was just working out.'

I try to keep the smile on my face. 'In your jeans?' I look down at his jeans where his bare feet poke out. I meet his eyes, and for a second, they soften: but only for a second. He pushes the door open and I follow him into the spacious hall, with hardwood floors and white walls, dotted with photos of his family and life back in Derry.

I follow him into the kitchen where he opens the old-fashioned fifties-style fridge and pulls out a bottle of beer, twists off the lid and throws it into the bin. He turns to stare at me, and drinks deeply. I stare back, lean my back against the kitchen island and wait for him to finish.

'So. Explain.'

'I didn't steal your idea. We already had the software concept when we were . . . together.'

'Right. So, the reason you left the country in the middle of the night – the night, incidentally, that I told you about my idea that would change my career – and wouldn't return any of my emails or calls was because . . .?'

'I knew we were going to go after Greenlight.'

'So, you knew that I would probably lose my job?'

'Stop being so melodramatic. You're not going to lose your job. Can I have a drink?' He shrugs his shoulders like a sulky child. I walk past him, open the fridge and pull out a bottle of white wine, screw off the lid and swig from the bottle.

'Jesus, Sophie,' he says, sounding more Irish as he uses the word; he walks over to a cupboard and passes me a wine glass, which I fill to the top.

'You're not going to lose your job. It will just be . . . changed.'

'What if I don't want it to be changed?'

'You sound like a toddler.'

'I do not!' he replies, sounding exactly like a toddler.

'Your company was going down the pan – you know it and I know it. Our acquisition will save it.'

'How can you stand there all high and mighty? You left, Soph, in the middle of the fecking night, no call, no explanation and the next thing I hear is . . .' he air-quotes, '"Goodbye and all the best."' He opens the fridge and grabs another bottle of beer. 'And then, then . . . I find out that you're heading up the team analysing our data! And you turn up, looking like . . .' he gestures up and down at me with his beer bottle, 'that, and tell me that my idea, my big idea that was going to save our company, was actually used to buy it out!'

'I told you, we already had the plans for the software. It wasn't your big idea, we'd already pitched it.'

'So why not just say that?'

'Because I couldn't!' I shout at him. 'Can we, God, can we sit down? I'm knackered, and my feet hurt.' I take off my shoes and tread barefoot through the hall and into the lounge, the cool floorboards easing my soles. I sink into the pale-blue sofa and continue to drink my wine, waiting for him to follow me. Leaning my head back, I roll it to the left and right, trying to ease some of the tension.

'Why did you leave, Soph?' His voice is quiet, like he almost doesn't want me to answer. I sigh.

'I didn't know you worked at Greenlight until then.'

'You did! I told you about work, talked about it all the time. I—'

'You talked about computers all the time and you never called it Greenlight.'

'I did, I . . . shit. I always call it—'

'Emerald City,' we say in unison.

'But you must have guessed, must have—'

'Why? Because there is only one loan company in Washington?' I laugh. 'Believe me, I've replayed our conversations a million times, and you might find it hard to believe, but I simply never clicked. Besides, if you think about it, we didn't really talk about work that much.'

'You could have just told me.'

'No, I couldn't. I'd have had to come off the project.' I smile at him. 'Conflict of interest.'

'But nobody knew we were together. It was just us.'

'I couldn't risk it.' I shake my head, feeling the effects of the wine as I do. 'And then if you came out with your "big idea" they would have thought that I'd told you. I'd have lost my job.'

'So, the job meant more to you? More than what we had?' I look away from the hurt look on his face, his eyebrows creased, and eyes softened. I drink the rest of my wine.

'Yes.' He looks as me disbelievingly. 'Don't look at me like that. I've worked hard to get where I am. You don't know what it's like to have nothing, Samuel. You have a huge family that loves you, you can walk into anywhere and light up the room with your smile and crap Irish jokes; I'm not like you. I need my job.'

He leaves the room and returns with another beer and the bottle of wine, then fills up my glass and puts the bottle on the floor. 'So that's it? That's why you left?' He sits next to me and leans his elbow on the back of the sofa and his head on the heel of his hand. 'Because of my crap Irish jokes?'

I laugh and shake my head sadly. 'If they knew that we were, you know, I'd never have been able to close this deal, and I'd never be able to make partner.'

'And me? Did you care at all what I was going through? That I had no idea what I had done wrong?'

'I never stopped thinking about it. So here we are . . . a sulky Irishman and – what was it? Ah yes, the biggest bitch you've ever met.'

'Yeah, sorry about that. I'd had a few jars.'

'It's OK. I mean, not OK, but I understand why you would think that.'

We sit quietly for a few minutes; my stomach is churning from drinking the wine so quickly. 'Oh!' I get up and smile at him. 'I have something for you.'

'P45?'

'Funny. Wait there.' I go back into the kitchen, grab my handbag and return to the lounge. It smells of him: the same fabric softener and remains of this morning's aftershave. 'Open your hand and close your eyes.'

'I'm still pissed off at you. You know that, right?'

'Fine, but just do it.' He leans forward and puts his bottle on the floor, then closes his eyes. I resist the urge to kiss him and instead, put the box into his hand. 'OK, open it.'

'You're not proposing, are you?' He looks down at me and I realise that I'm kneeling on one knee.

I roll my eyes and sit back on my haunches. 'Just open it.'

I watch his hands, the knuckles dotted with pale freckles that are so faint I can't quite see them, but I know they're there. I know that he has a small scar on the inside of his left palm from trying to slice an apple when he was making apple pie with his gran but that he tells everyone it happened in a bar fight. I know that he has a slight callous on the inside of his thumb because he scrapes his index fingernail against it when he's thinking; I know how his hands feel when he holds the back of my neck.

'I'd forgotten how you do that,' he says, looking into my eyes.

'Do what?'

'Pull at your ear when you're thinking.'

'Do I?' I smile at him, pleased that he doesn't hate everything about me after all. My hair is caught in my hoop earring and I pull the tendrils free as he unwraps the red ribbon and opens the box. Carefully he pulls away the tissue paper and stares at its contents.

'Is that the same one?' I nod, feeling embarrassed and draining the remains of my glass of wine. Tentatively, he lifts the leaf up and stares at it.

'I never stopped thinking about how I must have hurt you. I wanted you to know that.'

Samuel replaces the leaf into its box and closes the lid. 'Thank you.' He leans forward and reaches for the side of my face, stroking it with his thumb. Everything inside me wants him. I rest my forehead against his.

'I'm sorry,' I say.

'Thank you. I'm sorry for calling you a bitch.'

And then I kiss him.

Week Two

Samuel

For feck's sake! For the fourth time this week, I have had to turn around and walk the other way in this building. I mean, would you look at me? I'm actually trying to camouflage myself behind a potted tree while she swings from side to side on one of the wheeled chairs, blond hair swishing neatly with her as she taps those manicured fingers on the desk.

'Samuel?' I flap the large green leaf out of my way, and pretend to look for something at the base of the plant.

'Kat, hi, just looking for my, erm, my cufflink.'

'You're not wearing cufflinks, though.'

'Well no, but, I lost one last week and I thought I might have lost it here.'

'In the pot plant?' she asks, smirking.

'Stop busting my balls, OK?'

'So, you and the Brit-bitch, eh?' she asks as I step out of the foliage and rearrange my hair.

'Brit-bitch?'

'Are you offended? I hear you and her were—'

'No. I mean I met her briefly, way before all this stuff went on.'

'Is that so?'

'It is,' I say with some conviction. 'Brit-bitch is a bit . . .'

'What? Harsh?'

'No, I was going to say lame. I would have thought of something a bit catchier, like "Britch", you know, has a better ring to it.'

'Britch? I like it.' She looks over to where Sophie is punching numbers into a calculator. 'She really is a piece of work, isn't she?'

I'm wary of my answer. Kat is well known for orchestrating discord in the office. 'I don't know much about her really.' I look away from the way her fingers are punching the numbers and ignore the nagging feeling inside that pushes a vague memory of Kat at the bar the other night to the forefront. I turn my attention back to Sophie and wonder if she is working out if I am a viable asset or – if the rumours are true – I'm surplus to requirements. I pull out my phone to check for messages and then turn to walk away.

'I'll let you know if I see it,' Kat adds.

'Eh?'

'The cufflink?'

'Oh right, thanks.'

This is ridiculous. I re-read the last paragraph of the self-help book which Sarah left last time she was here.

'I am a handsome, successful man, I do not need anyone to make me feel worthy. I am master of my own destiny . . . and I sound like a twat.'

It's not self-help that I need. I need Jon. Jon was my first love: is my first love. I don't know when our love affair began – maybe it was when I first saw his hair, or the way his leather trousers fitted in a way I could never get mine to, but I knew it was love.

My hands are almost shaking with anticipation as I reach for the dial; I have no control of my body as the beat begins. I stand, legs slightly apart, bent at the knees and head bowed in reverence as I begin to live on a prayer. I use the gravelly part of my voice that empowers the struggle of Tommy's life as he worked on the docks; I lean forward and sing into my bottle of beer, 'wahoooing' all the way there, my mood lifting considerably.

There is a knock on the door, so I pause the playlist. It's unusual for anybody to visit me at this time in the evening. My stomach growls and I hope that it might be girl scouts selling cookies; instead, it is her: the Britch.

I can feel the comfort and security that Jon has given me ebb away as I look at her. I have always been overwhelmed by her beauty. That's the wrong word to use. My da always said I was a 'namby-pamby'. I once showed him a piece of poetry that I'd written at school. My English teacher, Miss Clarke, had almost cried when she'd read it. She'd said that if there were more boys in the world like me then there would be less fighting. When I told Da this – after he had finally stopped laughing – he clipped me round the ear and told me to man up. As I look at the flush in her cheeks and the way she looks up at me, I can hear Da's voice: 'Treat 'em mean, keep 'em keen.'

'What do you want?' I ask.

She wants to explain, she says, and then she does this thing: she bites her lip, no, not bites, she sort of pulls her bottom lip with her teeth, and I know she's nervous. I feel myself wanting to hold her but then I think about Da and the poetry and Jon . . . Jon wouldn't take this shit. I let her in and she follows me into the kitchen.

When I was a kid, I used to watch this American sit-com and every episode, I was jealous of the kids in it because they always had bottles of Coke in this big old fridge. We only ever had two-litre plastic bottles of supermarket-brand coke, which Da used to swig from. When I moved in here, this fridge was the first thing I bought, that and six bottles of Coke that needed a bottle opener to open . . . I even got them customised: 'Share a bottle with Samuel'. I reach in and grab a bottle of beer, ignoring the bottle of wine that I should be offering to her. It's a small victory and I hide my smile as my hand passes it; her favourite bottle of white is hiding next to the milk and she isn't going to have a drop. I rearrange my face and turn to her.

'So, explain.'

I listen as she tells me that she already had the software pitch outlined before I told her about my idea, but I'm fighting the memory of that night. The strawberry stains on her fingers as they sliced the fruit into bowls – neat, precise quarters: whole hearts dissected. I remember I could still taste them later as we kissed and the way I could still smell them on the sheets after she'd left.

How does she do it? I sigh as Sophie passes me, taking the wine and my small victory with her, dismissing my complaints and making the whole mess sound like an argument about leaving a damp towel on the floor rather than stealing my ideas and leaving me, quite literally, in the dark . . . Now she's going on about my job just changing. I don't want it to change. It's not fair.

'What if I don't want it to be changed?'

'You sound like a toddler.'

'I do not!' She raises her eyebrow at me.

'Can we, God, can we sit down? I'm knackered, and my feet hurt.' She drains her glass and refills it before turning on her heels and heading for the lounge.

She plays with her ear as she sinks into the sofa and it kills me: that tell that lets me know she's concentrating on what she is going to say.

I glance at her glass of wine; her slim fingers edged with rose-pink nails grip on to the stem: she's drinking too much too quickly. I notice the edges of her words have softened, their clipped consonants filed down, the spaces in her sentences becoming shorter and her gestures more animated. She kneels in front of me, asking me to close my eyes. Her hair has caught in the small silver hoop earrings. I'm still angry, I tell her, but the need I feel to unhook her hair and hold her is contradicting my words.

I open the small box and inside is proof: proof that I was right to feel about her the way that I did. I can feel my heart pulsing, my blood quickening, bringing fire and warmth to my body when I didn't realise it had been cold. She must see the way I'm looking at her and I worry that the intensity of my feelings is scaring her. Her smile is fading, and she looks pale. I lean forward to reassure her that there is nothing to be scared of and then she kisses me . . . and I feel like I've come home.

There is a girl lying in my bed. A girl who has a small chicken pox scar on her left eyebrow, a girl who in the short time I have known her has made me feel hatred and love, betrayal and loyalty, fear and security. I know she can't see the way that I'm stroking her hair, the way I'm watching her snoring gently, and the way that I'm smiling: slightly sadly, because I know that she is not entirely mine. I pull my arm from under her and kiss her on the forehead, step into my shorts and go about the business of cleaning up last night's mess.

The washing machine whirs into action, as I try to light the gas on the cooker and place the kettle on top. The big American fridge hums next to the old dinosaur of a gas stove. There are times when I have almost gone for the convenience of an electric cooker, an electric kettle, but there is just something about the routine of manually lighting the gas, the whoosh as it ignites, the whistle of the kettle on the hob, that makes this place, so far from home, feel like home. While the kettle heats up, I stare out of the kitchen window as the sun starts to rise, turning the kitchen walls the colour of those bubble-gum-pink lollies that I used to eat as a child. I spoon coffee into two mugs and smile as I replay the events of the night before: her embarrassment and the way she had started hiccupping; how her hand had flown to her mouth to try and hold in their sound and the way she had started giggling when they wouldn't stop. The hard-nosed businesswoman laughing and snorting like a little girl. How she had fallen asleep on the sofa and the feel of her as I carried her up to the spare room. The way she had snuck into my room while I slept, smelling of soap and toothpaste; the way her skin felt beneath me and the things she said.

I close myself in the downstairs study and reach for the phone. I have no choice. I have to do it.

Week Three

Sophie

The smell of coffee wakes me up. I stretch with contentment, allowing myself a few minutes of luxury as I replay last night. The lilt of his accent from downstairs fills the room as I glance at the clock. I should be going into the office to double-check everything is in order, but I can't seem to find enough urgency to get out of this bed. I roll over on to my stomach and bury my head in the pillow, breathing in his smell, and I know that this is right. I was right to come over last night and I was right to, well, I was right to knock on his door.

As a door closes quietly downstairs, I hunt for my clothes but instead put on his shirt like some clichéd romance film and wander downstairs. His voice continues from behind the study door and so I finish making the coffee, adding milk and stirring his three spoons of sugar into his cup. The door to his study opens.

'Jesus, but you gave me a fright!' he says, looking startled. He looks back at the door then to me with a half-smile, as if he can't quite remember why I am here.

'Do I look that bad?' I ask, raising my eyebrow and passing him the cup. He notices the shirt and gives a soft chuckle as I pick up my mug.

'Too tacky?' I ask, sipping at my coffee.

‘No, not in the least . . . especially when there’s a button missing.’ I look down as he walks towards me, taking the mug from my hand.

He’s snoring softly as I creep from the bed, put the shirt back on and go in search of my bag and, more importantly, my phone. I might not need to go into the office, but I do need to check my emails.

The lounge door closes quietly behind me, muting Samuel’s snores as I retrieve my phone. There are fifteen missed calls from Gemma, my assistant. I sigh, shake my head and scroll through the missed calls: there are missed calls from Bob, too. This strikes me as odd, given that he’s on paternity leave. I open my email account and see that there is a meeting scheduled for when I get back to the UK. Something about these things makes me feel uneasy: something is wrong. I bite the skin around my thumb and then call Gemma . . . if I’m being paranoid, I don’t want to bother Bob when he’s not at work.

‘Where have you been?’ she yells down the phone.

‘I’ve, um, I’ve had a sickness bug, why? What’s the matter?’ My blood is starting to feel cold inside my body.

‘The shit has hit the fan, that’s what. Have you spoken to Bob? He’s been trying to get hold of you, too.’

‘What do you mean?’ I hear the jangle of her charm bracelet, picture her twisting her purple hair around her finger, picture the inside of the office.

‘I mean that some guy from Greenlight has been telling a load of lies about you!’

My hands start to shake. ‘What kinds of lies?’

‘That you stole the idea about the software.’

‘That’s ridiculous.’ My mouth has gone dry. ‘Tim knows that it was my idea.’

‘Well, I heard him talking on the phone and apparently Greenlight are going to start legal action against us. They’re saying that you had an "inappropriate relationship" with someone there when the deal began, to gain inside information. They won't go ahead with the merger unless you're disciplined, I mean, you know, fired.'

'Who, I mean, do you know who started the rumours?' I ask, not wanting to hear his name but knowing it couldn't have been anyone else. I close my eyes. '*But nobody knew we were together. It was just us,*' he'd said.

'No. But they have minutes from a meeting that has this idea on it, and it was just after you went over to Greenlight the first time. I heard them in the meeting, Sophie. They're going to fire you.'

'I'll get the next flight. Don't tell anyone we've had this conversation, do you understand?'

'Of course.'

I deserve this. My eyelids close and push back the tears that are forming. Of course I deserve this. It's ridiculous to think that I could just turn up here after I left him without an explanation and everything would go back to how it was. He thinks that I'm the woman who stole his idea. He's blinded by my armour, I'm hidden from him . . . he can't see me.

I'm lost.

And this time he can't find me.

I call for a taxi, and as quietly as I can, I collect my things from the spare room then hurry back into the lounge where I write him a quick note:

Samuel,
I understand why.
Soph x

And with that, I close the door on Samuel.

*

The next flight is in an hour. I shower away the smell of him from my skin; I brush away the taste of him from my mouth, each action applying a fresh layer of skin, adding another layer of protection. I throw my things into my case, drink a tall glass of water and leave the room without a backward glance.

As I wait for the lift, I hum the hymn that is leaking from one of the hotel rooms: 'Lord of the Dance'. Memories of myself as an awkward thirteen-year-old standing in assembly at school chip away at the confident businesswoman that I have become. I wait for the lift to open, ignore the arguing couple whose responses and gestures tell of a lifetime together: he moves an apologetic hand; she drops her shoulder a split second after, subconsciously knowing his every move, his every gesture. Do they know how special that is? Pressing the button again, I straighten up, avoiding the haunted reflection that looks questioningly back at me from the mirrored doors. My reflection splits in two and I walk through the doors and ask for the ground floor.

I step out into the lobby and for a second, I can smell him, see his smile, feel his touch. The images try to scratch at my new skin, to bury themselves beneath it, but I push them back. This time I will heal. I shake my head and walk over to reception. My nails tap agitatedly on the desk while I wait to check out and ask for a taxi to the airport.

'Which one?' the receptionist asks.

'Reagan National Airport, please.'

'Sure thing.'

As we pull away from the hotel, I fight against an invisible cord that tries to drag me back. The sound of his voice calling my name repeats over and over in my head. My fingers reach inside my handbag, pull out my headphones and force them inside my ears; music plays as I close my eyes. The taxi pulls me further away, the cord being cut in two – cutting the link between us.

I can register the words that they are saying but I can't *hear* them. They are snowballs hitting my face: sharp words that melt and disintegrate, leaving me cold and shaking.

I have now been awake for hours; my body has no idea whether it should be awake or asleep. I've come straight from the airport, needing to set the record straight before any more damage is done. I'm wearing the same clothes I wore when I left DC and I smell of sweat and desperation.

'We have to let you go, I'm sorry,' Tim says neutrally, as if his words are not ricocheting around the room piercing my skin like shrapnel.

'But I put this deal together!' I throw my hands up, revealing sweat circles beneath my armpits. They look away, embarrassed by my emotions. I don't blame them; I would look away too. I catch my reflection in the tinted glass windows. My hair is a mess: my curls, unleashed from their serum-straightened restraint, are veering away from my head at all angles. I've never cried within these walls, but my reflection shows uneven smudges beneath my eyes.

Behind me, I can see necks craning to see through the glass-partitioned wall, sniggers of staff who have been jealous of my success smirking and throwing smug glances at each other.

My façade is starting to crumble with every desperate word that I say, with every response that they launch back at me.

'There is no other option here. Greenlight simply won't entertain a deal with you involved. You're lucky that they aren't taking matters further . . . that *we* aren't taking matters further. They have shown us minutes from a meeting where Samuel McLaughlin pitched the software idea not long after your . . . time in Washington.' He raises his eyebrows at me as if he is a disapproving headmaster. 'I'm sorry, but there is just no room here at Sandwell for . . . loose lips, shall we say?'

'But the software was my idea.' I can feel myself unravelling, my words coming out in a tone that is close to pleading. 'I can't help it if Samuel had the same idea.'

He shakes his head and looks down his small piggy nose at me, arranging his features, somewhere between looking stern and amused.

'So, it's just a coincidence that two people from opposite sides of the world just happened to have the same idea at the same time?' he says incredulously.

'Yes!'

This time I don't need to decide what emotion he is trying to convey. It's clear in the dip of his head, his chin dropping into his long neck: pity.

'Well, it sounds like you are perfect for each other.' He shuffles some papers on his desk. 'I'm sorry, Sophie. I'm afraid your time here at Sandwell has come to an end. Of course, you may keep the company car for another month and we will be offering you a generous severance package. That is . . . if you're happy to keep this incident as quiet as possible.'

My head nods without my control.

It's over. Everything that I have worked so hard to achieve has been taken from me. I know that no argument I can make will change their minds, and I refuse to beg.

'Very well. I wish you every success in the future.'

Somehow, I find an appropriate response. My words are formal, proper and devoid of the emotion that my face is revealing. I wipe away my embarrassment with the heel of my hand and pack up my things.

The office hushes as I walk out of the meeting room, and glances dart towards me; the air is rich with gossip, effervescent with anticipation.

Gemma half-rises in her seat. The movement is hesitant, conflicted, but resolved by an apologetic smile towards me, then a dismissive turn of her back.

I keep my head up, my legs keep walking, my back remains straight, even though inside I feel like I'm falling apart.

Rain is hammering against my front door as I push it open, drop my case to the floor, and let it slam against the frame. Silence follows its protests, cowering in every corner of the house.

The fridge hums inside the kitchen and I open it, staring at the contents. Grabbing a bottle of white wine, I twist the top off and go to take a sip; the memory of him is almost too close to bear. In rebellion I take a swig anyway, this time continuing to drink without a glass. My phone begins to vibrate. I take it from my pocket and without looking at the screen throw it against the wall. Tiny pieces of it shatter on to the floor, emails and data, photos and contacts surround me, and I start to laugh. Look at it; look at how pitiful my life is: a few broken pieces of glass, memory chips, plastic and gleaming metal. Look at how useless it is. I take another swig of the wine then pull out my laptop. I log on to my email and close the account, allowing myself the small victory of taking charge of the decision rather than having a faceless name denying me access. I take another swig: delete, delete, delete – I close all my social media accounts. By the time the last of the wine slides down my throat I have erased Sophie Williams. Sophie Williams is dead. I unplug the landline from the wall and throw it into the bin, then I sit down and cry. Each tear that falls strips away the façade that I've worked so hard to put up; the business woman with clipped vowels walks away without a backwards glance, leaving behind a girl with scuffed shoes and a hand-me-down uniform.

Week Three

Samuel

The door thuds. A quiet, hushed thud, the type you would make if you spread your arms, leant back and sank into soft snow, an angel created, a memory cherished. My eyes open and I know. I know she's gone.

I rush to the window just in time to see the taxi pull away, the blue sky reflecting back at me from the rear window. I bang on the window with my fists. The sound is angry and urgent inside this room, but outside, I know, it will not even drown out the insistent tapping of the woodpecker in the large conifer across the road. 'Shit,' I say as I push my feet through my jeans.

Optimism instructs my eyes to look for clues around the house. Maybe she has just left to go and grab us a coffee? Groceries for a romantic breakfast in bed? Hope fills me until I see the note left on the table.

How can she possibly know? And what does she think she understands?

I have no idea where she is or where she would be going, but as I leave the house, I hope against all the odds that she's at the same hotel as last time.

'Feck sake,' I groan as I stand in front of the hotel. Rotating doors: my nemesis. My eyes narrow at them as I take a confident step towards the slow-moving glass rectangles. They have hindered my path many times before, but today is not going to be one of those days. Here are the reasons that this is not going to happen to me today:

1. I am not carrying an oversized bag over my shoulder that could get myself and said bag trapped.
2. I have not drunk a bottle of ten-year-old ouzo and felt confused enough to do three whole rotations before my sister pulls me out (after she has recorded it to upload to YouTube).
3. I am the only person about to enter the revolving doors, therefore reducing my chances of being trapped once again while Sarah jams the doors and films my inability to escape for yet more YouTube uploads.

I take a deep breath, loosen my shoulders and walk into the gilded chamber to be deposited into the hotel lobby without incident. I straighten myself and give my glassy-eyed opponent a nod of respect.

I follow my feet, which are encased in pale-blue baseball Converse, in a fashion probably more suited to younger soles; slightly worn on the inside because I always walk – according to my sister – like I'm deliberately trying to trip myself up. Their hastened steps stop at the desk; I face a small receptionist with caterpillar-like eyebrows – no, not caterpillar-like . . . It takes me a moment to place where I have seen such beasts before, then it dawns on me: the tail of my childhood pet cat, Marmalade. I'm mesmerised as they arch up and down, in the same way that Marmalade's tail would swish and curl at the sound of the tin opener, and wonder what the deal is with women and their thick eyebrows at the moment. She is talking to a tall, unkempt man in a crumpled black suit. It is much travelled, that suit, I can't help but observe.

'Excuse me?' I interject. In my head, an image pops up of Marmalade's tail shooting up in fear as I squirted water at him with a home-made water pistol: the latest in the highest end of the Fairy washing-up bottle range. 'Please could you tell me which room Sophie Williams is staying in? I'm her, um, brother.'

I have no idea why I said that, when clearly we both have very different appearances and our accents are nothing like the same. 'Half-brother.' Shite. That would still probably give us the same accents. 'I mean, step-brother, um, twice removed.' I look at the eyebrows, unfurling above two amused-looking eyes. The transatlantic suit wrinkles and shifts.

'Is she expecting you?'

'Yes.' I nod convincingly. I watch as the minute hand on the clock above the desk clicks onwards.

'Four-Five-Four.' The eyebrows reward me for my hard work. I grasp the information, run towards the lift and press the up button. And press it again. And press it again. Until the doors finally open.

I hurry out of the lift, looking to the left, to the right, taking in the Jackson Pollock-esque prints, the emergency exit posters, the cleaning trolley, the arguing couple – their middle-aged faces showing to the world that they've had this argument before and their relationship is over even if they don't know it themselves yet. I walk past the doors; each room is hidden and each occupant a mystery. Only one room's secrets escape, as the hymn 'Lord of the Dance' spills under the doors: one moment of its notes climbing higher and higher and I am thirteen again, standing in our church, pretending to look at the hymn book and not down the top of the girl in the pew in front of me; she always missed a button on her blouse, revealing a glimpse – a promise – of a lacy bra. The sound stops just as I arrive in front of her room: 454.

My fist hammers against the door. 'Sophie!' I yell, my hand becoming sore. The couple quieten, their argument forgotten, foreheads touching: a compromise met. 'Sophie!' I shout again.

'She's just left,' the woman tells me. The husband puts a protective hand on her shoulder, guiding her into their room.

The lift announces its unexpected arrival and I quickly step inside, urging it to descend faster. I rush to the desk and interrupt the receptionist and the crumpled-suit man again, asking if she has checked out.

'She's just left,' Marmalade explains.

I run out on to the kerb, scanning up and down the street: the people, the buildings, the traffic, the homeless man counting the change in his hat. All of this has blurred edges because all I can see is the back of her head through the taxi window, and indicator lights blinking as it edges away.

My feet chase, my mouth shouts her name over and over again, my hands pull at the back of my hair, but the taxi is already picking up speed.

I run back into the hotel.

'Where was she going?' I ask marmalade brows.

'The airport,' she answers, looking irritated as I interrupt her hair-swishing and furtive conversation with crumpled-suit man.

'Which one?' I ask. Something about my desperation must soften her opinion of me.

'Reagan National.'

The traffic is slow. My eyes fill with tears of frustration and I pound the steering wheel.

Tock, tock, tock . . . time stands over my shoulder as I park the car and escape the seat belt. Tock, tock, tock . . . I push my way past excited groups of travellers, through the doors, and scan the screens for the next flight to London:

it's boarding. I sprint to the gate, but the air steward tells me that I can't go through. No, he says, I can't buy a ticket: the flight is full.

Actions that I have been performing all my life become difficult. I find that I'm having to concentrate on sucking in air and releasing it. I'm having to tell my legs to support my body, having to tell my hands to not respond to the heavy grasp of the security guard as he pulls me away. I have lost her, again.

Week Four

Sophie

I sleep.

Mornings and nights roll into one, until I eventually venture out of my bed and into the shower.

I make a coffee, but the smell feels like mould: claggy and dense. Instead, I open a can of bitter lemon, resisting the urge to glug a shot of vodka into it, and add some crushed ice from the fridge dispenser, then drink it quickly, quenching a thirst that I didn't know I had.

It's strange having nothing to do. Time stretches in front of you, taunting you. I open another can of bitter lemon, refill my glass and carry it into the lounge where a stack of paperwork sneers at me from my glass-topped dining table. I lean against the door frame and sip my drink, daring myself to go over and take a look, like curling the edge of a plaster that needs to be ripped off. My waste-paper basket is full and as I scan the room, I notice that there is a thin layer of dust coating every surface. I wander over to the television screen and draw a smiley face on it then laugh out loud into the stillness, wondering how many of my 'colleagues' are laughing at me right now. I swipe the screen with my sleeve, and do the same for the inside of one of the box-shaped shelves of the TV storage unit – complete with slanting books and random glass ornaments, none of which really mean anything to me.

When I was growing up, my house was stuffed with heavy pieces of memorabilia. Mum would buy any old tat from the most mundane of day trips and fit them in hidden, cluttered spaces. She used to say they told our story; anyone could walk into our house and our whole life's story would be there for anyone to see. It would bother me. Why would she want to share our memories with everyone? Surely the most precious of memories should be kept safe, away from prying eyes . . . but what was kept hidden and safe were the secrets, ugly and wounding. Perhaps if she had displayed her bruises and broken bones like her souvenirs, then she would still be alive.

The thought of Mum startles me. I don't normally allow myself the indulgence of thinking about her; it hurts too much. But I hear her voice as clear as if she was standing right beside me as she read me my favourite bedtime storybook, *The Alice in Wonderland Collection*: '"Why, sometimes I've believed as many as six impossible things before breakfast."' I can feel her arms around my shoulders, feel her body shift, smell my damp hair after my bath as she reached her arm and turned the page. I picture us at the breakfast table as she poured milk into a jug, sugar into a bowl as we listed the 'six impossible things' we could do before we eat. 'Grow wings,' I announced, pushing my arms either side of my body as she smiled at me, passing a spoon into my hand. '*Change your hair colour with a blink*.' She over-exaggerated a blink, looking disappointed when her hair remained brown. My stomach churns, the bitter lemon only just making it into the toilet bowl.

I push the thoughts of Mum away and distract myself by tidying the house, cleaning the surfaces and throwing out the paperwork, trying to avoid eye contact with the figures and spreadsheets that have made up the last year of my life. I vacuum, polish, scrub the toilet; domestic chores that were once secondary to my life, seemingly now becoming my priority.

I turn on my laptop and place a supermarket delivery, suddenly feeling ravenous. I fill the little cart icon with salads, blue cheeses and meats; I begin to add popcorn, ice cream, rich, creamy pasta sauces, pâtés and wine: lots of wine.

My delivery arrives later in the day. Dusk is already scraping the daylight away and I keep my head down, avoiding all attempts at polite conversation from the delivery man, and close the door behind him, drawing the door-chain across. I carry as much food as I can into my bedroom, scattering the feast on top of my bed. Reaching into the back of my wardrobe, I pull out my collection of old black-and-white films, classics from an era of gallant heroes and women with elegant hats and cigarette holders. A car alarm sends flashes of colour into my room and noise penetrates my silence. I press play on the DVD player and turn up the volume, reach for my wine, grab a handful of popcorn as the flashing lights stop, and retreat into a life of black and white.

Week Four

Samuel

'What do you mean, you think it's best that I take some leave?' I stride back and forth across the office. Bob Golding, the big chief, shifts in his seat; his stomach is pushed as close to the desk as is possible for him to be able to reach the keyboard and his phone. I'm reminded of one of those tubs of slime that you used to play with as a kid, the ones that made a fart sound when you pushed your fingers inside. He shifts again, and I wonder briefly how much food he must have to consume in a day to get that big.

'Just until the complexities of your contract are checked, and the matter has been investigated.'

'There is nothing to investigate! Sandwell have confirmed that they had already been outlining their final pitch before I even met Sophie Williams. So, let's say I had mentioned my idea, it wouldn't have made any difference anyway.'

'Well, of course they would say that! We can't disprove it either way. We are liaising with their head office about the matter, but since Ms Williams has been let go, they are having problems contacting her.'

'What do you mean, let go?'

He fidgets again, the sleeves of his white shirt straining against the tops of his arms as he pushes his gold-framed glasses further up his hooked nose. 'Oh, I thought you knew, Samuel. She's been fired.' He pats down his oil slick of hair with his left hand, revealing a skin-tight silver bracelet without a jangle. 'We categorically stated that unless she was taken off the project, we would not entertain the merger. It's a trust issue, you see. A lot of people believe she – how can I put it? – used you to get information about your idea and—'

'I don't see how this has any impact on the issues in my contract. I'm entitled to receive six weeks—'

'You may not be entitled to anything, Samuel. That is why we need this investigation to take place.'

'She didn't steal my idea.'

'From what I gather from the office gossip, your relationship was short-lived, so how do you know? Can you tell me you are absolutely certain that this woman is not capable of coaxing information out of an employee of this company for her own gain?'

I picture the way she had replied to me when I'd asked her how she could leave me after the time we'd spent with each other: *I'm not like you, I need my job* – wasn't that what she'd said?

'I believe your relationship ended abruptly?' His thick Deep South drawl coats my memories of the hiccupping origami-girl with poison.

'With the greatest of respect, Bob, that is nothing to do with my job or this investigation.'

'Of course, of course. My apologies. I'm sure that her departure from our shores straight after she heard your idea has no connotations whatsoever.'

'How long?' I ask, not allowing myself to reply to his comment.

'A month at least.' He sneezes, then blows into a tissue from his top drawer, his buttons striving to contain his great mass inside the cotton restraints.

'Fine,' I answer, and slam the door behind me.

*

My eyes hurt as I search through fifty-seven Sophie Williams Facebook profiles. I'm beginning to think that the whole world is becoming insane: profile pictures presenting dogs in outfits; an entire week's worth of posts from one Sophie, dating and describing each and every time she had eaten, what she had eaten and where she had eaten it; as well as several hundred different types of pouts and eyebrows, all kind of merging into one, singular female in her early twenties.

There is a rhythmical knock on the door, a call and respond beat – the kind that implies the knocker is a friend.

'What the hell, Sammy boy! Open the goddamn door! I can see your shadow through the curtain.' I open the door to see Bret – quarterback tall and sun-bleached blond – frowning at me. 'Well, you took your sweet time about it. You don't call, you don't write . . .'

'Not in the mood, man. I gather you've heard about my . . .' I finger-quote the words, '"leave"?'

He follows me back into the lounge and to my desk. 'Yeah, I've heard nothing but that all morning. So, what's going on, really? The last we spoke you hated the Britch and now I hear from Kat – who by the way has been telling everybody your entire relationship details from start to finish – that you're head over heels with Ms Williams. She said you were stalking her from behind a plant?'

'Yeah, well, a lot can happen in a week. How the hell does Kat know all about . . . shite.' The blurry memory of her at the bar the night I called Sophie reminds me. 'Never mind.'

'So? What's going on?'

'I love her.'

'Whoah, hold on there. Rewind. The woman you've done nothing but complain about for the last four months? The woman who stole your idea?'

'She didn't steal it.'

'Uh-huh, well, you've sure changed your mind. I was with you at the bar that time when you called her. You told me the whole story, remember? Jeez, man, how many Jameson's did you drink?'

'A lot has happened since then. She came here, she explained she had no choice last time – they already had the idea, so . . .' I shrug as if having my heart torn in two wasn't that big a deal, 'conflict of interest.'

'And you buy that? Buddy, I know how crushed you were when she left but—'

'She stayed. The night.'

'Right, but does that change the game? Really? It's not as if you've not batted an innings on that pitch before.'

'Your sports metaphors are getting worse.'

'I thought holes and balls might be a little crass.' He flashes his American pearly whites in a grin, perfect dimples forming in his tanned cheeks – a far cry away from my pale complexion and freckles. 'All right, Sammy boy, what's the state of play?'

We make our way through the first six-pack as I fill him in. 'I've rung Sandwell and nobody will tell me a thing; her phone just goes to answer phone, I can't find her anywhere. I'd get a plane but what would I do when I get there?'

He pulls his massive frame from the sofa, does a couple of squats, links his fingers, turns them and stretches them before cracking his knuckles.

'Let's find your gal then, Sammy boy.'

'I've tried . . . look.' I reach over and grab the notebook covered in unsuccessful Facebook searches.

'I thought you didn't do social media.'

'I don't. It's full of fake people with fake news and fake—'

'All right, all right. Sorry I mentioned it. Have you tried Twitter? Insta?'

'Not yet.'

'Right. I'll log on to my accounts. Order us a pizza, will you? I'm starving.'

Daylight fades, lights blink on, curtains yawn and stretch. Bret leans back, defeatedly throwing a cold pizza crust into its box.

'Mate, it's as if she's disappeared.'

'But she has to be somewhere!' I march up and down the lounge. 'We just have to find her.'

'I hate to say it, Sammy boy . . . but maybe she doesn't want to be found.'

Week Five

Sophie

It is half-eleven in the evening and I am currently throwing up. Again. Too much wine and stilton. My time has been spent lying in bed drinking, eating and watching old films. It's amazing how exhausted you can feel when you're doing nothing.

I stare at my pale reflection, my hands gripping on to the sides of the sink. This has got to stop. I wash my face, dry my hands and go into the kitchen. I blink at the light's harsh intrusion and open the fridge door. The remaining wine is still sitting there and so I pour it down the sink, retching again as the smell hits me, bringing up only bile this time.

Morning comes with the realisation that I need to pull myself together. I pull up the roman blinds and stare outside as buttery light sugar-coats the edges of the harsh, black pavements like lemon curd on burnt toast. Hot jets of water awaken me further, as I shower and change, straighten my hair, adding make-up to my face for the first time in a couple of weeks; I even venture out to the corner shop and buy some newspapers and a litre bottle of ginger ale.

I sit with my legs tucked beneath me, the soft-grey chenille sofa cushioning my body, as I try to remember the last time I read the papers in my own lounge as opposed to a coffee shop or on the train. Job pages leap forward, leaving the world's tragedies behind, and I begin circling prospective opportunities, but the pages have become blurred. It takes a moment for me to notice that I am crying again. I close the papers and hold my head in my hands. A feeling of helplessness fills the void inside; the void that I didn't know was there. I know I'm not ready. I need to wait until my name isn't bouncing off the lips of everyone in acquisitions and finance. I know what I have to do. My hands are shaking as I plug the phone back into its socket and dial the familiar number.

'Hi,' I say, noticing my voice has a rougher tone to it: it's injured and scraped. 'It's me.'

'Sophie, now is not a good time. Caitlin has just stuffed sweetcorn up her nose and I can't get it out.' My sister's life is always peppered with one disaster after another. 'No, Jess!' I hear a muffled scream as she moves the phone away from her ear. 'Put the worm down! No! Not down the toilet. Soph, can I call you back?'

'Helen, I, I, just needed a chat,' I say, feeling the need to be by her side.

'Just a sec. For God's sake, Greg! Can you just watch them for a minute? I need the loo.' I hear the background noise of Greg's deep voice, the thuds of Helen's steps up the stairs and then the noise is dulled by the click of what I presume is the bathroom door. 'This is the only place I can get some peace and quiet.' I hear the noise of the toilet seat slamming down. 'So, what's up? I haven't heard from you for ages. How is it in the world of finance and the big smoke?'

'I've messed up, Hel.' I'm crying again.

'Soph?' I can hear the surprise in my sister's voice, the sister I have barely spoken to in the past month. 'Sophie?' I am sitting slumped against the wall, holding the phone against my shoulder as my words are stifled by claustrophobic sobs.

'Can I come and stay for a few days?' I ask.

'Where else would you go?' Relief floods my body as I hang up the phone.

It feels good to be driving away from the city. The further away, the more relaxed I become. The grey sky lies above me like a duvet, folds and creases smothering the cold toes of spring. I push my foot down harder on the accelerator, the call of the familiar urging me forward. Funny that I should feel this way, when I felt the exact opposite when I left.

For step-sisters to become as close as we did is unusual: two broken families forced to become one new one. I didn't want them to come and live with us; it had been just Mum and I, since I was three. I have no recollection of my dad other than the few family photos that Mum insisted on keeping around the house, even though he had left her. She even – morbidly, ridiculously – framed his letter telling her he didn't love her any more and that this wasn't 'the right life' for him. I remember being embarrassed by that letter and dreaded having friends over in case they saw it. I mean, how do you explain that you weren't 'right' for your own father?

I take a sip of my bottled water, thankful that the hangover is starting to go. The motorway stretches out languorously towards the countryside as I think about those early days when Helen and her dad Ian moved in.

I had always wanted a baby brother. I remember playing with my baby doll called Damian. I used to cut up my dad's old clothes and make him romper suits out of his blue shirts and pretend to give him milk from an old pop bottle. Helen was the opposite: an older sister.

We lived in a semi-detached cottage deep in the hills near the Mid Wales coast. Next door was an elderly lady who smelt like cabbage and lavender. It was cold all the time, except in the middle of summer, if the sea breeze was kind. I remember peeking from behind a crack in the door as Helen unpacked her pretty cotton nightdresses – mine were all thick and thermal. She must have known I was there, watching the way her long brown hair curled at the ends and noticing how she seemed to have a permanent smile on her face. I had scurried into the room after my bath – embarrassed to have to share the room with someone I didn't know, as well as someone who was four and a half years my senior – but she had smiled and passed me one of her nighties.

'You can have this if you like . . . it was my favourite, but it's a bit small for me.'

'Thanks,' I had whispered and then clambered under my covers, my five-year-old eyes avoiding her smiling ones. She settled herself into the bed opposite, turning on the bedside lamp.

'Do you like stories?' she asked. I had nodded, afraid to break the spell that had woven its way into my cold room. 'Oh good! Do you mind if I read it out loud? I love sharing stories . . . my mum used to read out loud to me, all the time, and we'd try and guess what was going to happen next. Sometimes, we would have to look up the words that we didn't know in a dictionary and then we would write them down on paper and make a word-wall that covered my whole bedroom wall . . . could we do that? Is that OK? Do you mind?' She still talks like that, like there aren't enough minutes in the day for her to say all the words that she wants to. My eyes had widened. I couldn't believe that she actually wanted to read to me. My very own real big sister.

'This one is *Treasure Island*. It's really, really old with some big words, but that will make a good start to our word-wall.' She had smiled. 'Oh look!' She opened the book and pointed to a map: 'A treasure map!' I leant forward, my eyes widening like saucers as she pointed out the words 'Spyglass Hill' and

'Skeleton Island'. 'It begins with: "To the hesitating purchaser" – hesitating means if you're not sure about something and purchaser means the person buying the book – so that's us. They can be our first words; would you write them down for me? I know, I'll come and sit by you on your bed and you can copy the words down in my best notepad, how does that sound?' I had given her a shy nod and she had scrambled over clutching the book in one hand and her notebook with a pen down its spine under her arm. That's how we spent most evenings, even when the arguments began, and the sounds of smashing crockery almost drowned out her words.

Hours pass, and the swish of the window wipers and the classical music from the radio is starting to have an effect. My eyes feel heavy and even though I'm not far away, I decide to pull into a retail park to get some caffeine. My indicator ticks in between the squeaks of the wipers, as the rain hammers harder on to the screen. A lorry is turning right in front of me and I have to slam my brakes on, my belt cutting across my chest with a jerk. I hit my horn and continue around the bend. I didn't see it coming: the white car.

The sound of metal upon metal screams in my ears and for a moment I'm confused as to what it is that I have hit or what has hit me. The airbag – full and startling – has already begun to deflate and the moment of security has collapsed. The rain continues, regardless of my turmoil, as I sit dazed for a few moments. Mozart is still playing on the radio and my heart is still beating, albeit faster than usual. I reach my shaking hand towards the door handle, as a stabbing pain shoots through my abdomen. My breath is taken away by the pain, my eyes watering in response. The door is stuck. I undo the belt, climb over the gear stick and out of my car. I watch as my feet step out on to the endless tarmac, the sooty reflection of the sky blackening the puddles around me. My brown boots take steps; I am aware that I am already soaked and that there is a woman yelling at me. I blink twice, mascara dripping from my eyelashes, and then there is nothing.

Week Five

Samuel

I follow my feet as they run. My heart rate increases with every step, my body waking, my thoughts becoming clear. I don't look at my surroundings; I don't care about the colours of the sky, or the reflection on the water.

My thoughts are tied up with images of Sophie, of the day of the dancing umbrella.

I run towards the tidal basin; the Washington Monument stands tall and poised like a marble pencil which dips into the clear ink of the water. The air is filled with the perfume of cherry blossoms and it brings my thoughts back to the here and now. Each tree arches towards the water, leaning and linking themselves together: a family of pink clouds raining their petals gently over the spectators. I slow my pace into a walk and then reach up and take a blossom. It is so delicate that it feels as though I am holding nothing; only the gentle whisper across my palms lets me know that it is there as it rolls from side to side. I take off my backpack and nestle the blossom in between the folds of my wallet. I know I am being sentimental – foolish even – but this small act makes me feel closer to her. I replace my backpack and start to smile. I'm thinking about the look she will have on her face when I give it to her, because I am determined: I will find her.

The run has cleared my head. I take a shower, clear up, put the kettle on and carry a parcel from Mam into the lounge. Tearing it open, I smile at the contents: another food package. Bisto gravy granules are resting on top of a packet of McVitie's chocolate digestives – simple things that you can't find over here. I eat a biscuit in three mouthfuls and then go back to my laptop. I check my email account for replies from the messages I've been sending to as many of her colleagues as I can track down. I scratch the back of my head as I re-read a sentence from an email that I've had from someone called Gemma. 'Have you tried her sister?' it reads. I rub my hand over the rough stubble on my chin . . . I remember her sister was called Helen, but apart from that, I don't have any more information about her. I rattle off a quick email to Gemma, asking if she happens to know Helen's surname or address. I hit send, then check the Sandwell website again for any mention of Sophie. I'm certain she would be going for another job in finance; she seemed too strong to just let this setback stop her. As I begin to scour through the financial newspapers, I ignore my dry mouth which should have been quenched by the tea I'd intended to make.

Instead, I settle myself away from the desk and on the sofa. Leaning backwards to reach for a pen from the desk behind me, I start circling jobs that she might be interested in, making a list of the office names, websites and phone numbers.

A ping from behind me lets me know I have an email. I get up, lean over the desk and click the mouse on the icon. It's from Gemma: she thinks the sister's name is Helen Yates.

I wander back to Mam's hamper, rip open a packet of 'Tayto' crisps and begin searching for Helen Yates. I pinch my finger along the crease of the crisp packet and aim the tip of the crease into my mouth, sliding the remaining fragments into my mouth. There are hundreds of Helen Yateses: Helen Yates' hairdressing; Helen Yates Isle of Man; Helen Yates tattooist. I screw up the crisp packet and throw it across the room towards the bin – it hits the side, but the shot falls short. I turn back to the screen. I need more than a name; she could be anywhere.

My neck cracks as I rotate it from side to side, then I realise that Helen Yates is probably her married name. I hit the keys and enter Helen Williams into the search bar. I scroll through the results, but again I'm left with nothing. My mouth is parched from the salted crisps, and my eyes feel dry from looking at the computer monitor for so long. I get up and walk to the window. The wind is playing with the leaves on the ground like a spoilt child, picking things up and throwing them down. The sun is setting, the blaze of it surrendering to the eagerness of the night, darkness pushing into the scene, demanding its spot in the limelight. I draw the curtains and head to the kitchen to make a cup of tea. My feet tread along the hall, the noise from the wind outside whistling through the gaps in the walls, my feet sticking slightly to the hardwood as I step through the door, pausing to reach my hand to the wall and flicking on the light switch.

I'm momentarily distracted by a sound: like an elderly man taking in his last breath. And then I'm hit by a ball of white-hot light. The feeling is less of being thrown from the room than of being pushed out; I think of the leaves outside as my feet leave the floor, my body tossed from the room, my head cracking against something hard.

I'm on the rugby pitch; I've been tackled hard. My breath is short, and I'm paralysed by the shock of the impact. The noise of the stadium roars in my ears. My face is pushed into the grass, but as I breathe, I can't smell it; instead I can smell smoke. Get up, Sammy, you great eejit. It's Da, but what is he doing on the pitch? I try to move but I can't; pain screams from my leg, from my head. The captain is having it out with the ref, Irish voices calling for a penalty. Get up, Sammy Boy. This time it's Bret. Something isn't right; Bret shouldn't be here, Bret should be in DC. DC. I'm in Washington DC. I'm at home looking for Sophie.

As though I've hit the rewind button on the remote, I watch as my hand leaves the light switch, I see myself reversing back through the hall, into the lounge, I open the curtains: the leaves are still playing, I smile, I walk backwards to the computer, the crisp packet flies from the side of the bin back into my hand, I walk backwards to the table, I rummage in the parcel, I reverse back into the kitchen, I turn on the gas, I put the kettle on top of the stove, I watch myself rewind up the stairs and into the bathroom for a shower. Then I stop, press play and watch as I walk back down the stairs, into the kitchen, turn on the gas and place the kettle on top of the stove. I turn the knob that is always sticking. The knob that I've been meaning to fix. And then I walk out of the kitchen . . . the lighter still sitting in the kitchen drawer, unused.

I try to open my eyes.

I'm screaming. I can hear my voice. I can feel the heat.

Then I feel nothing.

Week Six

Sophie

It doesn't feel like the same day. This morning seems like a lifetime ago and so does the car crash, and yet just two hours have passed. How can my life have changed so dramatically in such a short space of time? Six months ago, I had a job. Six months ago, I was a successful thirty-year-old who knew exactly where she was going and with whom: six months ago, I wasn't pregnant.

'If I just . . . Ah, there we go. See that little blinking light? That's baby's heartbeat.' The technician turns the screen towards me and smiles. A real smile, one of those smiles that reaches every part of the face. I try to replicate this gesture, to smooth out the muscles of my cheeks and stretch out the frown that I can feel is corrugating my eyebrows into uneven arcs. She notices – or is perhaps hit by – my expression and I watch as the radiance from her face leaks out of her, and I'm filled with immediate remorse, that the deep crevices of my forehead can have such a destructive impact. She clears her throat, pushes her black-framed glasses further up her small, button nose and returns her gaze to the screen. 'Here is the yolk sac, and if I just measure the heartbeat . . . there we go, one hundred and fifteen beats per minute, nice and strong.'

'Oh,' I reply. I know this word – not even a word, really,

more a sound that you make if you suddenly realise that you've run out of milk – does not explain my feelings correctly. I know it is insubstantial and yet it is the only word that I can say. 'Oh,' I repeat as I attempt to swallow some saliva, but my mouth is dry. 'Oh, I, I didn't know there would be a, a . . .' I look into the hopeful eyes of the technician but my startled reflection glares back at me through her lenses, '. . . yolk sac,' is my disappointing conclusion. It's as though I have shot her. I can see the colour drain from her flushed cheeks. I try again. *Come on, you can do better.* 'So, I guess I'm like a chicken?' I inject some humour into the situation, but my tone is flat, and my sentence comes out as a statement rather than a question.

It's strange to me that I'm able to function at this level when I've just found out this news. I can't even find the right adjective to describe my reaction (distraught? overjoyed? confused?), let alone understand why I am functioning, why I'm able to consider the technician's feelings when I am so filled with emotions but at the same time so devoid of them.

'Would you like a picture?' I'm momentarily confused and think that she wants me to grin into a camera, but then I understand that she's talking about the thing on the screen: the swirl of greys that has a heartbeat.

'Er, I guess?' Again, her face looks as though it's about to crumble, like I've just told her that Santa isn't real. 'Yes, of course, that would be perfect.' I hear my voice reply, but it seems to be speaking a language that I don't understand, a language, I suppose, of motherhood.

She smiles at that and I stare at the screen again until the the picture disappears.

The car is a mess, and one side is beyond repair, but it still turns over and will get me to Helen's.

Deep down, I knew something was wrong . . . I think about the image on the screen, think about the heartbeat: nice and strong. Perhaps 'wrong' is not the right word to use? Something was different? That's better. I knew that something was different.

The car and I limp our way along the roads. We ignore the toots from angry horns as they overtake, laughing at the state of us: one wiper working, an all but flat tyre on the passenger side and a painful screeching sound coming from the engine, until, with relief, we arrive at Helen's house.

'Where the hell have you been?!' Helen exclaims, as she envelops me in a fried-onion-smelling embrace.

'Long story,' I mutter into her hair.

'Where is your stuff?'

'Can I use your loo first before you give me twenty questions?'

'Yes, come in, you look awful.'

'Toilet first, Hel, explanations later.'

'Right, yes. OK. Kids will be back in an hour!' she shouts behind my retreating back as I rush up the stairs, past the chaotic array of family photos that pose and grin at me from the walls, and into the bathroom. I dig around in my bag for the test that I bought from the pharmacy and pull down my jeans. Sitting down on the toilet, I tear open the white wrapper with my teeth, take the plastic end from the white stick and wave it in the vicinity of my urine which I can no longer contain.

I have a theory: the test results in the A and E department could have been mixed up with anyone's, and as for the scan, these things are filmed all the time – what's not to say that what was on the screen was just a recording of some other unfortunate soul? And the pains that may or not be my uterus growing are probably, actually, just nasty period pains. What

I need is proof that hasn't been tampered with by anyone else.

Purposely, I ignore the pink stain that is creeping across the two clear plastic windows and instead wash my face and hands. From time to time, I glance suspiciously across to the window ledge at the test until I can't put it off any longer. Replacing the towel on the radiator, I take a step towards the window ledge. I watch my hand pick it up and turn it over. I'm met with two very strong, very clear pink lines.

I am pregnant.

It feels like I'm drowning in this knowledge. I repeat it over and over in my mind, but it can't seem to anchor. I can't seem to keep hold of it, as if the word is being pulled by an uncontrollable tide: finally, it sinks, finds ground. There is a baby inside me, right now.

I look down at my stomach and give it a little poke.

'Hello.'

It doesn't reply . . . but somehow, I know it's listening.

A small smile plays at the corner of my mouth as I realise why it is that the coffee Helen has placed in front of me has turned my stomach. I ask Helen for tea instead and she looks at me quizzically; my hand is resting on my stomach.

Looking around at the chaos that fills the kitchen, I stare at the painted handprints that are stuck to the grubby fridge; the smears on the stainless-steel kettle and the plastic plates and beakers that are sitting haphazardly on the draining board: a vast contrast to the sleek lines that shine from my own kitchen. I never feel unsettled here, though, never feel the need to spray anti-bacterial spray over everything, leaving everywhere faultless and perfect, because it is perfect: perfectly Helen.

She gulps down coffee that is clearly still too hot, glancing at the clock intermittently as though it will be sucked into a black hole at any minute; her daughters Caitlin and Jessica (ages three and five respectively) will be home within the hour. I have always loved coming here: the way the house smells of cooking and scented candles; the way that Helen and her husband Greg (a huge bear of a man with a mass of curly brown hair that is always a little too long, a little too wild) argue continuously but always end the conversation by whipping a bottom with a tea towel and a giggle, or a one-liner that makes her face light up even though she is rolling her eyes. Helen's life is something I have always enjoyed – from afar. I have never wanted it to be mine, never been envious, just . . . enjoyed it.

'I've been fired.' I watch her reaction from over the rim of the cup. She spits out her coffee in a dramatic explosion that showers the kitchen table.

'Fired?! How the hell has that happened? Did you sleep with the boss and his wife found out? Or did you, you know, sleep with your assistant? And she did you for sexual harassment, because I've always said I wouldn't judge you, but—'

'Christ, Helen, when was the last time you read a decent book or watched something other than the soaps?'

'Too tired to read, and back off – the soaps are the only things on telly when the kids are around that don't involve coloured ponies or presenters that look like they have had too much caffeine.'

'Point taken, and no, nothing that exciting, I'm afraid. I've been accused of stealing information from the company we were taking over.'

'What? Did you?'

'Helen! No!'

'Sorry. Knee-jerk reaction, but you must have done something, or you wouldn't be sitting here – you'd be demanding your job back.' Seeing my wobbling lip, her face drops.

'Oh my Lord, are you about to actually cry?'

I laugh through my tears at that, as she gets up from the table and fetches some kitchen roll with pictures of onions across the bottom. I wonder if the designer had a wicked sense of humour or if they just had a penchant for them. I blow my nose into it as I consider whether it is a pretty enough vegetable to be used decoratively, and decide that, no, it is not. This thought makes me cry a little harder as I realise that I now have the time to consider this useless fact. Six weeks ago, the thought wouldn't have crossed my mind. Helen is sitting opposite me with a look of utter horror.

'Oh, Hel . . .' I rummage into my bag and pull out the test, noticing as I do that the pink lines look even more vivid than they did ten minutes ago. Helen snatches it from my hand and stares at it, biting her bottom lip just like she used to when she was worried as a child.

'Oh. Wow! I mean, wow! Congratulations?' she says tentatively.

'Thanks.'

'Did they fire you because they found out you're pregnant and tried to frame the whole stealing thing on you because they didn't want to pay out for maternity pay? Because I've heard all sorts about discrimination against working mothers and—'

'No. I've only just found out. Today. After I crashed my car. They did a routine test because I was having some stomach pains.'

'You crashed your car?!'

'Seriously?' I hold out my hands in exasperation. 'That's what you are bothered about?'

'Well no, obviously, but you know how I love that car.'

'Helen!'

'Well, I do, but, oh gosh, come here.' She kneels in front of me and holds my hands. 'Who's the father?'

'Samuel.'

'Hot Irish Samuel?'

'Hot Irish Samuel.' I give a little shrug of my shoulders as though it was a foregone conclusion that it wouldn't be anyone other than him.

'I thought you were on the pill?'

'I am, but I had a sickness bug the week before I went over to DC. It's not like I was thinking much about contraception then. There hasn't been anyone since Samuel.'

'Are you together? Again?' She looks up at me hopefully.

'No.'

'Why not? You said that you were going to sort everything out, tell him about why you couldn't stay together until that deal was sorted.'

'Because he thinks I stole his idea.' I blow my nose again noisily and wipe away the tears before taking a sip of tea – grimacing because there is too much milk in it.

'But if you explain—'

'I did, but then—' I look up at the ceiling and try to control the watering of my eyes. I take a deep breath. 'He's the one who got me fired. Slept with me then, well, got his own back, I suppose. I don't blame him really.' Helen's eyebrows shoot up into an angry triangle. 'Don't look at me like that, try to see it from his point of view. He thinks I stole his idea and then took over the company that he was going to turn around, took it over with – from his point of view – his own idea.'

'Did you explain that to him, before you, you know?'

'Of course I did, but, well, it seems that he didn't believe me. I understand why he would do it. He's hurt and betrayed. Don't forget I buggered off and didn't tell him anything.'

'I told you! I told you to ring him and apologise.' She purses her lips and crosses her arms.

'Again, Helen, really? I told you so? Bigger picture, Helen, bigger picture.' I reach into my bag again and let my fingers run along the edge of the cardboard frame. 'Speaking of which . . . do you want to see it?' Her face lights up and she claps her hands as I pass the picture with a shy smile. 'It's apparently the size of a baked bean.'

'Bean . . .' she smiles at the picture, 'nice to meet you.'

Week Six

Samuel

SPRING

Week Seven

Sophie

As I lie in Jessica's bed, covered in pink cartoon ponies, I listen to the sounds of Helen's house: the hum of the central heating, the click and hum of the fridge below and the gentle snores of Caitlin lying opposite. I look up at the fluorescent stars on the ceiling and place my hand on top of my stomach. Can I do this? Can I have this baby, this Bean? I turn on to my side; the bed creaks and springs twang in resistance to my adult weight. My eyes close and I breathe in the smell of fabric softener mixed with something else, something sweet, something which is alien to me.

I replay the last time I saw him. I think about the way he looked at me and I feel his betrayal cutting deeper than it did before, because now I have Bean. Do I want a man who can do that? Sleep with someone, make them believe that they were loved, only to betray them the next day? I meant what I said: I do understand why he would do it and, as crazy as it sounds, I could forgive him for it, but now . . . now there is Bean and I can feel that forgiveness – that understanding – slipping through my fingers.

The night is spent drifting in and out of sleep, like all the nights over the past week. At half past three I creep downstairs, pausing next to Caitlin for a moment, watching the rise and fall of her chest; the way her cheeks are slightly flushed and how her chubby hand remains gripped around her snowman doll even though the rest of her body is relaxed. She looks so vulnerable and precious that the realisation of Bean becomes ever more threatening. I leave the room quickly, trying to discard this terror that feels heavy and brittle, but it does not stay in the room with the sleeping child. This terror follows me into the kitchen. It won't be quietened, but becomes louder, irrepressible; it spreads its thorns into hidden places and panic fills me. I wander quietly into the lounge and pull the cord on the lamp, filling the room with a sepia hue.

The room is mismatched. Pieces of odd furniture are marked with fading felt-tip pens; toy boxes line the edges with dead-eyed Barbies making a bid for escape. The book shelf is filled with dog-eared stories of rabbits and tigers, pirates and princesses; among them I spot a few familiars, a few glimpses of the Helen I grew up with, but they are few. The real Helen has become suffocated, smothered and pushed back, retreating behind the urgent needs of these garish books. My stomach cramps, a reminder that Bean is here and with me . . . is this what it will do? Will it suffocate me? Turn me into something, someone I'm not?

I wander over to the fireplace and pick up one of the photos of me, Mum and Helen; it can't be long after she'd moved in with us. We are standing in the garden; the wind is blowing my hair and I remember that it had smelt of candyfloss . . . Mum had been trying to make fudge and the sugar had burnt so we had to go outside because of the smoke. He had taken this picture. I close my eyes and prod the memory until it hurts: the smell; the sound of the sea in the background and her laughter. Grief hits me like a wave; I let it crash over my head, let it fill my ears and my lungs until I can't breathe. I collapse on to the floor and cry, for the injustice of what happened to my mother and for the injustice of what is happening to me. Like glue, the memories ooze through me, thick and profuse.

I was fifteen when she died. When he took her from us. My life was torn apart, but not in the way that Helen's was. The community tried to support us, especially when the journalists started hounding us, trying to get an insight into the mind of a killer. The guilt Helen felt almost ruined her. She had always been a good girl, always dotted her 'i's and crossed her 't's'; she couldn't cope with the shame. She thought people were looking at her, pointing the finger; she lost her friends, she left university, she lost everything except me. Even now, Helen is always wary of strangers, always suspecting that they may be after her story.

We left Wales, we left the house that eventually became mine once I turned eighteen and we started again. To everyone other than Greg, she is just Helen Yates; they have no idea who her father was.

'Aunty Sophin?' I'm pulled back from the memories. I try to quickly compose myself as Caitlin stands by the door frame. Beneath sleepy lids, her wide blue eyes look tired; the battered and bruised snowman dangling from her hand. 'Why you cryin', Aunty Sophin? Did you fall over and have a bump?'

I nod as I try to silence the aftershocks of my tears which are still shaking my body. She scampers towards me, chucks the snowman to the floor and cocks her head to one side. 'What is broken?' she asks with her hands on her hips.

'My heart,' I say quietly and give her a brave smile.

'Oh, I kiss it better. Put your arm like this.' I follow her instructions and stretch my arm out where she plants a kiss on my wrist. I laugh despite myself.

'Why have you kissed my arm?'

'I didn't kiss your arm, silly Aunty Sophin, I kiss your sleef.'

'My sleef?' I question.

'Yes. Mummy says I wear my heart on my sleef.' She climbs on to my lap and begins to twiddle her blond hair. 'I like it when you live in my home, Aunty Sophin. Are you going to live here?'

'No, sweeetie, I'm just visiting.'

'Oh, then you go back to your home?'

I hear Mum's voice as she crouches in front of my grazed knee, my cries turning into hiccups.

'*It's just a scratch. Let's get you home – you'll feel better once you're home.*'

I kiss the top of her head and marvel at how, in the space of a minute, a three-year-old has managed to bandage my old wounds and help me back on to the road of recovery.

Week Seven

Samuel

'Samuel? Can you open your eyes for me? Samuel?'

Week Eight

Sophie

I flick through Helen's pregnancy book. By week eight, according to The Book, if I could see inside my stomach, I would be able to make out the tip of Bean's nose, the folds in the eyelids. Bean's arms and legs are stretching out and bending towards where a tiny heart beats. It looks like a little person – albeit with a giant head.

I put the book down, grab a mirror and sigh at my pallid skin and lank hair, and begin to put my hair up and add some make-up.

'Right then, Bean, this is the plan.' I open my mouth into an 'o' and begin adding mascara to my lashes, then replace it in my make-up bag. 'We're going to go on a road trip – if you'll let me off the hook this afternoon, that is.' I swallow down another wave of nausea. 'We're going away, just me and you. I'm taking us home. My real home . . . our home.'

I haven't been back to the cottage since just after Mum died. I own it outright and yet it has been sitting empty for the last fifteen years. I've made arrangements for the gas and electric to be reconnected and called a local odd-job man (Handy Huw) to visit it and make sure that the water is safe and that the heating is working after being shut up for so long.

'But surely you'd be better off staying close by? Renting

something here so I can help you?' Helen asks as she pulls a pile of damp washing out of the washing machine. 'Do you think this will dry on the line yet?' She peers out of the kitchen window where petals of daffodil light fall intermittently through the clouds.

'It's supposed to rain later, I think,' I tell her. She sighs and begins putting half of the laundry into the tumble dryer. 'I've thought about it, Helen. I can't face going back to London, not for a while, at least. I've registered the house with a renting company – fully furnished, so I only need to get my clothes and stuff out. They've already got a couple interested.'

'Won't that be weird? Having some stranger living in your house?' She slams the door with her hip and presses buttons that whir the machine into action.

'Strangely . . . no. It's just a house.'

'Not a home?'

I shrug my shoulders as she opens a wire airer, hanging a variety of pink and purple pyjamas over it. 'But the cottage, Soph? Are you sure? Won't it bring back memories of . . .' She shakes out a tangled pair of dungarees and folds them over one of the bars. 'What I mean is, you're obviously in a bit of an emotional state at the minute and I'm just worried that being there, on your own—'

'I'm not on my own. I've got Bean with me, haven't I, Bean?' I imagine it practising, this little person, moving its arm and giving me a little wave. Oh, before I forget,' I add, 'they're picking up the car later. Could you give them the keys?' I grin.

'You're sending the company car back in that state?' Helen laughs.

'I am. It serves them right.'

'Fair enough, but the cottage, Sophie . . . it's a lot to deal with.'

'I know it sounds strange, but I want to feel close to her. I need my mum, and the cottage is the next best thing. And Handy Huw says that it's habitable.'

'Habitable? God knows what kind of state it's in. And Samuel?'

'I don't know what I'm going to do about Samuel.'

I indicate off the main road and start the steep climb into the hills, lowering the window a fraction and letting the thick, kelpy tang of the sea air fill my new car. It's not brand-new like my others, but it felt good to buy it, to have another piece of independence. The trees are still mostly bare. Their age-old arthritic fingers are stretching and turning their gnarled knuckles towards the sun as another new year pulls them away from death and into new life. Green hills rise up, like sleeping giants, while in the distance, toy-like sheep and tractors roam and play, and bubbling streams slice their way between the fields that stretch towards the Irish Sea.

Our cottage is in Mid Wales, towards Aberystwyth. I used to hate being so far away from the town when we were growing up. Helen and I would despair whenever there was an event of any excitement in town because we were very rarely able to go, especially if it ended late at night. We wouldn't be able to get home – bus routes this far out were few and far between, Mum didn't drive and taxis just cost too much – but as I drive deeper into the valley, down narrow lanes and up steep inclines, I couldn't be happier that I am far from all of the hustle and bustle that I used to crave.

I pull up to where the gate closes over the lane, with a sign announcing 'private property'. I smile at the memory of my childish self giggling with Helen about the word 'privates' and open the car door, holding on tightly to the handle before the wind snatches it away from me. Strong winds lift my hair, pulling it and teasing it across my face, blurring my vision as I coerce the rusty bolt into submission. Long grass tangles beneath the gate, as it groans with indignation at being woken so early. The frayed rope which holds the gate open has seen much better days, and I climb back into the car with some urgency, fearing that it may snap at any moment, sending the gate into my newly purchased car. I rev the engine and pass through it unscathed, closing the gate behind me, fighting against the wind once more. The cottage inches into view and I suddenly feel sorry for neglecting it for so long.

It is a long, low building made of large, chalky stones. Our red door stands to the right with small windows either side, each pane split into six small rectangles. To the left, the neighbour's black door crouches beneath three more windows, their wooden frames battered by the sea air. The slate roof has seen better days, but the two chimneys still stand proud at either side of the roof. Next door seems empty and a tired 'For Sale' sign hangs defeatedly from its post.

I remove the key and sit with the engine ticking and the sea breeze filling the view with chaotic gusts.

'So, Bean. This is home.'

I tread carefully towards the door; my fingers struggle with the lock until it yields and the door swings open. I prop it open with my bag and then return to the car and retrieve the rest of my things, as well as shopping bags filled with a couple of days' worth of essentials.

The door slams closed behind me. I secure the latch and stand in the middle of the small square of carpet at the foot of the staircase. To my right is the low door into the lounge and to my left is the kitchen. There is a dream-like quality when I step into the lounge; distorted memories fly at me from every direction. Even though the room has lost its feeling of home and security, it still embraces and repels me in equal measures. I'm so overcome with emotion that I feel breathless and unsteady. I turn my head and face Mum's empty chair, the wooden legs chipped and marked and the beige upholstery almost threadbare. She would sit with her legs folded beneath her to one side, a book on the arm and a cup of tea balancing precariously next to it. My legs feel weak and I sink into the beige sofa opposite, as the smell of mould and disgruntled dust is expelled from the tarnished material. I feel her loss engulf me, but not in the way it has in the past. This time I feel myself folding into it; I nestle against memories that I have blocked out because the pain was just too acute to bear. I let myself remember Christmas mornings in this room, the smell of pine from the tree and the feel of the waxy holly that she used to lay beneath the log burner. I look towards the window where an overgrown bramble taps and claws at the glass above the sill where Mum used to arrange sweet peas in a crystal vase. Anger starts to rise, speeding up my heartbeat and shaking my limbs: the vase had been smashed, broken shards trapping daylight inside them, sparkling and gleaming. It had seemed so wrong that they could still sparkle when the light inside her was gone; the shimmer and glint had been taken from her, but that vase was still full of light. I remember kicking the pieces across the room into the darkness, away from the sunlight. I close my eyes and let the memories consume me: the ridiculous scarecrow outfit she had made for me for a book day at school; the way I screamed at her – brimming with teenage indignation – at how unfairly life was treating me; the way she would smile when he was kind to her; the way she would look at him as if he had given her diamonds instead of a backhanded compliment.

I'm shivering. I don't know how long I've been here or when sleep claimed me; the skin on my face is tight and my eyes are swollen, but I feel better, lighter. The wind has calmed a little as I go outside into the small garden. Hedges and grass still frame the overgrown lawn and swing tyre. There are a few broken fence panels too, which have become part of the land, smothered and hidden by the undergrowth. I bring in some logs from the old coal bunker and set about lighting the burner in the lounge.

The amber light begins to dance as the flames come to life and I stand up. My attention is caught by the crack in the plaster next to the door. My feet stop moving.

I'm petrified, just as I had been the day that crack was made. I stare at it; walk towards it; touch it. That day was a Sunday. Helen and I had heard his voice, slurred with rage rather than alcohol. As I ran into the room, he was holding her long, dark hair in his fist, her head leaning so far back that she didn't know I was there.

I watch the memory play out like a film in slow motion: his spittle flying slowly from his mouth; his lips brutishly forming the words of blame. I turn my head towards the door where I see my ten-year-old face, as bit by bit, my expression changes from shock to fear. My blond ponytail, kept in place by a plastic cherry hair bobble, swings fluidly from side to side as I shake my head, my mouth gradually forming the word 'stop'. Her crime that day had been ironing a double crease in his trousers. She was trying to make a fool of him, he had said. She had tried to tell him that she hadn't been able to find her glasses that day. In fact, he had broken them with the heel of his work boot while she had been crouched on the floor trying to pick them up.

My innocent face takes on an expression that the muscles of a ten-year-old shouldn't have learnt yet, an expression of absolute horror at the scene it's witnessing.

Helen's hand creeps into the shot, her fingers digging into the flesh of my arm as she pulls me out of the room, pulling me up the stairs, towards our bedroom. I heard the noise that had made the crack in the wall . . . but Helen saved me from seeing it.

I blink, and their images have gone.

My fingers stroke the hairline fracture in the wall. What had been her crime the day she died? Perhaps she had forgotten to buy his newspaper? I picture her optimistic smile as he walked through the door, his steak frying on the hob, his beer already being poured into a glass. Her beautiful smile fading, her heart thudding in her chest when she watched him looking for the newspaper, the image of the bare shelf in the shop filling her body with dread. Was that what had happened? Had he grabbed her by the wrist? By the hair? Or had she left the fridge door open so that his milk had turned sour? I picture her face blanching as she poured the milk into his cup of tea, the milk floating to the top in globules, the image filling her mouth with a sour taste before he smacked her face into the kitchen counter. Had she tried to flee the room apologising?

My stomach growls, bringing me back, and I put my hand to my stomach.

'Hungry, Bean?' I walk towards the arch into the kitchen. My mouth is dry and my heart thuds inside my chest, the vibrations climbing up my spine and into my ears.

'*Come on, Sophie.*' My mother's voice is soft but insistent. '*It's just a kitchen.*' I step into the last room my mother ever went into, the last room that she ever saw, the last room that she took her final breath in: the room where her life ended.

Another scene plays out in front of me as I step into the kitchen. It's a memory of before Ian, before Helen, but after Dad had left. She is younger and her hair is piled on top of her head in a bun as she stands by the counter with a mixing bowl. Mum is wearing a sage-green apron with little leaves on it. The kitchen is bright, the summer sun streaming from the windows as she pulls a chair next to her. I watch as my four-year-old legs clamber up, my podgy hand taking the mixing spoon from her hand. She ruffles my halo of golden hair as I start spooning cake mixture into pink paper cases. It was just the two of us and we were happy. We were happier on our own. My hand slides down to my stomach and I smile. We'll be happier on our own.

The memory slips away and instead, I let the horrors of the day she died creep their way in. My feet carry me to the spot where she would have been standing as he held his hands around her windpipe, her back against the edge of the draining board, the cupboard filled with cleaning products behind her legs. I let the tears fall freely as I picture her trying to fight him off. The weight of his stomach hanging over his jeans, the smell of his overpowering aftershave filling the room. My own breath catches as I stifle a sob at the thought that the last thing she would have smelt was not the sweet peas that she used to love, not the smell of my hair after a bath when I was three, not the smell of the wholemeal bread that we would cover in honey, but his stench: thick with rage and violence.

Maybe if I hadn't been at a sleepover that night, he wouldn't have done it. I shake this thought from my head. Her death wasn't my fault. I have no culpability here; but I do have regret. I regret that Helen found her, and I regret that Helen was alone when she called the police and when they questioned her about her father; a stranger from social services comforting her instead of me. I think that was what I was most afraid of whenever I thought about returning here to this house. But as I stand in the middle of this room, I don't feel alone; I feel like I have come home.

This room that I have been so afraid of is nothing more than mismatched cupboard doors that never hang quite right, a white plastic kettle, white fridge-freezer and a kitchen table which never stays still when you're trying to cut your food, unless you fold up some cardboard beneath the table leg.

I sit down and open a packet of salt and vinegar crisps and a can of Coke.

'We've got a lot of work to do,' I say out loud. 'We'll clean in here first and then make the bed, OK?' I tap my flat stomach, scrunch up the packet and crush the can. I roll my sleeves up and begin cleaning the kitchen with anti-bacterial spray. The kitchen cupboards are empty from that day so long ago when I closed up the house. It's hard to think I was just a teenager then; I had felt so grown up. Helen had tried to come in with me, but in the end, she couldn't set foot inside.

Instead, I filled bin bags and loaded them into the boot of Helen's old white Citröen, and she transported them to the skip in town.

The house and Mum's life insurance, which I inherited, was put into a trust fund for me until I turned eighteen. Mum had made changes to her will a year before her death, making Helen my legal guardian and trustee of my inheritance, in case anything happened to her. Helen paid the bills on the house until I was old enough to decide what I wanted to do. We moved to England, not far from where she lives now. Mum had left a small inheritance for Helen too, enough for the first few months of living in a new place, but that soon ran out. Helen worked twelve-hour shifts in a factory making power tool parts, to pay the rent on a one-bedroomed flat, which we kitted out with bunk beds and charity shop furniture. I never intended to stay away for so long, but the longer I left it, the harder it was to return. It was no surprise that I would inherit the cottage; Mum had bought it with her own inheritance when her dad died (a heart attack, I think; she never talked about it much). He had left the house to her, not to my grandmother – much to everyone's disgust from the stories Mum used to tell. She never had much to do with Mum after that, and from what I could gather, there wasn't much love lost between them.

After I have cleaned, I make my way upstairs. The stairs still creak in the same places; I picture myself and Helen trying to avoid the loud ones, so we could sneak into the kitchen for snacks: the memories are vivid and comforting. I open the airing cupboard, and the dusty smell of the old towels that are still stacked there reminds me of how long this house has been closed and empty. I flick the switches and the central heating bangs and clanks into action.

Mine and Helen's bedroom is bare apart from the old wardrobes and beds. The window is curtainless, but the old net lace, yellowed by age and sun, flutters at the sides of the window where the elements battle to clamber through the gaps. The sun breaks through the clouds and bubble-gum-pink light stretches and pops against the back wall where blotches of old wallpaper leave silhouettes of the many pieces of paper that made our word-wall. I smile and take a deep breath as I leave the room and face Mum's bedroom door. My hand turns the porcelain doorknob, and as I step inside . . . I swear it smells of her.

Week Eight

Samuel

'Don't try to move.' I hear Sarah's voice. My body feels hot and heavy; the inside of my eyelids scratch as I force them open. The room feels small; I feel too big. 'Take your time. You've been asleep for a while, Sam . . . you've had an accident. You're in the hospital. You might feel a little groggy, you're on morphine for the pain.'

I try to reply but I'm pulled back under.

Week Nine

Sophie

I smooth down the white duvet and smile. I chose this bed with a purpose; a new beginning. It's different from anything I owned in the house in London: it is not practically making use of every inch of space and it doesn't boast an oversized headboard or a television at its foot. Instead, I have chosen something a little more . . . more. The frame is brass, not something I would normally choose. I love the way the pattern curls and twists itself – no beginning and no end – just an endless journey. I run my hand over the cold spheres of the knobs and let my fingers trace the loops and dives of the headboard.

The window is ajar. April exhales in a long, cool breath, the sea air setting a course towards summer. White lace billows inwards, swollen, like the sails of a ship, towards the heavy white curtains which try to anchor it. I know the idea of having everything white may sound alien to some people. But there are so many different types of white, and I love how they sit together: the fresh, almost milky tone of the painted bureau against the harsh, electric white of the mirror-frame. The floorboards I have kept bare, just as Mum had originally had them, before He had complained that the floor had been too cold and covered them with a hideous blue patterned carpet. There are thick white rugs either side of the bed and almond-white French vintage-style bedside tables, with bowed legs and a deliberately weathered look. Each piece of furniture I have chosen carefully, filling this room with things that I love, that I enjoy, that make this my room. Looking over at Mum's old brass carriage clock, sitting on the bookcase, I realise I need to get going. I allow myself another moment to enjoy being in this room; this room that I have been so afraid of for so long.

'So, as you're quite late seeing a doctor, we may as well make this your booking appointment.' Doctor Flint's eyes crinkle at the corners as he looks at me over his wire-framed glasses. He had glasses like that when I was younger – are they the same pair? I have been in here for about twenty minutes talking about my family history and about the foods I can and can't eat.

'Let's find out your due date, shall we?' He picks up a cardboard circle and begins to turn part of it around. 'What was the date of the first day of your last period?'

'Oh, um, the sixth of February.' He turns the disk around and then smiles at me over his glasses again.

'So, your little bundle of joy—'

'Bean.'

'Bean, is it?' he chuckles.

I nod, feeling curiously proud.

'Right then, well "Bean" is due on the thirteenth of November.'

I'll have a baby before Christmas. This thought scratches my mood. It runs its nail around my fragile bubble of contentment, pushing it slightly so it starts to drift from my grasp. I'm going to have a baby: a real-life baby. I think of last Christmas, which I spent on my own. I'd eaten a supermarket turkey and stuffing sandwich and had spent the day researching the profiles of some of Greenlight's employees – seeing which staff we would want to keep, and which ones would be dead wood. It hadn't been a sombre day: I didn't feel left out or sad; I just had work to do and that was that. Helen had invited me over, of course, but I'd declined; I didn't want to waste valuable time travelling over the festive period.

'Sophie?' I look down and notice that my hands are twisting the bottom of my scarlet top around like a bobbin. The memory is vivid: I can see the slight smudge of mascara under Mum's eyes as we sang 'Wind the Bobbin Up'; I can smell her perfume – floral and powdery – and her smile, as we 'clap, clap, clapped'. 'Sophie?'

I'm crying. Again.

'I'm sorry, that's wonderful news, I just . . . miss my mum. And, I miss my life, and I miss my job, and I miss Samuel, and, and . . .' I start sobbing: pathetic, noisy, uncontrollable sobs. 'And, and . . . I miss wine!' I take the tissue that he is offering and blow my nose noisily.

'Anything else, Sophie?'

'Yes . . . Stilton.' I smile a little at this and then start laughing.

'Mood swings are perfectly normal,' he says sympathetically.

'This . . .' I swish my sodden tissue around, '. . . is normal?'

He smiles kindly. 'I'll book you in for your twelve-week scan and then I'll see you for your next check-up in around six weeks' time. But if you have any other concerns in the meantime, please feel free to make an appointment.'

As my car bumps towards the cottage, I imagine Bean looking around in confusion as its home, a bubble of liquid pink, is rattled up and down. What does it sound like inside there? Can Bean hear the engine? Are the sounds of the radio sea-like echoes of the outside world, softening into whale-song tones?

I pull up outside the cottage and take the key from the ignition. There is warmth in the sun on my skin as I step out of the car, slamming the door with a thud. My steps are swallowed by the moisture in the ground; the grass reaching and clinging to the heel of my brown boot, wrapping itself around it. The 'For Sale' sign next door has been taken down, I notice, as I bend down to untangle the grass from my heel. The sudden bang of a door rips its way into the soft sounds of my garden, tearing away my solace and filling me with a sense of violation. I look up to see who or what has encroached on my privacy. Through the door walks a man. A man that I know but who doesn't belong here.

Week Nine

Samuel

'How are you, my boy?' Da's voice fills the room.

'Jesus, Mary and Joseph, look at the state of your pillow! How do they ever expect you to get better when your pillow case is all ruffled?' I try not to let Mam know that her every movement is sending shots of pain up my back and my chest.

I wince as Da 'whispers' into my ear, 'I've got you some whiskey. It's in your drawer, but mum's the word, eh?' He slaps me on my leg, the only part of me that doesn't hurt.

'Mr McLaughlin, don't you think I can't hear you. It'll mess with his medication.' I close my eyes as I hear her open a drawer and take it out. My parents have always called each other Mr and Mrs McLaughlin respectively.

'For the love of God, woman, whiskey has been putting the Irish back on the road to recovery for hundreds of years.' Da's voice is sinking into the floor, becoming quieter and more distant.

'It's put them on the path to ruin, too, now behave yourself.' Mam's voice shrinks away as I close my eyes again.

'Will you both shut your holes? He needs to rest,' Sarah says, but her voice skips away.

I slip into an opiate-filled dream as memories play in black and white like a Charlie Chaplin movie. Blacks, whites and greys flicker as the tape rolls, organ music playing as I see us: me walking hurriedly along the pavement while Sophie sits inside a café opposite, her big, sad eyes with fluttering eyelashes staring at me. She is wearing a twenties outfit, her blond hair arranged in sleek curls framing her face; she looks away bashfully. I give her a little wave and doff my bowler hat as my hand reaches for the door. I try the door but a white light consumes the shot, sending me somersaulting back. I reach for the door again. The white light sends me backflipping away. Again and again, I reach for the door, and again and again I am sent spiralling away. The sky darkens around me as the film comes to an end with the image of me sitting in the dust as the camera closes in on my pale, desolate face, a single tear running down my cheek: a small, circular shot of film, the rest of the frame black.

Week Ten

Sophie

Charlie Evans. Gorgeous, kind Charlie Evans. Charlie Evans, who took pity on me as a shy, awkward fourteen-year-old girl when I was being teased at school for my hand-me-down uniform and home-cut hair, who began sitting next to me at lunch, putting up with me hanging around him – even though I was two years younger. He introduced me to his girlfriend Olivia, listened to my opinions and ruffled my hair like I was his younger sister. The teasing stopped and I was left alone; I had a friend. That was until Jeanette Jones started telling everyone that I was in love with him.

After that, Charlie would blush every time I looked at him, would avoid me when I walked towards him at lunch time, because the whole school knew. And once again, I was the awkward girl with the scuffed shoes who buried her head in books.

And now, Charlie Evans has moved in next door.

I stood there, my foot still tangled in the grass. He had stopped short and looked straight at me. His expression slowly changed, his eyebrows folding into a scowl, whereas at school, they were raised; like he was always in a state of alarm. He lifted his chin as he no doubt tried to remember where he knew me from, the gesture defensive and wary. I smiled at him, trying to embody the London me, the straight-backed, perfectly groomed version of me that didn't have her heel stuck in grass and wasn't desperate for a wee.

'Hello!' I said, my confident London voice coming out over-enthusiastic, like I was trying too hard. He gave me a short nod in response. His light-brown hair needed a cut; waves that used to bob up and down as he walked seemed stiff and unwashed. I used to love how he walked, almost rocking on to the balls of his feet with every step. It always looked as though he was eager to go wherever it was he was going – even double French.

'I thought next door was empty,' he answered, turning his back and walking back through the open door. My welcoming smile dropped, and irritation replaced it. I bent down and released my foot, trying to keep my legs clamped together as I regretted not making a dash for the loo before I left town. I fiddled with the key in my own front door, as he dragged out a roll of carpet. In my peripheral vision, I could see him hauling it towards the skip which I had ordered, ready for the kitchen fitters.

'That's my skip.' The words were out before I could help them. He stopped the dragging motion and turned to face me.

'Pardon?'

'The skip,' I replied, holding my head a little straighter, my shoulders a little further back, enjoying the sense of control I was feeling. 'It's mine. But feel free to use it, if that's all that you need to get rid of. I don't mind.'

'Right,' he replied, and with a slight grunt, chucked the carpet into the skip, wiped his hands on his jeans, walked into his house and slammed the door behind him.

Bean seems to really like chocolate milk. Who would have thought that I would prefer to drink this than coffee? I suck on the straw and drain the last of the carton with a slurping rattle as I smooth down the pages of The Book. My baby is approximately the size of a sherbet lemon now; the skin is covered in soft hair; eyelids are now fully formed and sealed. Bean is apparently moving around quite a bit, too. I picture it doing a little somersault to celebrate. Bean's fingers now have tiny nails. Cute.

I hear a bang from next door and ignore the little niggle of annoyance. Charlie Evans has turned into a knob, I have decided.

I close The Book, put it on the floor and walk over to Mum's old battery-operated radio. I fiddle with the dial until it tunes into a classical station, then settle myself down into her chair. *Great Expectations* sits in my lap again, but I keep getting distracted by thoughts of Samuel. The urge to fetch my laptop from upstairs is proving harder for me to suppress than I would like. I keep ignoring the whispers from Bean that he has a right to know.

'We'll be fine on our own,' I say. 'What kind of father would he be to you? He slept with me because of revenge, Bean, not love.' I dismiss the way he had looked at me: the anger in his eyes in the meeting; the way he smiled. I clear my throat and return my attention to the book, re-reading the passage again.

My hand drops to my knees, the pages remaining open.

'Do you think he would like it here? You know, if things were different and he didn't hate me? Didn't sleep with me and then destroy everything that I had worked for?'

Deep down I know the answer to that. He often talked about his mam's house, about how nothing ever matched, how nothing ever worked without a swift kick or bang in the right place . . . maybe I should call him? 'Should I call him, Bean?' I imagine the tiny human floating around in a pink pool, the thick cord anchoring it as it kicks and nods its head. 'What would I say?' I sigh and return to my book. 'We're better off without him.'

I'm starting to get bored. I have cleaned the kitchen twice, which is pointless because I have chosen a new one and it will be fitted tomorrow. Pip and Miss Haversham have been discarded again and instead I have begun a crossword.

'Three down, six letters, Bean . . . sequence of notes that are pleasing to the ear . . . Melody.'

I fill in the blanks and then sigh. 'It's no use, I need to do something.' I call Helen on the same phone that I called my first boyfriend on . . . My initial nostalgia of watching the dial turn lazily after my index finger slides into the hole, is replaced with impatience.

'Hey, what's up?' she asks.

'Nothing, I'm bored.'

She laughs at this. 'When have you ever been bored? I thought you were enjoying the peace and quiet of the Welsh countryside?'

'I am. I'm reading *Great Expectations* and doing a crossword.'

'Simultaneously? You always were an over-achiever.'

'Funny.'

'How's the old place looking?'

I smile at this and look around. The old patterned carpet was replaced with a thick, deep grey yesterday and the new pale-blue sofa looks much softer and more welcoming than the tattered brown one that sat there previously. I've kept Mum's chair but have made an appointment to get it re-upholstered to match the heavy latte-coloured curtains.

'Nice, different. I think you'll like it.' Helen hasn't been back here since the day Mum died.

'Soph . . . I still don't think I could—'

'Give it time, Hel. Once I've had the new kitchen put in – did I tell you about the oven? Remember how we hated this one? The way the grill was on top of the hob and we nearly burnt our eyelashes every time we made fish-finger sandwiches? I've chosen a cream Aga to replace it, do you remember how Mum always wanted one? And proper oak cupboards, not like that sticky stuff she tried to cover them with that time. It'll look completely different, not dark and dingy like it is now. Oh, and once the furniture for the lounge comes, it won't look anything like it did before.'

'Sophie, how are you planning on paying for all of this stuff?'

'Rent from the London house, my "if you leave quietly" severance pay and . . .'

'And?'

'I'll worry about that in a couple of months. I've got a lot on my mind.'

'What, like seven across and Estella?'

'Point taken. I'll have a think about my finances.'

'You know, if you talked to Samuel, he'd have to help.'

'I don't need his help. Bean and I have decided we're fine on our own. Haven't we, Bean?' I ask.

I picture Bean's legs kicking a few times to agree with this point, but I can't feel them yet.

'I have a neighbour,' I add, changing the subject. 'Do you remember Charlie Evans?'

'Charlie Evans? Kind of. Didn't you have a thing for him?'

'No. I. Didn't. He was a friend, that's all . . . He was kind to me when, well, you know, when I was having that horrible time at school. The year Ian lost his job. Anyway, he's turned into a complete wanker.'

'Ouch, do I detect a touch of sour grapes?'

'There are no grapes, he was just a friend.'

'Yeah, well. I think Charlie should be the last thing on your mind.'

'He is.'

‘Good.’

‘I’ve not given him another thought.’

‘Glad to hear it.’

Rain is sliding down the windows wearily, as though it can’t really be bothered to put the effort in. I run my finger around my waistband and shift on the sofa as I write ‘Things I like to do’ in the centre of the paper and then chew the top of the biro, trying to ignore the banging coming from the kitchen. I know that this exercise would be a lot more effective if I was job-searching on the internet, but I can’t quite bring myself to open my laptop just yet, so instead, I’m brainstorming on an old lined A4 pad that I found whilst emptying the kitchen drawers. I circle the ‘Things I like to do’ a few times and draw a spider leg from it. I scribble out the word ‘like’ and replace it with the word ‘can’: ‘Things I can do’. Next to the leg I write ‘Have to work from home’. Beneath that I begin bullet-pointing; next to the first point I write ‘Accounting’. I draw another spider leg. ‘Needs to be good pay and flexible.’ I draw over the ‘A’ of accounting a few times. ‘Needs to be something I can do on my own.’ I draw over the ‘c’ a few times and then rip the paper from its gluey spine, yawning as I do. I glance at my watch, yawning again. Why am I so tired? I must have slept over ten hours last night. In the middle of the fresh page, I write the word ‘Accounting’. I don’t really know why I was trying to think of another career path; accounting has always been my fall-back, my constant.

I look out of the window as the sun pierces through the clouds, pulling them apart with its brilliance and sending them sliding away, inferiority heavy in their grey faces. The radio is turned up and Ed Sheeran begins singing about playing a fiddle and one of the kitchen fitters sings along in a key or so out of tune. I sigh and undo the top button of my jeans. My stomach feels bloated and uncomfortable, like I've eaten too much food. I feel fat, not pregnant.

''Scuse me, love, I don't mean to interrupt, but we've found this down the back of one of the cupboards.' He walks over and passes me a parcel wrapped in fading pink paper; it's covered in dust and cobwebs. I accept it with thanks as he leaves the room. My fingers reach for the tag; I'd recognise the handiwork anywhere. Helen has made it, the tag in the shape of a pocket watch:

> *Happy Birthday Sophie! Don't be late, we've got a very important date! Love Mum and Helen xxx*

The paper is brittle and tears easily, revealing a very old copy of a very familiar book. The cover itself is a dark blue, with Alice's image embossed in gold.

'*What is the use of a book, without pictures or conversations?*' Mum's voice asks me.

My mouth is dry as I turn it over in my hands and wonder why Helen has never mentioned this book to me.

Week Ten

Samuel

Sarah is asleep in the chair next to my bed. I'm glad about that. She looks awful. Her clothes are creased and the remains of what could be yesterday's mascara is smudged around the bottom of her eyes. There is no sign of Da and Mam. They have been by my side for days, making this room feel even smaller than it already is.

The last few weeks have been hard on them. I would hate to be stuck in this room when you have the choice to leave it.

I have no choice; I can't move much. It could have been considerably worse, they have told me – the nurses, the doctors, the people who come into this room and then leave it. I covet their freedom. Here is what could have been worse:

1. I could have been burnt to death. This, I agree, is a much worse fate than the second-degree burns that I have across the right side of my face, arms and torso. My neighbour, Eric, apparently pulled me from my house and called the fire brigade and ambulance. Without him, I'd be dead because my house is apparently now just a carcass.
2. I am not paralysed. My right leg is broken and currently in a cast hanging from some weird pulley machine.

3. I am still not paralysed. I have cracked ribs, and torn ligaments in my back and neck, for which I have to wear a neck brace which looks like I'm wearing half a stormtrooper helmet. So yeah, it could have been worse. I was lucky. But lucky is not how I'm feeling right now. I am trapped. My arms and face are screaming to be itched: they are sore, they are blistered, they are hot, they are painful. I'm desperate to get something to stick down the inside of my plaster cast and scratch like hell, but I can't, because right now I can barely move. I'm a prisoner. In fact, it's worse than being in prison because I can't escape it. I have been incarcerated in my own body. The painkillers are the only good thing about my life right now. They ease me in and out of consciousness; I long for the oblivion of sleep.

'Sarah?' My voice is hoarse and I have to repeat her name until she wakes.

'Mule? Are you OK? Do you need something?' She rubs her eyes and leans forward.

'I need you to check my emails.'

'Your emails?'

'I have to find Sophie.'

'Mule, you need to rest.'

'I will. Once . . .' I swallow. 'You've checked my emails.'

My eyes close for a moment.

When I wake, I hear an over-enthusiastic talk-show host babbling away on the television.

'For the love of God, will you please turn that down?' My voice sounds scratchy as I automatically try to turn my head towards the person sitting by my bed.

Sarah has been replaced by Bret, who stands up and retrieves the remote control, turning down the sound.

'You're awake.'

'Well, I bloody am now.'

'How are you?'

'How the feck do you think I am?' I look at him, my eyes tracking the easy fluidity of his movements, the way he strides across the room and then slumps back into the chair opposite the bed. I need a drink. I hate the idea of having him help me sip through a straw, but the brace around my neck makes it difficult to drink out of a cup.

'Can you get me a drink, please?'

'Sure thing, buddy!'

I close my eyes. The painkillers are wearing off; the heat inside seems to rise, the itching writhing around: rats in a sewer.

'Here you go, mate.' I hate that it hurts to turn my head towards him, that I can't see where the straw is.

'How the hell am I supposed to drink it from here when I can't even see it?' I snap.

'Sorry, mate, I thought you could reach it.' He moves forward and passes me the straw. The water is warm; more heat inside my body.

'Thanks.'

He chuckles. 'Man, I love your accent – "tanks".' He laughs again. I close my eyes. Everything about him today is irritating me. 'Sammy Boy, take a look at this.' I open my eyes again but can't see where he is standing. The exasperation grates on my insides, igniting the pain, and stoking the burns until I almost cry out.

'Jesus! I can't sodding well see it until you bring it in front of the brace!' The door opens and closes behind me and I can sense the arrival of yet another doctor.

'All right, keep your hair on, mate. It is in front of your brace, look.' He moves further in front of me and I can see the mobile phone screen with the baseball scores on. 'I'd be on your guard today, doc,' Bret says over his shoulder. 'He's not in a great mood.'

'Of course I'm not in a great mood! You keep doing things behind my back!'

I close my eyes again as Bret laughs and jokes with the doctor. I gather by the sounds of Bret's phone that he is showing him something on YouTube. I open my eyes, but they are behind me. Again. 'For the love of God, can you not keep standing behind me! I can't turn my fecking neck!'

'Samuel? Can you see the screen of this phone?' There is something different about the tone of the doctor's voice as he asks me. The inside of my skin feels like it is crawling, like my veins are filled with ants scurrying around my body.

'I'm not behind you, mate.' Bret's voice has lost its booming certainty, its wise-cracking lilt, and is replaced with a voice that is edged with anxiety. 'I'm here, look.'

I can see the tips of his fingers in the top left corner of my vision, but I can't see the rest of his hand. He takes a few strides forward, concern on his face. The doctor follows his path and begins barking orders at me, shining a light in my eyes and asking me to look up, to look down, to look left, to look right. Bret stands at the bottom of the bed avoiding my gaze until he excuses himself.

The tests come thick and fast. The specialists are called; I'm wheeled into darkened rooms; I'm lifted on to beds and pushed into a scanner. Words zigzag around these rooms like the old computer games that would consist of a small ball bouncing from one side of the screen to another. Boing. Retinal damage. Boing. Peripheral vision loss. Boing. Deterioration. Boing. Tunnel vision. Boing. Beyond treatment. Boing. Eventually blind. Boing. Boing. Boing. I stop listening to Sarah's questions. I stop listening to explanations. I stop listening.

It could have been worse . . . I have a year of sight . . . if I'm lucky.

Week Eleven

Sophie

I'm meeting Helen in town. The Welsh rain batters the windscreen relentlessly, and as I turn up the blowers, I notice that my nails are different shapes and sizes; they have become brittle. My reflection in the rear-view mirror stares forlornly back at me. The smudge of mascara under my eyes, my wet hair clinging to my scalp, the roots looking even worse in the dim light. My jeans are digging into my stomach and I undo the top button, the flesh beneath the denim exhaling. I picture the English woman with the green umbrella and begin to cry. Where is she now?

A fist knocks on the window, and I wipe my tears away as Helen waves, runs around the bonnet and climbs into the passenger seat.

'Good to know that Wales is as pleased to see me as I am to see it.' She turns to look at me, rain dripping from her fringe and on to her glasses, then she takes them off and wipes the lenses with the cuff of her jacket. 'Jesus, are you OK?'

'Yeah, just morning sickness again.' I smile and reach for her as we try to give each other an awkward hug over the seat-belt buckles. 'Are you hungry? The Rose and Crown has been renovated, we can go there.'

'OK, if you feel up to it?'

'Oh, I'll be fine in a bit.' I blow my nose. 'Bean likes to keep me on my toes, don't you, Bean?' I tap my stomach.

'Ooh, you're getting chubby!' she exclaims, seeing my open button. I nod and smile . . . who knew that someone telling you you're getting fat could cause so much pride?

The rain has finished throwing a tantrum, the slaps and crashes turning into sniffs and snivels. I blow my nose and open the window a fraction. Rain on dry earth mixes with the sounds of the seaside and damp tourists as they shake off the downpour. I begin the steep climb, my foot pushing down on the accelerator, the engine protesting at my low gear.

'How are the girls?' I ask. Mismatched houses stand watchfully as I leave the main part of the town, each one stepping further back from view, as the houses gradually become grander and more hidden.

'Oh, they're good. Never give me a second, though. I swear if I make one more playdough My Little Pony I think I'll go mad.' I notice that Helen is avoiding the landscape as the grand houses peter out and give way to the old council estates, the corner shops, the pubs with bouncy castles in the beer garden.

I'm distracted by the sight of a woman pushing a buggy up the hill; the way her gait stops and starts, stops and starts. As I pass her, I glance at her tired eyes as she pushes a bottle into the baby's mouth which is hidden from my view. I pull in to the car park and wonder why the woman hadn't just fed the baby before she left.

We settle ourselves by the log burner, our drinks fizzing inside the glasses as we scan the menu and order.

'So . . . how's the place looking? How are you keeping? Are you having heartburn? Because you can have as much Gaviscon as you want. I should have bought some, I'll get plenty in next time you come to visit.' The ice cubes in my glass clink against each other as I listen to Helen's stream of questions.

'No, not yet and it's great . . . the bedroom is finished.'

'What colour have you gone for?'

'White.' She snorts into her glass. 'What?' I ask.

'Nothing. It's just you're about to have a baby, and white, well . . . let's just say baby poo isn't white, Sophie.'

'I'll put the baby in another room.'

'Right.' She swirls her straw around the inside of the glass and smirks. 'Of course, keeping your duvet cover blemish-free will be in the forefront of your mind when you've had an hour's sleep in two days.'

I ignore her and carry on. 'I've just had the kitchen redone. Actually, that's why I asked you to come.'

'Oh Sophie, I can't. I'm not ready to, I don't think I can go back there. I know you want me to, but I just can't. I—'

'I know. That's not it. I mean, I do want you to come though Hel, it's nothing like how it was before. But I understand if you need more time. I wanted to see you to ask if you could tell me about this?' I rummage in my bag and slide the book across the table. The colour drains from Helen's face and tears fill her eyes.

'Where did you find it?' she whispers.

'It was hidden behind one of the kitchen cupboards.'

She reaches for the tag which is resting on top of the book, and her fingers follow the outline of the pocket watch.

'I made this. I made it the day before she died.'

'Why did you never tell me about it?'

Helen's eyes shift from the tag and begin to scour the room, resting on the bar, the ceiling, the floor, the couple walking into the pub, looking at anything except me. I reach my hand across the table, taking her fingers in mine, but she snatches them back.

'Sophie, I can't, I'm not ready to explain. I need to go. I'm sorry.' She picks up her things.

Her reaction has thrown me. I was just expecting a memory, a forgotten story, but Helen is more than a little flustered. She drops her bag, the contents spilling over the floor. I watch her scrabbling her things together.

'Helen, stay, we can talk a bit more.'

'I can't.' She shoves the last of her things into the bag, stands and grabs her coat.

'Let me take you back into town at least.' I pull out my keys but she shakes her head.

'I think I'll walk. I need to think, to clear my head—' She pulls me towards her, her fingers digging into my shoulders as she folds me into her embrace, an embrace that is filled with the weight of the past.

I'm about to go to bed when the phone rings.

'Do you remember that KT Tunstall song about the cherry tree?' she asks, the word cherry sounding like sherry. '"Woo-hooo-ooh, woo-hoo!"' she sings down the phone.

'Helen, where are you? Are you home?' I ask, the slur in her words instantly worrying me.

'I am, safe and sound. Do you know how much faster the train journey goes when you're drunk? I might do it every time I travel. I went into a bar and drank an entire bottle of wine on my own. Just me and the bottle, no kids, no Greg; I haven't done that in years. I sat on the beach and watched the whole of the sunset.'

'Weren't you cold? It's April.'

'I needed to clear my head, and I didn't stay on the beach that long. I went into a bar and had a pornstar martini. I think I might have had three, actually.' She burps as I begin making a cup of tea. 'Do you think he killed my mum too?' she asks, the switch from pornstar martinis to murder fracturing the air in the room and pausing my movements: the sugar stills on the teaspoon halfway towards the cup. 'I mean, the death certificate said she died of pneumonia . . . but what if he did something first?'

'I don't think you can cause pneumonia, Helen.' I stir the sugar into the cup and add milk.

'You can. I've googled it. It can be caused by pulmonary contusion,' she stretches her voice into something official sounding. 'Chest trauma.'

'I'm sure there would have been an inquiry, if there were any signs of—'

'I don't even have a photo of my mum, did you know that? Not one. At least you have that.'

'I do.' I lower myself into a chair.

'There was flour all over the floor next to her body,' she whispers. 'I cleaned it up before I rang the police . . . I didn't want to spoil your surprise.'

'My surprise?' I ask, eager for more but not wanting to break her train of thought.

'I loved her very much, Soph, but I had to look after *you*. Everyone was always asking how *you* were, how sad it was for *you*, how awful it was for *you* . . . Do you know that I didn't sleep more than two hours at a time until I was twenty-five? I was always too scared to let myself rest for too long in case something happened and I missed it. It was my fault.' Pain grazes her voice, quietening her: she feels so very far away.

'Helen?'

'It was all my fault.' I hear her sniff and then the phone is dead.

'Just give her time . . .' Mum says. *'She'll tell you . . . just give her time.'*

Week Eleven

Samuel

The gauze has been replaced across the right side of my face and it's healing nicely – apparently. I look down to where the male nurse, who smells strongly of garlic and sweat, is wrapping fresh bandages around my arms, whilst laughing at whatever hilarity the sit-com family are involved in today. I look away. I hate it here. I'm now on a ward filled with the lives of strangers, the sounds of their day-to-day existence, heightened by the restrictions of my vision.

Only Sarah knows the truth of what is happening to me. I've asked the doctors not to mention it to my parents until I've had a chance to explain. I'll tell them soon, but not here, not surrounded by unfamiliar people . . . I'll tell them once I'm home.

So here is what it feels like: raise your hands and circle them into binoculars – just like you used to when you were a kid looking for pirates on the horizon or looking for Prince Charming to rescue you from the tower. Now take them away from your eyes . . . see how the room expands, see how it is filled with colour, see how free you feel. Pop your binoculars back on, but this time use just one hand and close your other eye – it's easier for me to explain if we do it this way. Now slowly start to close your fist. You should see your world shrinking and disappearing; you have just lost what lies in the corner of your eye. Take your fist away and enjoy the sights around; you don't have a fist squeezing your life from you. I, on the other hand, can't twist and turn away from the fist that has grabbed me by the scruff of the neck, like Daniel Byrne did when I was eight. I can't use brute force to escape it like I did back in the day. This fist has a hold on me that I can't escape, and it's only going to get stronger.

I have a song stuck in my head and I can't get rid of it: 'Unchained Melody' by the Righteous Brothers. It's the one from the saucy clay-moulding scene in *Ghost* – the line about time going by slowly – it's like the record is scratched and it keeps replaying the same line over and over again. Time is still going by slowly. My sight is going and I'm wasting it, stuck in this hospital looking at peach curtains and magnolia walls. My sight is being wasted on magnolia. Jesus, I want to go home. I need to see Ireland, then I need to find Sophie. But until my temperature goes down and I've fought off this infection, I'm stuck here in the peach and magnolia with the sounds of loud Americans.

Sarah is trying to arrange my flight home. A long flight in a neck brace: now, that sounds like fun.

The itching beneath the gauze and beneath the plaster on my leg is driving me insane. I need to get out of here. A quiet nurse with a soft, whispery voice appears in front of me, making me jump. The pain screeches up my spine and my eyes water. This is becoming a regular thing, people sneaking up on me, except they don't: I just can't fecking see them.

Let's do another experiment, so at least you can 'see' where I'm coming from. Take your left hand, keep your fingers together, cross your body and hold that hand – pinkie facing forward – against your temple; now stretch out your right arm, again, like you did when you were a kid pretending to be an aeroplane. Got it? Now slowly bring your arm forward so it's pointing straight out in front of you . . . how long did it take you to see your fingers? Put your left hand back down and go back to aeroplane mode and do the manoeuvre again . . . see how much sooner you can see the arm moving?

I forgive the nurse because she is here to give me my meds. I watch her flick through a few pages of my chart. I give her a smile and a thanks, but her response is of pity and understanding, a sort of head-tilted, tight-lipped, poor-you kind of smile. I close my eyes and wait for the cool feeling that calms the itches and blows out the fire.

My mind drifts away from this room with the beeps and gasps of the machinery, from the coughs and footsteps of the staff, the hushed discussions of blood pressure being too high, of higher dosages, of let's see over the next forty-eight hours, of the distant ping of the lift arriving; instead, happiness floods through my veins as I let my dulled senses take me to Sophie.

Week Twelve

Sophie

Gale-force winds are battering the house. I know that this house can take the beating Mother Nature is giving it – after all, it's been empty for all this time and it's still standing – but the howling and the shadows outside have unsettled me. A stray piece of TV cable is complaining outside my window, tapping at the pane; I imagine Cathy on the moor asking Heathcliff to let her in. My cold fingers reach out of my bed and click on the bedside lamp. Soft light gently touches the corners of the room; shadows that had been scowling and hiding from view are caressed and cajoled into a yawn and a stretch.

I shift into a sitting position and put my hand to my chest where I can feel the scrape of heartburn.

'So, Bean, you've stopped making me sick and replaced it with this instead? That hardly seems fair.' I poke my stomach. The Book says that if I poke my tummy, Bean will wriggle about in response. I grin down at my pink fleecy pyjama top, imagining Bean frowning and fidgeting into a more comfortable position. I burp and shift again. 'I get to see you tomorrow.' My voice resonates and meanders through the air, peeks under the furniture and strokes the walls, awakening the house and giving it life. I rub my chest again and wonder if I have any Gaviscon downstairs. The mattress flexes beneath my weight as I shift and pull my dressing gown around me, noticing the belt ties don't hang as loosely as they once did.

The smell of fresh paint and treated wood greets me as I open the new kitchen door, made of heavy oak, and step into the room. Gone are the cracks and the mismatched furniture, and instead a creamy-white Aga stands proud like a parent amongst the family of oak cupboard doors. The wall behind it holds an old beam which had been hidden behind plasterboard, and it arches above it like a puzzled eyebrow. Outside, Cathy is still screeching through the hills, whispering her way through chimneys and hissing in the ears of hidden cracks, but in here, the new double-glazed windows are keeping Cathy away, making her presence feel distant. Warmth radiates inside this room, like a heartbeat pulsing inside what was once a cold, dead space.

Reaching for the kettle, I fill it, add a tea bag to the cup and then sit down at the table which I found in town. It's been 'up-cycled' and still has scratches and stories beneath the varnish. I run my finger along one of the cracks. It feels smooth, the texture of the original scrape now healed and treated; hidden almost. I think of Helen and how hard she has tried to hide her scars; how my asking her about the past has made her begin to pick at the varnish.

I'm going to see her next week. The few conversations we've had since the night of the pornstar martinis have been brief and formulaic: I ask how the kids are, she asks how my pregnancy is going, I mention the weather, she agrees it is too wet or too windy. Neither of us mention her phone call; I wonder now if she even remembers it.

I get up and make the tea. I'm just adding the milk when a loud bang slams against the front door, making me clatter the teaspoon on to the counter. My body reacts, adrenaline spiking as it explodes from my core, that prickly feeling that scurries over your skin like sunburn.

Rational thoughts take over. It's just the wind: it's not a pack of wolves scraping at my door, it's not a masked criminal with a machete. It's just the wind. I take a few deep breaths and glance down to where my hand is lying protectively over my stomach.

'It's OK, Bean. It's just the wind.' I take careful steps towards the door and peer out of the peephole. My heart is banging, the sound of it loud in my ears. 'Cover your ears, Bean,' I say. The Book says Bean can open and close those tiny fingers this week; I imagine little hands covering perfectly formed ears, a cute little face looking up towards me for reassurance. I squint my left eye and look through. The night is surprisingly bright, the wind's howl and rage sending any stray clouds scampering apologetically on their way, but this image is distorted. The image of my car, headlights catching the reflection of the moon, seems far away and enclosed by the circle of darkness impairing my view. I can make out part of the skip to the right of my car, but that is all I can see. No matter how hard I try to change the angle of my head, the image remains confined, as though it is inside a tunnel.

I pull my head away and rub my stomach. Bean's worried face plays on my conscience. My boots stand next to the door; I stare at them. I look back outside through the tunnel: my car still sits; the skip hasn't moved. The boots are eager to go outside. I jump as the noise ricochets around the house; Bean's bottom lip quivers. I eye the boots with trepidation, then slip my feet into them and pull open the door latch, but the door swings away from my grasp, slamming against the frame. The wind pulls at my hair, slaps my face, yanks my clothes; the smell is deep and rich with earth and cut grass but the sea air lifts it, adds salt, sprinkles sea mist. An old terracotta plant pot – the culprit of all this disruption – is entangled in some twine and has latched itself to the trellis around the door; the wind is rolling it back and forth like a rolling pin as it flattens the patch of grass outside my front door.

My feet stomp forwards, sinking into the moist ground, while my hair lashes against my face, into my mouth, into my eyes. I push the strands away, bend down and pull the pot free, standing it upright. I glance around for something to fill it with, to keep it in its place, and notice some rubble sticking out of the skip. Battling my way against the wind and spray of sea mist, I dip my head into my chest and tread towards the skip. There is a rectangle of light cast on to the inky grass outside Charlie's house, and I stop my progress and look up. I can see the upper half of his bare torso; he must be sitting on a bed. The curtains are open, hanging limply either side of the frame, but he seems oblivious to the chaos outside. My feet stay rooted, my view obscured for a moment by a cloud fighting against the gusts of wind as it covers the moon. I'm intruding by standing here watching him, and yet I can't move. I've never seen so much pain on a man's face. He is staring forward, but his face is crumpled in anguish; his whole body is crying, his shoulders juddering under the force of it, and his chest heaves up and down as though each breath is a struggle.

I take a step back; this moment is so intimate, so raw, that my intrusion prickles under my skin. I begin to move back towards my house, looking down at the green wellies, urging them forward, choosing my steps carefully, mindful that a fall could injure Bean. A flicker in the corner of my eyes distracts me and I squint back up at the window. The cloud is pushed away from the moon, a silver spotlight shining on my silhouette as he stands in front of the window looking down at me. Embarrassment floods through my body, heat pulsing through my veins as our eyes meet. We stand there opposite each other: me, Bean and the Welsh wind, a trio of chaos facing him; but he, I now understand, is very much alone. We stand there, mesmerised, as he opens his arms as if welcoming me – or perhaps sacrificing himself – but then he is gone; the curtains are drawn, and his agony is hidden.

When I wake, the sun is streaming through the curtains and the destruction of last night seems hard to believe.

'Good Morning, Bean.' I yawn as my tummy rumbles, almost in response. I wander downstairs and open the roman blind in the kitchen, filling the room with melted-butter light, then I toast two crumpets. Tentatively, I place a decaf coffee capsule in the coffee machine and eye it with an anxious frown. It clicks into action, the surge of steam filling the room with its heady scent as I grin and stroke Bean in thanks. The cup sits inside my hands as I enjoy the aroma and watch the sun peeking over the trees. I eat my breakfast, trying to swallow down my excitement that today I get to see Bean properly.

Has it really only been six weeks since I last saw it? Bean was barely visible, a tiny circle in a blob of black, but what I now see on the screen is a baby. My baby. Bean is tall, the technician tells me as she measures a femur. My due date is correct. She smiles and goes on to talk about heart rates and measurements, but I'm mesmerised by this baby moving around . . . She laughs and points to the screen where Bean is scratching its bottom. She pushes down harder on my abdomen and I watch Bean wriggle and try to move away. I'm hungry for every second of this glimpse at my baby. Bean begins to hiccup. Real hiccups. I watch the screen in awe as this little being moves; I watch Bean's heart working away; I follow to where the technician's finger shows me that my baby has had a drink. But the moment is over too soon. I want to stay watching the screen, but the screen is blank, and my stomach is being wiped with blue paper towel.

Week Twelve

Samuel

'That's good, your temperature is back to normal, you're healing nicely.' The doctor, medium build, medium brown hair, medium enthusiasm, smiles at me. 'I can't see any reason why you can't fly back to Ireland, Samuel.' Thank the Lord, I want to shout. My hands reach for the wheels of the wheelchair and I manoeuvre myself forward.

'That's great news, thanks,' I say.

Sarah smiles. In contrast to the medium-sized doctor, Sarah fills the room. We are almost the same height, but she rarely wears flats, preferring instead to add another couple of inches to her already impressive height. 'Are you sure he'll be OK? What about—'

'For the love of God, Sarah, the man says I'm good to go.'

'I know that, but—' She pushes a chunk of hair behind her ear.

'Anyone would think you don't want me home.'

'Oh, shush your mouth now. Mam has been on the phone to half of Derry giving them orders to stock the kitchen with your favourite dinners; I'm just worried about you being stuck on the plane if something were to go wrong.'

'Sam will be well supported with the brace, so you shouldn't worry. It's going to be uncomfortable, though, no doubt about that. How long is your flight?'

'Seven hours, give or take . . . I'll be grand. I'll pop a few of those sleeping tablets and I'll be home before I know it,' I say. In truth I'm dreading it. I mean, the pain is bad enough sitting here – it will be excruciating on the plane. But it'll be worth it. I just want to go home. I need to find Sophie.

'And how are you finding the glasses?'

I have been prescribed some 'prism' glasses. They supposedly help me see parts of my blind spots but, I'll be honest with you, they just make me feel ill. Parts of my vision are replaced but then it's kind of blurred, and the new bits of sight sort of jumble up with what I actually can see, plus I look ridiculous. I'd rather just get used to the restrictions.

'Ah, not so good, Doc, they just make a mess of what I already can see.'

'You may appreciate the benefits of them when you've left the hospital. You might find you bump into people, and walking through busy places will be a very different experience from what you're used to.'

'Honestly, I'll be grand.'

This is a lie. I can already tell that the fist is squeezing harder. I can't see above me, I can't see below me. The world is closing in, but for the moment I can still see most of the room, even if it is being suffocated by darkness. Things will be better once I'm out of this brace. At least I'll be able to turn my head easily. I'll be able to lean it back; I'll be able to lean it forward.

The doctor leaves, his medium-ness disappearing into the fog before the door is closed behind him.

Sarah decides to push me through the hospital and takes me outside where there is a garden of sorts, an oval lawn and borders around it. She finds a bench, parks me to the side of her, and sits down. I know that she has positioned me so we can talk; she won't be aware that the darkness has claimed the garden from my sight. I manoeuvre the wheels so I can have a little segment of the garden flourishing in my field of vision. It suddenly seems important to me to be able to drink in bursts of colour after drowning in magnolia for so long, but the warm sun aggravates my burns so I turn the wheels again, facing away from the flowers and the sun, instead filling my vision with the towering building that has kept me hostage for so long.

'Have you found anything on Helen Yates?' I ask Sarah as she steps into the darkness to reach for my drink, re-emerging by my side with a can of Diet Coke and a straw.

'Not yet. Anyway, don't you think you've got enough on your plate without looking for this Sophie person?'

'I've got nothing on my plate. My plate is empty.'

'But if she left and she hasn't been in touch, Samuel . . .' She puts the straw in my mouth. 'It's, well, it's a pretty strong message that she's, well—'

'Well what?' I ask out of the corner of my mouth.

'Not interested.'

'Of course she's interested,' I say automatically, although the way that Sophie has managed to completely disappear makes me wonder how she'll react when I find her. 'Just look at me! What woman wouldn't be interested?' Sarah laughs at this and slides into the tunnel walls – segments of her red hair lick out of the tunnel like fire before she reappears holding her phone.

'Oh, hold on, don't forget your glasses now. Geek chic, I think it's called.' She slides the frame on to the bridge of my nose and steps back, taking a few shots, laughing at my expense as she does. Crouching in front of me, Sarah shows me the photo. The gauze from my burns has now been removed and what remains is a purplish red mark which looks like a giant penis-shaped birthmark across the right side of my face. My leg is still in plaster, and to top this look off, I'm sporting a pair of thick glasses that would best be suited to my Uncle Pete – and let me tell you, Uncle Pete is not an attractive man.

'I take your point. Perhaps it would be wise to wait a bit until I declare my undying love?'

'Undying love?' Sarah's amusement fades and she raises an eyebrow at me. 'You're not even joking, are you?'

'No. I love her, Sarah, I need to find her.'

'But if she's left you twice . . .'

'For the love of God, can you not just do as I ask?'

'OK, calm down. So, tell me . . . why do you love her?'

So I do. I tell her about our week together, about the week she came back to DC . . . about the colour of her eyes and the way she hiccups when she laughs.

Sarah is quiet for a moment.

'There is something that might help,' she says eventually, and I know that she is keeping something from me.

'What?'

'I checked your emails . . . You know, you really should come up with a better password than "mule-means-cool". You were using that when you were eight years old.'

'Just get to the point.'

'There's one from someone called Gemma. It says that she received an invoice from a car repair firm that Sandwell uses, billing Sophie for damage done to her company car. The repairs were done in Shropshire . . . is that any help?'

'Why are you only telling me this now?'

'Well, we've had quite a lot going on, Mule, and I don't know if chasing after some woman who has dumped you is what you need right now.'

I ignore her.

'Shropshire, where the hell is that?' I say. 'It sounds familiar.' A quick search on Google shows it is in the West Midlands . . . and then I remember.

'I don't see her very often . . . she lives in Shropshire.'

A slow smile creeps across my face.

Week Thirteen

Sophie

I'm startled as the knocker on the door interrupts me. I've been sitting at my laptop for the past hour and have begun to set up a web page for my accounting business. I haven't googled Samuel once.

The knocker raps again, insistently, the kind of knock that means this is not an emergency and yet one shouldn't ignore its importance. I peek through the spyhole and Charlie's face appears at the end of the tube. The sun is fractured into thousands of beams, just the way that I used to draw a sun when I was a child: yellow rays shooting outwards in every direction. It hovers over his shoulder, stinging my eyes. I pull away from the door and try to shake the image of the last time I saw him as I open it.

'Hello,' I smile brightly.

'Your car is in the way,' he answers. My smile fades.

'In the way of what?' I ask and fold my arms over my chest. I picture Bean copying my actions, a scowl furrowing on a tiny brow.

'The van. I'm having a delivery.' He has washed his hair, I notice, as he turns and nods towards where a large white truck is growling behind the gate.

'Right, I'll just grab my keys.' He nods his thanks before I turn my back on him, stride into the kitchen and delve inside my handbag, which I'm alarmed to see contains an obscene number of empty crisp packets. 'Bean . . . we're going to have to cut back on the salt and vinegar.' The keys dangle from my mouth, clattering coldly against my chin as I push my feet into my boots, closing the door behind me.

Charlie is walking towards the delivery truck, his hair bouncing up and down like it used to at school, that same eager walk that I've seen so many times. He stops at the gate and climbs over it easily as I open the car door and sit inside. My jeans are uncomfortable, so I undo the zip and smooth down my loose white shirt, then I start the engine and manoeuvre my car so that the gate can be opened, and the van can get past. I climb out, lock the door and watch as Charlie follows it. Two burly men jump down from the truck and begin to unload. Charlie issues instructions as he pushes his front door open. His voice is soft but authoritative, a voice that is used to handling people, making them feel valued but getting the best out of them.

'Are you having something nice?' I ask, making my way towards him, determined to get at least a small piece of civilised conversation from my new neighbour.

His eyebrows shoot up in alarm as if I've appeared from nowhere.

'Just some old furniture,' he replies. I stand next to him and watch as the delivery men go back inside the van, this time pulling out a sofa.

'Mind yourself,' he says, shifting himself backwards to let the men past. Bean and I shuffle backwards too.

'Have you moved far, or did you stay locally?' I ask, as he turns his head towards me, again as if he had forgotten I was standing there. The mild Welsh wind blows his hair into his eyes and he flicks his head and runs his fingers agitatedly through it, a glint from his ring finger surprising me.

'Manchester.'

'Didn't like the city life?'

'Something like that.' He glances down and then looks away.

'I'm fresh from the city, too – London.' Charlie glances back with an expression that tells me he wouldn't care if I had just said I've moved from Pluto. He looks down again and then climbs into the van, dragging what looks like a computer desk towards the end as the two men return and lift it down, carrying it back into the house. I put my hands in my pockets, unsure of whether to stay or go.

'So why did you leave London?' he asks as he leans forward and pulls on a rolled-up rug. He slings it on his shoulder, jumps down and carries it back into the house, leaving me pondering his question.

'Why did you leave Manchester?' I counter when he re-appears.

'Long story,' he mumbles, looking away from me.

I watch as he carefully climbs back into the van, lifts a duck-egg blue glass picture frame and passes it to one of the re-emerging men.

'That's a beautiful frame,' I say. 'Really unusual to see glass tinted that colour.'

'My wife made it; it's Perspex, actually,' he replies, and I see a glimmer of light behind his preoccupied eyes.

'Wow! She is a very talented lady.'

'Was.'

The word slams against my chest. The air which felt light a moment ago, air which had been filling and expanding my lungs without me even noticing, now feels heavy, dusty. How is he able to breathe with all this weight in the air?

'I'm so sorry. How did she—'

'Car crash.'

He looks down again. I follow his gaze to see what it is that is so interesting on the ground that he feels he must keep looking at it, but instead of seeing something nestling in the grass, I see a bright red polka dotted pair of Minnie Mouse pants staring out of a triangle of open jeans, my white shirt flapping away, oblivious to the embarrassment it is causing me. The heat in my cheeks is instantaneous.

'I'm pregnant,' I say loudly in explanation for my state of disarray, and smile. He looks up then and meets my eye.

'And you moved here alone?' he asks, his expression somewhere between disbelief and revulsion. I nod hesitantly, the smile frozen on my lips. 'Sounds like a pretty stupid thing to do,' he replies, turns his back and goes inside his house.

I feel like I'm walking through nettles as I tread back to my doorway; his words have stung, and my body itches as they echo through me. I slam the door and slump into Mum's chair. What kind of man says things like that? The tears come, but they are short-lived. I'm not some weak, stupid woman without a plan. I know I can do this by myself; I don't need help.

The sounds of twilight filter in through the open kitchen windows as I sip my water, the ice chiming as I tilt the glass. The word 'Google' is winking at me from my monitor. I drain the rest of my drink and crunch on an ice cube. My fingers begin to tap 'Samuel McLaughlin Greenlight Finance' and my hand hovers over the enter key. It's as though I'm daring myself to do it, the way I did before I jumped off the pier when I went on a residential school trip when I was ten. *Go on. You can do it. You'll be fine. You've seen water before.* I hit enter and within moments his face fills the screen. He's still at Greenlight, then. I reach forward and follow the outline of his jaw but another knock at the door makes me pull my hand away. I exit the screen and close the lid. The knock is different this time, a tentative knock, one that could be ignored but doesn't want its feelings hurt.

For the second time today, I peek through the tunnel, but there is nothing at the end of it except the beginnings of a beautiful sunset, oranges and reds mixing together as though the sky has been tie-dyed.

I open the door and there is a wooden box, about the size of a ring binder. I lift it and take it into the kitchen where I place it on the table next to my closed laptop. My fingers run around the edges of the box until I find the catch and open it.

Inside, wrapped in delicate blue tissue paper, is the duck-egg blue picture frame.

Week Thirteen

Samuel

Ah, it's good to be home at the best of times, but after the journey that I've just had, it's even better. My mam and da's house is crammed to the gills with family that have come to see me. When I say come to see me, what I basically mean is Mam has invited all and sundry to visit as if it's Christmas Day; the oven is on and the thick, rich smell of roast beef hangs in the air.

I'm sitting next to the electric fireplace, which gives the illusion of a flickering open fire, my crutches leaning precariously against it. The old pictures of me and my sister in various school uniforms at various ages stand on top, as they have for years; the edges of the frames are chipped and worn, but smell of the polish that Mam uses religiously twice a week. On one sofa – beneath the photos of myself in my graduation cap and gown, my sister in her hockey kit and my parents' wedding photo – is my gran, my sister, her husband Duncan (who I used to play rugby with) and my niece (Gertie, three) and nephew (William, five), both of whom have inherited Sarah's red hair and who are sitting on each of Duncan's knees. Sitting on the floor by their feet are my cousins Jill, Jane and Janet, all in their late teens, with the same thick, dark curly hair and huge blue eyes. My Aunty Katherine is sitting opposite them on the other sofa, where my Uncle Pete has now joined her.

On the coffee table are mugs of thick brown tea in chipped mugs that don't match, a biscuit tin the size of London Town itself and a ripped open bag of Haribo which is spilling its contents on to the floor.

I can describe all of this because it is home. But I can't see it. Most of this is down to the position my neck brace keeps me locked in. All I can see right now is my sister, Duncan, the tops of Will and Gertie's heads and some of the photos above their red curls. Their legs dangle into the abyss and the dark roof leans down on us.

The kids on the floor; the tea on the table; my mam as she lifts the whistling kettle from the hob and fusses with the strings of her apron; Da as he sits at the back of the room peeling carrots to go with the mammoth joint of beef; they have all been sucked into the walls of the darkness. My family, which always feels so big, now feels small and out of reach. How am I going to tell them that I can't see? That I'm going blind?

The pressure of the tunnel feels heavy today, more like a mine than a passageway; its darkened walls are leaden and dense, and I feel it pushing in on me. I'm not strong enough to hold the roof above my head; I'm not strong enough to fight the gravity which longs to pull it crashing down on top of me. Every sound in the room adds an extra layer of pressure: with each voice it feels heavier, with each laugh the weight leans on top of me – the scrape of a cup, the creak of the springs in the sofa, the crack of a biscuit, the scrape of the vegetable peeler against the skin of the carrots – each sound becomes a burden and it pushes me down. The heat of the room squeezes the walls of the mine closer; the smell of the beef surrounds me like impenetrable fog. I feel like I can't breathe the air as it mixes with the different perfumes of my nieces, which are cheap and sweet. The plug-in air freshener creeps into my mouth and my jaw aches as though I've eaten something sharp, like the time I made lemon curd at school – the citrus had been so strong that Mam's eyes had squinted when she ate it, but eat it she did . . . the whole bleeding jar. I need to get out of here. The tunnel is too small for my family to fit in; they're sucking out the oxygen.

My mouth is dry, and as I try to reach for my crutches, my hands are shaking. Sarah's face peers around the edge of the darkness, her eyes narrowing as she looks at me.

'Get me out of here,' I say, my breath coming in sharp bursts.

The sounds are sliding off the roof; the chatter has stopped as Sarah shouts over her shoulder for Mam to get me a drink of water. The creaks in the sofa have stilled but the silence pushes down even harder on the ceiling, the rafters beginning to buckle under the pressure, and I'm frightened that it's going to collapse and I will be buried here, buried in the dark, the sounds of my home suffocating me.

'Don't be so daft, you're not blind!' Da laughs, clears his throat and walks over to the kitchen sink to swill out his mug. 'We'll get you to Specsavers, they'll sort it out.'

'They've got a lovely range of frames, Samuel,' Mam chips in. 'You can get some of those designer ones, and they have two for one on. You'll be grand, love, you'll look distinguished, so you will. Mr McLaughlin, pop the kettle on, we'll have a cuppa and have a look on the website.'

'Da, sit down,' Sarah orders. I see Da turn to look at her, nodding his head. 'Right you are, Sarah love, right you are. No need to get your knickers in a twist.'

'The doctors in DC have done some tests,' I begin.

'Well, there you go! You need Irish doctors for Irish eyes. Bloody Americans, always making a mountain out of a molehill.'

I take a deep breath and try to curb my irritation at Da's inability to listen to anything negative about his family.

'I'm losing my peripheral vision, Da. I can't see the clock over your shoulder, I can't see the right side of Mam's body. It's like looking through the end of a telescope. All the edges around the centre are dark, like I'm looking through a tunnel.' I ignore Mam's sharp intake of breath, 'And that tunnel is going to close. I won't be able to see anything when it does.'

'When?' Mam asks, her voice quiet and shaken.

'Within a year . . . if I'm lucky.'

'A year? That's plenty of time, Sammy, my boy.'

'Plenty of time for what?' I ask with trepidation.

'To write your bucket list.'

'Shush your hole, Mr M! He's not dying . . . are you, Sammy, are you dying?'

'No, I'm not frigging dying!'

'But his eyes are, that's right, isn't it, Sammy? Let's give them something to see before they pack in, eh?'

And with that, Da claps his hands together as if I've just told him to get last orders in and Mam makes a pot of tea.

Week Fourteen

Sophie

I can't do up my trousers. This is now a fact. I look at my bed where a cascade of different coloured material confirms this. I chew my bottom lip and stand nakedly in front of the mirror.

'I'm pregnant,' I say and notice the panicked sound within my voice. Turning to the side, I look at my profile where there is undeniably a bump. I run my hand over it. 'I'm really pregnant. Oh God.' The enormity of not only my stomach but the situation makes me feel dizzy and I slump on to the end of the bed. I take a few deep breaths and concentrate on slowing my breathing down. I know this is the beginning of an anxiety attack; I used to have them before exams and when I would hear Ian's voice raised in the night, knowing that Mum would be 'having a little accident'. I continue to concentrate on controlling my thoughts, on rationalising them and relaxing my muscles. My pulse slows down, and the dizziness subsides. 'Get a grip, Sophie,' I say to myself.

My hands grasp the end of the bed and I push down on the mattress as I get up, pull open my underwear drawer, put on a pair of black knickers and then fasten on a matching bra. Except the bra doesn't fit. 'You have got to be kidding me!' I go back to the mirror where my boobs are impressively spilling out of each cup. Typical. My whole life I've wanted bigger boobs and now that I have, there is nobody around to see them! I rummage through my trousers and grab a pair of leggings, then stomp downstairs into the kitchen, where I open various drawers until I find a pair of scissors and make incisions either side of the waist elastic. I pull them up. They will have to do for now.

I fan myself with my hand – it's the second week in May and the forecast has said that temperatures will hit twenty-three degrees this week. I sit down and pull the laptop towards me, then spend an hour ordering a vast array of maternity clothes. Satisfied that by tomorrow my wardrobe will be filled with new, comfortable clothing with hidden panels and adjustable waists, I pull on a pair of bright-yellow rubber gloves and begin scrubbing the pan from my midnight feast. I've been having a lot of troubled sleep this past week and came down in the early hours to make a cheese toasty . . . the odd thing is that I wasn't really craving the cheese itself, more the burnt bits around the edge.

My inbox pings and I lean over to see a confirmation on my delivery time for tomorrow just as someone knocks on the door. I pull at the fingers of the rubber gloves, but they feel tight and stuck. I bite the end of my right index finger and try to pull the glove off again; it moves slightly but not enough to release my hand. There's another knock on the door. 'Coming!' I shout as I continue to wrestle with the gloves. I put my hand in between my thighs and start pulling against the yellow rubber. Another knock. I wipe my brow with the back of my forearm, my face becoming red with exertion. I can feel a little movement inside the glove, but my hand is still not coming free. The door knocks again insistently. Still trying to release my hand, I open the door. There – looking slightly alarmed – is Charlie, and he is holding a box full of vegetables.

'Hello.' He looks up at the sky as he talks, and I wonder

if this avoiding eye contact is a trait of his. 'I ordered vegetables.' He thrusts the box towards my rubber-gloved hands, thinks better of his action and instead, still not looking anywhere in my direction, places the box on my doorstep. I look down at it with confusion. I haven't seen him since the previous week when we had a stilted awkward, conversation as I thanked him for the frame. His reply had been that he had never liked it anyway. Honestly, I can't decide whether he is rude or just odd. 'There were too many,' he adds, still looking up at the sky. I look into the box and see a small collection of vegetables.

'Oh. Um, thanks,' I say, still fiddling with the rubber gloves.

'You've been away.' He says this as a statement, his eyes still looking skywards.

'Yes, I've been over at my sister's for a couple of days. Helped her at the school fair.' He snorts.

'What?' I reply indignantly.

'It's just that you don't seem like a school fair kind of person, that's all.'

'I will have you know that it was quite a prestigious affair. ITV News was there because Gina Little was auctioning the name of a character in her new book for charity . . . Apparently, she used to go to that school when she was a kid. And I made muffins to sell – she even took one from our stall.'

'OK.' He raises his hands up defensively. 'I take it back, you're perfect school fair material.'

'Could you do me a favour?' His eyes glance at my face momentarily then back at the sky. I wonder if he has autism. 'Could you help me get these gloves off? I think my hands have swollen in the heat, or maybe from the pregnancy, but I can't get them off.' I stretch my yellow Marigolds out towards him. He glances back at me and then down at the gloves. Charlie reaches for the wrists, still with his strange eye-darting movement. He gives it a good tug and the glove releases my ensnared right hand, folding itself inside out.

'Thanks so much,' I say, offering my other hand. It is at this moment that I realise. I am standing in front of my burly neighbour wearing a pair of cut-at-the-seams leggings, a rubber glove and a black bra from which my newly enlarged bosoms are heaving out. 'Oh God!' I shriek, snatching my gloved hand back from his grip and frantically grabbing the nearest thing that I can see to cover my modesty: a Savoy cabbage and a head of broccoli. I hold them over my chest which is rising and falling at an impressive rate. 'Go!'

He takes a step back and blinks in a panicked fashion, then risks a brief look at my chest, the hint of a smile playing at the corner of his mouth. I push the box with my heel into my house and shimmy myself backwards through the door, closing it with a bang.

Helen's face disappears from my laptop screen before she reappears with a glass of wine.

'It's not that funny,' I scold her lightly, even though the more I replay the image of myself holding the cabbage and broccoli, the funnier it seems.

'It is,' she laughs. It's a relief to hear her laughing. Last week we only talked once about *Alice in Wonderland*, and that was as she carried my case into the girls' bedroom.

'I'm sorry about the way I just left, Soph,' she'd apologised, her hand resting on my arm, 'but I've tried long and hard to put that part of my life behind me. I'm afraid of what will happen if I start thinking about it again . . . do you know what I mean?' I was fairly sure she didn't remember the drunken phone call after she'd got home last time. I replayed Mum's words and didn't question her: giving her time. I'd nodded, just as Jessica had run into the room, grabbed my hand, and pulled me into the kitchen to show me the recipe for the muffins she wanted us to make. I'd suggested we make jam tarts instead but she had made gagging noises and said her mum hates jam tarts.

I remind myself how horrific it must have been for Helen to find Mum, to know that her father had killed her. It's enough for me to hold back my questions . . . for now at least.

'How's the business?' Helen leans towards the screen as she shifts in her chair, opening a bag of crisps.

'Good, I've got my first client.' I look down at the pile of receipts on the table. 'One of the B&Bs on the front contacted me. You know you're back home when you get a reply from the card you put up in the corner shop.'

'Figures.'

'Muuuuuummmmmy! I've had a poo!' is announced from within Helen's house.

'Give me strength,' she sighs, rolling her eyes and draining her glass. 'I've got to go.'

'OK . . . see you soon?'

'Sure. See you soon.' She kisses her two fingers and places them on the camera. I return the gesture but the screen is already blank.

Week Fourteen

Samuel

I've come to the library for two reasons. Firstly, there is only so much tea a man can drink. God love her, but I think Mam believes if she gives me enough caffeine my sight will be fixed. And two, I need to find Sophie and the WiFi at home has the speed of a snail.

The walls of the tunnel are thinner today; I think the fresh air and being outdoors help to lift the feeling of claustrophobia. I've just been to the park with Sarah and Duncan and the kids; Sarah enjoying pushing me around literally rather than metaphorically. I can move around on crutches if it's for a short time, but for a trip to the park, it's back to the chair. I'm sitting in a quiet corner, searching for Helen Yates in Shropshire. So far, I've got two from LinkedIn, five from the phone book, and a list as long as my arm from people called Helen Yates on Facebook who don't list their whereabouts.

I look up at the muted TV screen that has the news subtitles running across it. The edges of the screen are hidden in the darkness. My stomach does an involuntary flip. I won't be able to watch the telly soon, won't be able to watch films, won't be able to see technology advancing as special effects change. I stare at the screen for a moment. Some romance writer is buying cakes at a school somewhere; I see a hand passing her a cake, but the owner is hidden from my view. I feel cheated. I won't be able to see the news soon, and this crap is what I get? I read the words 'Gina Little auctions off character in latest bestseller'. I turn myself away and roll the wheels outside, so I can begin my phone calls.

'Hello, is this Helen Yates?'

'It is,' replies a Liverpudlian accent.

'Great, my name is Samuel McLaughlin and I was wondering if you have a sister called Sophie?'

'I'm sorry, no. I'm an only child,' is the reply.

'Ah well, thanks for your time.'

I make fourteen more calls, but the answers lead me nowhere.

'Mule! Do you want gravy on your chips, Mam says?'

'Yes, please!' I reply, hobbling along to the kitchen where the smell of the deep fryer clings to our clothes as much as the food will cling to our arteries. Duncan pulls out a chair for me and I lower myself into the seat. The table is piled as it always has been with condiments; my family are condiment mad. Sarah always has salad cream with her chips, Da has brown sauce on his Sunday roast and Mam will not eat any chicken produce (even Southern-fried) without cranberry sauce. There is always bread and butter on the table – not spread, butter – and most meals are covered with vinegar.

I tap my fingers gently along the table to find the knife and fork and smile at Mam as she puts the plate down in front of me. I've been in this brace for eight weeks. I've got a check-up next week and I'm hoping that Dr Medium was right and that I've only got another four weeks in it. At least then I'll be able to see where my dinner is.

'Be careful now,' she warns, 'Mr McLaughlin has just made the gravy.' I look down to see my dinner – pie and chips – but I can't see the plate at all; it's too close. I can see the edge of the plate of bread and butter, piled high like the leaning tower of Pisa, and I can see the tomato sauce. This has happened a lot since I've been home. Some meals I can negotiate with – chippy is good, my fingers can find the chips easily; sandwiches too are inoffensive – but sit-down meals are another matter. Dinner continues around me: pass the sauce, no more salt Gertie, did you see that weather forecast? It's going to get hotter next week. All of this continues as I navigate my hands holding the cutlery and guess where they are landing on my plate. Nobody seems to have noticed.

A chip goes down the wrong way and I try to reach for a drink (a glass jar with a straw inserted into the lid, as is the current trend – 'Why would you want to drink out of a jam jar?', Mam asked when she came back from the supermarket), knocking it over in the process. She starts fussing, getting up and ripping huge wads of kitchen towel to wipe up the mess as I continue to splutter.

'Sorry,' I say, taking a piece of kitchen towel and wiping my mouth.

'Worse things have happened at sea,' she replies. The same phrase she has always used.

'Tell me a bit about this girl you're trying to find, Sammy,' Da interjects, and I'm grateful to him for his attempt at ignoring what has just happened. I stall, trying not to think of the small gasps she made, the way her legs wrapped around my naked skin, the taste of her, the—

'Sammy? You look like you're in cloud cuckoo land.' Da's voice brings me back; I clear my throat and shift, hoping that the beginnings of my erection aren't on show.

'Paddle boats,' I blurt out.

'Paddle boats?' Gertie and Will say in unison.

'Paddle boats . . . I took her out on paddle boats.' I picture the way she had laughed so hard she had started snorting when I said I had to get off them because I felt so seasick; I can't help but smile.

'But you get seasick, Sammy. Remember when we took him on that boat trip, Mr McLaughlin?' They both start laughing. 'You've never seen a child throw up so much! It was everywhere.'

'The wind took it and it hit the reverend right in the chops!' Da punches the air like I've just scored a try.

'I wanted to, you know . . . show her my romantic side.'

'I never had you down as the romantic type, Sammy,' Da says thoughtfully, 'although there was that time you started writing poetry, but I thought we'd sorted that out.'

Ma sits in front of me, right in the centre of my view. She inclines her head and smiles.

'Ah, Mr McLaughlin . . . our boy is in love.' Gertie and Will make puking noises.

'Well, it's about time, Sammy,' he answers as Mrs McLaughlin claps her hands excitedly.

'So, when can we meet her?'

'I'm working on it,' I answer.

Week Fifteen

Sophie

My fifteen-week check-up has gone well, no problems at all except for when I stepped on the scales; I've put on half a stone already. It's only the third week in May and yet my time with Samuel seems so long ago. As the time passes, I worry more about whether the decision to do this on my own is the right one, but then I think of the hurt I felt. I let down my defences before and look at what happened to me. I have Bean to think of now; I need to protect us. I'm setting up my new life. The website 'S B (for Bean) Williams Accountants' is almost ready; I've had a couple more interested potential clients.

The air conditioning in the car is on full as I drive home and I still feel hot even when all I'm wearing is a blue jumpsuit – one of my purchasing mistakes. What is the point of a maternity jumpsuit when you have to unbutton a million buttons before you can take it down so you can go to the toilet? Fashion over practicality. I laugh at myself as I notice a chocolate Mini Milk stain on my chest . . . how many times have I worn crippling heels and a white suit, even though I know my feet will hurt and I will inevitably have to avoid anything vaguely colourful on the menu, just so I can look the part?

*

I stare at my back garden, a jungle that I have been trying to tame for the last hour. Sweat dribbles down my back and expands into crude circles under my arms. This time next year I will have Bean here, and my child will need a place to play. The difference between the grass and weeds is indecipherable and there is no hope of being able to get a lawnmower anywhere near it. The hedge at the back scratches and fights in all directions as the fence panels sway and groan, their backs broken, their discs slipped. I'm trying to clear a way for Handy Huw to be able to get his rotovator into the garden. There's an old gate that we never used to the right-hand side, which is barely hanging on by its rusted hinges, and in front of it there's an old fence panel that has fallen over where our old garden table used to sit. Brambles have woven their way through the slats and attached to the furniture I know is behind it. The veins and innards of this overgrown monster have taken over my mother's garden.

The bruises of Ian's abuse could almost be forgotten when we were out here. The garden would be filled with the scents and colours of the plants she would grow from seedlings in the small greenhouse; a skeleton is all that remains now, the glass skin broken and exposing its brittle bones.

My palms are itching inside the rough gardening gloves and my lower back is starting to ache as I snip away with the shears. I cut away, and little by little the panel becomes freed of the monster's grip. The sweat slithers down my back as I begin to pull at the wood. A small piece splinters away but the rest, I worry, is too heavy for me to move.

'What now, Bean?' I ask as I take thirsty gulps of lemon squash. Bean loves all things citrus at the moment. The Book says my baby might be sucking its thumb this week; this thought brought me to tears. Mum still sucked her thumb all the way through her adult years. Never in public or in front of Ian, but she did in front of Helen and me, her middle finger running left and right as though she was rubbing a moustache as she sat with her feet tucked beneath her while reading cheesy romance novels. I can hear Charlie moving around in his garden: the sounds of a radio and some kind of gardening machine – not a lawn mower but something like it. I pull at my earlobe. The garden needs doing. Handy Huw cannot get into my garden. The fence needs moving but I can't move it. I need help. I lift my arms and grimace at the patches beneath. Oh well . . . it's not like he hasn't seen me looking worse. I wade through the monster's tendrils and peer through a crack in the fencing between our two gardens. The machine sound has stopped, and I squint my eye and look through the knothole in the wood but can't see anything other than something propped up next to it. I sidestep along the fence and peer through another gap, registering that his garden is in a much better state than mine.

'Looking for something?' I snap my head back and look up to where Charlie is leaning, bare-chested, over my fence in the exact spot that I was just peering through. Once again, this man has caused my embarrassment to roll its eyes, begrudgingly adding wood to the fire as my cheeks flame. It must have been his torso blocking my view, which means he's just watched my progress from where he is standing peering over at me with an expression that is either amused or irritated. I can never tell with him.

'Hah, um, yes. Glad you're in, actually,' I say, shading my eyes from the sun with my hand and trying to salvage some dignity. 'I was wondering if you could help me move this fence?' I point to the wood in question.

'Now?' he asks, as though I've just interrupted an important meeting to ask if he wouldn't mind massaging my feet.

'Yes, please,' I say, smiling, I hope, gratefully. 'Handy Huw is coming tomorrow, and he needs to get a rotovator or something in through that gate.' I signal towards the gate in question with my thumb.

'Well, we can't have Handy Huw stuck outside with his tools, can we?' I'm not sure if he's being kind or sarcastic. He disappears from view and my feet are confused as to what to do next: do they walk towards the front door and open it, or do they wander back to the broken fence panel because the conversation has ended? They needn't have worried, because he then strides through my doors into the garden.

Seeing him inside my house shocks me and I chastise my baby-brain. I must have forgotten to lock my door.

'You should lock your door,' he says, but I'm not really listening because, I'll be honest, I can't take my eyes off his chest which is bare, tanned and very, very nice. My libido has just woken up from a very long nap, and it is hungry.

Week Fifteen

Samuel

I've been at the hospital for almost the whole day. And the news is good: the ligaments in my back and neck are healing well, and I'll be out of this carcass in three weeks' time. But. The bad news is bad. My sight is diminishing 'much faster than we'd hoped'. This phrase bothered me.

Than they'd hoped? They'd hoped? They have only just met me. They are not going to spend the rest of their lives in darkness; they won't have to learn to walk again, learn to eat again, learn to fecking wipe their own arses again.

I check my email. I don't have time for Gemma to take all day to reply to her emails; I imagine she probably doesn't even work in Sophie's office now anyway. I press refresh again, but the screen tells me cheerfully: 'Yay! Your inbox is empty.'

'Mam! Did you post those letters?' I shout from the lounge. I'm holding my arm up in front of my face while I swipe the screen. I'm searching for repair garages in Shropshire and there are hundreds of the bastards. I've called every Helen Yates I could find, private-messaged the ones on Facebook and come up with nothing. My last resort was to write to the few Helens that I found in the phone book who I called but couldn't get an answer from.

'Mr McLaughlin!' she shouts. 'Did you post Sammy's letters?'

'I'm having a shite, for the love of God, woman!' The toilet flushes and Da shuffles into the lounge; I can hear him wiping his hands on his jeans. 'I sent them yesterday. What is it you're doing there, Sammy?'

'Looking for garages in Shropshire. Sophie had her car fixed there when she first left London . . . it's the only place I know she's gone to.'

'Isn't that like looking for a needle in a haystack? Shropshire is a pretty big place, I think.' I ignore his reply and continue alternating reading my phone, putting it down and lifting a notepad up so I can write notes. 'Ah, Sammy, give me the whatsit.' He snatches the phone out of my hand and sits down on the sofa, hidden in the tunnel's walls. 'She worked for a big hotshot bank-thing, right?'

'Yeah. Sandwell.'

'So, let's ring Sandwell and offer them some business.' I can feel that he is winking as he says it. 'How do you—? What the—? Mrs McLaughlin! Fetch me that laptop, would you? I can't see a thing on this phone of Sammy's!'

'Da, I can do it, just—'

'You need to rest your eyes, Sammy – it's probably staring at this thing that has buggered yours up in the first place.' I sigh.

'Would you like biscuits with your tea, Samuel?' Mum fusses as Da starts pounding the keys on the laptop.

'Right. Here we go . . . oh, two, oh . . .' he starts punching numbers into the landline phone next to him. 'It's ringing.'

'Ah, hello. My name is Paul O'Grady.' I close my eyes and would shake my head if I could. 'I'm running a promotion for our garage and was wondering if your company would be interested in a free trial? We're a new business and . . . right, right, right you are. And just so I know who our main competitor would be, who is the firm that you use?' He pauses, covers the handpiece and whispers that they are transferring him. 'Hello!' he begins again. They won't tell him, but then again, Da usually gets his way. 'Fast Fix, you say?' Ma stands in front of me and claps her hands together. 'Grand, grand. Thanks for your time.' He replaces the phone.

'Mr McLaughlin, I always said you should be a spy.' She winks at him and leans into the darkness where I hear a peck on the cheek.

'Now then . . .' It's a wonder the buttons still work on that laptop, I think as he punches the keys again. 'F-A-S-T, space, F-I-X, space, S-H-R-O-P-S-H-I-R-E . . . here we go. There are seven, Sammy. Now then, that's narrowed our search a bit, hasn't it?' The springs in the sofa creak and clap him on the back for a job well done.

Ma returns with the tea, which I have to drink in the lidded jam jar.

'Sophie's eyes look like the colour of tea,' I say, smiling.

'Really, has she got cataracts? You'd make a blinding pair, you two!' Da laughs, the bass rumble filling the room.

'Ah, would you shush, Mr McLaughlin? What colour do you mean, Sammy?'

'Like amber,' I reply.

'You've turned into a right soft touch, Sammy. What else did you get up to after the paddle boats? Paddle boats! I ask you!'

'We read Tolstoy together.'

'Tolstoy? Best get you up and sorted and back on to the rugby pitch, I reckon . . . Blind rugby! Now that would be an extreme sport I'd enjoy watching!'

'Sweet Jesus, wash out your mouth, Mr M! Now pass me that laptop while you drink your tea . . . let's find where this Sophie who has stolen our boy's heart is hiding.'

Some time later, Mam tries the last number on the list. 'Thanks anyway,' she says into the phone. We have called every one of the Fast Fix garages in Shropshire, but each call is a dead end.

'What's yours will always come back to you,' Mam says, kissing the top of my head after the final call. 'You'll find her.'

Week Sixteen

Sophie

Sleep hides from me, crouching behind vivid memories and unknown questions. This time last week I barely knew Charlie at all. I think it is safe to say that our relationship has changed quite a bit.

Charlie had flipped the fence panel with relative ease. I had been distracted as he pulled on his T-shirt while walking through my garden, so didn't see it at first. He carried the panel away to the side of the house while I stood, my skin prickling with goosebumps: it felt like the heat of the day had been inhaled by the past and ice filled my lungs as it exhaled.

The memory had been so buried that I felt dizzy with its resurrection. The day I had left for that night at my friend's, Mum had looked disappointed. She had forgotten all about the sleepover, she had said with a bright smile; never mind, we'll do it at the weekend; do what? I had asked; nothing important, she had said with a dismissive wave of her hand. But it wasn't nothing. The night she had died, there had been dreadful storms – I remember me and my friends shrieking at the lightning. When I was thrown into hell the next day, I remember thinking that the world must have been angry that night and that it had tried to let me know. Maybe pulling that fence panel down that night was the world trying to protect the last piece of her.

What the broken fence revealed was the round garden table which we had spent countless sunny afternoons sitting around with the Scrabble board. But I couldn't see the cast-iron swirls of the table top because it was obscured by a tablecloth; the rose pattern and lace around the edge just visible beneath its dark green covering of moss. Each of the three high-backed wooden chairs was covered in dense green foliage which tucked and folded itself like seat covers over the frames. In front of the three chairs I saw cutlery: knives, forks, spoons, their silver tarnished to bronze, sitting slightly out of place but preserved. In the middle of the table were the remains of a china teapot, green-tea innards pouring over and spilling on to the table, and at each place setting, a china cup and saucer, each cup filled with the same vibrant green moss as the chairs. I felt myself keel over, a loud keening noise escaping my lips: it was a tea party, the tea party she had always said we should have, the tea party from *Alice in Wonderland*, preserved and sheltered by the moss and wood of the fence panel.

I was aware of his warm hands guiding me inside, of him holding me as I sobbed into his chest, his unfamiliar smell feeling alien and yet comforting. Time passed as I began to talk. And once I started, I just couldn't stop. I told him about Mum and Ian, I told him about moving to London and meeting Samuel, I told him how I had left him and how hurt I was that he betrayed me but that I knew I deserved it. I told him about Bean and the way I felt having this baby entirely dependent on me. The sun arced slowly across the sky: just as it would in Paris, dipping past the Eifel Tower; sinking behind the Sphinx in Egypt; hiding behind the Colosseum in Rome.

As dusk began to blink heavy eyelids, and the darkness of night closed around us, he listened to me. He poured bitter lemonade into iced glasses. He closed the windows as the insects began to creep in with the end of the day. He made sandwiches. He washed up: he listened.

'Thank you,' I said as he passed me another tissue.

'You're welcome,' he answered with a small smile.

'Thank you for listening. I don't know how I would have coped with finding that today if you hadn't been here.'

'You would have coped anyway.' He gives a short nod of certainty. My eyes were stinging, and my body felt drained.

'Well, thanks anyway.'

'I'd best get going . . . I'll help you. In the garden. Tomorrow. If you want.' His sentences were deliberate, his pauses considerate. 'I'll bring breakfast.'

I give up trying to sleep and find myself in the garden. I don't need much light; the sky is filled with stars and the moon is proud and glowing. I look at the tea party that my mother has made, gently stroking the china and touching the ends of the forks. I think about the way Charlie cried when I saw him through the window and I think about my mother. I rip away the image of the night time and the overgrown garden like the page of a children's book, and instead, imagine new pages filled with coloured pencil sketches of Mum, smiling in this garden in the summer. Pages flutter past and I see her unfurling the rose-patterned tablecloth, a butterfly dancing over her shoulder, her hair blowing away from her face. On another page, I see her placing the cutlery while swatting away a lazy bumble bee. Wind grabs the paper, turning it over, and there she is: licking her finger where some of the sugar has escaped its pot. Pages flash past until my hands smooth over the final drawings and I see her standing with her hands on her hips, her face turned towards the house as a side profile of myself slides a school bag from my shoulders.

My morning coffee is warm in my hands as I reach for my phone, punching in Helen's number.

'Hi, it's me. I'm sorry to ring so early, but, I, we, need to talk.'

'Are you OK?' she asks. Greg's sleepy voice groans in the background.

'I'm fine.'

'Is the baby OK?' Helen asks just as Charlie knocks on the door. I hold the phone in the crook of my neck and unlock the door. He doesn't say hello, he just walks in carrying a tray of something smelling of cinnamon.

'I've baked,' he announces as he walks past me and into the kitchen.

'Sophie?' I shake my head and turn my attention back to Helen. 'Who's that in the background? Is it hot Irish Samuel?' she whispers excitedly.

'No. It's Charlie from next door.'

'Well, you didn't waste much time!'

'What, no! It's not like that, we're friends.'

'So what's he doing around your house so early? The kids aren't even up yet.'

'I know, I'm sorry, but I've found something. In the garden. Do you remember the table?'

'Breakfast,' Charlie calls. 'It's going cold.' I still can't quite get used to his bluntness.

'Just a minute!' I shout. He pops his head around the door frame and scowls. I stick my tongue out at him as he disappears into the kitchen.

'Helen? Are you there?'

Her voice is wavering, but she replies, 'Yes, I'm here. What did you find?'

'The table was covered by a broken fence panel. It hadn't crashed completely on top but had protected it. The table has been preserved; it's covered in moss and completely overgrown, but . . . Helen, the table was set. Like a tea party . . . do you know anything about it? Because I keep thinking about the present and the label, "don't be late for a very important date" – it has to mean something. Helen?'

'It does . . . it was . . . Look, I'll explain everything, I promise. Just give me a week or so to gather myself, OK? I'll come to you. I'll come to the cottage and I'll explain everything . . . Just let me get to grips with it first. Can you do that?'

'Sure.' I swallow the huge lump in my throat. 'I'll see you soon, love you.'

'Love you too.'

I follow the smell of cinnamon into the kitchen and stare at Charlie as he opens cupboards and pulls out plates as though he has always lived here. I'm not sure how I feel about this. Yesterday was different; the situation needed control and I was oblivious really to the way he made himself at home, but today, it feels intrusive. I'm still holding my mobile in my shaking hands, gripping the phone as I picture Helen on the other end, the sacrifice she will be making to come here. My eyes fill with tears as I sit down, a cinnamon bun placed in front of me. As I tear a piece off and feel the sugar and soft dough melt in my mouth, thoughts of Helen are swept aside. I actually groan with pleasure. Charlie sits down opposite and looks startled, a piece of bun halfway to his mouth.

'Sorry,' I mumble with my mouth full. He puts the food into his mouth and stares at me, then swallows. 'Do you,' I swallow, 'want an iced coffee?' He wrinkles his nose in disdain.

'I don't do cold coffee, but I'll have an espresso from your space-aged machine, if you don't mind?'

'Right, sure. I'll just . . .' I get up, the feeling of unease returning; I feel like I'm a guest in my own house. He gets up, dusts his hands on his cut-off denim shorts, which look like they've been hacked off by a pair of blunt scissors, and heads for the garden. I have an irresistible urge to blow a raspberry at his retreating back.

Is that what Samuel felt like when I went back to DC?

Did he feel like I was an intruder when I stayed the night? Helped myself to wine from his fridge? The image of him kissing me returns. Was it really just an act, Samuel? Did you really sleep with me to get your own back, to prove a point?

I bite down on my lip and carry the drinks outside, to find Charlie touching the moss cascading out of the teapot.

'I think this is moss campion . . . it has pink flowers in June.'

'I want to keep it,' I say, passing him his espresso, which he takes with a begrudging mumble of thanks. 'I want to keep it as it is.' I stroke the chairs and imagine pink flowers tumbling down; the cups filled with petals.

'So how are we going to get Handy Huw in with his rotovator?' he asks.

'I don't know,' I reply. He nods and passes me his coffee, then walks over to the next panel along to the dilapidated gate, looks it up and down and disappears back into the house. I stand sipping my coffee and looking at the table in all its fairy-tale glory. His return startles me and it takes me a moment to register that he is holding a sledgehammer as he stomps back to the panel and, in six heavy swings, sends it crashing to the ground in a pile of splintered mess.

He stamps back towards me.

'Huw can get in now.' Charlie smiles, drains his cup and leaves.

Week Sixteen

Samuel

I can't breathe, I can't see, I can't live like this. I grip my phone tightly in my hand but what I want to do is throw it against the lounge wall and watch it smash into my twenty-year-old rugby-playing self. Instead, as I lower my hand, I let the black hole swallow it. I have found and rung every number for the staff at Sandwell and the answers are always the same. Nobody knows where Sophie is; three of them – new employees – hadn't even heard of her.

Insanity is nudging me, whispering to be let in; I can feel myself slipping into the darkness, the tunnel closing around my insides in the same way that it is closing around my vision. My small circle of sight is collapsing, and my ability to see is caught in the embrace of the snake which contracts and squeezes, taking my will to live with every movement.

I can still see my phone screen, but I have noticed that the fog around it is rolling in. Where it used to be surrounded by life and colour, it is now smudged in soot. I'm powerless to stop it.

Just over two weeks and I'll be out of this brace, my leg will be out of the cast and for that I'm grateful. My sight will be a little easier to cope with once I can move around, but for now . . . I'm still stuck here.

The house is quiet for once; the family have taken Will

and Gertie to the beach. For the first couple of hours it was a relief. The silence smiled and relaxed into the sofas; the ticking of the clock grew cocky and commanding, taking over the house like an old general. But now I have nothing to do but watch Da's old James Bond films on their small TV. My heart quickens when I realise that I won't be able to see the whole screen of my fifty-inch flat screen by the time I return to DC – the edges will soon be eaten away by the encroaching darkness – but then I realise that my TV isn't there anyway; it's buried beneath the pile of rubble that used to be my home. I will never be able to watch a film at the cinema again . . . too much would be hidden in the tunnel walls.

My eyes close and I replay the way she'd laughed at my jokes as we drove to the cinema.

'What do you call a man with a piece of wood on his head?'

'I have no idea.'

'Edward.'

'What do you call a man with three pieces of wood on his head?'

'Still no idea.'

'Edward Woodward.'

'I don't get it.'

'What is there to get? Edward Woodward, the actor? The Equalizer*? We didn't have Sky until I was seventeen, so we were always stuck watching stuff from the eighties. The classics, my Da always called them . . .* The A-team*?* Knight Rider*?'*

She'd shaken her head.

'You've got to have heard that joke when you were at school?'

'Sorry, no, I guess we were too busy watching the Eisteddfod.'

I think back to the way she talked, how when she'd had a few glasses of wine her speech pattern would change, her London accent slipping into something much softer.

Feck's sake . . . she's Welsh!

Week Seventeen

Sophie

The tape measure unravels as I count out the twelve centimetres. My thumb holds its marker and I bend and twist the reel over the curve of my stomach.

'You're getting big, Bean,' I say, discarding the measure and rubbing my hand over my expanding stomach, which now sticks out further than my boobs. Although I can't be sure if that is all Bean and not down to Charlie's food parcels.

Ungainly fat raindrops plod down against the window panes and I reach over the sink to pull the window closed, my tummy leaning against the counter, restricting my movements.

I recognise Charlie's knock and open the door.

'Vegetable lasagne,' he says by way of greeting from beneath his hood. He is holding the glass dish with a pair of pink oven gloves.

I can't help but smirk at him – this blunt-speaking, broad-shouldered man wearing something so feminine.

'Do you mind if I put the match on?'

I shake my head as he hangs his coat on the back of a chair, grabs the remote and flicks on the new flat-screen. My kitchen is instantly filled with sounds of a football stadium as England take on France. I'm not particularly interested; it's the wrong-shaped ball.

We haven't talked much since my outpourings of last week; our contact seems to be restricted to food deliveries and his overseeing of Handy Huw's handiwork.

They managed to get the rotovator in, and between them, the lawn has been completely dug up and levelled, and the turf arrives tomorrow. I had mentioned that I had been thinking about getting fake grass.

'Fake. Grass?' Charlie had said scornfully.

'What do you mean by fake?' Huw had asked, his hairy belly hanging over his dirty shorts. 'Like a different type to what's local?' His Welsh accent had softened the words, making them inoffensive and gentle. The more time I spend at home, the more I can feel my own words slipping back into their native tongue, the accent I had been so determined to lose, cuddling up against my new life like a faithful dog.

Helen had never had the same lilt as Mum and me; she and Ian had moved to Wales the year before he met her. Mum had met him at the school Christmas fair while he sold home-made Christmas tree ornaments; he was personalising them on the stall with a wood burning pen. I remember her saying what a lovely idea and look at how he is with his daughter. So nice to see a father and daughter together like that. We didn't know that Helen had had to stay up until midnight most days that week engraving the patterns, so he could make money from the stall.

The lasagne is delicious, and we eat in companionable silence. I tear a piece of garlic bread away, the butter running between my fingers. I get up to wipe my hands just as my phone rings.

'Go on, Harry,' Charlie yells at the screen just as I pick up my mobile.

'Hello?' I answer; it slides from my grasp and smashes on to the newly tiled floor. 'Shit! Shit! Shit!' I crouch down but

I know it's beyond repair, the innards spilling out of the shattered screen.

'You said you needed a new one with a better network,' Charlie says matter-of-factly. 'Yes!' he exclaims at the TV as a goal is scored.

'I know, but—'

'At least it's happened now before your website goes live.'

'I suppose.'

I wipe the butter from my fingers, then try to reassemble some of the parts, but it's no use. The phone is knackered. I slide out the SIM card and return to the table.

Charlie takes a sip of non-alcoholic red wine and grimaces. 'You should get a better number for your phone.'

I load my fork with lasagne. 'Why? I've already put this one on my website.'

'But you can choose one that's easier to remember . . . something catchy, something accountanty.'

'Accountanty?' I query. 'I'm not sure what you mean.'

He shrugs and changes the subject. 'When's your sister coming?'

'Next week,' I answer with my mouth full. His lack of concern for etiquette has rubbed off on me and I feel more relaxed about table manners and manners in general. And that is a very good thing. Because I have just broken wind. Loudly.

'Have you just?' he asks, his nose wrinkling in disgust.

'No!' I lie, my cheeks burning with the embarrassment of it.

'You have. I can smell it.'

'I haven't, I—' Another blast escapes from my seat. Charlie sits back and folds his arms across his chest and raises his eyebrows.

'It's Bean,' I say, looking at my food, unable to meet his gaze.

'That's a good name for it, you know: "Beans, Beans,

they're good for your heart, the more you eat the more you—'''

'Yes, yes, I've heard the rhyme before.'

'The same thing happened with Olivia.' My embarrassment slides away and the room fills with the weight behind his words. 'She would let rip all day long when she was pregnant with Jack.'

'Oh, you have a son?' I look at him and watch as he almost winces at the pain which flashes across his face.

'Did.' He stands up and begins scraping his plate into the sink.

'I'm sorry,' I say to his back as he puts on my oversized yellow washing-up gloves.

'It's not your fault. You weren't the one driving. My wife Olivia was.'

How do you answer a sentence like that? I pause, appropriate responses pushing their way forward only to be swallowed down by their ineptness.

'Did they both die in the crash?'

'Jack did. Olivia died three days later from internal bleeding.' I remember Olivia, his girlfriend at school. She was a tiny little thing with long dark hair that almost reached her bottom; I always thought it looked too heavy for her to carry. I get up and gently place my hand on his shoulder. His body is warm, the kind of warmth that would stay even in the depths of winter; I can feel his muscles and bones moving beneath his skin: how can so much hurt be contained inside so thin a layer? He stops washing up and we both look at our reflections as the rain slides down our cheeks; our faces look like they're drowning.

'She had been drinking,' he tells me in barely a whisper. 'Not much, but enough. She'd been to her friends for a play date and they had opened a bottle of prosecco.'

'When did they die?' I ask.

'Six months ago. Jack would have been four next month.'

'I'm sorry,' I say. Two words that can mean both everything and nothing.

Did he blame her? How do you grieve for somebody you loved but who killed your child?

We stay like that for some time, the rain continuing to slide sad tears down our reflections.

Week Seventeen

Samuel

I'm not an idiot. I know that I'm going to need help soon, that my sight will be gone, and I will have to learn to cope with life as a blind person, but I'm just not ready yet. I don't want to listen as Mam talks about guide dogs and how lovely it will be to have a dog around the house, one that's trained, not like Dotty, our last dog, who ate all Da's slippers.

Mam came into my room yesterday all excited because she had found me a watch on eBay that I'll be able to tell the time on. Isn't that clever, Sammy, you'll be able to feel where the numbers go by little bumps. Isn't it clever? I know she's only trying to help, but I hadn't even thought about that, hadn't considered that I wouldn't be able to see the time. Do you think you'll have a cane, Sammy? Ooh, look at this, it folds up all nice and tidy, you'll be able to fit it in your pocket. I know that eventually, yes, I will need all of these, but I'm sick of hearing these questions, these scenarios and images of myself holding a cane, bumping into things, linking arms with my mother so I can cross the road. I try to push the thought away that I won't be able to cook for myself. I say this to Sarah.

'Will you pull yourself together! I'm sick of hearing you giving up on life just because you're losing your sight. You could have died! You could be paralysed! You'll still be able to cook, Mule, you'll just have to learn to cook as a blind person.'

I ignore her and instead speak into my phone, asking Google to search for Sophie Williams Wales. Google looks for Sophie Williams Way. I repeat the statement, slowing my words down so it can be deciphered better. This brings up the same list that I have been ploughing through for the past week.

'Why are you still using your phone? I've shown you how to change the setting on the computer so that it will narrate the words for you.'

'I just prefer using my phone.'

'But you—'

'Can you just leave it!' I shout.

'Fine. But you're acting like a child. The computer is easier for you to see and hear, but if you want to waste your time trying to find Sophie on that, be my guest.' She storms off into the kitchen. The TV is on as always but from where I am sitting, from where my brace stops me from lifting my head, I can only see the top left corner of it. There is no talking, just high-speed background music; I don't know what is happening on the screen: I haven't a clue. My throat is filled with a lump full of fear and I don't know how I will ever swallow it. I feel the tears on my face before I even know I'm crying.

Mam walks in; I can tell by the sound of her wiping her still-damp hands from the washing-up on her jeans.

'Sarah! You get in here this instant! You've made your brother cry!'

I laugh through my tears as Sarah stomps into my view. She rolls her eyes at me.

'Some things never change,' she grumbles, passing me a tissue. 'He was mean to me first,' she says.

'That's no excuse.'

I wipe my eyes and stick my tongue out at my sister as Mam turns away.

'Mam! Mule's sticking his tongue out at me!' she grins.

'Will the two of you just behave?' she answers, her voice fading as she disappears back to the kitchen.

'Can you get me the laptop, please?' I ask, making a truce.

Sarah goes home and I spend the next few hours letting Google lead me to dead ends. The robotic voice reading out the entire internet address is irritating, but I suppose I'll get used to it. It reads out hairdressers, elderly ladies, surfing instructors; it feels like the whole of Wales is populated by Sophie Williamses. I know that looking for her like this is a long shot to say the least, but I can't stop. I'm getting angry with the robot, as though this voice belongs to a little man inside the internet, telling me things that I don't want to hear.

Mam delivers jars of tea and changes the channel to watch the friendly between England and France; Mam is in love with Harry Kane.

My sister bounds into the room, making me jump.

'For the love of all things that are holy, Sarah! I almost had a Tena lady moment!'

'Mule. Repeat after me.' She clears her throat. 'I, Samuel McLaughlin, agree, now and for the rest of my life, that my sister is superior to me in every way.'

'In your fecking dreams,' I mumble. Mam clips me around the back of the head.

'Say it.'

'No.'

'Say it and I'll pass you this piece of paper that happens to have Sophie Williams's phone number written on it.'

'That's not funny, Sarah. You know Sammy is in an emotional state at the moment,' Mam chastises.

'I'm not joking. It turns out that once I used my Irish

charm and told Sophie's assistant at Sandwell Incorporated what an utter arse my useless brother is, she gave me her number. No address, mind . . . I was treading on thin ice for a while, but once I explained how truly pathetic you are—'

'Give it here!' I say, standing.

'Not until you say it!'

She backs away slowly, flashes of the paper interrupting my vision of her face.

'Fine!' I cross my fingers behind my back. 'I, Samuel McLaughlin, agree that my stupid fecking sister is superior to me.'

'In every way,' she reminds.

'In every way, now give me the number.' I snatch it from her grasp and sit back down, flapping the paper in front of my face, scanning it.

My hand is shaking as I tap the numbers into the phone. It rings, the three of us ignoring the roar from the crowd on the screen as someone makes a play for the goal.

'Hello?' she answers, and I smile.

'Sophie?'

I've found her.

Week Eighteen

Sophie

It's the beginning of June – bare legs, children with sticky fingers and melting ice-cream cones dribble along the streets – but I'm shivering as though it's the middle of November.

I take some deep breaths and get out of the car, then steady myself with a hand resting on the hot surface of the bonnet as my head swims and my legs take a moment to find their anchor. This keeps happening. The Book says my blood pressure will be lower than normal, so to take care standing too quickly, but I keep forgetting. Bean is the size of a red pepper this week and as I glance down, leaning forward to catch my breath, my tummy is leaning against the car. Bean is getting bigger; there is no denying it.

How much longer can I deny the fact that this baby has a living, breathing father who doesn't know anything about it?

He has a right to know.

I push this thought away as the passengers from Helen's train pour out of the station, the flood of people slowing to a trickle until I spot her at the back.

'Hi!' I say over-enthusiastically, kissing her cheek and ignoring the pallor of her skin and the way she is avoiding my eyes. 'How was the journey?'

'Hot, stuffy and full of drunk rugby players.'

'Oh, the usual, then? We're just here.' I point to the car.

We make small talk through the journey to the cottage, the conversation dropping off as we approach the gate. I turn off the ignition as Charlie steps out of his door, gives an abrupt wave and then disappears back inside.

'So that's Charlie, I take it?' Helen questions as she follows me towards the door.

'Yep. He's, um, he's one of a kind.' I turn the key in the door and step inside. I turn to Helen, who I can see is on the verge of tears, her feet rooted to the spot.

'It's just a house, Helen.' I try to repeat Mum's words as I take her hand in mine. She gives me a tight smile and steps in.

I lead her into the kitchen and her face changes.

'Oh Sophie . . . it's beautiful.' Her fingers run along the work surfaces. 'It feels so different.' I smile as I pour us drinks and lead her into the lounge. 'Is that her chair?' she asks, striding towards it.

'Yes, I've had it re-upholstered. Do you like it?'

She nods, a tear rolling down her cheek. 'She would have loved it.'

'Are you . . . are you ready to go outside?' I ask. Her chest expands as she inhales, then smiles. 'Yes. I think I am.'

'So you helped her?'

Helen nods as she takes in the tea party table, touching everything in the same way that I had. We sit down on the old rug, my movements to the ground slower than they used to be.

'It was supposed to be an early birthday surprise because Dad wasn't going to be back until late. She wanted you to have something special for your birthday. We spent all day making things: marmalade, sandwiches . . . We found the tea set in the old charity shop in town, you know the one she loved? That was weeks before, that's what gave her the idea. She was so happy that day . . . We made you a birthday cake, nothing fancy, just a Victoria sponge, but we used the last of the sugar.' Her voice catches in the back of her throat and I put my hand on her leg.

'Take your time, I'm not going anywhere.'

'I had asked her if we could make jam tarts . . . "You can't have an *Alice in Wonderland* tea party without jam tarts," I'd told her.'

'But you hate jam tarts,' I interrupt, but her sad smile tells me all I need to know.

'I remember her opening and closing the cupboards, looking behind the cereal boxes, behind the tins, but we didn't have enough sugar. She tried to convince me that we could make Rice Krispie cakes instead, but I was adamant that I'd go and get some sugar.

'I went into town on my red bike, do you remember it? I was at uni then and felt stupid riding a bike with a basket on the front. It was a sunny day, the storm that came that night was nowhere to be seen. I saw your bus go past in town. I waved but you were facing the other way. I was too long in town . . . I went to the craft shop and bought some lace to go around the edges of the "Eat Me, Drink Me" labels. I was thirsty too, so I sat on the beach with a Coke. It was a red can – the full-sugar one – I don't know why I remember that.'

She looks into the distance for a moment. 'I finished it all before I cycled home. You must have already been and gone by then, we'd forgotten about your sleepover. By the time I got back . . . she was already—' Her voice is almost a whisper and I have to lean forward to hear her. 'She was already dead. And he had gone. I knew he hadn't left long ago because I could smell him, you know that Old Spice that he used to wear . . . I could smell it.' My mouth fills with water, the stench of the memory of him almost making me gag. 'There was flour,' she chokes on the words, 'on the floor.' I reach for her hand but she's oblivious; lost in the past, in the memories she's kept hidden away. 'I cleaned it up, I suppose I was worried it would spoil your surprise. She was so still, Sophie.'

She meets my eyes with hers. I want her to stop talking but want to hear every last thing at the same time. 'You don't know how still someone who is dead *is*. I know that sounds stupid, but she was just so *still*. Every living thing moves, doesn't it? Even just a little bit, flowers, leaves, trees, insects . . . I used to stare at things like that, at the way they moved . . . I'd never really noticed before how all things living move, even if it's just a fraction of a movement . . . they still move.' She shakes her head, collecting herself and straightening her shoulders. 'It was my fault. If I'd been quicker, if he'd had the sugar for his tea, he wouldn't have lost his temper. That's what he said in the trial, wasn't it? There was no sugar for his tea and he "just saw red". If I had gone straight home, she would still be alive, you would still have a mum. I'm sorry, Sophie. I'm so sorry.'

She begins to cry then. I've never seen her cry like this, as though she has collapsed into herself: her spine, her ribcage, her chin, they all seem to shrink and crumble; the pain she has been hiding away manifesting itself and revealing my sister. She is broken.

Anger and hurt surge through me.

'It wasn't your fault, Helen.' I say the words but I know they are sliding off her shoulders, floating away; she's not even trying to hold on to them. 'Helen, listen to me.' I grab hold of her shoulders, trying to pull them back up to where they should be, trying to stop them sinking into her waist. She looks up at me, her eyelids red and swollen. 'It's not your fault. *He* did this. *He* killed her, not you, not me . . .

Ian killed her. All you did was sit on a beach and drink a can of pop. Are you listening? All you did was drink a can of pop.'

I heave myself up and head into the kitchen, returning with a red can of Coke.

'Drink it,' I say, peeling back the ring pull. Her hand is shaking as she reaches for it. Hours of washing up and cleaning a house full of children has aged her skin, but they are still the same hands that held mine while we read stories and ignored the thuds from downstairs, the muffled sobs behind closed doors. The wind blows her dark hair back from her face as she lifts the can to her lips. I watch the gold chain around her neck rise and fall as she swallows it. Her eyes lift to meet mine.

'That is all you did . . . now tell me, where is the crime in that?'

Her shoulders lift a little, her arm unwraps itself from around her waist and her spine straightens back into shape, a smile beginning to form on her lips as she takes another sip. Her body expands, filling the cracks and holes, beginning to fix what was broken.

Week Eighteen

Samuel

I'm free. At least that's what it feels like. The brace has been removed, my ligaments are fixed; I can move my head up and down, my cast has been removed and I can walk easily.

This new-found freedom has helped me, for a small time at least. I can see more of the world now I can lift my head up and I'm embracing this freedom with a trip to the pub for lunch. Walking here wasn't too bad. This is a place I'm familiar with: I know where to cross the road; I know that there is a step going up into the beer garden because I fell down it on my eighteenth birthday. I'm trying to push aside the feelings of fear that keep welling up. How will it be, for instance, when my sight goes if I don't know that the pub I'm about to walk into has that step? How will I cross the road without getting hit by a car? Here, there are very few crossings with flashing green men; I don't need them yet because I know where I'm going, but how will I know when I cross a road back in DC? I know that there are flashing lights at some of the crossings, but I can't remember there being a beeper on all of them . . . is there braille? Will I have to learn braille? What about if I go on holiday to, I don't know, Crete? Will there be sounds to let me know when I can cross? I doubt it.

I go to the bar and order a pint then take it out into the

garden, remembering to step up and making it to one of the picnic tables outside. The sun is warm on my back as I open my laptop, plug in my headphones and type into the search bar. I'm going back over every step that we have tried so far. I've come here to research without the worried looks of my family. After the phone call they have acted different about my search for Sophie. Sarah thinks she hung up on me, Mam thinks she hung up on me and Da thinks I need to sow my oats a bit before my white stick puts girls off – before I don't know if I've pulled a looker or an absolute troll.

'Mr McLaughlin!' Mam had shouted.

'Don't you be getting on your high horse, Mrs M, I'm only saying it like it is. He can't go feeling the girl, now can he? How's he going to know if she's a beast?'

The conversation had continued but I couldn't help but think that Da had a point. How would I know?

I'm double-checking the Fast Fix garages in Shropshire, the robot voice reeling off the list. I take the headphones off as I try another search, but the reading of the web address drives me insane. I'm about to replace the headphone when I hear my name.

'Sam?' I turn my head towards a woman's voice that sounds familiar; she is saying goodbye to a couple of others, air-kissing and promising to speak soon. Parts of her friends are soon hidden in the mist as she walks towards me and I shift my head to try and get a glimpse of her face. The tunnel will soon claim my ability to see whole faces when they are close up; instead I will see segments.

'Isabella?' I smile up at her and hope she can't tell how strange it still feels to have a person's face surrounded by pitch-black, almost as if it is being focused through a camera lens. She looks good, but then that was always half of the problem. The other problem of our relationship was how similar we were and how little patience we had with each other. I was a mess when she finally ended it, though. Long legs, tiny waist, big boobs and an insatiable appetite, for sex as well as food.

'Long time no see.'

I bite back a witty retort as she sits down opposite. 'May I?' she asks. I presume she means to sit down, but she has moved too quickly to the right for me to catch her face. I do catch a glimpse of her long brown legs when she rearranges her skirt as she sits. 'I thought I was meeting my friends for lunch, but it turns out it was just a Diet Coke before a trip to the gym. Is it even worth the trip to the pub if all you're going to have is a Diet Coke? A little birdy told me you were back, so, how are you? I hear you were in an accident?' She reaches over through the shadows and touches the scars along my cheek, making me jump. I'd forgotten how physical she always was. 'Sorry, does it hurt?' she asks, taking her hand away and holding her straw between her teeth.

'No, not really, not any more. It's good to see you,' I say sincerely.

'You too.'

'So, what's new with you? Are you married? Kids?'

'Christ, no.' I hear her rummaging in her bag, and I take a sip of my drink as the smell of cigarette smoke fills the air. I watch her lips as she blows out a plume of smoke. 'I'm no good at relationships as you well know.'

'Yeah,' I smile at her, 'I remember.'

'You're not great at it either as I recall, we were always arguing.'

'That doesn't mean I'm not good at relationships, I'm just no good at relationships with you.'

'Fair point. So who is she?' I watch her suck on the end of her cigarette, exhaling the smoke and taking another sip of her drink.

'Who?'

'The girl who you are good at relationships with.'

'Ah . . . it's a long story,' I say, running my finger around the rim of my glass.

'I'd best order some lunch then, I'm starving.'

'Some things never change.' I smile at her.

'Why do you keep looking at me like that?'

'Like what?'

'Like you don't want to look at my face.'

'Even longer story.'

'Let's order pudding as well, unless you have somewhere else to be?'

I think of the robot voice probably still reading out the web address and I picture the worried looks passing over the dinner table last night as I knocked over my drink again.

'Is the steak sandwich here still good?' I ask, as I watch her lick her bottom lip then smile, afraid to move my head up and take a look at her eyes, in case I look odd when I try to focus. For one more minute, I just want to be the man she remembers, the confident rugby player who didn't have dark edges suffocating the world around him.

Week Nineteen

Sophie

Bean is moving. It feels like tiny bubbles bursting against the inside of my tummy, just below my belly button. I hadn't really noticed it until I was trying to go to sleep last night. The bubbles are popping rapidly this morning; it started after I drank a cold glass of apple juice. I love the idea that the cold liquid had woken Bean up, and that I was able to know what was happening inside that little cocoon.

I put my hand to my tummy again, but nothing can be felt from the outside. For a second, I can see Samuel's smiling face, picture him putting his hand to my stomach. I miss him. My hand reaches for my new phone and I tap in his number and add it as a contact. I don't dial it. But I like having it there.

It's my birthday today and I'm celebrating by meeting a new client in town, but my car is refusing to start. I turn the key again, but nothing happens at all. Great. Happy birthday to me.

'Damn it.' I knock on Charlie's door and he answers it in his boxer shorts. His hair is a mess and he is rubbing his eyes, blinking against the midday sun. 'I'm sorry to wake you.' I bite back the urge to add 'at lunchtime'. 'But my car won't start, and I've got a meeting with clients in town . . .'

'All right.' He yawns and rubs the back of his hair. 'I'll

just throw on some clothes.' I follow him inside. The house is a mess – half-drunk cups of coffee on various surfaces, clothes hanging on numerous pieces of furniture – and it smells of the overflowing bin in the kitchen. I haven't been inside Charlie's house very often – he is normally at mine – but I'm shocked at how quickly it has deteriorated. The last time I had been here, the kitchen had been old-fashioned and dated but it had been clean; this looks like another person entirely has been living here. I hear Charlie stomping around upstairs, swearing at something as I walk into the lounge. The brown leather sofas are littered with photos; there are some on the floor along with a duvet and a pillow. It takes me a minute to take in the scene; it looks as though he has slept in here, the photos surrounding him. I bend down and pick one up. It's of the Charlie and Olivia I remember from school, both smiling at the camera, young and in love.

'I'm ready.' His voice startles me and I drop the photo. His eyes watch it fluttering to the floor, and he looks me straight in the eye, almost challenging me to say something, but then the moment is gone as he turns his back, the car keys jangling in his hand.

The journey is awkward, the car filled with the unspoken and unexplained. His hand reaches for the volume on the radio, drowning out the questions, and we stay silent until we arrive. I hate not knowing what to say to him, hate how I can't seem to find the words to make him feel better.

The meeting goes well: a small café in town that has been made into an American diner. They've tried to do the accounts by themselves but saw my card in the corner shop and thought they'd make life easier for themselves.

Charlie attempts to make conversation on the way home, asking me about my old job and why I left. It's easy to talk about now, as if it happened to another person in another life.

'I can't imagine you, all high-flying and ball-busting.'

'Who said I busted balls?' I grin at him.

'We owned a restaurant. Me and Olivia.' He smiles as we drive through the narrow roads, the hedges scraping the windows as another car passes.

'Wow, was it hard, working together all day?'

'Not really, I was in the kitchen most of the time, she was in the restaurant. Olivia was good at that, always went out of her way to make people feel welcome. It was only small, seven tables, but we liked it like that. We weren't expecting things to change as much as they did when Jack came along, we thought we would just carry on as we were, but he didn't sleep. It was tough on Olivia. He just wouldn't settle with anyone else, not even me, so she stopped working and stayed at home instead.'

I think of the state of Charlie's house earlier, the pictures of his family cocooning his bed. My eyes fill with tears, and I blink them back and look out of the passenger window.

'So, what happened with the restaurant, when . . .' I don't finish the sentence; it doesn't need to be finished.

'I sold it. Bought this place instead.'

'Why here, though?' I ask as we drive through the open gate.

'I thought I would be on my own,' he answers as he pulls on the handbrake. 'Whose car is that?'

'It's Greg's. My brother-in-law . . . what is it doing here?'

The door is unlocked, and Charlie follows me through to the kitchen, where sounds of the radio playing 'Sweet Home Alabama,' and delighted squeals from Jessica and Caitlin are filling the house. The smell of home baking swirls around them as Helen spins Jessica around. Greg, huge, bearded and wearing my Laura Ashley apron, is carrying a tray laden with cups and saucers.

'Um . . . hello?' I announce myself. Helen stops twirling

and shouts 'Happy Birthday!' They all begin to sing 'Happy Birthday to You', Greg still holding the tray, Caitlin conducting us all with her fingers and Jess stuffing a sandwich into her mouth. Charlie stands awkwardly by the door.

'You didn't have to travel up! It's not a special one.'

'Nonsense!' Helen dismisses me with a wave of her hand. She kisses my cheek and reaches her hand out to Charlie. 'I'm Helen.'

'Yes. I know,' he replies. She frowns at him then shakes her head as he turns to me. 'You never said it was your birthday.'

'It's not a big deal . . . I'm thirty-one, not sweet sixteen or anything.'

'Obviously.' He furrows his eyebrows at me.

'Right, now close your eyes, Sophie!' Helen commands. 'Action stations, everyone else! Charlie, if you can wait there and then guide Sophie when I give you the nod.' The hustle and bustle of the house continues past me and out into the garden.

'OK!' Helen yells from outside.

'Should we go outside?' I ask Charlie as he remains still.

'She hasn't nodded.'

I bite back a smile. 'I don't think she meant literally.'

'Anytime now, Charlie!' Helen shouts as the girls snigger. 'And keep your eyes shut!' she adds.

'Why are women so complicated? You're all mad,' he sighs.

'*We're all mad here.*' I hear Mum's voice mimic the Cheshire Cat against the sound of her hand as she stroked down the page; I can smell the lemony shampoo she used.

'Right, hold on to my elbow then.' Charlie interrupts my memories and I take his arm and we make our way outside, Charlie giving me instructions, one step to the right, left, careful, up the step to the lawn.

'*Read the directions and directly you will be directed in the right direction.'* I picture Mum licking her finger as she turned the page.

'OK . . . you can open your eyes now!'

The old table weaves its magic, the moss campion's pink flowers cascading out of the teapot and spilling over the rims of the cups. The sun is glinting against the tarnished tines of the forks and reflecting off the small gifts wrapped in shining pink and silver paper which are nestling between the crockery. But next to that is another table. A pink tablecloth, laced at the edges, sits beneath a china tea set; blue and white cups and saucers are balanced next to a sugar bowl filled with brown and white sugar cubes. A three-tiered cake stand holds pastel-coloured macaroons next to a jam jar filled with marmalade, and in the centre of the table is a homemade Victoria sandwich surrounded by jammy tarts. 'Eat Me, Drink Me' labels are attached to each item. I drink in the scene in front of me, searching out Helen's eager eyes with my own.

'Helen, I—' She grins and puts a top hat on her head as I make my way towards her, Bean and I wrapping our arms around her and kissing her cheek. She smells of baking and sun.

'Happy birthday,' she whispers as she pulls herself away from me and reaches for a jammy tart. She passes one into my hand and knocks her pastry against mine as though we were clinking glasses together, before sitting down on her chair. Her eyelids shut as her teeth sink through the thick strawberry jam, and into the pastry beneath. A dusting of flour gathers at the corner of her mouth, which she wipes away with her thumb; cleaning away the past. She leans back and lifts her face to the sun.

The yellow stripe of a bumble bee bounces in front of me as I sit down, the same shade as the coat I had been wearing the day I met Samuel. I think about the woman who had been sitting outside the café that day, how alone she had felt, and as I reach into the birthday party that my mother had planned, accepting my final gift from her, I realise that I'm not alone any more.

Week Nineteen

Samuel

'So, what are you doing hanging about with Isabella Jackson, then? Come on, dish the dirt,' Duncan says under his breath. 'I saw you two looking very cosy in Costa yesterday.'

'We're just friends,' I answer, shifting myself on the sofa.

'Yeah right, I remember when you were "just friends" when I was first together with Sarah; your bed springs creaked.'

'She's helping me find Sophie,' I reply, my hand floating around, trying to accept the beer he is passing me. Mam, Sarah and the kids are busy sprinkling E numbers on to fairy cakes in the kitchen.

'I thought you'd given up on all that? She hung up on you, didn't she? And she's not answered any more of your calls. Mate, I'd think that's a pretty big hint that she's not interested, you'd be a fool to think anything else. And Isabella is . . .' I don't need to see to be able to work out that he is making big boob gestures or a woman's curvy outline; I can tell by the way his eyebrows are wiggling up and down.

'I'm not giving up on Sophie. I love her.'

'That may be so, but perhaps she doesn't love you. Sorry, mate, I love you like you're my own brother and sometimes you have to be cruel to be kind. I don't think she's the one.'

*

The next morning, I wake up to hear Isabella's voice downstairs. I can hear the rise and fall of one of her anecdotes and my father laughing uproariously at the punchline. He's always loved her. When we broke up, he walked into my room and gave me an earful, telling me that women like that come into your life once and that I should get my spotty arse out of bed and grovel or do something to make her want me back. Mam had taken the 'plenty more fish in the sea' approach; I don't think she ever really approved of Isabella after she'd seen her baby-oiled handprint on my bedroom wall. I close my eyes and listen to them, and it feels like the whole of Ireland is closing in on me. I can feel the houses, pubs, the schools, the whole population crowding around me, not letting me breathe, not letting me escape.

'Sammy!' Da's voice pulls me away. 'Get your arse down here! Isabella has something to tell you.'

My hands feel the walls for the banister as I make my way downstairs. Something has been left on the last step and I curse as my foot slips, and my heel hits the floor with a crack. I reach down, feeling and looking for the culprit. My hand clamps around plastic legs and brings a startled-looking Barbie out of the tunnel and into my line of sight.

'Barbie nearly killed me,' I say as I throw her on to the kitchen table.

'Do you know,' Mam begins, 'my friend who worked in the hospital said you'd be surprised just how many men "fall" on to Barbies. Strange world we live in.'

'Never mind that now, Mrs McLaughlin. Isabella has a lead on this Sophie girl Samuel's been harping on about.'

My eyes trace my way around the room until I land on Isabella, leaning on the far side of the kitchen, and she looks very pleased with herself.

'You missed one of the garages. This is a new branch and they've only just added it to the Fast Fix website. I rang them, and they checked their records for Sophie Williams and found that they did repair a car by that name.'

'That's great!' I shout, making my way to her but slamming my shin into a chair that isn't tucked under the table properly. 'Fuck!' I rub my injured leg. Isabella crouches down in front of me where I'm rubbing my shin. She's so close to me that most of my vision is filled with her face.

'That's not all,' she smirks. 'One of the mechanics picked up her car. He couldn't remember the number but . . . I've got a street name, Sam.'

Week Twenty

Sophie

Charlie has stayed at home today waiting for Handy Huw to fix my car; he really is quite handy. According to my calendar, it's not even officially summer and yet outside, the cars sweat, their leather insides melting and expanding; flowers lean heavily towards the hazy sun out of duty rather than enjoyment. It's the type of day where the heat dampens everything: the clothes on the line hang heavily, the trouser legs cramp, desperate to kick themselves forward, but the wind, exasperated by the heat itself, is too lethargic to massage their movements.

I've come into town to get a few things for the house. I buy a bunch of yellow roses to put on my new sideboard and swat away a fly as I stop to look through a bakery window. An alarm pierces through the seaside songs, slicing through my thoughts about fresh bread and strawberry tarts as a woman runs through the open doors of a boutique, her hair fanning around her in brittle waves, as if it had been in a plait but is now untied. Her white summer dress billows out from her thin frame as she tries to escape the advances of the security guard who is scanning up and down the street, his eyes latching on to her, his feet pounding the concrete in pursuit. My body begins to react. I step backwards as she turns her head, her eyes wild as they scan the road. The bunch of yellow roses in my hand is showered and fresh and the petals glisten inside the cool polythene.

I take another step back as she runs towards me. It all happens so quickly, none of us able to react in the way we would have wanted to when we replay this later. I would have turned and run; I wouldn't have stopped outside the bakery, and Charlie would have arranged for Huw to come on a different day.

But as it stands now, as she slams her hands against my shoulders, sending me flying backwards, none of the things we could have done matter. My feet leave the ground, my back arches and the yellow roses escape my grip.

It's strange the things you notice when your free will is taken from you. As my back lands with a crack against the concrete path, my thoughts aren't about the baby inside my tummy. I'm not picturing Bean sleeping with a thumb held in a rosebud mouth, the delicate spine curled into a comma; I'm thinking about my mother's vase and how the yellow roses would have looked nice in it. And as I watch one of the petals float through the air and on to my stomach, I'm thinking that I should buy a new vase.

I'm not thinking of those things that could have changed this outcome, because we didn't do any of those things.

As the midwife arranges the paper blanket over the bed in the assessment room, I tap a message to Helen but delete it. She would ring me and I don't want to talk. Instead I message Charlie:

> *I've had a fall, I'm in the hospital, could you come?*

My legs dangle over the edge of the bed as she checks that my blood pressure is OK and then asks me to lie back, put my feet together and relax my legs as she examines me.

'The swab is clear of blood, and you're not dilating.' She peels off the gloves with a flick that snaps into the quiet room, looping the stethoscope around her neck and placing the metal disk in various places on my bump.

'The little monkey is in a bit of an awkward position.' She smiles at me, but the smile is guarded. 'We'll take you for a scan now to check baby.' My mouth won't form the words to ask her if she could hear Bean's heartbeat.

As we leave the room, she holds on to my elbow and guides me towards a seat alongside the corridor where the ultrasound rooms are. The carpet tiles sit neatly, side by side, maroon twine twisting around vertical tubes.

The sounds around me, the chatter, the calls of patients' names, fade behind the images on the walls. Posters of babies in the womb taunt me and so I focus my sight on the inoffensive: the fire alarm, the signs for the emergency meeting point, the fire extinguisher, the fire door. I look back at the alarm: I could pull it; I could pretend that this isn't happening. But my chance is missed: the same technician who I saw at my twelve-week scan smiles at me, calling my name. My feet drag my body inside, even though my fingers itch to pull the alarm.

'We'll check baby first,' the technician says, 'then we'll take you down to get your back checked by a doctor. How are you feeling?' she asks as I lower myself on to the bed. How can I tell her that this baby means more to me than I ever imagined it would? That Bean is the reason I get up every day, that it's the only thing in my life that I have ever done that feels right. Without Bean, I have nothing. What will happen to me? Will I go back to London, back to the noise and the demands, back to days where I don't notice the things in life that are special? Without Bean I will be back to a life where I am alone, a life in black and white.

There is a gentle tap on the door just as she lifts my top up to reveal my swollen stomach. The idea that within it Bean could be hurt, that it could be in pain, fills me with an ache so acute that a small whimper escapes my lips, making the midwife stop her movements.

'Sophie, are you in pain?' she asks, her concern embedded in her frown. I shake my head, but I can feel that my legs are shivering beneath the blanket.

There's another knock on the door and a small crack of light breaks into the room. 'Sorry to interrupt, but there's someone here to see Sophie. He says to tell her Charlie is here?'

The midwife turns to look at me. 'Would you like Charlie to come in?'

I nod my consent, the door widens, and he steps into the room, sits beside the bed and takes my hand.

'I've brought you an overnight bag; there's a toothbrush and some toothpaste. In case you need to stay here. Overnight.' His voice is stilted, and it stretches around the words that are trivial, snapping at the words that aren't. Cold gel is squeezed on to my stomach, the scanner pushes down on to my skin; the screen fills with the image of my baby.

The picture swirls as she moves the scanner, and there, lying on its back, is Bean. The white outline of its skull, large belly sticking up, legs – cramped but perfect – shine from the screen, but Bean is still. She moves the scanner a touch and smiles, pointing to the screen where the flashes of Bean's heart can be seen.

'Baby is fine, Sophie, just asleep.' Charlie's hand tightens around mine as I begin to cry, relief escaping and rolling down my cheeks. 'Let's see if we can wake baby up, oh there we go.' Bean's mouth begins to open and close, 'Look! baby is having a little drink, and . . .' Bean shifts, kicking legs and moving arms, 'looks like it's having a natter there, look.' She points to its little mouth: open, close, open, close. 'Your baby is going to be a chatterbox!' I smile through my tears. 'Would you like to know the sex?' I've thought about this, but I have decided that I would rather wait. Bean is Bean and it doesn't really matter to me whether it is a boy or a girl.

'No, thank you. I'd rather wait.'

I turn to look at Charlie. I'd almost forgotten that he was there, but his face looks different, and I realise that I shouldn't have let him come in. His own despair is written on his face. I think about that feeling that I had just minutes ago and realise that what I have just experienced is a fraction of the pain he deals with. How does he have the strength to make it through each day?

'Charlie, I'm so sorry—' I begin, but he is already rising from his chair.

'I have to go.' He drops my hand and walks out of the room.

'Charlie!' I call, but the door closes behind him.

Week Twenty

Samuel

I have visited a new eye specialist. She is officially called a consultant ophthalmologist, but I have named her Mrs Cheerful. Mrs Cheerful gave me a series of tests, some testing how much of my sight (the picture at the end of the tunnel) I could see clearly, and another where she checked my field of vision (the tunnel walls). I came out with a score that put me firmly in the severely sight impaired bracket. I have a certificate saying this. This irritates me. Shouldn't certificates be to celebrate something? This thing should be a . . . a sentence.

She has confirmed what I already know: I'm losing my peripheral vision and I'm losing it quickly. Mrs Cheerful tells me (like it's a good thing) that I will get concessions for public transport use, as though the fact that I can never drive my car again is actually a good thing because I'll get money off bus fares. I even get money off my TV licence, she tells me in her cheery voice; I mean really? That should be free – I won't be able to see the TV!

I can still see a fair amount, really; if you make your fist binoculars again but leave a small gap about the width of a tiddlywink to see through, you can get the gist of what I can see.

Once I had my 'certificate', suddenly I was visited by

people from various disability departments. I've had white cane training. I'm not joking; someone came around to the house to show me how to use it, even though I keep telling everyone that I can still see. It has an end that looks a bit like a marshmallow and it rolls against the floor.

'Thanks, but I don't need it yet,' I told the woman as she showed me how it concertinas in on itself, so I can carry it inside my pocket.

'You may not, Samuel,' she said, 'but it helps people around you. If you bump into someone and they see you're holding a cane, they know that you are sight impaired . . . If they don't know the reason you have bumped into them, they might just think you're being an arsehole.' I wasn't entirely sure if she was implying that I was, in fact, being an arsehole – she had a point – but I still hate it. It prods about inside a world that is shrinking: darkness surrounds my every move, my every action; it's swallowing me whole. But. As I walk through the busy airport, I know it hasn't eaten me yet. I'm still alive.

'Sorry,' I say for what feels like the hundredth time as I bump into a teenager; the girl is wearing denim and the strong smell of cheap perfume clouds my senses. As I track my vision upwards, gigantic headphones fill my circle of light.

''S'OK,' she answers as I bump into another person, then another, until reluctantly, I pull out the cane from inside my pocket.

Da wanted to come with me; Mam wanted to come with me; Sarah and even Duncan had wanted to come with me . . . they don't get it. I don't need their help. I want to do this by myself; I *need* to do this by myself. I have to believe that I can be blind and still independent.

You watch the news and it is full of poisonous stories of the decay of mankind, but as I tap my way through the airport, seven people have stopped to ask if I need any help. Because as much as I thought I could do this on my own, I'm realising that I can't do it without the help of others. This is not a bad thing: people are generally happy to help me, and I start to think that maybe my life isn't being taken away from me after all.

At the check-in desk, I'm offered a guide. I decline again. I can still see a small amount, I explain. I'm trying to do all the things I would normally do. I walk into the bar. I can hear Da's voice: 'A blind man walks into a bar . . . and a table . . . and a chair.' I smile to myself as I order a pint and sit at a table where I can watch people pass me by. From here I drink it all in: the woman in an orange puffer jacket that completely swamps her; the tired children swinging from their parents' hands, the garish holiday shirts; the crumpled business suit hanging over the arm of an overweight man. I try to commit it all to memory so that when my sight does completely go, I will be able to still picture it.

My flight is called. I drain my drink, extend my cane and tap my way towards the gate. A flight attendant appears by my side, making me jump.

'Would you like some help boarding the plane, sir?' her eyes and perfectly outlined eyebrows ask me.

'That would be great. Yes, please.'

'We'll get you on before the other passengers if that's OK?' She has a small hooped earring and I think of Sophie and why I'm doing this.

'That would be grand.' I smile. You know, as I take her arm, I'm thinking that if I didn't have Sophie, then this blind thing might have its benefits after all; my eyes might be broken but it looks like my smile still works.

This is the part of the journey I have been worrying about, stepping on toes and knocking into people, not being able to find my seat, but I needn't have worried. The perfect eyebrows help me on to the plane first; I fold up my cane, listen to the chatter of the other passengers and then watch through the window. As Belfast shrinks away, and the plane heads towards the middle of England, I'm reminded of the telescopes that line the seaside promenade, the ones that you have to put twenty pence into: the view black until you hear the clunk of the shutter opening, the horizon revealed inside a small circle . . . How long will my twenty pence last? When will the shutters close and the out of order sign be hung around my neck?

When we arrive, I'm guided out of the building by Ken, who tells me about the house in Italy he is renovating; through passport control I learn that his mother is Italian, and he has always wanted to move there. As he walks alongside me to the taxi rank, he tells me he is going to propose to his girlfriend. I shake his hand, wish him well and then give the address of the hotel I'm staying at to the taxi driver.

The room is small. Really small, but this is a blessing in disguise. I can navigate myself around it without too much bother; the bed takes up most of the space. My head is killing me from the airport beer; I'm guessing that my brain has to work twice as hard to be able to keep me on the straight and narrow . . . Will I have double tunnel vision if I get plastered?

I'm drifting off to sleep, my head sinking into the pillow, as my sight returns to me. My eyelids block out the darkness as my mind's eye opens and smashes down the tunnel walls. Jumbled up stories of myself fill me with technicoloured pleasure, but my pleasure is stolen from me by the siren, the sound forcing through the walls and into my room, shaking me and opening the tunnel door. I look around the room, the disorientation of sleep mixing up my childhood memories of pretending to hunt the horizon for bandits with the inside of a kitchen roll. I feel along the bed for my cane and sit up. I can't find my shoes, panic fills me as I hear the other rooms in the hotel opening and closing, rushed footsteps descending the stairs. I decide that I'll have to go barefooted. The memory of the white-hot light scorches my body and terror propels me from the room, my hand skimming walls as the kitchen-roll tube leads me outside. I don't know where to go; I have no idea where the meeting point is. I follow the sounds of others until I look down and see a hand, the wrinkled skin paper-thin, resting on my forearm.

'This way, I think,' he says. I open my mouth to thank him, but no words come out.

It was only a fire drill. We all return to our rooms grumbling about the inconvenience, but for me it was a lesson. My life is changing, and I need to accept it. I need to learn how to cope with a life without sight; I need to find out the types of things that I can use, the types of things that can help me.

The next time I go anywhere on my own, I will ask about the escape routes . . . or fire could take more from me than just my sight.

SUMMER

Week Twenty-One

Sophie

I frown up at Charlie's house: windows with heavy eyelids are closed against the summer's day. The wind drags fingers through the wispy leaves of the trees surrounding our building, and the house groans but stays asleep. I tread quietly back to my door, trying not to feel alone, trying not to miss my old life, trying not to become that girl who was desperate to be noticed.

The fear I felt when I stared at the screen, before the spark of Bean's heart, has stayed with me. It has taken me by the hand and pulled me towards the new person that I must become. In London, I needed to be good at my job, to succeed, but now I need something different; I need to be a good mother, to be independent, to enjoy my life.

Bean and I go for a short walk in the mornings, then work on the accounts until lunchtime. Our evenings are made up of stories about Samuel. I talk about the man I fell in love with and it's becoming harder to defend my actions to Bean: why isn't Dad part of our life?

But then I think of my own father, the note – it wasn't the right life for him, what's to say that this would be the right life for Samuel? I think of Ian's hands around Mum's throat, of Samuel's betrayal, of how much happier Mum and I were when it was just the two of us. Around and around my head the thoughts go.

And so, our summer nights together, looking at the table and chairs, sipping iced tea, are now becoming harder to bear, because deep down I know that no matter what he has done . . . he has a right to know about Bean, and Bean has a right to know Samuel.

I pick up the phone and dial Samuel's number again, but again, I hang up before it has a chance to connect. Each time I ring, I stay on the phone a fraction longer. Soon, I tell myself, soon I will. The Book says that Bean will be practising facial expressions, raising little eyebrows when I tell it about the way Samuel had taken me for a midnight picnic; I imagine my baby smiling as I retell some of his jokes. I've started calling him 'Your Dad'. Your Dad likes eighties rock music, Your Dad took me on paddle boats even though he gets seasick . . . next to you, Bean, Your Dad was the love of my life.

Charlie has been distancing himself. I knocked on his door again yesterday, but he didn't answer. I peg out the washing and notice that the curtains are still drawn, but with the size of my new knickers, I can't say that I'm not a little grateful that he won't be seeing those bad boys billowing in the summer breeze.

I smirk at my reflection as I walk past the mirror in the hall. My reflection is rubbing her back. She looks like a real pregnant woman: not the woman of a couple of months ago who just looked fat, but a real pregnant woman, like the ones in magazines and films. How would this woman look if she were still in her London life with her designer clothes and heels? Would she still be working? Her stomach resting against a desk covered in numbers and rich coffee? Would she notice the small nudges from inside telling her that Bean is just waking up or would she be too engrossed in her work to care?

I wink and grin at the pregnant woman then close the door behind her.

My fists knock on Charlie's door. His curtains are drawn still; I knock again but I worry that it's useless. I turn my head to where his car still sits and give his door a final thump. But again, there is no answer.

The next morning, Charlie's house seems to have woken up. His door yawns open, his curtains are stretching widely, and Charlie is carrying bags of shopping into the house. I hesitate when I get out of the car, not knowing whether to try and carry on the way things were before the scan or to return to the position of slightly awkward but friendly neighbour. I lock the car as he comes back outside and make my way towards the house.

'Your guttering.'

'My guttering?' I question.

'It's leaking.'

'Oh right . . . I'll ask Huw if he can fix it.'

'I'll do it tomorrow.'

'Oh, um, thanks. That would be great.' He nods at me and turns to walk away. 'Do you—' He stops still with his back towards me. 'Do you want some dinner?'

'Yes, that would be lovely,' I say, unnecessarily loudly, making a fool of myself in my eagerness to please him. I clear my throat. 'As long as it's not too much trouble?' I add, my voice fading to a murmur.

'I'm OK,' he says over his shoulder but the way he says it, the seriousness of his response, makes me think he wasn't talking about the dinner. Charlie strides back towards his house. He's spoken the right words, but the hunch of his shoulders and the state of his appearance does little to comfort me.

Week Twenty-One

Samuel

I get out of the taxi and look up and down the road. I reckon there are about eighty houses along this street. The grey clouds are miserable, looking down on me with glum faces, and lazy drizzle leaks from their eyes.

I feel like Hugh Grant in *Love Actually* trying to find Martine McCutcheon. I clench my hand into a fist and knock on door number one. If it was good enough for Hugh, then it's good enough for me.

I know I must be out of my mind and that it's a long shot, but it can't just be coincidence that Sophie's car ended up in Shropshire, the exact same place as her sister lives. I know it's a big place, but it feels like fate.

The reaction to a blind Irishman knocking at the door asking if they know where Helen Yates is, is not going as well as I'd hoped. Door number thirty-two has just been closed in my face by a worried-looking elderly lady. I must change my tactic. I can't just keep asking if they know her; I hadn't really thought about how odd that may sound. I could be a jealous ex or a stalker for all they know.

The sun comes out; I can hear the rain scampering away down drains as my cane splashes into a few puddles which hang about like bored teenagers around a local shop. I need a way of shedding my stalker-like approach; I need to make them feel important. My eyes focus on the black door and I reach for a knocker shaped into an owl's face. Weird.

'Hi,' I say as I'm met with a small, hairy-chested man. I get the feeling that he isn't wearing trousers, but I don't want to look down and check. 'I'm a journalist and I work for the *Shropshire Gazette*,' I say, keeping my fingers crossed that there is a newspaper of that name. 'I'm due to interview Helen Yates.'

'There is no newspaper called the *Shropshire Gazette*,' the hairy-chested man tells me.

Feck.

'It's new,' I say, making a mental note to google local newspapers before I try the next house.

'Sorry, you must have the wrong address, mate.'

'Ah, thanks for your time anyway.'

The street is long; so, so long. Numbers forty-one to forty-five are a miscellany of the British public. Number forty-one belongs to a man who opens the door a crack, revealing a key chain, still fastened; his suspicious eyes making me envisage a shotgun hidden behind the door. Number forty-two is a woman in a top so low-cut that my whole field of vision is filled with her cleavage; I chat with her for a while and tell her all about my job at the *Shropshire Star* (thank you, Google); the next house along, I'm met by the deep voice of a man encased inside a large woman's body . . . notwithstanding my limited field of vision, all I can focus on are the four protruding hairs on her chin. Number forty-four belongs to a tired-looking woman, desperate blue eyes ringed with dark shadows. Her children are arguing in the background and the look in her eyes makes me think that if I offered to take her children off her hands, she would let me, without a second glance.

The sun is relentless. I roll my neck around and shake the edge of my collar to let some air in, then follow my stick and the cracks in the block-paved drive to the next house, but there is a step that my stick doesn't find; I'm too busy looking at the strange gargoyle that has snuck into my vision. I fall flat on my face and my teeth bite into my lip as my chin scrapes the slabs. For God's sake, this is the fifth time I've tripped over the steps on this street. I hear a door fly open and the toe of a black work boot kicks through my absconded peripheral vision.

'God, mate, are you OK?' I pull myself into a sitting position as the man helps me up. He lets go of me and then pushes my cane into my hand. 'You're bleeding. Do you want to come in and get cleaned up?'

'Thanks, if it's not too much bother?' He walks off ahead as I begin to beat the cane along the drive. I hear that his footsteps have stopped and then his large nose is all I can see.

'Do you need me to, you know, help you?' I can hear in his tone that this is awkward for him. It's the first time really that I've felt like I'm different to everyone else. It's not that he is being rude or unkind, but there is that hint of the uncomfortable, of how to 'deal' with me.

'Would you mind if I grabbed your elbow?' I ask, swallowing down my pride.

'Right, I mean, sure . . . it's just up these steps.'

'How many steps?' I ask.

'Oh, I've never really counted them . . . four, four steps and then another small step up into the porch.'

The house smells and sounds like a home: the lingering smell of a hot oven, the sounds of the telly blaring kids' programmes from where I presume is the lounge. He leads me into the kitchen; the tunnel lets in images of kids' crayons, of discarded sweet wrappers and crockery draining on the sink. I can smell laundry detergent and a bin that needs emptying as the man guides me into a chair at the table. I hear him ripping sticky plastic back from something that I then realise is a packet of baby wipes. He hands it to me and I begin to wipe at the corner of my mouth. I feel awkward doing this; I have no idea if there is blood all over my face.

'You've got some, um, on your cheek.' I move the baby wipe.

'Left a bit.' I move it left a bit. 'Up a bit.' Upwards I go. 'No, no, back where you just were . . . shall I just?' He takes the baby wipe from me and he – coughing a sort of manly cough – begins to roughly wipe my face. This. Is. New.

'Thanks, you're the first man I've ever had a facial off.'

'It's the first facial I've ever given to a man, so we're even.' We both make guffawing noises to confirm our masculinity.

'Your front tooth is chipped, but your mouth isn't bleeding,' he comments as I hear the bin lid clang open. 'You might need to see a dentist.'

'Ah, that's been there years. Al Turner – illegal tackle.'

'Illegal tackle?'

'Yeah. I used to play rugby.'

'But you're—' His arm moves about, gesturing my sight.

'Oh, I haven't been blind all my life. Just this year . . . I had an accident. It's a long story.'

A lumbering silence fills the air; it's louder than the TV, louder than the washing machine on its spin cycle, louder than the repeating drip from the tap. 'I'm a journalist,' I say, 'I work for the *Shropshire Star*.'

'Is that so?' he says, his voice losing the ease of a moment ago.

'I've got an appointment with Helen Yates. Do you know her?'

'Can't say as I do.' Something in his tone makes me think he's not telling me the truth. I search for a glimpse of his face, but the telescopic image is now occupied by his back.

I choose my words carefully, making sure that my tone sounds offhand, like it isn't important.

'Oh, well. I'll go back to the office. I can't believe I've lost the address.' I start to get up, tilting the telescopic view around the kitchen, trying to catch a glimpse of something that will help me find Sophie, but each gem of sight is filled with clutter.

'Sorry I couldn't help you,' he says as he passes me my cane.

'Ah, not to worry,' I reply. 'Could I use your toilet before I go?' His hesitation hangs in the air; I hold my breath.

'Sure, I'll just show you . . . it's along the hall there on your right. Do you need me to . . .?'

'No, no, I'm grand, thanks, if you could just lead the way?'

I follow him and close the door behind me. I take my time scanning the room, careful not to miss anything that may help. There is a cabinet above the sink and I open it carefully. It's filled with the usual: unopened bars of soap, some razors, a packet of plasters, cheap supermarket paracetamol. If I could see clearly, I would be rummaging through these things, but I'm struggling to see in this dim light, in what is essentially a cupboard under the stairs. I move in closer, listening to the sounds outside the door – a small girl singing badly to an advert about ponies; a response from another child screaming to her dad to get Gemma out of the way – when, just peeking out from the side of my tunnel, I see a prescription sticker hiding behind a box of Tampax. I carefully pull it out of the cupboard and reach for the container. I'm nervous about knocking it over. That man outside the door is lying, I'm sure about it, and if he's lying, he's not going to be happy about a nosey Irishman messing with his wife's tampons. I tap my way back to the toilet, slide my hand along the top of the cistern and press the flush down, then return to the container. I clasp my hand around it and read the label in short bursts of letters: 'Hel-en Ya-tes.'

I return the container, close the door, thank my host and leave.

For now.

Week Twenty-Two

Sophie

It's early July and I'm shivering. White ghosts hang from the curtain hooks and they twist and turn as though their task is too arduous to bear.

Shivers slide from my body, the goosebumps ironing out into smooth, glistening skin. I kick off the blanket; Bean kicks too, the gentle bubbles of the last few weeks turning into a determined prod as I disturb its sleep with my tossing and turning.

Samuel is here.

'Sophie, you need to call a doctor,' Samuel is saying.

'I will . . . just five more minutes. Can you rub my back?' I ask. 'It hurts.' I hear the duvet rustle and I wait to feel his hands on my skin, but he doesn't push hard enough; I can't feel him. The shivers climb back up my spine and surge across my skin. I reach for the duvet, but the bed feels too large, the duvet too far out of reach, and it takes all my energy to grasp at its slippery corners, its weight cumbersome and stubborn. Samuel helps me with it and it slides on to my body like warm silk. He tucks it around me and I smile.

'I've missed you,' I tell him.

'You need to call a doctor, Sophie,' he replies. I'm desperate to feel his fingers clear my hair from my face, but he's gone. I'm on my own. Bean kicks me; it's the strongest I've felt it move before, and my eyes fly open. It's morning. The room is filled with light and for a moment, as I tap the bed, I almost expect to feel his weight sinking down on the mattress.

My hand reaches for the phone and I make an appointment to see the doctor.

I'm scared. Not of whatever is making me ill – I'm fairly sure it's a urine infection – but I'm scared of how much I wanted Samuel to still be here. I don't doubt that I can have Bean without him. I'm certain that I can bring the baby up by myself – women all over the world do this. What scares me is that I have made the wrong decision. That I am not fighting for something that I want.

The taxi journey to the doctor's is uncomfortable. Charlie's car wasn't outside and I'm glad that he is getting out and about. The hour it takes between my arrival at the doctor's, the diagnosis of the infection and being passed the white paper bag filled with my prescription, is leaden with gaps of time. Gaps that I can't help but fill with my memories of Samuel.

I flick through the channels but my mind won't settle. I've not been able to push Samuel from my thoughts for the last two days. It's as though that dream of Samuel has woken me up. I pick up my phone and FaceTime Helen. She'll tell me what I already know, I'm sure: that I should be fighting: for him. It's ridiculous, but I just need to hear it.

'Hi, Aunty Soapie!'

'Hello, sweet girl, I love your hair . . . did you do it yourself?' I bite my lip and look at Jessica's hair, which is tangled on top of her head.

'I did, but Caitlin keeps calling me pineapple head. Dad! Soapie is FaceTiming!'

'Pineapple Head' begins to be chanted from somewhere in the background.

'Is Mummy home?' I ask as the screen tilts and Caitlin's face – covered in chocolate and something that could be tomato sauce – pushes into the corner.

'Mummy's not here but Dad is,' she whispers loudly. 'He's talking to a blind man at the door . . . look, I'll show you.' The image of Helen's lounge jumps up and down and then is concealed by a door, some carpet, until I see Greg's feet.

'Oh. He's gone. I wanted to show Aunty Soapie the blind man.'

'Give me your mother's phone. I've told you not to answer it.'

'But Aunty Soapie's face was on it!'

'Just give me the phone.'

The screen is filled with a whiskey bottle being pulled out of a plastic bag, then by Greg himself, his nose looking even larger than usual this close up. I hold my phone away from my own face.

'Hey, a little early for the hard stuff, isn't it?' I ask.

'Some weird blind bloke has just given it me.'

'Blind bloke?'

'Never mind. How are you? Are you feeling better?'

I put on a bright smile, ignoring the pain in my back and the flush in my cheeks where the last of the temperature I've been battling hangs on.

'Much better, thanks. I was after Helen, but I'll call back later.'

'I'll tell her, she'll be back soon.'

'Dad!!! Tell her my hair does not look like a pineapple!'

'Sorry, Soph, I've got to go.'

The screen returns to my home screen, my question still needing validation.

Week Twenty-Two

Samuel

I've left it a few days before returning to this house, trying to think of a way to get back in there, but I've run out of time and I've run out of ideas. This is the best I can do.

The plastic handles from the shopping bag are digging into my palms, and I can feel their imprint leaving their mark on my skin. The bag is filled with chocolate bars and sweets for the kids and a large bottle of whiskey; he looked like a whiskey kind of man.

I unfold my cane, who I have decided to call Michael; the feedback vibrates through my wrist as he rolls down the steps. Following his guidance, I step on to the road, scanning the street through my tube of sight. The houses are all the same shape: they all have a door, they all have a bay window downstairs and two windows above them. The street stretches away from me, coating the inside of the tunnel, each house straight-backed and ready to salute: a parade of uniformity. But inside, they are filled with the chaos of people I don't know, people with different lives, different problems, different hopes.

Michael follows the cracks in the pavements; he warns me that there is a bin next to the lamp post and he tells me where the edge of the kerb is, but I still manage to trip. Michael, myself and the shopping go flying, all of us landing with a clatter on the road. I gather myself and stand back up with a groan.

I still have enough of my sight to be able to scan the ground if I dip my chin, and I spot him lying apologetically in the middle of the road. Part of me wants to leave him there – it would serve him right – but then I see how pitiful Michael looks lying on the road amongst the contents of the shopping bag; it's as if he's been abandoned. My head tilts so I can push the gloom away enough to be able to see the road and the step, then follow my feet until I'm standing next to my cane. I look at my shoes, the same pair of high-top trainers that Sophie had laced up for me. That man could see his beautiful girlfriend without her being framed in a circle of darkness. That man could chase after her, throw her over his shoulder while she shrieked in protest, her feet making little kicks as he ran up the stairs. They are the same shoes, the same feet, but they belonged to a different man.

These feet are standing next to a blind man's white cane, this man's feet; this man's cane, is surrounded by shadows that are trespassing into this man's world, shadows that will soon swallow it. The man who could run in these shoes is dead.

A honk from a car's engine shakes my insides as it swerves around me. I push the bottle of whiskey and the chocolates back into the bag, grab Michael and let him sweep the road in front of me until he guides me to a bench. I sit down and think of the time I spent with Sophie and then I replay it, adding the tunnel, adding the cane, adding this new person that I have become.

I don't belong here. I don't belong in DC. I don't belong in Wales, either. Maybe it's time I went home and began to start living my life, my new life, a life that Sophie and the man I used to be don't belong in.

What am I doing here? Trying to get into a family home

that, for whatever reason, holds secrets. He seems like a decent man with a young family. Sophie isn't here. The message from Gemma could be wrong. Sophie might not even have a sister called Helen Yates.

I knock on the door with my other hand, having successfully negotiated the steps without further injury. It swings open and the man from last time stares at me, the gentle, friendly manner replaced with a stern expression. His eyes seem to be drawn together by his eyebrows, and below them a deep groove cuts across the bridge of his nose.

'Hi,' I say, smiling. He responds by stepping forward slightly. His hair is brown and bushy, and I'm reminded of a grizzly bear. 'I hope it's not too inconvenient, I just wanted to thank you for helping me the other day.' I stretch my arm forward; the plastic bag swings hello. 'Just a few things, to say thanks.'

The nose groove relaxes a little and the eyebrows loosen.

'Oh. Cheers, it was nothing.' He looks down at the bag and takes it from my grasp.

'Well, thank you anyway, I really appreciated it.'

'Pineapple Head! Pineapple Head!' is being shouted from behind him.

His head turns back towards the inside of the house as a clatter and a cry from a child forces its way through the gap in the doorway and into the street.

'Look, about what I said, I'm not—' I begin to try and explain when the scream from inside gets louder and more urgent.

'Thanks for this.' He nods towards the bag. 'But I've got to . . .' His words come out in short breaths.

'Sure, I understand,' I say. He nods, takes a step backwards into the house as though he's afraid to turn his back on me. 'Well, thanks again.'

I take out my phone, the screen of which is starting to

get closer to the edges of the darkness, and call for a taxi, then make my way back to the bench. Two women are walking towards me as I follow Michael along the path. One of them is holding a lead, a pug trotting lazily beside her. They are looking over at me and I smile at them. I turn my head where I can see the bonnet of my taxi and its indicator flashing as it turns into the street. I stand, extend Michael to his full height and let him tap the edge of the pavement, checking for the edge of the kerb.

'Cute dog,' I say to the woman.

'Sicko!' she gasps.

'Yeah,' the other adds, 'some people really are blind. It's not a joke!' and off they totter on their air of self-righteousness, leaving me and Michael watching their retreating backs with a blank look of disbelief.

Week Twenty-Three

Sophie

It has taken days for the infection to abate. Now I feel fine again physically, but the longing I had felt for Samuel after my night of fevered dreams hasn't been cured. I keep thinking of the yearning I experienced during that moment when I thought he was here, and I question again if I should be fighting for him. I'm a woman who has spent her adult life fighting for what she wants: is an assumption of his betrayal, or the fear of being hurt again, enough to justify letting him go?

'Of course you should find him!' Helen had said, exasperation mocking my question.

'But what if—' I had begun.

'What if what? What if he listens to you and realises why you left? What if he finds out he's about to be a father with a woman who loves him, what if he realises he should never have betrayed her?'

'I told you, I deserved that.'

'Whatever. Just ring him, Sophie.'

I pick up the phone and dial his number, but again I hang up before it connects. Am I strong enough to hear him tell me I'm nothing to him – can I cope with that yet? I stroke the curve of my stomach and feel the shift beneath my skin. I imagine him laughing at me as I try to explain my actions.

How will he react when I tell him I'm pregnant with his child and never told him? And if he can forgive me, what if I can't? What if our betrayal sits between us . . . would our relationship ever really work?

The sound of Charlie's door opening and closing pulls my thoughts away from Samuel. I'm worried about him. You know how they say that the eyes are the window to the soul? Well, if that's true then Charlie's soul is disappearing. Our roles seem to have changed; I seem to be cooking for him, visiting him, and he puts up with it.

I balance the tray tottering with sandwiches and chips on my bump and knock on the door. He opens it without greeting.

'Hi, um, ham salad OK? I was making some for myself and . . .' My sentence trails off like a reluctant bride's train: there for decoration, hanging on but not necessary.

I overlook the mess in the kitchen, step over the discarded tea towel on the floor and ignore the smell from the stagnant water sitting in the sink. He eats the food I put in front of him and he answers my questions, but rather than his answers being delivered in his usual curt manner, he answers them slowly, as though he can't process his thoughts quickly enough.

'Can you believe it's mid-July already?' I ask, the sandwich halfway to my mouth. He blinks slowly and slides his focus away from his food and up at me. His eyes are bloodshot and his eyelids heavy.

'July,' he repeats in reply. I swallow my food and worry that there is some significance to this month and Charlie's actions.

I try to make small talk about the weather, about what has been happening on the news, the latest gossip about new restaurants that have opened in Mid Wales, about new dishes that the critics are raving about, and he listens, and he comments, but it's like he's not really here. Charlie pushes his food around the plate as though he's not going to eat it, but somehow he does. He is functioning in the same way that we all do – his chest is moving up and down as he breathes, his feet take one step after another the same way that mine do. He can see the seasons changing; he is seeing the new flowers that are showering my garden with summer; he can see the beauty that the world has to offer – but then he's not seeing it at the same time. He gives every appearance of living and breathing, but it's as if, inside himself, he is dead.

Week Twenty-Three

Samuel

When I woke up this morning, in the house where I grew up, with the familiar sounds and smells of home, I felt happy. This is a strange feeling to acknowledge when even in the last week I have noticed how much darker my world has become. I feel like I can start to live again now that I have left behind the person I once was.

I have spoken to Bob Golding, my boss from Greenlight, and I imagined his pallid chins rolling over the top of his collar as he talked; his voice even sounded fat – how is that possible? The investigation found that I hadn't broached any infringements, as I knew they would. This means that they can accept my voluntary resignation and I will now receive the severance pay that I had been denied the last time I had made this offer, that morning while Sophie lay asleep in my bed, the morning I had called Bob and told him I wanted to take voluntary redundancy.

I wonder how different my life might now be, if I hadn't been distracted by Sophie in my shirt, if I hadn't fallen asleep after, if she hadn't somehow misunderstood how the company had found out that we were together and left without speaking to me about it. Would there still have been an explosion? Would I still have put the kettle on the stove without lighting it, or would we have been doing something else? Would she have been the one to notice that it wasn't lit? Would we both have been there? The image of her being hit by the white light turns my stomach. I've got to stop this. I have to start my new life, and that life doesn't have her in it.

My faithful friend Michael leans against my bed and I reach out for him; he guides me into the bathroom. Hot steam fills the room as I turn on the shower and carefully step into it, my muscles relaxing as I close my eyes while the strong jets pound my back, the water washing over my face as I try to wash away the thoughts of Sophie.

The door to the bathroom opens and closes. We only have one bathroom and so the lock is never used; we have an unspoken rule, even if someone is in the shower. Ma had a code brown once when Sarah was in the bath; I don't think I've ever heard Da laugh so much. It was the twenty-ninth of March and in our house, that date is known as The Day Mrs McLaughlin Shat Herself. We have a curry every year to celebrate. Anyway, from then on, the door stays unlocked. Besides, Da always needs a shite when I'm in the shower.

'Could you not have waited ten minutes?' I ask as I lather shampoo into my hair. The shower curtain is pulled back, my eyes flying open in shock as the shampoo runs into them, stinging like a bastard. I attempt to cover my tackle with one hand whilst trying to wipe the shampoo out of my eyes. 'Jesus!' I shout, turning my face to the streams of water, washing the suds away as Isabella stands there.

'I think we've waited long enough,' she answers as I look over my shoulder at her. She disappears from sight, and I hear the lock complain as it is guided into its latch.

She pulls her dress over her head, steps out of her knickers that are more elastic than material and steps into the shower. She has always been stunning to look at and I feel myself responding to her. I'm still half-turning towards the shower but she takes my hand and turns me around.

'I don't think this is a good idea,' I say, trying to address her face, but my eyes are hungry for more. *If all we're going to see for the rest of our lives is darkness*, they say, *then we're damn well going to enjoy what's standing in front of us.*

'Ah Sammy, I'm not proposing marriage,' she answers as she reaches for me. 'Just a little fun.' She smiles as she kneels.

It's been a while since I've had a little fun and I'm sure it's going to be over before I have time to think about whether it's a good idea or not.

'Stop,' my mouth says, taking over the decision. My eyes do not enjoy this decision and they frown and tell me that it will serve me right when they stop working. *What are you doing?* they say. 'I can't. I'm just not ready.' She looks up at me with a puzzled expression and then gets up.

'For the love of God, Sammy, what did she do to you?' She strokes my cheek and looks sadly at me. I cower further away from her reach at the same time as I register the sound of the lock being opened – Mam had insisted on a lock that could be opened from the other side of the door – but I'm too late to react.

'Jesus, Mary and Joseph!' Mam shrieks as she is met with what I'm sure is a clear view of Isabella's – it has to be said – magnificent breasts.

'Waahheeeey! Sammy boy!' Da's voice booms from behind.

'Mr McLaughlin, you avert your eyes this instant!'

'Good on you, my boy!!' he shouts. Isabella is laughing and reaching for a towel as the door closes on Mam reciting the rosary.

Bret's face fills the screen; the edges of the monitor are held in place by the closing passageway. It's been so long since I've seen him that I'd forgotten just how American he is.

'Sammy, everyone sends their love, buddy.' He grins his pearly whites. 'The place isn't the same without you – are you sure you're going to leave? I know how difficult it's going to be for you, but we'll all help.' I smile at him. His words are genuine, but I know that if I went back there, they would all soon be taken up with their own lives, their own priorities.

'DC isn't for me any more,' I tell him. 'At least not for now. I need to get to grips with things before I think about going back to work.'

'Did you get the insurance money from the house yet?' he asks as he slurps a health food shake that I know he got from the gym we used to go to together. I think about how we would run first, how he would stride ahead of me. I have another gut-wrenching moment when I think about how much I loved to run. Will I ever be able to do that again?

'Not yet, but it should be here soon.' I push the thought away. I'll still be able to use a treadmill.

'What are you going to do with it? Buy somewhere over there?'

'Nah, not for a while.' I don't tell him that the thought of being in a house on my own, once the fog rolls in, terrifies me. 'I'm enjoying Mam's cooking too much,' I laugh. 'So, what's new with you?' I change the subject.

'I, my friend, am in love.' He puts the drink out of shot and leans towards the right so that the screen is filled with the side of his face.

'Are you indeed?' I grin, knowing full well that the only thing Bret falls in love with is the measurements of his biceps. He holds up a picture of a car and I burst out laughing. I hear Da opening the front door and making a huge fuss as Isabella arrives. Bret is telling me about his new car as Isabella comes into the lounge. She stands behind me then leans forwards and kisses me on the cheek, halting Bret's talk about sweeping indicators and virtual cockpits.

'Seems like I'm not the only one,' Bret says. 'Hi!' His voice booms through the tiny speakers as he leans towards his own screen.

'How d'you do.' Isabella smiles and I can see Bret's eyebrows rising as he takes in her full figure, her heavy dark curls and long eyelashes. 'I'm Isabella.'

'Ah, just like that nymphomania—'

I interrupt Bret before he says another word about the stories I used to tell him about Isabella.

'She's an old friend,' I interject, trying to telepathically urge Bret to shut up across the thousands of miles over the Atlantic Ocean.

'Riiiighhht . . .' he responds. 'I hope you're taking good care of our Sammy?'

'I'm trying to.' She leans forward and bites my ear as I try to lean my head away from her, and then she leaves the room to join Mam and Da in the kitchen.

Bret starts to talk in an overly loud whisper.

'Didn't take you long,' he whispers as I glance towards the open door. 'What happened with Sophie?'

'It's nothing serious,' I say but I can hear the doubt in my voice. Isabella's visits are becoming more frequent after our bit of fun in the shower. 'And as for Sophie . . . I just can't torture myself any more. My sight is going, man, I've got enough to deal with. I've got to tell you, I think I was starting to lose my mind a bit.' I tell him about the phone call and the trip to Shropshire.

'You sound like you were starting to go all stalker-like, buddy. I think you're right. You took the chequered flag, I think it's time to throw in the towel. I mean, if she hung up on you . . .'

'Yeah, that's what I'm thinking . . . except for the sports metaphors, obviously. Anyway, lots to be keeping myself busy. I've got to learn to cook.' I laugh.

'But you can already cook,' he answers, looking puzzled.

'Not as a blind person, mate, not as a blind person.'

'Oh yeah, I forgot about that.'

Michael catches my eye and I wish that I could forget about it too.

'Right, Sammy boy.' Da slams a pad of paper on to the kitchen table as Mam opens and shuts the oven. Even in the bloody summer, we have to have a roast. 'Your bucket list: number one?'

'Drive a car,' I answer, the words leaving my mouth without much thought.

'Right you are . . . number two?'

'See a match, a real match. Not on the telly.'

'Three?'

'I want to see a show.'

'A show?' He hesitates.

'Just write it down,' I snap. 'Jesus, Mam could you open a window? I'm melting in here.'

'Four? Sammy? Four?' Sophie's image pushes its way into my thoughts: the way she looked at me when she first opened her eyes in the morning.

'Christ, I need some air. Can we do this later?'

'Sure, but—'

'Da! Just give me a minute to think, will you?' I grab Michael and leave the room, trying to escape the six things on the list that all involve Sophie.

Week Twenty-Four

Sophie

There is a stillness to this evening. The sky is blood-red and starlings in their hundreds swoop and dive across the sky as though they are one pattern. I describe them to Bean, who is now the length of one of the rulers at school.

'The type that Lewis Slater used to twang elastic bands at my head when the teacher wasn't looking,' I tell Bean as I make a salad. My hair is escaping a plait, resting in between my shoulders; my loose lemon camisole leans forward as I take the baked potatoes out of the oven. The heat of the day is still and warm, but it is a breathable heat, not like the oppressive heat of the first rush of summer at the beginning of the month. I put the plates on a tray and carry it around to Charlie's house. The door is open and as I walk into the kitchen he is sitting staring blankly at the wall. He blinks as I walk into the room, as if trying to re-focus his eyes.

'Hi,' I smile. 'Just baked potatoes today. Have you got any sour cream?' I ask him, trying to nudge life into this room where grief floats around like an empty ship adrift after a storm.

'Why are you here, Sophie?' he asks, blinking slowly and meeting my eyes. His eyes look clouded and unfocused, as though he is drunk, but I can't smell any alcohol. Bean doesn't like the smell usually and my nose will wrinkle at it.

'Well, it's dinner time and—'

'I mean, why are YOU here? Why are you making me food that I don't want, talking to me about things I don't care about?' His voice is rising and there is spittle at the corners of his mouth.

'Charlie, I know that you're hurting—'

'No, you don't know. You don't know anything about me. You're just using me to fill your dull little life. You have nothing to do other than to poke your nose into mine, because you have no life of your own.'

His words are ricocheting off my skin. I feel their small nips and bites, but I know that he doesn't mean them. I place the plate in front of him, but he takes his hand and swipes it to the floor. The sound does more than shatter the silence; the silence implodes. 'Get out,' he says.

'I'll just clean this up—'

'I don't want you to clean it up. Can't you see how difficult it is for me to see you, to see you talk about your bump in the same way that Olivia did? You're not her; why are you forcing your way into my life? Do you think I don't know how you used to watch me in school? Don't you know what everyone in school used to think of you? You think that by leaving and getting a ball-breaking career that it changes who you are? You're still the fucking same: a leech. You attach yourself to whoever will take you and just won't. Let. Fucking. Go. I bet Samuel sighed a breath of relief when you left Washington. I bet he couldn't believe his fucking luck. I bet he—'

I don't let him finish his sentence because my hand has slapped his face. My hand stings and my insides are crawling; they want to escape me; the anger that I have always said could be contained has broken free. Is that how Ian felt? Like he couldn't contain it? Maybe I'm just as damaged as he was.

'Get. Out.'

He needn't have said the words because I am already leaving, backing out of this house that I don't belong in, a life that I don't belong in.

My whole body is shaking. Bean is still; is Bean scared of me?

I slam the door behind me, my back sliding down its ridges as I sink to the floor. My palms turn over and I look at them as if they are holding a knife, as if they belong to someone else. The sun is beginning to sink, the blood-red sky seeping through the windows, staining the clean surfaces, tainting everything I have tried to create with doubt.

Week Twenty-Four

Samuel

'Are you sure this is a good idea?' I ask Da, who is sitting in the passenger side of his car. Da seems to think that the old dirt track we used to go tobogganing down when we were kids never gets used, so it's OK for a blind man to drive down. It leads on to the field that we used to make dens in and where I popped my cherry on a very cold night with Carol; I can't say the ground shook for either of us unless you count the herd of cows that wandered past us after my cherry had been very quickly dispatched.

'Ah, will you stop complaining, Sammy, and turn the key?'

'I'm just saying that as I can't even see you, or the steering wheel, this might not be the grandest of ideas, you know?'

'Stop being a wet blanket and turn the fecking key.' My head shakes in response while I feel for the key and turn on the ignition. The car splutters and coughs rather than the purr that my car in DC gives out.

My vision through the window is small and filled with the bumpy lane stretching in front of me and the green grass of the field up ahead, but I can't see through my passenger window and I can't see through the side mirrors either; I know that this will be the last time I drive a car. 'What are you waiting for?' Da asks.

My foot feels the resistance of the accelerator pedal

beneath my sole as I add a little pressure, the car beginning along the bumpy track. 'Jesus! You're driving like my Great-Aunt Nelly.'

'I've never heard of a Great-Aunt Nelly,' I tell him, pouring all my concentration into the small hoop of fields and mud in front of me.

'Well, if we did have one, this would be how she would be driving.'

I press my foot down a little harder and feel around for the gear stick, sliding it from first gear into second; it grinds in protest as Da swears under his breath. From the black hole where my peripheral vision should be, a growling sound starts up; I hear something pass us and it takes a moment for it to swerve into my vision: a teenage boy on a quad bike veers in front of me.

My foot responds by hitting the brake and we lurch forward, the seat belts tightening sharply across our bodies.

'For Christ's sake, Sammy, you're not going to let that little shite Timmy from down the road overtake us, are you? Put your foot down, you great Jessy.'

'I could have hit him! You need to tell me if something is coming from behind me, Da, I can only see what's in front of me! I can't see if Little Timmy or Little Tommy or anyone comes from the side, OK?'

'As long as you don't make me the laughing stock of Ireland. Now put your foot down on the accelerator – do you want to feel like you're driving like a man or my Great-Aunty Flo?'

'We don't have a—'

He grabs Michael and pushes him down on to the accelerator, and we hurtle down the track.

'That's more like it! Ha, ha! Off we go, Sammy boy!'

'Da! Move Michael away from the pedals!' I screech as we bump our way down the lane, the tyres dipping into potholes, with the sound of mud splashing up the sides of the doors.

'Michael? Who the feck's Michael?' The image of the open gate is sucked closer towards us as the car jolts and bounces its way through the dirt towards the field.

'The cane, Da, move the cane!' We speed through the open gates and on to the field, splashing into a deep puddle that sprays mud on to the window. I need to look down to find where the wipers are but I daren't look away from the little greenery of the field that I can see.

'Wipers, Sammy!'

'I can't find them!' My hand begins flicking the sticks around the steering wheel, one of them activating the radio, which begins blaring out Bonnie Tyler's 'Holding Out for a Hero'. I finally find the wipers and they begin swiping the mud away at a furious pace. 'Move the cane, Da!'

'I can't! Mikey is stuck!'

'Oooh, whoooo, whoooo, whooooo! Ahh! Ahhh!' Bonnie sings.

'Michael!' The car continues to bounce, the low gear screeching alongside Bonnie's questions about where all the good men have gone.

'Ah, Michael Caine! Ha! I get it, Sammy.' Da seems oblivious to the way I'm gripping the wheel.

He pulls the cane away as I slam on the brakes. The adrenaline is pumping through my body, making me breathe in short gasps while my heart hammers inside my chest. I sit still for a moment and stare ahead where Timmy has stopped his quad bike, the image of him encircled in darkness as he revs the engine at me. He adjusts his helmet and sticks up his middle finger at us.

'That little—' I say.

'Buckle up, Michael,' Da says as I slip the gear stick into first, take my foot off the brake and begin hurtling after

Timmy from down the street with Da shouting, 'That's it, my boy! Show him not to mess with an angry blind McLaughlin driving a car!'

Timmy drives his quad bike around in a semi-circle as I come hurtling after him; he tears off towards the summit of the field and dips down beneath the horizon. We bump and creak our way after him, the mound of the hill coming into my view before we hurtle over its peak and career downwards where Timmy is flying off ahead, giving lewd hand gestures over his shoulder. We gain on him, my fingers gripping the wheel, my head leaning as close to the windshield as I can get it. We begin to catch him up, but the front of the car suddenly dips, and we find ourselves trapped in the clutches of a hidden ditch, the back wheels spinning and the car remaining stationary. Timmy zooms away, flies past us and gives us a wanker sign as he does.

Da, Michael and I sit speechless until we burst out laughing, the type of laughter that crunches your stomach muscles and takes away your breath. Da claps me on the shoulder.

'That's one of your bucket list ticked off, eh, Sammy?' He smiles at me and I see tears in his eyes; I'm not sure if it's from the laughter or because of what is happening to me.

In all this time, I hadn't really thought about what it was like for my parents to see me losing my sight; how difficult it would be for them to watch their son lose the world in front of us. Our laughter peters out as a thought hits me out of the blue; I will never see the face of my children. I will never get to hold my baby in my arms and look at its features and say it has my nose or my eyes. That's even if I have kids. Who would want to take this burden on when they could find a person who is able to look into their face and tell them how beautiful they are?

Sophie is better off without me.

Week Twenty-Five

Sophie

I have thrown myself into my new business, trying to hide Charlie's words in between the neat rows and columns of numbers, but they refuse to be hidden, peeking out at me when the total doesn't match the receipts. His words cling to the backs of my eyelids when I try to sleep, they lie on my tongue when I try to eat, they reverberate around Bean's cocoon, and I wish I could grab them with my hands and hide them away.

The image of my hand slapping his face refuses to go. I can't remember any thought process before my hand left my side; it was just instinctive. The Book says mood swings are normal; it is normal to act out of character, everything feels heightened and this is all down to my hormones. I worry that my mood swings may not go once Bean comes. I'm hanging on to this excuse: it's my hormones; it's not learnt behaviour; I won't become a result of the things I saw as a child.

My hands grasp the coffee cup and my feet are tucked up beneath me as I stare at the TV. The curtains are drawn, and my half-eaten dinner is congealing on a plate on the floor.

I don't think I have ever felt so alone.

My mother's voice resonates inside me: '*You can never be alone in this house.*' She had said this while she was polishing the cheap memorabilia that were scattered around the room, shuffling picture frames on the window sill, picking up small ornaments that she had bought on various day trips. '*This house is full of memories and each one is a reminder that you are not alone.*' She smiled at me as she ran the cloth over the old teak sideboard which doubled as a makeshift bar at Christmas, picking up a snow globe with a Welsh dragon trapped inside. '*Do you remember the day we got this?*' I can hear her voice as if she was still in this room.

My hand slides away from the coffee cup and I wipe away a stray tear. '*It was that horrid day out to Llandudno when you were four . . . do you remember? It had rained all day, so we ended up in that little gift shop. You started crying when you saw the dragon, because he was facing the wrong way and couldn't see what was going on around him.*'

I answer her, even though my words are falling on silent walls and empty chairs. 'You said if we took it home, he could watch us for the rest of his life. You said that, Mum, but do you know what I used to think?' I rub my face. 'I used to think that it would have been better off staying in the shop than watching the things he did to you.'

My new sideboard sits against the wall, the edges of the wood leaning further out than the rest of the oak, in the shape of a fat 'T'; all that is on it is the blue frame that Charlie gave me and Bean's scan picture sitting neatly inside. What things could I display on it? What story would my possessions tell? I put the coffee cup down and walk towards it, sliding my hands along the smooth surface. What would I cover this with? Nothing from the London house meant anything to me. I trace my finger around the frame and across Bean's picture.

'That's what we'll do, Bean, we'll put our favourite things on here, only the good things in life. Nothing bad.' I open one of the drawers and pull out a pack of Post-it notes and a pen. I write on the first one my happiest memory so far: seeing Bean at my twelve-week scan. I write it down and then stick it on top. I write on the next one: the day I kicked Samuel in the ankle. I smile and stick that below the first one. I feel Charlie's words start to lose their sting as I replace them with good memories; good things in my life.

My back aches as I look at the sideboard, which is now covered with the things that make me happy: Helen and Greg's home; the way Caitlin drags her snowman teddy around with her everywhere she goes; this house that I've made my own . . . and Samuel. There are lots and lots of happy memories with Samuel: the way he walks, almost as if he might trip himself over at any minute, the look in his eyes as he proposed that I stay in Washington, the awkward way he had asked me to stay at the end of the week. Once I start to write these memories down, I can't stop. His smell, his accent, the scar inside his hand, how he had been dancing the day I had watched through his window . . . the sideboard is covered with my memories of him.

Mum was right. I don't feel alone any more, but she has shown me more than that: she has shown me that my head is filled with Samuel; that I am happiest with Samuel.

'Shall we call Your Dad, Bean?' I ask quietly, daring myself to speak the words out loud. I rub my stomach tentatively. 'I wonder what he will think of you.'

I glance up at the giant clock-face that counts down the days to Bean's arrival. It is the middle of the night in DC. I'll call him tomorrow . . . and this time I know I won't hang up.

Samuel's mobile is now out of order, as is his home phone. I swallow down my irritation. If I had let the phone connect those few weeks ago, I would be closer to finding him now. I google the Greenlight number and hear the dialling tone connect as I swallow down my nerves and take a few deep breaths. Bean is kicking me impatiently. I picture the reception desk; I picture the doors that I had walked through: a confident businesswoman in killer heels. I rotate my foot, an old flip-flop dangling from my swollen foot.

'Greenlight Finance, how may I help?'

'Hello.' My voice from a lifetime ago rings out into the kitchen. 'Please could you put me through to Samuel McLaughlin?'

'I'm sorry, ma'am, Mr McLaughlin is no longer here. Shall I transfer you to his department where another member of our team can help you?'

'Y-yes, please.'

This doesn't make sense. Why would he leave? Why would he have left after everything he had said about his job and how he had betrayed me to ensure that he kept it?

'Good morning,' announces the sing-song voice of a young woman.

'Hello, I was hoping to speak with Samuel McLaughlin. I've worked with him before and I would like to—'

'I'm sorry . . .' the sing-song has stopped and is replaced with something gentler, 'but I'm afraid Samuel is no longer with us, just a moment.' I hear her hand cover the receiver and urgent muffled conversations in the background. Her hand slides from the receiver as she tells a colleague that she'll be right there.

'I'm sorry, is there anyone else who can help you today?'

'Could you tell me what happened to him? To Samuel?'

'I'm sorry, I'm new here, just a moment.' The muffled tone fills my ears again before she continues.

'There was an accident.' She comes back on to the line. 'At his house, I believe. Is there anyone else who can help you today?'

'An accident?'

'An explosion. I'm sorry, but Samuel has gone.' There is no song, there is only remorse in her tone. Bile rises in my throat and my hands start shaking. 'Is there anyone else who can help you with your enquiry?'

'No. No . . . could you tell me when Samuel, when he left?' She's talking to someone else again.

'March. Is there anything else I can do to help you today?'

'March,' I repeat. The daffodils would have been out . . . why am I thinking about daffodils? The walls are closing in around me, my breath is being sucked out of my body and I'm finding it hard to form any more words other than a quiet 'No'. No, she can't help me. My shaking hands reach for the keyboard as I type in Samuel's Washington address into the search bar, followed by the word explosion. There is a report in the *Washington Post*:

Authorities in DC Investigate Report of Explosion

At approximately five o'clock on March 15, an explosion ripped through a property in Hangart Drive. Authorities said it appeared to be related to a gas leak.

The owner of the house, Mr Samuel McLaughlin, was dragged from the burning house by a neighbor. He is said to be in a critical condition and is being treated in the Washington Hospital Center.

I scroll down to where a picture of Samuel's house, or what is left of it, is being hosed down by firemen.

My fingers punch in the words 'Washington Hospital Center' and I call them, gently stroking Bean, trying to keep my child and myself calm.

'Washington Hospital Center.'

'Hello? I was hoping you could help me. I'm trying to find a friend of mine.' The memory of his face, as he held out his hand to me when I was sitting in the puddle, steals the breath from my lungs and I have to concentrate on gulping air back into my body. 'He was admitted in March?'

'What name, please?'

'Samuel McLaughlin.' His name doesn't roll around my mouth the way it used to; it sounds brittle, fragile.

'There is nothing on the screen to say that he is a current patient and I'm afraid I can't give out any personal information about any of our past patients.'

'I understand, but I know he was taken to hospital in March and I know that his injuries were severe, but I don't know any more than that. Please, if you could give me anything about him, anything at all, I would be . . .' I close my eyes, their surface burning inside their sockets.

'I'm sorry, but I can't give you any more details. Perhaps if you contact his next of kin?' These words punch me in the stomach. Next of kin.

'I don't know where his . . .' I force these words out of my mouth, these words that are associated with death. 'I don't know who his next of kin are.'

'I'm sorry, but there is no more I can do to help. Maybe ask his friends? They might know?'

'I will, thanks for your help anyway.' I'm being polite. How is it that I am still managing to be polite when inside I am full of chaos?

I hang up and look down at my stomach.

'Oh, Bean, where do we go from here?'

'Would you tell me, please,' I whisper into the silence, repeating Alice's line as I did as a child, 'which way I ought to go from here?'

'That depends a good deal on where you want to get to,' Mum replies.

But deep down I already know. Washington DC.

Week Twenty-Five

Samuel

The McLaughlin family are clambering towards their seats en masse. The Kingspan Stadium is filled with the smell of grass and beer, the excited chatter mixed with the anticipation of the game. We used to do this a lot when I was a kid, come to see Ulster play. And when I played here, they didn't miss a single game: Mam, Da and Sarah always screaming my name, always telling me to get up off my fat arse.

Michael is leading me to my seat. I've had to pass my plastic pint glass to Sarah to carry as I side-step my way to my chair, my backside sliding against strangers' knees. What must I look like to them? A blind man coming to watch the game. We take our seats and I collapse Michael and put him below me.

The doctors knew my sight would deteriorate quickly, but I didn't think it would happen so suddenly. The fist has begun to lose patience and has started to squeeze harder and faster; in the space of the last few weeks, the darkness has begun to creep closer. Like hot tar, it oozes from out of the shadows and swallows the world in front of me. I haven't mentioned this to anybody just yet and I wonder if they've noticed how much more I'm relying on Michael, how much more I have to move my head to let my surroundings in. Sarah's hand takes hold of mine and she passes the plastic cup into my grip.

'Cheers,' I say and take a sip. I hear her passing drinks to her kids as I stare out at the pitch, taking in as much of it as I can. I'll be able to see most of the match if I move my head quickly enough with the players; it's the rest of the stadium that will be stolen from me. The sky above it will be sucked away into a black hole. I will be able to hear my sister's cheers and I'll be able to hear Da's insults and Mam's gasps at a tough tackle, but unless I turn my head right towards their direction, their expressions will be hidden from me. My time is running out.

As the players run on to the pitch, we all clap and cheer, the noises of the stadium knitting together just as they always have, the whoosh of heat that comes from thousands of gasps, thousands of cheers, thousands of 'ooohs' as a player takes a hit, all the sounds weaving into each other to produce a whole 'image' that is just as complex, has just as many components as the view on the pitch, and it is just as intoxicating.

The game begins, and I watch the kick-off easily enough. White shirts with black collars chase after the ball, but the ball . . . well, the ball is just too fast for me to follow. Play soon slows down; I can watch the phases, the ball hunkered down beneath the players before it is thrown backwards, but then I'm lost again amongst the flashes of white shirts being guarded by the opposing reds. My eyes search the pitch until I find it. I never thought it would be this exhausting. I've lost track of the ball again.

'You all right, Sammy boy?' Da asks.

'Yeah, I'm grand, thanks, tremendous game so far, eh?' I answer as I scan what I'm fairly sure is the twenty-two-metre line.

'Only, well, I only ask because you're looking the wrong way, son.'

Arses.

I turn towards Da's face. The crowd roar and I can sense that most of them are in the halfway position of standing to cheer for a try and sitting back down when the opportunity is snatched away from them. He isn't looking at the game; he's looking at me in a way that I haven't seen for a long, long time. He's looking at me just like he used to when I was a child – when I was Joseph in the school nativity and forgot my lines. Or when I got my arse kicked in a scrap when I was ten. The expression that tells you that your father would live that moment for you if he could.

'It's hard to keep track of the ball,' I say and turn my face back towards the pitch.

'Well, why didn't you say so sooner, you silly arse? I always wanted to be a commentator. Now, turn your head towards the five-metre line, can you see they're about to throw in the line-out?' I feel Da's arm around my shoulder as he begins possibly the worst commentary in a match that I've ever heard before, but, at the same time, one of the best.

I'm drunk by the time we get back into the car, which is more like a minibus, really. Gone are the days when we would all just squish in, Sarah sitting on my knee while as many cousins as we could manage would sit shoulder to shoulder, rugby shirts on top of rugby shorts. My limited sight is even more distorted, even harder to keep hold of, but I don't care. Da, Sarah and I are singing rugby songs and Mam is telling us to hush up before we get ourselves arrested for disturbing the peace.

'What's next on your list, Sammy?' Da asks in the over-loud way that we all do when we're drunk.

'A show,' I say.

'I get you, but that'll be just me and you, lad,' he winks over his shoulder at me.

'Not that kind of show, Da,' Sarah says as she rummages in her bag and passes packets of crisps to the kids sitting behind us who are whinging about not having another hot dog. 'Sam likes musicals.'

'What?' Da yells.

'Mr McLaughlin! Lower your voice or I'll end up crashing the car and killing us all, and then where would you be?'

'Where would I be? Dead, I'd imagine! What do you mean, Sammy likes musicals? What, like *Jesus Christ Superstar* and all that malarkey?'

'I was thinking more along the lines of *West Side Story*?' I say and then burp behind my hand as Mam takes a sharp corner. 'You'd like it, Da, I hear there are more deaths in it than an episode of *Game of Thrones*.'

'This is your fault, Mrs M,' Da says and turns his head back towards the windshield.

'And just what do you mean by that?'

I turn my head towards Sarah, who rolls her eyes at me; I grin back at her.

'You were always too soft on him when he was a lad, always putting magic bloody cream on his grazes . . . and now listen to him! Musicals! Paddle boats! What's next, Sammy? Flower arranging?'

'I don't know, maybe.' I wink at Sarah, who laughs.

'What do you think you might do, as a career?' Sarah asks as Mr and Mrs McLaughlin bicker in the front about how Ma's uncle was a florist; the fact that it never did him any harm is currently under question.

'I don't know. I'm all right for a while but I'll need to do something with myself. I might see if I can get back into a bank. It's weird, a few weeks back, the idea of losing my sight felt like, I suppose a bit like I was terminally ill or something. But now . . .' I look through the tunnel and out of the window where the Irish summer sun warms the dust that is being blasted up the sides of the car and smile. 'Now, I don't feel like that . . .'

'So how do you feel?'

'A bit lost.'

I think about the look in Sophie's eyes the first day I met her . . . If only she could find me, the way that I found her.

Week Twenty-Six

Sophie

As I walk past the tall buildings lining the street, my pregnant reflection looks at me with confusion. My large stomach gives my walk a suggestion of the waddle that is sure to arrive in the next few weeks. The Greenlight building frowns at me: what is this woman doing here in her loose summer dress and her flat sandals? What business does she have here?

The offices are the same as they were when I came here in February: the same noises, smells and air of urgency that I don't think I have ever noticed before; everybody seems to be in a rush.

My stiletto-less feet walk to the desk and I ask to speak to Kat. A tall, willowy woman with large glasses and hair scraped into a bun smiles at me from behind the high mahogany desk.

'I'm afraid she no longer works here.' I fleetingly wonder if that was anything to do with the merger. They were stupid to let her go; her performance in the last year had outshone her colleagues.

'In that case, may I speak with . . .' My mind goes blank – my baby brain rooting through the lists of employees that I had spent hours and days scouring. Then I retrieve one: 'Bob Golding, please?' The willow looks down at me, lingering on the sweat glistening on my top lip.

'I'm afraid you will need to make an appointment.'

'If you could just call him and tell him that Sophie Williams wishes to speak to him.'

She glances down at my stomach with a slight look of revulsion. Bean kicks inside my ribcage, pushing me forward. 'Urgently,' I add.

'As I've said, you will need to make an appointment.'

'Very well.' It occurs to me that I don't have a diary in my bag; instead I have a bottle of Diet Coke and a packet of crisps. I pull out my phone, swipe the screen to my diary, which is filled with gaps and the occasional antenatal appointment. I tap my blunt nail against the screen. 'I can fit him in tomorrow.' She does little to hide her smirk as I say this, and I wish that I had worn a suit. I was wrong to think that my voice alone could command the same respect that my armour and I had worked so hard to achieve.

'I'm afraid Mr Golding has a very busy schedule.' She looks at the screen of her monitor and begins to rap her fingers over the keyboard. 'He can possibly fit you in on the fourteenth?'

'Of August?'

'Ye-es,' she says slowly.

My cheeks redden as I grimace at how stupid I sound; today is the third of August. 'But that is three weeks from now. I need to speak to him . . . Please, if you could just call him, tell him my name?'

'Mr Golding is in meetings all day.'

'Sophie?' I hear a loud male voice call my name. I turn, and it takes me a moment to recognise Bob Swift, back from paternity leave and back, it seems, at the head of our merger. I glance at the willow fleetingly, hoping she can now see the woman I am beneath the rounded stomach and loose dress.

'Bob,' I smile, hold out my hand and let him shake it before air-kissing me. I worry that I might smell sweaty, but he reeks of coffee and long hours; he vibrates with it. He looks down at Bean and laughs.

'Well, congratulations! When are you due?'

'November,' I reply and ask about his own baby.

'Total nightmare, doesn't sleep, wants to be held constantly . . . wife looks about fifty. Truth be told, glad to be over here for a few weeks, get a decent night's kip!' Bob speaks as though he can't afford the time to start his sentences with pronouns. 'Was just about to grab lunch, want to join?' he asks. I agree, and we walk to a café not far from the one where I first met Samuel.

Bob rattles off his order before I even have a chance to read all the options, and then I remember that when I worked, I always ordered a chicken salad. Did we all do that? Choose the same thing because we didn't have time to read the whole menu?

'So, back in DC?' he asks, filling his glass with water from the jug, swigging it down quickly. I watch his Adam's apple bobbing up and down.

'Just for a short while. I've started up a new business.' The Adam's apple stops bobbing for a second. 'I was hoping to meet up with a few old colleagues that I worked with at Greenlight during the merger, but it seems a lot of them have moved on.' I reel off a few names, attaching Samuel's name like a comma, an afterthought, instead of the thing that can change the meaning of the whole sentence.

'Samuel McLaughlin?' My heart pounds and I feel light-headed for a moment. Will he tell me that he is dead? I'm not ready to hear it; I force aside the words that could fall from Bob's mouth. 'Yes, I'd heard that you two were involved.' I furrow my brows together. I'm about to try and lie, but what would be the point?

'We were, but Bob,' I say almost desperately, 'I left him the moment I knew where he worked. It wasn't easy and I'm not proud of the way that I treated him. I, I didn't even tell him why I left. I didn't steal his idea, and I didn't tell him about ours,' I add, taking a sip of water.

'Knew you wouldn't. Always believed in your integrity. Dreadful business, those fools firing you. Preposterous.'

Our food is served, but instead of asking about Samuel, instead of demanding the answers about his accident, I let Bob lead the conversation. I cower behind the taste of the ripe tomatoes and the garlicky dressing; I let them taunt me, I let them persuade me to enjoy them; I try to concentrate on the way they pop inside my mouth, their sweetness oozing from their centre; but the picture of Samuel's house burns the back of my throat with every mouthful, and the words of the newspaper report slide down my spine every time I swallow. I know I need to ask. I need to find out what he knows about Samuel, but I'm scared that he will tell me the truth, and any hope I have will be pulled from beneath me and I will fall.

Bob calls for the bill: my time is up.

'I heard Samuel had been in an accident?' I ask as I dismiss his attempts to pay with my hand.

'Yes. Terrible.' He drains the rest of his drink and glances at his watch.

'An explosion or something?' I say casually as we say our thanks and leave the café.

'Yes. So young, too. Ever meet his friend? . . . Bret something or other, left him in a terrible state after . . . well, after Samuel departed. Much better now, though, full of energy, that chap.'

'So, he's . . . he's?' Bile rises in my mouth and my throat seems to be closing around the words.

'Flew him back to Ireland, I think.'

I gasp and reach out for the wall behind me.

'Good lord, Sophie, are you OK? You're as white as a

sheet! Should I call for a doctor?' Bob asks, looking up and down the street as if he can hail one like a taxi. I blink, the scene around me blurring around the edges and then straightening itself, like a drunk in front of a policeman.

'I'm fine, thanks, just the heat. I think I'll go back to my hotel . . .' I smile at him, 'take advantage of the air conditioning.'

We air-kiss goodbye and my sandals – gold and cheap – walk me back to the hotel, where I lie on the bed, turn on my side and face the wall before I close my eyes and let the realisation of Samuel's death wash over me.

Grief slides a hand into mine like an old friend. It's been a while since we were this close and I feel myself leaning into the embrace in the same way I did when Mum first died. How easy it is to let it cover you and block out the outside world, blunting your senses and protecting you. It feels good to be back, but this time it is different because Bean is here, and my baby doesn't like it. I try to calm it, I cup my hands around my bump and make gentle shushing noises, but Bean begins to kick furiously; it wants to get out. I can't stay, as much as I long for the solitude and the quiet of grief's embrace. I have to get out.

Week Twenty-Six

Samuel

Isabella is here. Again. I'm not sure how to handle this relationship: relationship isn't the right word to use; 'thing' is more appropriate. I don't want a relationship with her and I've been trying to tell her this. She says she doesn't want one either, but that doesn't stop her from constantly turning up here. I know that maybe I should be making the most of my sight, making the most of my life. I know I said I was going to move on from Sophie, and I have, but she's still here.

When I sleep, when the murky edges of my life disappear, and the subconscious sights fill every corner of my mind, Sophie is always there: full of colour, full of happiness. And when I wake, it takes me time to accept that my life has to go on without her. Now that I've made the decision to let her go, I feel like I'm almost grieving . . . does that make sense? I know I must carry on, but it feels as though there is a hole inside me. No matter how many times I tell myself I'll learn to live without her, the way that I look forward to dreaming means that I'm not quite ready to move on entirely . . . not just yet.

'Move up, Sam,' Isabella says, wiggling herself down into the small space next to me, the sofa sinking and tilting her body towards me. 'So, your mam tells me you're off to see a show tomorrow?'

'I am.' I look over to the window. There is a splatter of pigeon shite dribbling down it.

'On your own?' she asks, the heat from her thigh making me want to move away. I try to manoeuvre myself further up the sofa, but she just moves with me. I resist the urge to sigh.

'No, Sarah is coming with me, we're staying in London overnight.'

'You should have told me, Sam, I could have made plans to come with you.'

'I don't think that's a good idea.'

'Afraid you couldn't resist me in a hotel overnight, on our own?' The tunnel encapsulates her one eyebrow arching provocatively; I tilt my vision to her mouth which gives me a slow but deliberate smile.

'It's not that, and for your information I think I could. Resist you, I mean. Isabella, it's great that you're here, and I—'

'You're not going to give me the "it's not you, it's me" speech, are you?'

'No, nothing like that, because, well, it is you.'

'Sorry?' She laughs loudly.

'Well, it's because you're you . . . you're not Sophie.'

'The infamous Sophie who hung up on you and left you twice? That one?'

'It's not like that.'

'Really, well then, if she wants you so much . . . where is she?' She begins to lift the cushion and looks astounded when Sophie isn't hiding beneath the barley-twisted edges. 'Maybe she's hiding . . .' She stands and I lose sight of her but hear her footsteps walk over to the curtains, the whoosh of the material letting me know that they have been dramatically pulled back. 'Nope, not hiding there.'

'Stop it. I know she doesn't want me, but that doesn't stop me wanting her.'

The sofa gives beneath her weight as she slumps back down.

'Well, that's just killed the mood.' She elbows me in the rib, a smile in her voice. 'I may as well take this off then.' She begins a movement that I've seen many of my exes carry out. (Do they teach this at school maybe? Is it part of Sex Ed lessons, the ones when they split up the girls and boys? We got taught that masturbation is a normal, healthy part of growing up; did the girls get taught how to take off a bra fully clothed?) Anyway, she shimmies about and the fragments of my sight catch a glimpse of black lacy bra through the opening in her sleeve. The clasp of her bag clicks as she hides the garment inside. I focus on the edges of her sleeves and feel her tuck her legs under her bottom and lean in to me.

'So, go on then . . . tell me about this show. Or you could tell me about Sophie.'

'I don't want to talk about her, but . . . ah, feck it. Do you want a drink?'

'White or red?'

'White.'

We both go to get up.

'I'll get it,' she says. Part of me wants to argue but let's face it, my life is easier if I let her. I catch sight of her back as she walks away, a film shot of her swaying her bottom and pulling her hair into a ponytail.

'Tell me why she left you!' she shouts from around the corner. I hear the fridge door open and close, and the clink of the glasses.

The telescope darkens around her figure as she walks back into the lounge; the wine glugs into glasses. I smell it, but it takes me a while to find where the glass is. Before I can worry about it, she is holding my finger and clasping it around the stem.

'Thanks,' I say. The dynamics of our relationship have changed in just a few moments. 'She left me because she thought that I had betrayed her, at least I think that's what she thought . . . I've never been able to tell her that I didn't.' The wine slides down my throat. I continue to hold the glass; the act of placing it back on the table requires too much effort.

'Betrayed her how?'

'I told her about an idea for some new software . . . God, it sounds so insignificant now.' I run my finger around the rim of the glass, which barely escapes the blackness.

'When was that? The first time she came over?' I nod, glancing up, the edges of her profile dimmed by the insatiable shadows that continue to prowl around my world. She takes another sip of her wine.

'Yeah. We never talked about work that much, stupid as it sounds when it was the reason that, well, that meant we couldn't stay together.' I stretch my legs forward, most of which the tunnel has swallowed. 'She left, just up and went in the middle of the night when she realised it would jeopardise our jobs.'

'Why didn't she just explain?'

'She couldn't, it would have meant that I would know her firm's plans to use the same software, to take it over.'

'Ah, so when she came back, you thought that she'd stolen your idea?'

'Yep.'

'Maybe she did?'

'Nah . . . she's, she's just not like that.'

'How do you know?'

I shrug my shoulders. 'I just do.'

'You don't get off that lightly, tell me why. I've just thrown myself at you in my really bloody expensive underwear which is riding up my crack as we speak.' I laugh and try not to picture the underwear riding up her crack.

'Sophie is . . . complicated. She's so vulnerable and so

independent at the same time. She can walk into a place like she owns it, she will be so confident, but then once you get to know her you would see that it is all an act. Sophie's a bit, well, a bit lost really. But after she got to know me, after that week . . . ah, it's hard to explain. I felt like I had saved her somehow. That sounds wrong, it's hard to explain what we had without sounding like a twat.'

'OK, so explain why she left you again.'

'I may have got wankered when she first came back and shot my mouth off about her being a manipulative bitch in a bar.' I rub my forehead and try to erase the foggy memories of that night. I explain how hurt I'd been, that maybe she had played me. I told Isabella how I'd rung Sophie and told her she was the biggest bitch alive. 'One of the girls I worked with was there – Kat. She wasn't with us, but I think she must have told someone that Sophie nicked the software idea from me.'

'Ah Samuel, what were you thinking?'

'You don't know what it was like seeing her walk into that meeting. She was so . . . so frigging professional and cold. She looked me straight in the eye when she told us that her company was taking us over. Do you know what that was like after the time we had spent together? I can tell you the sounds she makes just before she falls asleep . . . like little puffs of air; how she has dimples when she smiles and that they are the width of my index finger away from the corners of her mouth, how she pulls at her earlobe when she's thinking about something . . .'

'So, she left you because you got drunk and called her names?'

'No. She left me because she thinks I was the one who told Greenlight that she stole my idea.'

'Ah . . . I see. So that's it? You're just going to let her go through the rest of her life thinking that you betrayed her?'

'Sophie's made it clear that she doesn't want to speak to me.'

'She lost her job and I'm guessing her reputation. It's no wonder she doesn't want to speak to you.'

'I've tried to find her, you know how hard I've tried.'

'Not hard enough, or we wouldn't be having this conversation.'

'If our time together was as special for her as I think it was . . . maybe she'll find me?'

Week Twenty-Seven

Sophie

I sit down on the blanket opposite the fountain. The grief I feel is consumed by the memories of the last time I was here.

'I know it's not quite the same, Bean, it was dark when Your Dad brought me here, but it's just as beautiful.' I open the plastic bag, my hand shaking as I take out the sandwiches . . . one Marmite from the jar I brought with me, the other salmon from the deli. I pull out a plastic flute and pour a small bottle of sparkling water into it, taking a small sip and trying to convince myself that it is just as nice as the real thing. My fingers peel back the plastic film from the salmon sandwich and I smell it suspiciously. The smell doesn't turn my stomach . . . Bean, it seems, likes it. Tentatively I take a bite and Bean shuffles. Huh.

'So you've got Your Dad's taste buds, hey?' My voice snags on the edges of the words 'Your Dad', and I feel myself unravel. Sobs expand inside my chest and Bean kicks against me as it is crushed by the pain that I'm trying to swallow down.

The next day, I drive us to the same cinema, Bean's shifts and kicks reminding me to breathe, to eat, to live. The film is different but I sit in the same seat as he did. Bean enjoys the popcorn and sleeps while I stare through my tears at the screen.

I walk us along the tidal basin; I reach up and grab a leaf, the colour vibrant and green this time, not the burnt umber of autumn . . . I'll keep it, maybe frame it and add it to the sideboard when I get home. The image of the sideboard covered with my memories of Samuel pinches the air from my lungs. I reach out and grab the edge of a bench, my knees buckling, my body slumping against the wood.

'This is where we were when he asked me to stay, Bean, and over there . . .' I whisper, pointing to where other couples are pedalling away across the water, 'that is where he took me on the paddle boats. You should have seen his face, Bean, he was almost green with seasickness.' I close my eyes as tears fall from beneath my lids.

On the morning of the last day, the day I'm due to meet Bret, I take Bean on a trip around the city on a horse-drawn carriage. I don't care how odd I must look, this pregnant Welsh woman in her loose clothes and pale face. Instead I point out the same sights he did; I tell Bean that his favourite movie is *Die Hard*; then I laugh to myself, whispering that he also had two copies of *Love Actually*.

Bean is tired, the diner is busy, and we are squashed behind a small table at the back. My flight is tomorrow; this is my last day, and I know it is time to say goodbye. I need to find out as much as I can so that when Bean asks me, I can answer my child's questions.

Bret walks towards my table; I can see it is going to be quite a squeeze to fit him in. I smooth down the white maternity blouse which hugs my new and improved boobs tightly; beneath the table, the material flares neatly over my ever-growing bump.

'Thanks for agreeing to meet me.' I smile as he lowers himself into the chair, which doesn't look strong enough to contain him. I don't stand; my feet hurt too much. He gives me a tight smile and crosses his feet.

'Well. We were starting to think that you had disappeared from the face of the earth. Do you have any clue how many Sophie Williamses there are on Facebook and Twitter?'

I don't know how to respond to this. Questions flit behind my nervous fingers as they twist the napkin between my hands. A waitress appears at his side and he orders a Diet Coke. I shake my head and reach for the sparkling water that I have been nursing for the past twenty minutes. 'Samuel tried so hard to find you. I never quite understood why he would want to after you left him again.'

'I didn't steal his idea if that's what you think.' This comes out abruptly, and I wish I could suck the words back in. Nerves are fuelling my defensive nature.

'I know. Sammy put up quite a good defence of your honour. But he wasn't the one who threw you to the wolves, either. You broke him when you left. Do you know that?'

'I had no choice,' I reply as I feel the first hot sting of tears behind my eyes; ready to fall but not yet released.

'Yes, you did.' I flinch but he isn't looking at me; he's gazing around the room as if there are more important things on offer.

'I thought that he had . . . got his own back, that—' My words don't flow from my mouth as they should, but instead they tumble out in a disorganised heap, landing on the floor like wet washing from a machine.

'Then you don't know him at all.' He looks me straight in the eye; his words are crisp and neat, the edges sharp.

My hand reaches for my glass. My nails are short; my rings are still in my jewellery box at home now that my fingers have swollen. Bret is still referring to Samuel in the present and I take comfort in this small mistake. I take a sip of water and Bean fidgets against the coolness of the liquid.

'I know what you must think of me, but please understand that, that he did mean a lot to me. I was devastated when I heard about the accident. I cared for Samuel, very much.' Bret leans back, appraising me.

'You know about the accident?' he asks, his voice catching. This is obviously something that hurts him.

'A little. I read it in a newspaper article . . .' My words are controlled, not betraying the feeling inside. They don't give a glimpse into the way that beneath them, my skin feels like it's peeling away from my bones.

'A newspaper article?'

'In the *Washington Post.* There was an explosion, it said?' My mouth is dry and I take another sip of water.

'There was. He hadn't lit the gas hob, it had been leaking gas for well over an hour before the spark from the light switch lit it. He was thrown from the room and knocked unconscious. His neighbour dragged him free.'

'I told him that needed fixing,' I say; the phrase sounds annoyed, not regretful. 'Was he burnt?'

'Yes.' I bite the inside of my lip. I can't taste the blood; I can't taste anything other than guilt.

'Did he suffer?'

'Yes.'

'When did he . . . when did Samuel go back to Ireland?'

'You know he's in Ireland, but you haven't been in touch? What do you want, Sophie?' he asks, folding his arms across his chest.

'I want to say goodbye, I want to say sorry and I want to get on with the rest of my life.'

'And what if he doesn't want your apologies? What if he's moved on? What if he's found someone else and—'

'What do you mean, found someone else?' Jealousy and confusion battle against each other as the words erupt from my mouth.

'Samuel is recovering slowly, but—'

'Recovering?' I can feel my eyelids blinking, trying to process this information.

'He was in a neck brace for twelve weeks, so yes,' he adds impatiently, 'he's still recovering, and he is just adjusting—'

'He's alive? But I thought . . . I thought he was dead.' Euphoria and relief fill me: my body contains these emotions; I don't know how they are still inside of me, but they are.

'Dead? No. Sammy boy is alive and kicking.'

'And he's in Ireland?' I'm smiling, leaning forward.

'Yes. Look, Sophie, I know you had this thing together, but Sammy, well, he's really gone through the shit these last few months and—'

'But he's alive.' I nod maniacally.

'Yes, he's definitely alive.'

I open my handbag and rummage furiously around the insides, finding a pen and a notepad. I pass these to Bret.

'Please could you tell me where he is staying?'

Bret takes the pen apprehensively. 'I don't know the address. He's staying with his parents.'

I can see there's another reason for his reluctance to give me the address, but I need to see Samuel. He's alive. 'Please, Bret.'

'Look, I'm happy that I have been able to fill in the gaps. I'm genuinely pleased about that, but . . . things have been really hard for him. He's just starting to pull himself back together. I'm not sure that if you were to walk back into his life that it would be best for him. Best for Sam.'

Bean gives me a sharp kick that almost takes my breath away. My immediate response is to rub my stomach, but it has just occurred to me that Bret hasn't noticed that I'm pregnant. Bean is obscured by the tablecloth. I don't want Bret to be the person to tell Sam about Bean; I want to do that myself. A little buzz of excitement fizzes through me as I imagine his face when he sees me, when he sees our child.

'Please, I have to see him, please, Bret.'

'Look, how about I contact him? I'll tell him you want to see him.'

'But . . .' I think of the look on Samuel's face as I pass him the scan photo, the way his eyes will search the edges of his baby's nose, his chin, his feet; looking for the similarities in the way that I have for the last six months.

I pull the paper back towards me and write down my email and my home address, as well as my phone number.

'Sophie, you have broken the guy's heart twice. He's just been through hell and back, what kind of friend would I be if I open the doors and let you break him again? I'll tell him you want to see him.'

'But—'

'From what he's said, you've always decided the way your relationship ends. Let him decide this time, eh? You owe him that much.'

I nod slowly, knowing this battle is lost but knowing that I will find him, whatever it takes.

Week Twenty-Seven

Samuel

My August bank holiday is lost in the shadows that block out the sun. The tunnel walls have their own colours, I'm starting to notice. As the real colours from the outside world diminish, the colours of the darkness swirl and tilt. There are shadows within the shadows, marking out dancing silhouettes within the walls of the alleyway that play along with the yellows of the sun, the greens of the grass, the red of Sarah's hair that flies intermittently into my closing circle of sight.

The Distance is my best friend. In The Distance I can see the promenade in all its seaside town glory: the waves of the sea lapping against the hulls of the boats in the harbour; the buoys bobbing up and down like giant gob-stoppers and the hotels and B&Bs that stand tall and proud along the road. Those things take up the small circle of sight and fill it with parts of the whole landscape. But the parts of Ma's face, parts of the things closest to me, block out the rest of the vast surroundings and the dancing shadows play with them instead.

Michael taps along with the rhythm of the Bank holiday festivities; he jumps down steps and rolls along the path confidently as though he's enjoying it. I try to relish his enthusiasm but today is a dark day for me.

My moods seem to take me over lately. Yesterday I was happy to carry on with my life like this. I've begun to learn how to use screen-reading software to help me when I return to work. I've been listening to crime thrillers on Audible, the images in my head as good as any film that I've seen lately.

I cooked pasta, only burning myself once, and navigated the bus into town to buy some new clothes before I have to spend the rest of my life with my mam and sister dressing me. Da offered, but I'm not sure the white shirt with rolled-up sleeves tucked into jeans with creases ironed into them is the look I want to go for. At least this way, I will have a few things that are my own taste.

The boxes containing the things that were salvaged from the fire have arrived. Bret had been keeping it all in his garage: a few clothes, some pictures that Mam has already found new frames for, and my backpack that I used to wear when I went for a run.

I've joined the gym before the fist closes so I can learn to navigate my way around without the need to grab on to any Lycra-clad gym-goers. Running on the treadmill has given me a new sense of freedom. I'm out of shape, that's for sure, but it won't take me long to get it back. I need to work out regularly because I can't move around as fast as I used to. I find that I'm sitting down more than I ever would have before the accident, and Mam's constant plates of biscuits and beef-dripping-roasted-food have added a roll of soft skin that wasn't there this time last year.

I've a mint ice cream in my hand. I don't need to look at it to know it is mint-green because I can smell it; I can feel the sticky texture as it dribbles down my fingers.

'Your ice cream is melting, Mule,' Sarah tells me.

'I know. I'm blind, not fucking stupid.' As I've said, today is a dark day.

'All right, keep your hair on, and don't swear in front of the kids.'

'I didn't know they were close. I can't see, remember.' This is a lie, I know they are close because I can hear Will jangling his coins in his pocket. Clink, clink, jangle jangle. The noises are like nails scraping across the blackness, like it is trying to claw a way through the walls.

'Fine. If you want to behave like a mardy tit, then you can do it without me.'

'Fine.'

'Fine.' I hear her grabbing her things together. 'I'll see you later.'

'I won't see you,' I snap back.

'You know, lots of people have disabilities, Mule, but not all of them have to make everyone around them feel shit about it.'

She leaves. I drop the ice cream. It hits the leg of my grey shorts, bounces off and lands on to my flip-flopped foot. For feck's sake. My hands are sticky, and I haven't got a tissue. Michael slips from my hand as I reach for him; it seems he doesn't want mint ice cream on him either.

Perfect. I'm guessing I look like I've got a venereal disease oozing out of my boxers. I pull Michael up and drag him along towards home.

'Sorry,' I say as I bump into a woman whose bright blue dress fills my sight. The circle traps the swirls and colours of the fabric for a moment before I straighten my posture. I pull Michael reluctantly up the kerb. 'Sorry,' I say again. This time I've shoulder-slammed into another woman but as I zig-zag my focus on her, I realise she is pregnant. 'Are you OK?' I ask. 'I'm so sorry.'

Bret's face fills the circle of light within the screen. He looks different, not his usual perfectly toothed grin.

'Nice to see you,' I say. I wonder if I will say that once the dancing shadows take over.

'You too.'

'So, what's new?' I ask as I twist off the top of my bottle of beer. I tilt the bottle towards the screen and say 'Cheers' as Bret clinks his bottle towards the screen. He wipes his mouth with the back of his hand and smiles at me.

'Not much . . . How's things with you and . . .' he moves his head around the screen as if by doing so he will be able to see more than my camera is letting in, 'Isabella?'

'Ah, nothing, mate. I told her I'm not ready.'

'Because of Sophie?' he asks, leaning forward.

'Look, I know what it sounds like, man. I know I sound like an idiot, but . . .' I scratch the back of my head, 'I just can't get her out of my head . . . you know?'

'Yeah. I get it.'

'Thanks for sending my stuff over, by the way—'

'Sammy! Mrs McLaughlin has lost my fecking bag! Can I borrow this one of yours?'

I smile at Bret. 'My da,' I say by way of explanation. 'Yes! You might want to empty the crap out of it, I've not sorted it out yet.' I've not been keen on opening it and finding reminders of my old life. I know that there are my spare running shoes in there, and a few parking tickets . . . my old sports bottle. Everyday things that we all have, and I know it's not like I'm not going to need them again, especially now that I go to the gym, but those things all hold memories that are too raw to touch just yet.

'Jesus, Mary and Joseph!' Da storms into the room. I narrow my eyes and track his movements, following the length of his arm to see what he is holding. The brief glimpse at his expression leads me to believe that it may be poisonous. 'I thought you were joking!'

Bret begins laughing on the other side of the Atlantic.

'Your dad sounds just like you!! I "taught" you were joking!' he says, with the worst imitation of a Northern Irish accent that I have ever heard.

'Who the feck is that?' Da storms towards the screen and Bret backs away from the camera as though Da is going to grab him by the scruff of his neck.

'It's Bret, Da.'

'Oh grand, just a minute, Bret, my boy, I need to have a word with this stupid arse.' Bret nods and takes another swig of his beer. 'I thought you were joking about becoming a florist?' Bret spits out his beer and the small circle of screen is momentarily covered in what looks like a spray of piss.

'I was.' I lean forward to try and see what it is that Da is waving around in front of him. And then I realise. It's the cherry blossom that I had picked to give to Sophie. I reach out my hand and take it, filling my circle of life with the blossom that is now papery thin. The rose colours have faded into a pink ash, but as my world is filled with the tiny petals, I feel like my next breath is never going to come.

'I picked this to give to Sophie.'

'Are you listening to this, Bret? Keen sportsman like yourself, can you believe the stupid things this arse has been doing lately? Paddle boats and fecking flowers! I ask you!'

Da is oblivious to the way my heart feels like it is never going to take the next beat, that my lungs are never going to swallow the next gulp of air.

'Sammy boy?' Bret's voice is concerned and distant.

'Sam?' Da's face obscures the petals. 'Ah, I'm only joking with you, Sam.' His voice has taken on a quieter tone.

'I, I will never get to see her face again.'

'Actually,' Bret clears his throat, 'about Sophie . . .'

Da sits down next to me and starts rubbing my back like I've swallowed something down the wrong way. Bret leans forward. 'She was here, in DC . . . and she was looking for you.'

'When?' I ask, sitting up. The air has found its way back into my lungs and my heart has begun to beat again. 'What did she say?' A volley of questions begins falling from my lips.

'She, well, she looked different,' he says, taking another sip from his bottle.

'How?'

'More . . . girly?'

'Why, what did she look like before, Bret? Was she butch?' I can hear my dad processing the idea of me as a florist and Bret's description: putting two and two together and getting one hundred and four.

'More . . . relaxed,' Bret continues. 'She wasn't wearing her usual kind of clothes . . . She looked a bit more . . . a bit more like the woman you used to describe her as, rather than the version I saw in the office every day.'

'Why did she want to see me? What did she say?'

'Well, she didn't at first.' The air becomes too heavy again, my lungs sighing with the effort to breathe. 'She, well mate, she thought you were dead.'

'Dead?'

'She's only just found out about the accident, she said.'

'Where is she, have you got a phone number?'

Bret hesitates.

'No.'

'What?' The disbelief takes my voice a few octaves higher than it usually is. I can feel Da looking at me with a puzzled expression.

'I've got her address. I didn't want it to be that easy for you, mate. I wanted to make sure you were one hundred percent sure you want her. That you want to put yourself through that again, especially as you seem to be getting your shit together, and with Isabella—'

'Isabella?' My dad laughs, 'Finally come to your senses, have you, Sammy?'

'There is nothing going on with Isabella, we're just friends.'

'More fool you, Sammy. I've told you before, when you meet a girl like that you shouldn't let her go.'

'I did meet a girl like that . . . and you're right. I shouldn't let her go.'

'I've got her address . . . she's living in Wales.'

I think of how hard it was to negotiate my way back from town and the fifteen apologies I've said today. I don't want to ask, but I know I need help.

'Da . . . do you fancy a trip to Wales?'

He slaps me on the back. 'Now you're talking, my boy!'

Happiness nudges me from out of the dancing shadows. Michael catches my eye and Da farts. Loudly.

Week Twenty-Eight

Sophie

I'm waiting. I'm waiting for the minute hand to pass the numbers on the clock-face, so another hour has passed. I'm waiting for my tea to cool so I can drink it. I'm waiting for the sun to set so it's the beginning of another day: the day when he gets in touch.

My waiting is disturbed by a knock on the door.

Charlie is standing at the threshold. I haven't seen him since I walked out of his house that day, and his appearance triggers an emotion far harder than the slap across the face I had given him.

His clothes hang from his body; his hair hangs limply from his head; his skin hangs from his face: he is hanging on to life. I take a tentative step forward and he collapses into my arms. The noises he makes are primal and it's like I've just stepped into a storm. Charlie's body convulses as he tries to let go of me but then he clings on a second later.

I guide him into the lounge, to the sofa; where he curls up into a ball and continues to gasp and battle for air. I sit next to him and begin to stroke his hair. I tell him he'll be OK; I tell him he will be OK; I tell him he will be OK.

August screams outside, the clouds smashing tears against the windows as my fingers weave their way through his hair, untangling it, smoothing it down. I watch the storm outside throwing leaves across the garden, the branches bending in submission as Charlie's sobs turn into gentle snores. I stroke his hair while he sleeps, and I wait.

My back begins to hurt, Bean fidgets, and so I shift myself and quietly step away towards the window.

'I'm sorry.' His voice is hoarse and brittle. I turn around. He is still in the same position, curled up, just as Bean must be, I suppose.

'You've nothing to apologise for,' I say.

'I . . . I—' He begins to pull himself up from the sofa, but I return to his side and crouch down as best as I can with Bean in the way.

'Shush . . .' I answer. 'Let me make you a drink, OK? Then we can talk.'

I pass him his tea and he drains the cup, even though it must be scalding.

'Let me help you, Charlie.' The time for small talk has long since gone; it left the building the minute he stepped into my house.

'I don't know if you can,' he says. 'I don't know if anyone can.'

'So, let's find out.' But he just stares at me blankly. 'I'm not sure being here on your own is what you need.'

'I don't want to be anywhere else.'

'OK . . . so let's see what we can do from here to help you.' I don't know how this new relationship works, so I take my first step towards being the person who tells him the things he needs to hear, even if he doesn't want to hear them. 'You need to eat, Charlie. When was the last time you ate something?'

He shrugs his shoulders, but the way he has just drunk his tea makes me think that maybe he hasn't been drinking either.

'OK, well I think our first step is to at least get you eating and drinking.'

'I should go,' he says, looking away from me. I begin to panic; everything in me thinks that letting him out of my sight right now is a bad thing, so I use an old tactic.

'Good idea.' He looks up at me, his eyes still haunted and hurting. 'You go and have a shower and a shave, and then I'll cook us dinner.'

'I—'

'Is an hour long enough? For you to get cleaned up, or shall I do dinner a little later?'

He digests my words, he takes in my plans, but as I watch him, I'm not sure if I've pushed him too much.

'An hour is plenty.' Charlie starts to get up, his back stretching out from the broken curve that his spine had formed, but his shoulders remain stooped, his head still balancing on top of his neck, still hanging on even though his chin is almost sunken into his chest.

Charlie returns with a gently closed front door and an air of reluctant defeat. We sit and eat; I put on some classical music in the background and I fiddle with the tear-drop pendant hanging from my silver necklace. His mouthfuls are small, and he eats as though he has tonsillitis, like every mouthful that is swallowed hurts.

'Are you waiting for a call?' he asks, sipping a glass of water to help dislodge the mouthful of pasta that he is struggling with. Now is not the time to tell him about Samuel. He is barely surfacing above the grief that is wrapping around his body and squeezing the life out of him – how can I tell him that not only have I found Samuel, but that he is alive after I'd thought he was dead? How can I tell him that I have everything that he has lost? Instead I push my phone away from me, the constant refresh of the screen an addiction that I need to break.

'Oh, I was waiting for a call back from a gas company. I'm thinking of changing supplier.'

He places his knife and fork together across the plate. He hasn't eaten much, but he has drunk two glasses of water. It's a start at least.

'Charlie, I think that maybe . . . maybe you should see someone? A doctor?'

'A doctor can't bring them back.' He looks into his glass of water and swills it around in circles.

'No . . . but a doctor might be able to bring you back.'

'What if I don't want to be brought back?' he asks.

'You must do, otherwise you wouldn't have come here.' I reach for his hand. 'Let me help you.' His hand feels cold to my touch and he moves it away from me.

'My wife . . .' he dips his finger into the water and circles the rim of his glass with his finger, 'could get a can of Coke to balance on its edge when she took her hands away. It was her party trick. Jack used to think it was magic, but it was more to do with having the balance levels right.' He doesn't smile as he says this but his face changes, like the memory is hidden just below the surface. It evens out a few of the lines in his face, but it doesn't quite reach a smile. 'And she could hula-hoop.'

'Hula-hoop?'

'Yeah, she did it on our first holiday together.' The memory irons out the tension around his eyebrows, around the deep crevices that surround his eyes. 'There was a huge pile of them in the kids' area. She picked them up and began looping them around her arms and her waist; she could do it for ages at a time without dropping them, all the kids on the campsite loved it.' Pain returns, digging itself back into the muscles around his mouth, pulling back the softness that had formed in his lips. 'She did it when she was pregnant, too. She was about four months gone and Jack was only just starting to show, but the hoops still glided around her, Olivia's hips were barely even moving.' His head lifts involuntarily and his gaze is almost challenging, as if he's daring himself to look at me while he is saying the words. 'She was wearing a bright pink crop top and it kept riding up, her bump was sticking out beneath it.'

'She sounds like an amazing woman.'

'Not really, not to anyone else. But she was to me. And now she is gone and no amount of trips to the doctor can change it. No trip to the doctor's is going to change that she decided to have a drink when she knew she had to drive later. She was pregnant . . . thirteen weeks.' The words are barely a whisper, but they taint the atmosphere, their meaning dulling the light in the room, sending it scampering away.

'I'm sorry.'

'It's not your fault.'

'If I'd have known, I would never have asked you to come to the hospital.' He shrugs as if it was no big deal.

'Was she over the limit, Charlie?'

'No, but—'

'Then was it really her fault? I've had a glass of wine while I've been pregnant, lots of women do. If she wasn't over the limit, then maybe it was just an accident.'

The word 'just' fires around the room, his face changing from hurt to anger in the time I realise I shouldn't have said it.

'I didn't mean—'

'I know what you meant.'

'No, Charlie, I don't think you do. I know that "just" isn't the right way to describe what happened . . . it was an awful, awful tragedy. But an accident means that it wasn't anybody's fault. It was just an accident. Maybe you need to forgive Olivia before you can start to get better?'

I have said enough. I may have said too much, but if I'm

going to help him, I need to be the one strong enough to say the things that maybe he doesn't want to hear.

Bean is getting bigger by the day. My stomach is starting to feel larger and I catch it on the side of the table as I stand. I walk to his side and reach for his plate, but he takes my hand. The feel of his skin on mine jolts the stillness of the room. The shock of this connection holds my feet to the ground; it makes the noises inside the kitchen louder than they were. The hum of the fridge is a loud vibration; the sound of his laboured breathing fills my ears; the dripping tap is so piercing that I wonder why I have never heard it so acutely before. My hand finds his hair as he lifts his head and looks at me. I meet Charlie's eyes, which are scanning my face. They follow the shape of my nose, my cheekbones; they are watching the way I'm biting my lip; they trace the shape of my neck, and they don't stop until they reach my stomach.

His hand begins to move, a small twitch at first. His eyes look back up at mine, an unspoken request, an unspoken answer; it reaches for Bean. His is the first hand to touch my child other than a midwife or a doctor. His warmth radiates through my skin and Bean squirms beneath it. A flicker of a smile pulls at Charlie's mouth as he begins to move his head towards my stomach. I want to tell him that it is too much for me, but as I watch his smile, as I watch him close his eyes and slip into the past where he has his hand on Olivia's stomach, where he has his family in his arms, it makes me stand still. He reaches his face forward and lays the side of his head on Bean. I close my eyes and join him in this precious moment and let myself pretend that it is Samuel who has his hand around my waist, Samuel's head leaning against our child, Samuel's lips that are giving my unborn child its first kiss. I run my fingers through Charlie's hair and pretend that his coarse waves are softer and finer; as I run my hands down towards the nape of his neck and twirl his hair around my finger, I let myself believe that I'm a normal woman, who is holding the man that she loves, while he embraces me and kisses our child.

The gate outside slams and reminds me that the real world is carrying on outside, but we keep our eyes closed and we pretend that our lives are just the way they should be, that Charlie is holding his pregnant wife and that Bean and I have Samuel.

All of us waiting for our lives to begin again.

Week Twenty-Eight

Samuel

Wales is a much darker place than I was expecting, but inside I feel light. Checking in to the small B&B had been a blast from the past. The elderly lady who had probably run this since the fifties still uses a carbon copy credit card machine. Da jumped into a conversation about how things should stay as they are, much safer, these things, than all of this contactless malarkey. We were asked if we would like a full English breakfast in the morning and Da smiled; that would be grand, he replied.

While he guides me by the arm to the room, he moans about three things: firstly, that he can barely understand her accent and why does Britain have to have so many? I roll my eyes and Michael taps his way up the stairs, while Da moans about the Geordie accent, the Cockney accent, the Manchester accent and that's before we've got into our room.

Michael and I are exhausted, and so we lie back on the bed and close our eyes. With my eyelids shut, the full expanse of the room widens; I push the walls of the tunnel away and I fill in the blank spaces. Da continues to prattle on and so I picture the small window that looks on to the seafront; I widen it, making it so large that it almost fills the wall. Outside, the long stretch of Aberystwyth promenade stretches alongside the Irish Sea; I squint and wonder if I can see the coast of Ireland. The day is so clear, the sky so blue that it looks as though I could swim to its shores.

'Sammy!' My eyes snap open. The room fills with dancing shadows, the blue of the sky replaced by a heavy grey. I leave Michael lying next to me: no need to wake him just yet. 'I said when are we going to fetch this girl of yours?'

'I need to get ready, I need to have another look at the map before I go.' I close my eyes again and my world fills with light.

'You're not suggesting you're going to go into the back of the Welsh beyond on your own, are you?' I sigh and open my eyes again, leaving the great expanse of the room behind and instead accepting this claustrophobic life that I can't escape from.

'Well, I'm not very well going to turn up on her doorstep with my da holding my hand.'

'I'm not holding your bloody hand, you great big arse wipe! But you've got to admit, Sammy, it's one thing walking through our town with Mikey boy guiding the way, but it's another thing traipsing up bloody mountains. What if you get lost? You'll not be able to understand the locals even if you ask for help.'

'I can understand them just fine, stop being so melodramatic.'

'Right . . . and what kind of first impression are you going to make if you fall flat on your great behind? Hardly going to be bowled over by you, is she? If you're crawling around on your hands and knees trying to find Michael, you'll look like a right numpty.'

'Thanks for the confidence, Da,' I say, swinging my legs over the side of the bed. I shake Michael awake and he stretches into his full height. Together we walk over to the window, but Da has left his case on the floor; Michael tries to warn me, but I don't react quickly enough and we go flying over it.

'Fuck!' I shout, throwing Michael across the room. Da bends down and grabs my arm, but I shake him off. 'I can do it,' I snap and pull myself upright.

'And you want to go climbing mountains?'

'It's your fault, you shouldn't leave your shit everywhere.'

'Well, I hate to be the one to tell you, Sammy, but there will be shit everywhere on the Welsh hillsides. There's fecking sheep all over the shop.'

A small grunt of amusement escapes me, and I begrudgingly reach up to take his hand.

'We'll get in the hire car,' Da goes on, 'and I'll drive you up the fecking hill, then we can park somewhere discreet and I can tell you where you need to mind your step and what you need to look out for. Don't worry, I'm not going to go holding your hand right up to the doorstep, but whether you like it or not, you need a little bit of help, so stop being a stubborn arse. The last thing your gal will want is you knocking on her door covered in sheep shite.'

He is right. I know that I have no choice, really, but it doesn't stop me from being angry. Actually, angry isn't the right word – defeated, possibly? Although that makes it sound as though I've given up, and I haven't. Maybe there isn't a word to describe how someone in this situation feels. I'm lucky to be alive and yet I don't feel lucky. I'm grateful for the small amount that I can still see and yet I resent that that is all I get. I'm happy, but every little bit of happiness I get is tinged with something dark. Happiness isn't something clear-cut any more; it is, and always will be, smudged around the edges. I will always be surrounded by that fire and no matter how far I travel away from the big smoke, *this* smoke will continue to spread, however hard I try to contain it.

*

'Do you think you need to change gear?' I ask, as the hire car screams up the hill.

'Giving me driving tips, are we now?' He crunches the gears and they lower their aggravated sounds into a more compliant grumble.

Michael taps nervously on my knee as I look out of the window. It's like summer has stayed behind in Ireland. Rain lashes down against the windows and the bright green that I saw in the pictures before we left home is dull and grey . . . the colour of old navy ships. I haven't thought about how the changing seasons would affect me. The sun, and the colours that summer brings, filled my vision with bright tones – even if they were seen through the tunnel – but what happens when winter draws in? What happens when there are weeks and weeks of weather like this? But then I think about how long it is until winter is here. My sight will be gone by then anyway . . . Christmas trees will flicker in the shadows and the faces of the people I know will become ageless; their images will be unchanging for me. 'Jesus, will you put a smile on your face? She'll likely slam the door on you if you keep that sour expression on your mush.' The road is narrow, and the hedges scrape the sides of the window as though they are trying to clamber in to escape from the harsh elements. Autumn is starting to wake up . . . will I get to see the leaves turn colour?

'So, your woman, Sophie. Tell me what is the best thing about her and the worst thing.'

I smile at Da; this is the way that they used to start dinner-time conversation when we were kids: 'Tell me the worst bit about school today and the best bit.'

'The worst thing is that she's defensive, she keeps people at a distance . . . it's hard to break through that, it's hard to know who she really is.'

'And the best thing?'

'Once she lets her defences down, once you break through, it's as though she's been waiting for you her whole life and only you get to see who she really is. It's like winning a trophy – no, not a trophy, an Oscar? It's like winning a . . .' I rack my brain. 'It's like winning.'

I think of how she snorts when she laughs, how she covers her mouth in embarrassment, the way her hands can turn a sugar packet into a flower, the look in her eyes when she sees something beautiful. 'That's it, Sammy, that's the look you want when she opens the door,' he says before I have time to answer. 'Like a lovesick idiot. That's what'll win her heart.'

'You think?'

'Worked for your mother.'

I laugh.

'But what about when I introduce her to Michael?'

'What she thinks of Mikey doesn't matter.'

'How can you say that?' I ask, returning my gaze to the circle of countryside flashing past the telescope in shades of sage and ash. 'Of course it matters what she thinks of him.' Michael stops tapping and sits still.

'Because if she looks at you with the same dopey expression, then she won't give a flying fuck about Mr Cane here.'

Sometimes there isn't a word to describe how you feel about your parents either.

'Oh, here we go. Looks like this is the place.'

He slows down the car as I scan the view in front of me. There is an old gate closing the road, leaving a small T-shaped piece of land, just big enough to be able to turn a car around.

The engine ticks as the ignition is turned off. I can see Sophie's building from here, it's far enough away to let me see it whole. It's a low building made of old stones and a slate roof. It has a red door to the right and a black one further over on the left; two cars are parked next to each other and the light is on in one of the bottom rooms on the right-hand side of the building.

'Stay here while I have a look.'

'I can see the building, Da. I'll be OK, I think.'

'Right, well, the first thing you need to watch is that the ground is going to be really uneven. Let Mikey take his time, don't rush. It looks like the land beyond the gate has been overgrown for a while, so there are bound to be things in your path. I think it may have been cut recently, so maybe let Mikey do that swishing thing rather than letting him rock and roll; he'll get tangled up otherwise.'

'I'll be fine, Da. I'll take my time, it's not like we're on a cliff face or anything.'

'Just . . . be careful.'

'I will.'

'Well. Good luck then.'

The seat belt unbuckles, and Michael and I leave the car, closing the door softly behind us. The ground beneath my feet is spongy and uneven and with each step I take, I can hear the squelch of the mud sucking under my walking boots. I pull the zip up on my waterproof coat as the rain pounds down from the sky, the warmth of the fat raindrops the only hint that it is still officially summer. I look downwards and focus on the end of the tunnel, to the top of the gate. I follow it with my hand until I reach the rope that holds it in place; I slip the rope off and open the gate wide enough for me to walk through, securing the rope back around its neck.

Michael swings about in front of me as I try to keep my eyes focused on the ground and not towards where the warm light shines from within the house. It takes me some time before my feet feel a smoother surface, and as I look down, I can see the remains of an old pathway that has recently been cleared. I lift my chin and look at the house. I know I should be going towards the door, but the light draws me in. Michael swishes in front of me as I make my way towards that side of the house; the ground has a slight incline that I make a mental note to be aware of when I walk back down, but then I stop, because I can see her. The tunnel is trying to swallow Sophie, but she hasn't been taken from me just yet. Her face is fuller, and her hair is longer, hanging loosely over her shoulders, but there she is. I thought I would never get to see her again. I make myself take notice of everything about her: the tilt of her head as she leans forward and takes her food off her fork; how she is wiping the corner of her mouth with her thumb; the way she shuffles her position on the chair. I try to commit it all to memory. The relief and joy I feel is clouded by the other component to this scene in front of me; it's probably just a split second that I have spent watching Sophie, a split second where I felt happy before I noticed she was sitting opposite a man.

I stand still, the rain easing off as though it knows I need a moment of time without anything else to contend with. I look at him; he's got that kind of rock-star thing going on, like he's been out partying all night but still somehow manages to look the part the next day. I, on the other hand, tend to spend the next day with the shits and the shakes. They are talking about something important; this isn't a conversation about the weather or when to book a holiday. Sophie looks upset by something he is saying. From where I am, I can't take in the two of them together and so my head switches from one to the other like I'm watching tennis. Sophie is trying to explain something and then she flinches. She doesn't jump back or anything, but it's there in the sharp breath she takes; it looks as though she's trying to apologise for something. My head switches back to the man. He is watching everything she does, responding to everything she says, but then he looks away as though he doesn't want to hear any more. I return my focus to Sophie, but she is moving. She stands, and I track her face, taking a moment to adjust to her movement. I stay focused on her face as she arrives at his side; she goes to move away, but he has done something to stop her. She looks upset; her teeth are holding her bottom lip. I track downwards to where I can see she has tried to take his plate away, but he has hold of her hand; this gesture is so intimate I feel breathless. I'm trying to keep up with the different components that are making up the whole: they're eating a meal together, her make-up and hair looks natural, so this is someone she feels comfortable with. I can't describe the pain that I'm feeling as I watch her hands begin to stroke his hair, but that is nothing to how I feel as I notice how much has changed for Sophie since we last saw each other.

She's pregnant.

My mouth begins to water as though I could be sick at any minute. I watch their faces as they look into each other's eyes, a look filled with raw emotion, one that you could only show to someone who you care for deeply. His hand reaches for her stomach and he smiles. As he wraps his arms around her, I can feel part of me falling away. The part of me that thought I could be happy without her is the first to go. As he leans his head against her bump, I can feel my hopes peel away from my insides, but what strips me bare is the look of pure happiness as she closes her eyes.

Her life has started again. Her world is expanding, her life filling with new things: a new man, a new home, a new life.

I watch her for as long as I can, even though with every second that I stand there I can feel each part of me that made living inside of this tunnel bearable begin to crumble into dust.

I study every aspect of this scene, putting myself beside her, leaning my head against our child as we stand in our new home. As much as watching this is killing me, I drink it in. I store away every detail: the tear of happiness rolling down her cheek that she leaves unchecked, the rhythm that her fingers follow as they flow through his hair, the way her bump must feel to him as he rests his head against it, the joy that is written on his face as he gently kisses it. I keep every detail because I know that for the rest of my life . . . this will be what I want; this will be what I am missing.

The rain picks up its pace again, telling me to move on, that this is enough for one man to bear. Da's feet tread quietly behind me and I try to straighten my shoulders, but I can't; they are slumped, the weight of the scene in front of me too heavy for me to brush off.

'Come on, lad . . . time to go home,' he says, the pain I'm feeling cracking his deep voice as though he's feeling it too. I nod and take a final look at the life I will never have. The gate slams behind us as Da leads me back to the car and to my new life: a life in darkness.

Week Twenty-Nine

Sophie

Charlie is starting to look better. I wave through the window as he walks past, his gait giving the impression of a man in a rush, the rise and fall of his steps reminding me of the horses on a carousel. He's eating more. I rub my large stomach: I'm eating more, too. I've tentatively suggested that Charlie think about starting up a new restaurant; I received a blunt 'no' in response, but I've noticed this week that his house is clean, the bags beneath his eyes are less bruised and our meals have become more extravagant.

I look up at the minute hand as it ticks time away with a nonchalant smile. It doesn't care that with every click of its tongue, more time is passing since I've heard from Samuel. The envelope icon sleeps at the bottom of the screen, and I click my finger, waking it. Samuel hasn't been in touch. This is a fact that pulls at my centre. It toys with my balance as though I have no anchor to keep me tethered, to keep me in the place where I know my message has been passed on. He would have been in touch if Bret had told him I was looking for him. I replay the way that Bret had spoken to me – would he have even told Samuel I was trying to find him? I was stupid not to push him for more information. My fingers tap in Bret's email address, but then I stare at the screen – what do I say that will make him change his mind?

Bean shifts and fidgets, my baby's kicks taking my breath away.

'I know you want me to tell him,' I say, looking down, 'but I want to tell him myself. I don't want some American man that I barely know telling Your Dad he's going to be a father.'

Charlie taps on the door then walks in as I close the lid on my laptop. I don't know why I haven't told him about Samuel yet. I'm finding it harder with the passing of time, like when you've told a white lie and don't quite know how to get yourself out of the fallout that it causes.

'I've sorted out the spare room.' He walks over to the sink, fills the kettle and scoops coffee into two mugs.

'Oh?' I'm left wondering why he is telling me this information. 'Have you made it into an office?' I hazard a guess.

'Yes,' he answers, shaking his head as though it's obvious. Did he always answer things so bluntly? Is it one of the things Olivia loved about him? He turns his head and pours the boiling water into the cups and adds milk. 'All of my paperwork is in the desk in there, anyway.'

He passes me my coffee and slurps his noisily. 'What are you up to?' he nods at my closed laptop.

'Nothing, just, you know . . .'

'No, because you haven't told me.'

I think of the straightforward way he handles things and so jump in.

'Right, well, the thing is . . . I've found out a few things about Samuel.'

I tell him about the accident and about my trip to DC. He blinks at this. Did he even notice my car wasn't sitting outside our house for a week while it was parked in an airport car park? I continue about my conversation with Bret and how I have been waiting for Samuel to get in touch.

'Right.' He drains his cup as though I've just commented

on the weather. 'Don't forget dinner at seven. I'm cooking my favourite.'

'Um, sounds lovely,' I say, thrown by his reaction to my story.

'Why don't you wear something posh?'

I swallow my coffee so quickly it goes down the wrong way. He frowns, walks over and thwacks me on the back. I hold out a hand to let him know I'm fine, even though I'm coughing my coffee everywhere. The coughing stops and I sneeze twice. I don't know why that happens, but it always does. 'Have you got a cold?' he asks.

'No, I always sneeze in pairs.'

'Strange.'

'I suppose so.' He turns to walk away.

'Charlie?' I call. 'What should I do? About Samuel?'

'Find him, I expect.'

And with that he closes the door softly behind him as I begin to smile.

I'm wearing the only 'posh' maternity clothing that I have in my wardrobe, which is a black knee-length dress with a sweetheart neckline. The swelling in my feet has gone down and so I slip on a pair of black high heels, which until now have remained in one of the boxes from my London home, and I put on more make-up than I have for weeks. Did I really spend this much time on my make-up every day? I rub my lips together and place the lid back on the lipstick case.

I knock on Charlie's door, feeling exhilarated from my day's work and the sense of occasion that a pair of heels and a bit of make-up can bring. He opens the door wearing grey trousers, matching waistcoat and a white shirt.

'You're on time!' he announces by way of greeting. Not the standard 'you look lovely', and I can't help but bite down a smile as I follow his retreating back into the kitchen. His hair is washed, and it bobs up and down on his head as I follow him. The table is set beautifully with a silver candelabrum holding three white candles. Grey napkins are folded beneath heavy cutlery, and crystal glasses catch the light, sending shards of rainbow reflections on to the walls.

'Do you want a small glass of champagne? It's not as if you've got to drive or anything.' His words sound neutral but there is colour behind them: a flash of red, a flash of anger. He takes a large sip of his glass and gestures for me to sit down.

'No, thanks.'

He nods and pours me a glass of sparkling water. I take a sip, picturing Bean wiggling about as the cool bubbles fizz their way through my insides. 'Thank you.'

He smiles and chats about the fish market in town and then serves me a starter of squid in a chilli and ginger glaze. As we begin to eat, he begins to talk. He tells me about the first time he saw Olivia at school and how when he finally picked up the courage to speak to her, she had scowled at him so viciously that it took him a whole year to find the courage to try again. This time she let him walk her home from school, let him come in and introduced him to her parents, all on the same day. As I asked him why she had scowled at him the first time, he cleared the plates away and refilled his glass, pouring sparkling water into mine. 'Her great-gran had told her that you would only find a good husband if he was scared of you first.'

I laugh at this. 'How old were you both then?'

'She scowled at me when I was thirteen, introduced me to her parents when I was fourteen.'

'Sounds like her gran had the right idea.'

He serves us goat's cheese moussaka with fresh garlic bread and a salad filled with herby olives and pickled asparagus.

The food is delicious, but listening to Charlie talk about his family is as beautiful as anything he serves. He talks about when Jack was born and how he had his first proper temper tantrum when he couldn't fit both of his feet inside a vase. He tells me about Jack's first day at school and his first Christmas play when he had to dance around as a flame. I sip my drink and listen to his stories as he becomes more animated with every glass of champagne.

As we begin to eat chocolate brownies drenched in a chocolate orange sauce, Charlie becomes more subdued. He describes how the last words he and Olivia had said to each other were about not forgetting to get milk from the shop.

'All the things I could have said to her, and that was it. Don't forget to get milk on the way home.'

'You couldn't have known that was the last conversation you would ever have, Charlie.'

'I know . . . but I was being a dick. She'd been in a foul mood that day, moaning at me for every little thing I hadn't done around the house. I can't help but wonder if that's why she'd had a drink at her friend's . . . because she was pissed off at me for not doing the washing-up enough, not picking up my clothes from the floor.' He pushes his plate away and pours the rest of the bottle into his glass. 'I held the phone for twenty minutes after the hospital had called me. It felt like hours, but I couldn't let go of the receiver because I knew that when I did it, it would all become real.'

Brandy is poured after he's placed the cheese board on the table. I watch him drink his glass and refill it; I get up and make coffee. He's forgotten that I can't eat half of the cheese on there, I think, but by now, his eyes are blurry, and he is beginning to repeat things that he has already told me. I begin to clear up the dishes and tidy around the kitchen as I hear, again, about how he had closed the restaurant, sold the house and looked for a cottage in the middle of nowhere.

'But you . . .' he points a wobbly finger in my direction, but he is smiling, 'you were already here.'

'I was.' I smile and lean my back against the sink, my hand covering my mouth as I yawn.

'I'm glad you're here,' he says. 'Thank you, Sophie, for everything.'

'You're welcome.' He stares at the wall, thinking about something else already. I glance at the clock: it's half-one in the morning. 'And thanks for a wonderful dinner. You really should think about starting again, when you feel up to it.'

He smiles with his eyes half-closed.

'Right, me and Bean are going to love you and leave you.'

'Yes. Sleep awaits,' he says, standing up and swaying as he sees me to the door. I turn to hug him, and he holds me tight, putting his hand on my stomach and saying, 'Goodnight, Bean. Look after Mummy for me.'

I kiss him on the cheek, thank him again and go home.

Bean and I try to get comfortable, but something is bothering me, like the feeling when you walk into a room and have forgotten why you went in there in the first place. I pull the covers over us, falling into a sleep which is splintered with broken dreams.

I'm awake again but it's still dark. I toss and turn for a while. It's getting harder to find a comfortable position and Bean is awake, kicking me so hard that my breathing becomes irregular. Something about the evening with Charlie is bothering me.

I flick on the light and reach for Mum's clock: it's not long after four. The salt in the cheese has left my mouth dry and heartburn simmers in my chest. I go downstairs to get a glass of water and some Gaviscon, flicking on the fairy lights that hang beneath the counter and thinking about how Bean will be here before Christmas. The glass is refilled twice, my thirst quenched.

A sense of occasion. That's what my evening with Charlie felt like, as though there was a significance to the meal, to the stories he was telling; as if he wasn't going to see me for a while, but was going away and was trying to say goodbye.

The glass slips from my fingers. Fractures of memories splinter with the glass on the floor: his smart clothes; the sharp creases in the arms of his shirt; the immaculately laid table; his favourite foods; the way the light caught on the candelabrum – polished and prepared.

It was a last supper: his last goodbye.

No.

This can't be happening. My hands are shaking as I pull open my door, run to his house and begin banging my fist on his door, but there is no answer. Ignoring the stitch that is running across Bean, I rush back into my house and call nine, nine, nine, asking for help. My words are garbled, but the urgency is unmistakable.

An envelope by the door distracts me, and I double over Bean to pick it up. My pulse is racing. I shove it in my pocket; I don't have time to read it.

My hands are shaking with adrenaline and fear as I pull open the kitchen drawer and grab a tea towel.

Outside, the sun has started to rise. I search the ground for something heavy and wrap a rock into the towel, smashing it through his lounge window. Glass shatters into the still morning and I push as much of it away from the frame as I can, while calling out his name. I sit myself on the ledge, feeling small pieces of glass grind beneath me as I swing my legs over. As I manoeuvre myself on to the lounge floor I feel a piece of glass scrape into my thigh and I scream out in pain.

'Charlie!' I shout as I limp towards the staircase. 'Charlie!' I hold on to the banister, quickly pulling myself up the stairs, the sound of heavy breathing my only reply. My hand reaches forward, pushing open his bedroom door.

Charlie is lying on his bed; he looks asleep, but next to his bed are prescription tablets which I grab in the hope that he has just passed out from the drink and maybe taken a couple of sleeping pills, but there is no sound from the inside of the container, and the bottle of brandy now lies on its side, empty. I lean my ear against his chest and wait for it to rise, but I can't feel anything.

'Wake up, Charlie!' I shake him, his head wobbling from side to side, before I put my ear to his mouth, praying that he will make a sound. 'Come on, Charlie.' There are no tears on my face, there is no dramatic music playing in the background . . . just nothing, but then I hear it: a tiny breath. I put my hand back on his chest and feel it rise slowly beneath my hand. 'The ambulance is on its way. I'm here, Charlie, we're here.' I hold his hand and bring it to my lips. 'You'll be OK, stay with me—'

'I'm sorry—' His voice is faint and I lean my forehead against his with relief.

'The ambulance is on the way. You're going to be fine,' I repeat, my London voice finding its way into this room, filling the space with false confidence and promises it might not be able to keep.

'I thought . . . I thought I wanted it.' His speech is slurred. I prop my arm around his neck and try to sit him up but his head lolls backwards.

'Charlie? Charlie!' I scream, shaking him by the shoulder. His eyelids flicker, his eyes rolling until they come to rest on my face. 'Wake up, stay with me,' I command.

'Sophie?' Tears are rolling down his cheek. 'I don't want to die.'

'You're not going to die. You're going to be OK, do you hear me? Charlie? You're going to be OK.' I kiss his forehead and move him into the recovery position.

The envelope crinkles as I shift my weight. What words are written inside? I pull it out of my pocket and wave it in front of his face.

'What does this say, Charlie?' I sit in the space left by the curve of his torso. 'Open your eyes! Talk to me. You need to stay awake, what does this say?'

He murmurs something but the sound is like a moan, a sigh – a word filled with pain. I lean forward.

'Charlie?'

'Friend,' he says.

I run my finger under the seal and tear open the envelope. The paper is so light – the crease has been pressed precisely; it crinkles and flutters in my fingers as I unfold it – and yet the words, neatly written in blue ink, are heavy, and their meaning filled with weight.

'*Dear Sophie and Bean*,' I begin. I take a deep breath and reach for Charlie's arm. I place my fingers firmly around his wrist, putting pressure on his vein so that I can feel it pulsing against my fingertips.

'*I've tried to start this letter so many times that it seems there is no right way to begin, so here it is.*

'*I suppose the first thing I should say is sorry. I know what I have done is selfish*— You're damn right it's selfish,' I mutter, wiping the tear away from my cheek, the paper whispering inside my fist as I bring it back into view.

'*It's unfair to leave you with this mess, but please understand that it's because of the strong, wonderful person that you are, that I know I can go. I have never met anyone else in my life as strong as you. I've never had a friend who I could trust my life with, or in this case, my death.*' The word hovers, tangled in my vocal cords, barely making it out of my mouth. Charlie's eyes open again fleetingly, searching me out before they close beneath heavy lids.

'*I'm so glad to have met you both. You have given me a purpose for the last few months when I thought I would never have one again. Having you as a friend has brought meaning to my life, Sophie. I see so much of myself in you – the person that I used to be, the person that I wish I could become again – but I know that it's too late for me.*

'*This letter should have been written a long time ago. I'd begun to hope that there is a life for me on this earth, but I know now that this isn't true.* You stupid idiot, of course there is!' I look at his face and see the glimmer of a smile on his lips. I take a deep breath and continue. '*I know that you will say there is, Sophie,* – smart arse,' I say to him, leaning in so I can just make out the sound of his shallow breathing. Satisfied, I carry on.

'*I know that you will always try to fix the problem and find the answers, but without Olivia and Jack, my life has no answers. I'm sorry but this is one puzzle that will never have the right answer. I don't belong here without them.*' My chest rises as I hold my breath, then let it out so I can continue.

'*All of my documents are in the spare room. It's all tidy so it won't be difficult for you to find the red box. Inside you will find that everything is in order. I've left the house to you and Bean in the hope that there will be some happy memories made here, not sad ones.*

'*Go and find your Samuel, Sophie, With much love and thanks, Charlie.*

'Oh Charlie, you stupid, stupid man. We've already started making happy memories . . . we don't have to stop.'

The grey light in the room begins to blink with blue; it fills with people, questions are thrown at me, a mask is put over his mouth and Charlie is carried out on a stretcher.

Blood is running down my leg and pooling into the hem

of my nightie, the pain in my thigh a dull throb. As I look down at the stain, it grows and spreads like the bruises that used to creep along my mum's body. Bean and I are guided out of the house as my home is, once again, covered in a blue-lighted morning.

Week Twenty-Nine

Samuel

So, what do I do now?

I plug in my headphones and try to dull this question with some techno gym mix that I downloaded last night. The treadmill can't see either and it's able to do its job, managing its day-to-day life without any bother. So can I. My running speeds up with the pace of the music, my breath becomes shallower, my body begins to ache, but I carry on, running down this black road that leads nowhere but takes me away from here.

It's times like this that I miss DC and the life I had there. I would have talked to Bret about Sophie as we ran; I would have been distracted by my job, by the speed of my old life. But then I remember that Bret wouldn't be at work for the next few weeks anyway because he always volunteers at the sports camp during the last two weeks of August.

Sleeping has become as much of a battle as the rest of my life; the images that used to fill me with colour every time I closed my eyes are now replaced with Sophie and her new family. The picture that I tried to burn into my memory won't be extinguished.

I set the incline to six percent and push my legs through the damage that sitting around for so long has done, replaying my conversation with Sarah.

'Nothing has really changed, Mule, not since before you knew she was looking for you. You'd accepted that she was gone, that you weren't going to spend the rest of your life with her.'

'I know, but Christ, if you could have seen the way she looked.'

'Is there any chance that it could be yours?'

'No.' I didn't tell her how I had sat down with my diary, circling the date Sophie was with me in DC and counting out the weeks that had passed since. I knew if that baby was mine she would be going on seven months.

Sarah came to visit me when she was seven months pregnant with William. I remember that she was seven months because I'd laughed at her wobbling through the airport gate and asked her if she was sure she had her dates right, and teased that she couldn't get any bigger surely? She'd burst into tears and said she had another two months to go yet and what kind of greeting was that? To tell her she looked like a whale? Sarah crying was a very strange phenomenon. If only I'd known that the secret to getting her to cry was calling her fat, I'd have had her under my thumb throughout our childhood rather than the other way around. Sophie was nowhere near that size. Even if she was that big, I still would have known, deep down, that she's not carrying my child. It was in her face; it was the way she looked as she stood there holding them both; the pure joy that she was feeling is something that I'm sure could only come if you have everything you have ever wanted, and in that moment, she had it. Sophie lives her life with her 'i's' dotted and 't's' crossed; if there was any chance that child was mine, she wouldn't have just not told me; she would want everything in order, everything correct and accounted for.

'You're sure?' Sarah asked.

'I am.'

'Well, I guess that's that then.' She rubbed my knee.

'Sarah . . . when we were kids, were you always picking on me because deep down you know you were a bit, well, on the fat side? Did you do it to make yourself feel better?'

'What?'

'Fat. When you were younger.' I tried my hardest to keep my face straight as Sarah stood up.

'I was not fat. I'll give you a fat lip if you carry on talking like that, broken heart or not.'

I shrugged my shoulders but could see that I'd hit a nerve. My ten-year-old self jumped up and down like Rocky.

'Fat indeed,' she scoffed from the end of the tunnel as she left the room. I chuckled to myself. 'If you could see the size of your own arse, Mule, you'd not be saying that! Too much time sitting around stuffing your face with biscuits!'

I reach for the treadmill controls and push the incline to seven percent. I'll give her fat arse.

My legs begin to burn and my breath is hot. I can't hold back the door that I have closed against the images of Sophie and her baby and her new life. The door flies open, and whether I want to see the images or not, they play out in front of me. My legs continue to pump harder and faster, through the way she had smiled when her eyes were closed, the light reflecting on the pendant of her necklace as she leant forward, the curve of her neck and the peace on his face as he kissed her bump. The images come thick and fast. I lose my footing, the tunnel tilts on its side and I crash into the walls. Pain courses through my legs and shoulder as I slam against the treadmill base.

People scurry to my side, like ants erupting from a colony, their hands touching me, their voices asking stupid questions: Are you OK? Are you all right?

No. I'm not. I'm not OK. I'm not all right.

The end of the tunnel has become blurred and smudged;

tears are obscuring my view, like heavy rain against a window pane.

I'm fine, I tell them, but the ants are everywhere; they are surrounding me. My hand taps around the floor as the ants pull me up: I can't find Michael. Panic fills me. The ants swarm, and as I try to stand, they cover me entirely, dragging me away from Michael and the man I used to be.

Week Thirty

Sophie

Charlie is home. Charlie is alive. Kind of.

He has managed to convince the hospital that his attempted suicide was because he is obviously grieving and that it had all got too much for him. He had drunk too much, that's all. Just a drunken mistake. No. He doesn't want to die. Yes, he is relieved that his neighbour found him. Honestly. He'll be fine. They'll be in touch, here are some leaflets, phone numbers, you must go to your counselling sessions. Please contact us anytime.

'Charlie?' I call, trying hard to keep the fear from my voice every time I walk into this house. The cardboard against the window is taped awkwardly as though it's ashamed to be there, and I ignore it the same way some people would when they walk past a homeless person if they haven't got any change, almost as if they haven't seen them, but I feel its eyes on me as I concentrate on looking the other way.

'I'm in here,' he replies as if nothing has changed, as if I haven't spent the last God knows how many nights without sleep, fearing the sound of the letter box which may deliver another envelope.

Since that night I feel like I'm spending my time worrying about what I can say, what I can't. Should I ask him if he's OK? Should I pretend everything is OK when it's not?

Every action, even making a drink, is calculated. Should I offer him one? Is that what he wants, for me to be here asking him if he wants a drink, or should I just leave him alone? Maybe I should stay away, but then, should I be here in case he needs me? I can't go after Samuel yet; I can't leave Charlie alone.

The whole evening was planned, right down to the conversation we had had earlier that day when he mentioned that his paperwork was in the room that he had cleared out, but what is more worrying is the will. That you could plan your own demise in a day is one thing – we've all had days when life gets too much – but he had to have seen a solicitor days before.

The note was written before I arrived that night. The handwriting was clear; there was nothing to suggest that it had been written after he had been drinking. If I had slept through that night, he would be gone. And what's to say he won't make that decision again? What if he decides he was right in the first place and that he does want to die?

In the lounge, he is hanging a picture of Olivia and Jack on the wall. A week ago, I would have thought that this was a good sign, but the thing with living around someone who has thought about their suicide so methodically, is that you cannot trust anything they do afterwards. I watch him humming to himself and seeming to get on with his life, but I am filled with fear that he is doing this for my benefit, so I will believe him, leave him alone with the pills, or a knife in the kitchen drawer or the gas from the cooker or the rope that is in his cupboard from when he replaced the tattered one on the gate outside. These are the things that tease and worry my thoughts when I'm away from him, and I don't know when that feeling will stop, if it ever will.

'That looks nice,' I say instead, as if this is all normal.

‘I thought I should stop hiding the photos away. I’ve spent enough of the last few months avoiding them.’

‘That’s a good idea.’ I smile. ‘I’m about to make some lunch, if you want some?’

‘No thanks. I’ve just had some soup.’

I try to ignore my suspicious mind as it tells me there is no smell in the house to confirm it. ‘OK. I’ll pop in later then.’

‘Sophie, you don’t need to keep coming here every five minutes.’ He adjusts the picture and steps back to look at it, checking that it’s hanging straight.

‘I know, but—’

‘I’m sorry. For what I’ve put you through.’ He puts his hands into the back pocket of his jeans and looks at me.

‘It’s fine.’

‘It’s not,’ he answers.

‘No. No, it isn’t, not really,’ I reply, breathing out a loud sigh. ‘I don’t know what to do,’ I say honestly, as has always been his way.

‘You don’t have to do anything.’ He reaches into a brown box and brings out another picture and smiles at it. ‘I took this at half-six in the morning on Jack’s third birthday. Olivia was so cross with me for taking it.’ He turns the photo towards me. She is looking away from the camera at whatever Jack is opening and she is in mid-yawn. Her hair is sticking up on one side and she has the remains of last night’s make-up under her eyes. ‘We’d stayed up late the night before, blowing up enough balloons to cover the carpet. He loved balloons. It had taken ages for him to give any attention to the bloody presents that we’d spent a small fortune on.’

‘I can see why she didn’t want you to take that, though. I’d hate to be caught with bed hair and my mouth wide open.’

‘You’ll have plenty of mornings like that.’ He nods to Bean.

'Luckily, I won't have anyone to take the photo.'

'Well. You need to go and find what's-his-name then.'

I had been starting to feel a little more relaxed as we had been talking, but his flippancy about Samuel's name had jarred somehow. I know he knows his name, because he had told me to go and find *'your Samuel'*. I think of how convenient it would be for Charlie if I was to go away for a few days.

'I will,' I reply, 'but not now.' I look at him directly, letting him know that I am under no illusions of what my disappearance for a few days could mean. He throws his head back and laughs.

'I'm not going to try to top myself again, if that's what you're worried about.' He rummages inside another box, pulls out a wooden frame and slots the picture inside.

'That's exactly what I'm worried about.'

'I'm fine,' he mumbles as he puts a nail in his mouth and reaches for the hammer.

'Look,' I say, taking the picture frame and holding it while he begins to hammer the nail into the wall. 'I need you to tell me how to help you.'

He hammers the nail five times then reaches out his hand to me; for a fleeting moment I think that he is reaching out for help, but it is just the picture that he wants.

'I don't need you to do anything. I'm fine.'

'Well, I can't leave you alone for more than a few minutes without worrying, so you'll be doing me a favour if you just tell me what I can do to help.'

We stare at each other for a few minutes.

'Stop coming around so much, you need to trust me.'

'I can't.'

'I'll call you. When I feel . . .'

'Suicidal?'

'Empty.' He looks away then. I can see he is uncomfortable talking, but this is a big step towards him opening up.

'What . . . hungry?' I smile, making light of his sentiment, trying to let him know that talking about it isn't such a scary thing to do.

Week Thirty

Samuel

Sweat sticks last night's clothes to my body as the shivers take hold. Michael is lying next to me, his own shame and exhaustion evident as he mirrors my actions and lies motionless and prone. The sharp edges of my bedside cabinet arrive beneath my tapping fingers; the bottle crinkles and cracks as I bring the water to my lips. The house shakes with me as I hear Sarah storm up the stairs and throw open my door.

'Come in why don't you?' My voice is gravelly and whiskey-soured.

'What the hell were you thinking?' she shouts. I flinch at her volume and pull myself up. 'It is *not* OK to take my husband to a strip bar!' she yells.

'It's not like we forced him,' I answer sheepishly, even though I have a vague recollection of him trying to get us to go home.

'No, Mule, you didn't force him, but you and Da were so pissed, apparently, that he didn't think you were in any fit state to get home safely, if at all!' Sarah is blazing at the end of the tunnel, but I look away from her, preferring to fill the tiny gap of sight with a piece of my navy curtain.

'It was Da's idea and can you . . . lower your voice a little?' I fumble with a packet of paracetamol and pop two in my mouth, chasing them down with the water.

'Well, Mr and Mrs McLaughlin aren't speaking to each other this morning, so you can have all the peace and quiet in the world!'

'Samuel Rupert McLaughlin! Get your backside down these stairs right now!' Mam shouts.

'Jesus, she hasn't used "Rupert" for a long time.' I can hear the smug smile in Sarah's voice. 'You're properly in the shit.'

'Feck's sake.' I lie back down and cover my eyes with my arm. Images from the day before fill me with a wave of nausea.

I remember opening the whiskey early on and Da telling me I was too young to be drinking the doom away before lunch time.

'If you want a drink, let's go and have a pint in the pub.' He had taken the bottle from me, making me eat a sandwich with bread as thick as bricks.

I'd let him lead me, not caring who he stopped to talk to, not caring if they were looking at me with *that look* that is supposed to be sympathetic but just feels cruel. I just didn't care about anything.

Beer kept flowing. Da became louder and more theatrical, getting in drinks for old friends who came to join us. The more drunk I got, the less empty I felt. I liked listening to them talking; it reminded me of the way things used to be around here before the gastropubs took over. Most of the community would meet every Saturday night in the local pub, even if it was to pop in and buy eggs from behind the bar, or to fetch home someone because their tea was ready; every weekend this family of neighbours would stop to speak: everybody knew everybody. As I listened to their stories, their jokes, the images of Sophie and her child began to slip away. Michael led me back and forth to the toilet; even though he was a little unsteady, a little clumsier, he still looked after me.

Duncan joined us later. It had felt late, but I think it would have only been early evening. Connor, my old school friend, had come crashing through the door wearing a veil and heels. He was on his stag night; that's how we ended up in a strip club.

My memories of the club are hazy. Michael had struggled to negotiate the steep steps that took us down into a room where dark clouds covered the end of the telescope; the only light leaking through was made of purples and blues. Deep bass tones had reverberated through Michael and thudded in my ears as I stumbled towards the bar, edges of tables bumping into my sides as half-filled glasses wobbled and spilled on to the tables.

As another wave of sickness floods through me, more than one image of Duncan's hands beneath me, helping me stand, fills me with embarrassment. My vomit had landed on tables and shoes because I couldn't navigate my way to the men's loos quickly enough. The sound of my retches mixed together with the blues and the purples at the end of the tunnel.

I have memories of sounds after that, Da apologising on my behalf, telling them I was blind drunk and laughing loudly at his joke, a joke that he had told several times throughout the night. There were angry male voices and Duncan's calm tone, offering to buy them a round of drinks.

'Do you know what would have happened if that group of men had got hold of you?' Sarah asks, and I can hear the worry in her voice.

'Jesus, Sarah, let it go, would you?' I turn on my side as Mam calls me again and threatens to throw cold water over me if I don't go downstairs right this instant.

'Fine. You want to throw away the rest of your life drinking yourself to death, be my guest, but don't fucking take my husband with you.' The door slams, her feet pounding against the stairs, as she leaves us and our sickness in peace. Michael and I groan and pull the duvet over us as we slip into fractured dreams about the night before.

The dreams end abruptly as I bolt upright, cold water dripping from my eyelashes and sinking into last night's clothes.

'I said downstairs, Samuel, and I meant it.' I hear Mam slam down the empty cup and charge out of the room, her familiar powdery smell following her like an eager friend.

Da is at the table and by the fractions of his face that I can see, he looks how I feel. Mam is slamming things around the kitchen; cutlery crashes inside drawers, the lid on the teapot shaking with fear as she pounds it into place. The kitchen is rich with the smell of bacon and my stomach turns over in response.

'Sammy,' Da greets.

'Da,' I reply. Mam pushes a glass of something fizzing into my hand; my nose moves towards it, the familiar smell of Alka-Seltzer turning my stomach. I push it away from me as Mam bangs another glass down on to the table, for Da, I presume.

'Now, if you two can drink the Swan out of whiskey then you can bloody well drink that. That and a bacon butty will sort you out and then you pair of eejits are going to sit at this table and you're going to listen to what I have to say.'

Mam, it turns out, has a lot to say.

As I nurse a cup of black coffee, and force a mouthful of bacon down, Mam begins. 'Right, first things first, Samuel, you're not dying.'

'I know—'

'Shush!' she snaps, and I scan the room to find where the slight nostril snort of amusement is coming from and see parts of my sister's red hair from beside the door. 'You two great idiots, with your bucket list, are swanning around as if you've got a month to live. Sammy, whether you want to accept it or not, you need to prepare for when your sight goes, and that means applying for a guide dog and—'

'Guide dog my—' Da begins.

'Mr McLaughlin, you shut your piehole! You've done enough damage!' The table wobbles as her hands slap the surface. 'There are lots of things you need to learn to do as a blind person, Sammy. Like how to post a selfie.'

'What? I know how—'

A fuzzy image of Da laughing his head off as we staggered through the lounge replays in my aching head. He was showing Mam the selfie I'd taken of us but hadn't managed to hit the selfie mode. Instead – as Mam is demonstrating by pushing Da's phone screen into my face – is a pair of tits. Good ones, but tits nonetheless and I'm not talking about me and Da.

'Christ, woman, it was only a strip club, not the red-light district,' he grumbles.

'I couldn't give a flying fish about the strip club,' Mam answers. I've given up trying to track her movements as she bangs about the kitchen. I focus on Sarah's hair instead as she twirls it around her finger like she used to when we were kids.

'Sammy, you need to get your life together. I'm not having you living here for ever; I brought you up well enough for you to stand on your own two feet. Just because you're going to be blind . . .' her voice catches as she says this, 'doesn't mean you stop being independent. It's time to get on with your life.' Something is slid across the table and my palms skim across the plastic tablecloth and pick up a note, but I can't read it without slowly moving my head across the words: it's a number for a social worker.

'I've spoken to her this morning. She can help you so

much, Samuel, she can help you learn to look after yourself; teach you to iron, to cook . . . to get your life back.'

Sophie holding her family in her arms punches me in the stomach, shaking the bacon and the coffee.

'I haven't got a life to get back,' I say. Michael straightens his back and we walk out of the room, closing the door quietly behind us and returning to our bed.

Week Thirty-One

Sophie

I'm trying to give Charlie some space. It's hard not to keep knocking on his door. Every morning that I notice the curtains are open and hear the sound of his radio fills me with relief. Will I ever stop worrying about him?

Darkness fills the room as I balance my laptop on Bean. We huddle beneath the duvet, my fingers tapping away as I try to find anything I can about Samuel.

Stepping back into the world of social media fills me with apprehension. I set up new accounts, putting a picture of a leaf as my profile picture.

The sheer magnitude of social media settles around my shoulders like a cloak. The weight of it presses down on me, becoming heavier, and with every page I open, with every photo I scan, another patch of material is added: the smiles, the dogs, the babies, the food, the pouts, the memes, the proposals, the weddings, the lost and the lonely. How do so many of us do this, walk around with this cloak pulling us down, dragging behind us as we walk, the material itching us until we scratch ourselves raw? We try to make the cloak pretty, make it look brighter with a filter, happier with interesting scenery, look perfect as we gaze into our partner's eyes. But with every new piece of material we add, no matter how special and perfect it is, we can't stop the cloak from becoming heavier.

But Samuel never wanted to wear it. *'I don't do social media,'* he said. *'It's all fake.'*

I yawn and glance at the clock – it's half-two in the morning.

He's not there.

My search continues as I scroll through Sarah McLaughlins, but there are so many, some without profile pictures, some with, but none of them look like the Disney character he had described. I jot down a few possible matches, but as I click on them, they don't live in Derry.

The cloak is too heavy for me now and so I slip my arm out of the sleeve as I close down Facebook, unfasten the buttons as I log off Twitter and finally shrug it off and on to the floor as Instagram disappears from view.

Bean fidgets beneath my skin and I change position as a heel catches my ribcage. My baby is as uncomfortable as I am and I shift the laptop next to me, pull down the duvet, and lift my nightie. I laugh as a foot stretches out and then jolts against my tight skin, moving my whole stomach, but my baby is still not comfortable. My stomach arches up on one side; the clear outline of bone protrudes from my stomach then snaps back inside. I gasp as the bone pushes outwards again, the whole bump stretching further away from my own body than I ever imagined it could, and then the baby beneath it rolls over to the right side, the entire tummy moving from the left of my body to the right. My hand flies to my open mouth as I let out a giggle that is more shock than amusement as Bean stills, comfortable in its new position.

'Oh Samuel, you're missing it,' I mumble and then I have an idea. When, and I do mean when, I find Samuel I don't want him to miss these moments; I want to be able to show them to him. I smile, grab my mobile and choose the video camera option. I give Bean a good poke and film my tummy as our child pushes and turns beneath my skin. I replay it and sigh as I put the phone down and look at the clock again. I compose another email to Bret, but just as I have so many times, I delete it before I hit send. I've said all that I can to Bret; I'm not leaving my fate – and Bean's – in his hands any more.

I stroke my bump. My body is uncomfortable now, the weight of Bean making my hips ache and pushing against my bladder. It takes a long time before I finally begin to drift off to sleep but just as I do, I hear Samuel. *'I was never late for dinner because we could hear the bells from our den.'*

My eyes flash open and my heart speeds up; I have a clue about where Samuel grew up in Ireland, that he lived by a church.

My hand fumbles for the light switch. I know how ridiculous this is – it's one tiny straw to clutch at – but I reach for my laptop and carry on regardless, tapping in 'churches in Londonderry' into the search bar. There are a lot of churches in Derry.

But it's a start.

Week Thirty-One

Samuel

My arms find their way through the sleeves of my denim jacket; my left hand finds its way into my pocket as my right grips on to Michael. We are going to the doctor's and we are going on our own.

Our first problem is when we get into town, we need to cross the road, but as my fingers push the button and we wait for the green man, I find it hard to locate him. As the fist squeezes tighter and tighter, it is taking me longer to see the things I need to, even though I've become an expert on 'crossings'. Mam has been noting the best ways for me to cross town, making use of pelican rather than zebra crossings as most of them will have a sound when I need to cross.

'Did you know that the name for a pelican crossing comes from Pedestrian Light Controlled Crossing – isn't that clever?'

'Hmmm,' I'd replied. I don't really know what response she was expecting me to give. It seems that Mam has become an expert on all things 'blind'; it's like her new fecking hobby.

The green man flashes at me, but I don't trust it. I concentrate on the hums of the engines of the stationary cars and only when I'm certain that they are not about to move do I step off the kerb.

My life has become something I don't recognise. This time last year it was something that strode alongside me without a care in the world; that life – the one that revolved around a man who could see and was surrounded by light and life – has died, and when it did, it left me with its shadow. Michael rolls along the street and I bump into an overweight man, his heavy carrier bag swinging into my leg; both of us say sorry at the same time. The shadow skulks around me and the tunnel, it slithers across the buildings and trundles behind me as I follow the familiar route to the eye specialist building; no matter how hard I try to get rid of it, it follows me everywhere I go.

The doors into the building swing open easily and as the reception desk flickers into view, I don't see the edges of a buggy that is hiding in the darkness beneath my feet and I trip over it, regaining my balance before I fall. The apology has already left my mouth, the question if the toddler is OK happening before I have instructed my mouth to open. Apologising is becoming as much a subconscious action as breathing is. I don't need to think about it any more. The toddler is fine, no harm done – look, he's still fast asleep. I put together the small parts of the baby's face to make a whole, and I smile. His name is Henry, she is telling me. I step back to try and fit the pieces of her face together; she's pretty with green eyes and lip-glossed lips, but the look of love that radiates from her as she looks at her son knocks me off balance almost as much as the buggy had. Sophie will have that look soon; she will look at her sleeping child and will feel complete happiness: something in me changes.

The realisation is so powerful, so unexpected, that I find myself standing still, smiling at this woman, this stranger who has just told me more about my relationship with Sophie than I knew myself.

I love her enough to let her go.

Sophie's happiness is enough for me to begin my new life without her.

This realisation is like fresh air to me. I can breathe again; I can be happy because I know she will be happy.

Plans for my future begin to line up and take order as I follow the corridor. I need to take my life into my own hands. The shadow shrinks a little as I think about the changes I must make and the answers I need to find.

'Good to see you, Samuel,' Dr Morris greets me. I don't know if it is ironic that my reply is that it is good to see him too. My leg is bouncing up and down as I think of all the things I need to do. I need to get my shit together, so I can learn to be independent; I need to find a way of marking my clothes so that I can dress myself without looking like an idiot. How am I going to do that? I need to take control; I need to start living my life again.

I look up and down, to the right, to the left, into various pieces of equipment. I answer his questions, but all I can think of is how I'm going to change my life.

'When you see my finger, say now.'

'Doc? How can I make sure I don't dress like an idiot?' I ask.

'Concentrate, Samuel.'

'I am. But it's important, right? That I don't go out looking like a twat?'

'Say "now" when you see it, Samuel.'

'I will. How do your other patients do it? You know, the ones that are completely blind?'

'Um,' he sounds distracted, 'let's do that again. Say "now" when you see my finger.'

'How do they do it?'

'Well . . . I have one patient that has the store assistant cut a shape out of the label. Can you see my finger yet, Samuel?'

'No, a shape?'

'Yes, like a triangle for blue, a square for red . . . anything?'

'Not yet, oh – now. That's a good idea.'

The wheels on his chair whir as he pushes himself back.

'Where do I go to get a guide dog? Can I just go and pick one up? You know, if I take my certificate?'

He ignores my question. 'Samuel, it's not good news, I'm afraid.'

'What? I don't qualify for a dog?'

'It's not that, if we can just talk about your results for a minute. There is no other way of saying this. I'm sorry, but your vision has decreased even further.'

'I know. That's why I need to get a dog.'

'I mean, a lot more, Samuel, and a lot faster than last time we checked. I suspect, if it continues to deteriorate at its current rate, your vision will have completely gone within the next two months.'

His words sound dramatic, and if that man with the other life had heard them, I'm sure he would have been devastated, but this man, the one with the shadow that follows him around, is already prepared for this news.

'So, I'll get a dog then, though?'

'Did you hear me, Samuel? You will lose all your sight. Very soon.'

His words demand reverence, but I don't feel like I can bow to them. 'So, about this dog?'

He laughs as I grin. 'You have to do at least four weeks' training with a guide dog. It's not as easy as just picking one up; they will match you with a dog who responds well to you.'

'Oh. Right. Well, I better get going. No offence, Doc, but I don't want to waste my last bit of time looking at you. Not that you're not a handsome chap – I'm sure your wife is very pleased with herself, very pleased.'

'Now and then, Samuel, when I remember to put the seat

down, that is. Have you been in touch with your social worker?' he asks as I reach the door.

'Not yet, but I will.'

We make our way home: the green man flashes, the cars wait, Michael taps and swishes in front of me. Smells of grass and sun filter through as I follow the winding path through the trees, past dog walkers and pushchair pushers, past the sounds of kids playing football . . . then I stop. A leaf, tinged with orange and stained blood-red, floats past the tunnel. I reach out and it crunches in my palm. Autumn is on its way; I didn't miss it.

The leaf stays between my thumb and forefinger until I get home, where I transfer it inside my passport. It will stay safe until I'm ready to let it go.

Week Thirty-Two

Sophie

Steam rises from the hot water, as I rub soap suds over the heavy plates. Bean feels huge today and is creating a barrier between my body and the sink. The plate slides into the groove of the draining board slowly; I'm distracted by the tightening across my stomach, thousands of little ripples locking together like a closing fist. They've been happening a lot lately . . . the midwife says it's normal, that they are Braxton Hicks: practice contractions. I dry my hands and take a quick glance at the clock to make sure that there is no rhythm to their timings. Bean is about four pounds now, but not ready for the world yet.

'You just stay there for a few weeks, Bean, it's not time yet.' But as I say these words, the inevitability of Bean's arrival shakes me. Any time from thirty-seven weeks is normal, they say, and that is only five weeks away. I need to find Samuel before then.

I climb the stairs – my legs finding the whole process cumbersome – and into my bedroom, where I slump on to the bed and stare at the case I will take into hospital which is sitting beneath the window. It only contains my things so far: a grey dressing gown, some magazines, some lip balm and a loose black nightie which, I'm told, may get messy. I haven't really bought anything for Bean yet, just a few impossibly tiny vests and a fleecy blanket with a Winnie the Pooh motif in the corner. I haven't felt like I could leave the house for long enough, the constant worries of leaving Charlie alone keeping me close. I make my way into my old bedroom. The bare walls and the new carpet smile brightly, welcoming like a teacher on the first day of term. Bean stretches and kicks hard against my ribcage, telling me what I already know. I need to get this room ready. I need to acknowledge that Bean will be coming soon, an unstoppable force, no matter what is happening to Charlie, or how desperate my search for Samuel is, Bean won't wait for the world to be perfect.

I return to the kitchen, opening and closing my fingers to ease the ache that is surrounding my knuckles as I sit back down in front of the laptop. I smooth the paper listing the many churches I have found, the edges curling at the corners, my handwriting slanting towards the right. I've managed to narrow it down to churches with bells, but even so, finding Samuel amongst the names of these churches is a long shot. And even if I land on the right one, what am I going to do? Start walking up and down the streets, knocking on doors like Hugh Grant in *Love Actually*? I know it's ridiculous, but I can't sit here any more waiting for a reply from Bret.

His number told me he's not to be disturbed, as it has for the last week. I scribble down another street name, but the pen falls as the fist squeezes the muscles inside my stomach. I look at the clock again; there is still no pattern with the timings of these pains yet, but the intensity scares me, and for the first time since I've been pregnant, the fear of labour hangs around my neck.

The images of Derry churches shrink to the bottom of the screen as I minimize the page and bring up my email account. The mouse slides towards the new mail icon and I type in Bret's address, but this time I feel different: this time I know I'm going to send it.

I begin to write the email, but every time I do, I sound too formal. I delete the sentences several times until my fingers begin to fly across the letters; with each punch of the keyboard, with each letter that appears on the screen, emotions that I have never put into words order themselves into sentences. My fingers are typing so fast that it's as if they are in control of me and not the other way around. I tell him all the things I love about Samuel, and as I start to picture the things I'm describing, it's as though I have him back with me. My email to Bret becomes my release. I'm not bothered that if he shows it to anyone over there I will be a laughing stock; I don't care if he reads it and thinks I'm crazy . . . I just write. When I have finished, the email is pages and pages long and it is riddled with typos, but I don't care. I need this man who, right now, has my happiness in his hands, to know just how much I love Samuel.

My shoulders ache and I rotate them a few times to release the tension, then hit send. I have been sitting at the computer all afternoon. I push back my chair and decide to go for a shower.

Bean is asleep, and the pains have stopped. I watch the droplets of water glide over my body, over my enlarged belly button; my tummy bigger than I ever thought possible. The words of the email cascade over me just as the soft drops of Welsh water do. I think about the morning I had dressed in my armour, trying to rid myself of my mother's image, and the memories of Ian. I think about how much I have changed since that day, how amazing it is that those words could be written by a woman who had the most important thing to her ripped away in the most violent and darkest way imaginable. I close my eyes, the water tumbling over my eyelids as I picture Ian's hands around Mum's neck and think about the way he had squeezed, the way his hands would have been contracting around her throat. The same action that will help me bring life was the action that took it away. He took from both of us; he killed two people that night, destroying the woman and the girl. That girl died, the awkward girl who wanted to be accepted by everyone, to be liked, to be everybody's friend; that girl was reborn into a woman who locked herself away from the world, and instead, lived on a threshold, with one foot grinding her heel on the past, and the other striding into a future that was as cold and barren as the place she was trying to escape. Until one day, her foot got stuck. Until one day, a tall Irishman held out his hand and tried to help her step over the threshold into a new world that shone and glittered and beckoned her. But he couldn't hold her tight enough, couldn't keep her in the world with its light and joy, and she tumbled backwards, back into the world in black and white.

I think of the words of the email fluttering above me, flying over my cottage like a flock of starlings flying over hills and mountains, fluttering across the oceans, over forests and lakes, over towns and cities; the words written by a woman who now stands eagerly peeking around the doorway, desperate to take his hands, so he can lead her into the light.

Week Thirty-Two

Samuel

It's better to have loved and lost than never to have loved at all . . . Isn't that what they say? I take the leaf from inside my passport. I turn it over and the symbolism of this action makes me smile: I'm turning over a new leaf.

My life is going to carry on without Sophie.

I want her to keep her happiness, keep her freedom and to have a life that isn't locked into a world with canes and guide dogs and darkness.

My fingers find the catch on the window. The breeze holds the promise of bonfires, even if the sun is still hanging on to the frayed edges of summer. I hold myself still, listening to the sounds of my family below me, and bring the leaf to my lips. I kiss it, say goodbye to Sophie and my old life and let it escape from my fingers, letting it find freedom.

'I said keep your eyes closed!' Sarah laughs as she guides me down the stairs.

'You know I can hardly see anyway, right?'

'Oh shush, careful, there's a stray plastic soldier. Bloody child, I keep telling him to stop leaving things where you might step on them.'

'Ah, he's just a kid.' The air is thick with the smells of a Sunday roast and something else that takes me a moment to place. Realisation dawns as I hear Noddy Holder's declarations about it being Christmas.

Sarah pushes open the lounge door where an eruption of voices shout, 'Merry Christmas!' A cold glass is shoved into my hand; I bring it to my nose and smell Bailey's and Cointreau, our Christmas morning family drink.

I'm overwhelmed for a second by the kindness of my family. They all knew I would miss the sights of Christmas this year . . . so they have made sure that I don't.

Fairy lights blink at the end of the darkness and as I piece together the fragments of sight, it is filled with metallic baubles and plastic bells, cuddly snowmen and alarmed-looking Santas. The air is filled with the dusty smell of tinsel and the syrupy tang of the peaches Mam warms in the same pan she has always used; adding chilli flakes, cinnamon and nutmeg just as Granny used to. The peaches are one of those traditions that belong to us, that I would have liked to pass on to my own family. I remember my teacher, Mrs Chidlow, asking me what my favourite part of Christmas dinner was, and I had said Mam's peaches. My face had pinked with the sniggers of my peers as Jessy Gold made gagging sounds. Mrs Chidlow had frowned at them but patiently explained she didn't mean pudding. I had tried to tell her that the peaches were for tea; it was important that she understood this because it was the first year I had been allowed them. Mam had always batted me away whenever I asked for them before: 'Not for you, Sammy, they're too spicy; maybe next year when you've grown an inch more.'

But that year, I had grown two inches. Mam had ruffled my hair: 'Go on, Sammy, help yourself to some peaches. They'll put hair on your chest.' The spoon had felt both heavy and delicate as I scooped out a golden segment, flecks of chilli and peppercorns glinting at me with forbidden promise. My teeth sank into the flesh, the chilli burning my tongue, making my eyes water. 'Have it with a piece of that Cheddar,' Da had winked at me as he loaded a cracker with cheese and crowned it with a small piece of peach. It was like a rite of passage and I had copied Da's actions, right down to the way he sliced the cheese into four small triangles, facing away from each other like points on a compass. Da had stood up, refilling everyone's glasses, his paper party crown fluttering and crinkling with every tilt of the bottle, with every lift of a glass. Exhausted kids – cousins, second cousins, third cousins – stared blankly with heavy eyelids at the family Christmas film, their tired, podgy hands still dipping into boxes of chocolates, but I . . . I was eating peaches.

I scan the room until I see Mam and Da standing next to each other, the darkness framing my parents as they stand grinning and laughing. My throat contracts as I try to swallow down the emotion that is hot and dry, that prickles at the back of my eyes and is only satiated once the tears can fall freely; I never thought I would see Christmas again.

Fake Christmas is filled with laughter, too much food and too many drinks. We play charades, which I win due to the extra points I insist on receiving, claiming that I'm at a disadvantage. I don't let on that I can guess most of the clues even if I can't see them all, since the more wine that is consumed, the louder and more competitive they become and I'm able to guess the film, the book, the play from the things they shout out.

Mam leaves the decorations up for the whole week, the kitchen cupboards filled with Twiglets and Quality Street, which makes my trips to the gym even more of a necessity. I drink deeply from my bottle of water, throw my gym bag in the corner and follow Michael to Da and Isabella's voices in the lounge. Bret is laughing loudly from across the Atlantic as Da tells him about our Fake Christmas and Bret tells him about a fat kid who was at the summer camp who looked like a chipmunk.

'Ah, here's the lad himself.' Da claps his hands together. 'Bloody odd, those Yanks. Sports camp, I ask you! No offence, Bret.'

'None taken, Mr McLaughlin.'

I hear the rattle of the tea tray as Mam clatters cups on to the table. Sarah is crunching a biscuit behind me; I get a waft of something minty and adjust the image in the shadows to include a mint Club.

My arms fold over themselves as I lean over the back of the sofa and say a quick hello. Sweat continues to cling to my clothes and the wrinkle of Isabella's nose as she turns her head towards me (and thus, my armpit), lets me know that I need a shower.

'Can I catch you later, man? I need a shower.'

'Pfft,' Da begins, 'nothing wrong with the smell of a man's honest sweat. The sweat of the Irish working man is mixed in with the bricks and mortar that makes this city great.'

'Doesn't make it smell great, though,' Isabella interrupts, 'although I have to say, I always liked the way you smelt after a . . . good . . .' she gives me one of her looks that tells me her line of thought is anything but innocent, 'hard workout.'

'Blood and sweat of the Irishman, I ask you! What about the blood and sweat of the Irish women? Hmmm?' Ma asks.

'Exactly, Mam, what makes this city great is the ability of its women to push great fat Irish men's head out of their—'

'Sweet Jesus, Sarah love, that'll do. That's enough to put a man off his digestives.' I can almost hear Sarah's eyes roll as she collapses into the creaking springs of the armchair.

'Actually, mate, I need to speak to you now if that's OK?' Bret interrupts.

'Oh, um, sure,' I reply. My hand leads me along the back

of the sofa. I know it will take me two steps forward until I'm clear of the arm and then my body follows the feel of the material rubbing against my leg.

'I've had an email. From Sophie,' he says, leaning forward towards the camera, the screen filling with him.

'OK. But listen, Bret, I'm . . .' I drain the last of the water and crinkle the plastic in my hand, 'I'm letting her go. It's time to move on, you know?' The good thing about losing your sight is it becomes easy to ignore the tell-tale glances of your family. I can tell that my da is looking at Isabella, but I can also tell that Bret is wearing a serious expression.

'You might change your mind when I read you this. It's quite private, though. Would you rather I read it to you on your own?'

'Nah, you may as well read it while they're here, they'll only listen at the door anyway.'

'Bloody cheek!' Da says. The crunch of a piece of paper scratches against the speakers as I lean back and let my head sink into the soft cushions of the sofa. I feel Isabella's thigh pressing against me and I can smell the tea cooling in Da's cup.

'*Dear Bret . . .*' he clears his throat, '*It's been over a month since I saw you in DC and I can only come to the conclusion that you have decided not to tell Samuel about my visit. I know this, because the man I know and love would never have left things like this between us, because he is a better person than I am. He is just . . . better.*' Isabella's hand has slipped into mine; it's cold and small, yet she holds on to mine firmly. '*I have never had anyone look at me the way that he does, like every gesture I make is miraculous, as though he can see the good inside of me in every movement I make. I never thought it was possible to be looked at that way. He made me feel like I wasn't made of skin and bone, that I was made of something pure and raw and beautiful. I have always felt broken. I've always* been *broken; made of fragile things, things that could be trodden on or crushed or thrown away. But he could see something in me that I never knew was there, and the way he saw me changed the person I am.'*

'Lovely way with words, she has Sammy, lovely way,' Mam gushes.

Bret continues: '*I want to tell you how much I love him, but love isn't a big enough word. Love is only four letters: it isn't enough to describe the feeling that bubbles up inside me when I listen to him talking about his family; love isn't big enough to describe the way I feel when I recognise his traits as well as my own, like how I know he never nods just once, but always in threes—'*

'Oh, you do do that, Sammy,' Sarah butts in. 'You always nod three times. We used to think you had a twitch, didn't we, Mam?'

'We did, love, you're right.'

Bret carries on, ignoring the ramblings of my family. '*How I know that when he falls asleep he always sighs five minutes later—'*

Isabella snorts, 'You do . . . a bit quicker than that if you've just—'

'How do you know that, love?' Mam asks. 'Oh. I—' I feel Mam wafting her hand in front of her face.

Da laughs. 'Mrs M, you do turn a lovely shade of pink when you've put your big foot in your mouth!' Bret shuffles the paper. 'Sorry, Bret lad, you carry on,' Da instructs.

'Where was I? Right; *he always sighs five minutes later, and that he always eats his crusts before he eats the rest of his toast.'*

'That's because you always wanted curly hair, love.'

'Shush!' Sarah commands.

'*Love doesn't tell you how I feel when I lean against him, how he fixed me when I didn't even know I was broken. I know what you must be thinking – if you loved him that much why did you leave him . . . and the answer is simple really. I didn't want to break him. He was already perfect: he had no cracks; nothing about him was brittle or damaged; he was everything I wasn't. And then he met me, and I began to chip away at him; tarnished something that was pure and fun and caring and loving and instead made him angry and bitter.*

'It's taken me a long time to find the person who is writing you this email, to be able to accept that what he saw in me was there after all. It was just that he was the only one who could see it.'

Bret stops for a moment. 'Do you want me to carry on?'

I nod; words lie unspoken on my tongue for the moment. Sophie's smile as she held her family lingers and confuses me.

'I know now that I won't break him. I know this time I can fix the damage; I know this time that when he looks at me, I won't feel like an imposter. He was the only person who could see me when I was blind to everyone else.

'There is something else I need to tell him, Bret, something that will hurt him, but I know he will understand, I know he will be able to forgive me, but please, I'm begging you, please give him the chance to choose me.'

The paper crackles as he folds it, and the air stills, waiting for my reaction.

'When did she send it?' my voice asks. It feels detached from me; my mouth has a life of its own. The rest of my body is numb, but the words jump from my tongue and my voice carries the words around the room and across the world.

'Last week. I take it you changed your mind about seeing her after we last spoke?'

'No, no . . . I saw her all right.' My mouth opens and closes, and the words escape without my control. 'She's pregnant.'

'Whoa. Whoa . . . pregnant? Is it yours?'

Isabella shifts towards me and Da lets out a long sigh.

'No,' I say, not wanting to let that tiny bit of doubt unravel what I know I need to do.

'Are you sure, because I'm no mathematician, but man, it

could be yours, couldn't it?' Bret leans forward, optimism clinging to his words.

'She, look, it doesn't matter. I saw her with another man, she was happy; they were a family.'

'Then why would she send this?' I hear Bret wave the piece of paper about and see a glimpse of white flashing across the screen.

'I don't know.'

'Maybe she's having problems with the new one, Sammy?' Da adds.

'Sam,' Isabella says softly, 'that doesn't sound like an email from somebody having a few problems. It sounds like an email by somebody who is in love with you.'

'It doesn't matter, she . . . I saw . . . you don't know the way she looked. She was happy, in this little cottage with her perfect man and her perfect bump, and you heard what she said!' My body has caught up with the words that are forming, my heart is screaming, my lungs are gasping, and my eyes are full. 'I was the only person who could see her.' My voice rises. 'SEE her! How can I walk back into her life, back into a life where she doesn't need to be fixed – isn't that what she said, Bret? How can I go back to her when *I'm* the one that is damaged; *I'm* the one who can't be fixed, *I'm* the one who can't fucking see her! She wants me to choose her, that's what she says, right?' I get no response. 'Right?' I repeat. 'Well, I am choosing her. I did see her, and I know that her life without me will be better than one with me in it. I'm the one who will be brittle and damaged. You've seen how many times I fall or bump into things – how can I do that to her? She's better off without me.'

'But if you just speak to her? Let her explain?' Isabella pleads.

'Have you got a phone number, Bret my boy? If we can get this girl on the phone we can sort this out right now.

What do you say, Sammy boy?' Da claps his hands together as if Mam has just told him it's pie and chips for tea.

Michael pulls me up, and I hold on to him for support as I tell them, 'This is my decision.'

'What if I talk to her? Tell her about the accident, tell her about your sight?' Bret asks eagerly.

'No! If what she says in this email is true, if she loves me that much, do you think she will stay away if she knows about the accident?' I take a deep breath. 'I don't want to talk to her on the phone because I know I'm not strong enough to stay away if I hear her voice, if she tries to tell me I'm making the wrong decision . . . I'm not strong enough to do what is right . . . do you understand?' I say, wiping a tear away. 'I'm choosing to save her.' Michael pulls me across the room, away from temptation and away from the hurt.

'Sammy!' Da shouts.

'Sam!' Isabella calls but I slam the door behind me.

Week Thirty-Three

Sophie

I went into town earlier this week. I'd battled my way past buggies and hand-holding pensioners, past passive-aggressive voices of arguing couples, until I found myself inside a shop.

My hand stopped at a rail that had an outfit of the softest and palest beige and white stripes, with a small embroidered bunny popping out of a pocket in the middle. My fingers followed the tiny arms of the outfit and stroked the ridiculously tiny trousers that ended inside small, rounded pockets where Bean's feet would be cocooned. Bean shifted and stretched in approval. I looked at the sizes: 0–3 months, newborn, tiny baby . . . surely they were all the same thing? I held up the outfits but could see there was definitely a difference in size.

'Can I help?' A lady with a neat brown bob and smelling of powder and violets was smiling at me, reaching for the clothes. My first real shopping trip for Bean and I was already stuck. I looked at the wall behind her, where boxes of monitors, stair gates and car seats stood in a smug and organised array. I didn't have a clue about any of it. Sweat rose up through my pores as the sound of rushing water filled my ears, dampening the sounds of the shop.

'Yes, um, yes, please . . . I don't know which to get.' I laughed at myself nervously, trying to ignore the sense of panic I was feeling. My mouth was dry, my hands shaking.

'Not to worry, that's what I'm here for. When are you due?' She nodded towards Bean.

'The thirteenth of November,' I said quietly.

'Not long now, then?'

'Seven weeks.'

'I was five weeks early with my first . . . Everyone told me it would be late, being my first, but my Rachel is as impatient now as she was then. You're carrying a lot in your back, aren't you?' I had no idea what she was talking about, but I nodded and smiled.

'If I were you, I would go for the newborn size. No point in getting the 0–3 unless you're expecting a big baby, and you're only small yourself . . . what about baby's daddy?'

'Oh, he's tall.' I thought of the way his feet stuck out of the end of the bed. 'Very tall.'

'Let's hope baby has your frame then, eh?' She nudged me in a way that admitted me into the club. The women-who-have-children club. The club where women talk about leaking breasts and pureed food, dilating cervixes, epidurals and stitches; that brag about first steps and sleeping patterns.

'Um yes.' I smiled.

'Is there anything else that you need?'

I looked around the shop.

'Yes, I, well, the thing is, I need everything really. I haven't had a chance to buy anything yet and . . .' My words trailed off as the lady's eyes widened.

'Right. Well then. Let's get you and that baby—'

'Bean,' I said proudly.

'Bean, sorted.'

Since my trip to the shop, I have pushed aside the growing pile of invoices and receipts that I need to check – a lot of my new clients tend to keep paper records of their businesses which makes my life harder – but I have left them inside their respective folders and have decided to start on the nursery. My lounge is filled with boxes of deliveries. I've chosen a video baby monitor, an electric breast pump, a steriliser, a changing bag, a changing mat, a changing table . . . the list goes on and on. Charlie shouts a hello as I reach the paintbrush up towards the last of the cornice; lemon paint trickles oily colour over my fingers as I replace the brush in the tray.

'I'm in the nursery!' I shout as I reach for the roller and begin sweeping lemon over the wall in bold arches. He bounds up the stairs and frowns at the step ladder.

'What? I'm being careful.' I smile down at him as I continue swooping and diving with the roller.

'There's another delivery downstairs.'

'Oooh, that's the cot!' My feet lower themselves down the four steps of the ladder which Charlie has decided to hold on to even though the ladder is perfectly solid-footed and stable. He takes my hand as I step off, and I replenish the roller and continue my assault on the walls.

'Do you want me to help you put the cot up?' I pause my rollering for a split second; I can't subject him to that. He's doing well but I'm always conscious of what could send him spiralling back into the place with trips to the solicitor and neatly written letters. I know he has been going to counselling; every Thursday morning I look out of the window and check that he is getting in his car, that he is still going, that he is trying to get better.

'No thanks, I'm good. Ouch!' I gasp.

Charlie is at my side, the creases in his forehead puckering with concern.

'What is it?'

'Nothing . . . just Braxton Hicks.'

'Hmm. Give me the roller.'

'What? No!' I say indignantly. 'I'm fine, Charlie, I like doing this. It's therapeutic and it stops me from checking my phone for emails and missed calls every two minutes.'

'Still nothing?'

'Nope, nothing from Bret, not even a response from the advert I put in the *Derry Journal*.'

'Desperately Seeking Samuel?' he asks with a small smile.

'Still,' I answer him as I try to crouch down but give up and sit on my bottom instead, legs spread wide apart, taking the roller in two hands and pushing it against the wall above my head. My phone rings but my fingers are covered in paint and so I leave it to go to voicemail.

'I've got to go into town . . . my appointment has been changed.' I don't need to ask which appointment he's talking about, and I'm relieved that he is going even though it's Tuesday, not Thursday. Charlie is a person who likes routines.

The roller hovers over the wall.

'Please don't go back up that ladder before I get back?'

'I'll be careful.'

'I mean it, Sophie . . . you'll make me hurry and then I might drive recklessly,' he adds, raising his eyebrows at me, knowing that he has won the argument by playing a brutal card.

'That is so unfair.'

'I shouldn't have to say it. You should just listen in the first place.'

'Fine. I'll finish this wall and then I'll stop for a bit.' I rub my hand on my back where a pain is radiating along the base of my spine and around the front of my stomach. 'OK, Bean, I'll take a break.'

The water in the sink changes into banana milkshake as I rub the paint away and clean the brushes, my fingers swollen and my nails tipped with paint like a DIY French manicure. I wave goodbye to Charlie through the window and wince as the pain in my back burns inside my skin. The calendar tells me it's the nineteenth of September. I flick the kettle on and reach for my phone. There is a missed call and an answerphone message from an unknown number. My fingers glide over the screen as the kettle fills the room with steam and the switch clicks off.

A robotic voice begins: 'This is a message for Miss Williams. I'm calling about your energy supplier, did you know that you could be paying more than you should—'

I know it's just a sales call, but I slam my phone back on to the counter, my eyes filling with tears. I pour the hot water over my tea bag; the tightening across my stomach reminds me that I'm running out of time to find Samuel and I bite my lip in frustration. The phone rings again and I snatch it up, ready to give the robot what for, but instead I hear an American drawl asking if this is Sophie Williams.

'It is . . . Bret?' I ask, my heart hammering inside my ribcage.

'Hey, I'm sorry that I've not been in touch sooner . . . I was away and then, well, then I spoke to Samuel.' Bean kicks and turns as I walk to the table and sit down, my legs barely able to keep me standing. The late evening sun paints the walls pink as I try to calm myself enough to process his words which float around the empty kitchen.

'You've spoken to Samuel?' I ask. My face tries to react appropriately, but it doesn't know whether to smile or frown. My hand runs over Bean rhythmically, calming my own feelings by calming my child's. 'Is he OK? Did you send him my email?' Words fall from my lips like notes from a piano; a melody of rise and fall and desperation.

'He knows about the email but there is more I have to tell you, but before I do, you have to understand that Samuel doesn't know about this, OK? He doesn't know I'm ringing you. After I told him about our lunch I—'

'When did you tell him?' I sit forward. He takes a deep breath.

'The day you left.'

'But that was weeks ago!' My hand goes to my mouth as I realise what this means. Samuel doesn't want me.

'It was. Look, Sophie, he came to find you, but . . .' My hurt is followed with optimism, each emotion pushing the other aside, jostling for their moment in the spotlight. 'He knows about the baby, Sophie, he knows about your . . . new life, your new relationship. It broke him, Sophie.'

'But how? When? I haven't seen him – nobody really knows me here!'

'He saw you through the window; he saw you and your baby and your new . . . friend.'

'Charlie?'

'Er, yes, if that's his name? Samuel was, well, in bad shape when he got back to Ireland. But he's moved on. He wants you to be happy with your baby and . . . Charlie.'

'He wants me to be happy raising my child without him?' My volume rises as I try to make sense of what Bret is saying.

'Yes. He could see that you were happy. He wants you to be happy.'

'But that doesn't make sense! I want to be happy with him! I want him to be part of my baby's life, I want him to be there when Bean takes—'

'Bean?'

'I call my baby Bean.'

'Oh.'

'I want him to be there when Bean babbles first words, first steps, I want him to take Bean to the park, to push our child on the swings!'

'Hold on a minute, Sophie. Are you saying that Samuel is the father?' This sentence numbs me. The dust mites catching in the bruised light slow their movement and stay suspended, motionless. The clock ticks loudly and determinedly. This isn't how it was meant to be. This isn't how I wanted Samuel to find out, but I have no choice.

'Yes. Samuel is Bean's father. Charlie is my neighbour, my friend. Nothing more.'

'But Sammy said it couldn't be his. He saw you holding each other, he said you were happy.'

'Happy? I haven't been happy since the day I left DC, since he betrayed me.'

'Betrayed you? Sam never betrayed you. He tried to give up his job so you could be together, but they wouldn't release him from his contract until after the investigation.'

I think of the look on his face as he closed the door behind him that morning, the way he had looked distracted as I stood in front of him wearing his shirt. Had he just given up his career for me?

'Bret, I need you to give me Samuel's phone number and address.'

Another pain tightens my insides and I blink back the tears that have formed at the intensity of it.

'I can't, Sophie. I told you, he doesn't know I'm calling you. There are other things, things I can't tell you about Samuel, he's not the same person.'

'Please!' I rub my lower back again. 'Please, Bret, I have to speak to him.'

'I'll speak to him, I'll try to explain. I promise. I'm sorry, I, I'll be in touch. Take care.'

'No! Wait! I want to tell him, just give me his number. I can explain . . . Please, Bret, please.'

But the line is already dead.

Week Thirty-Three

Samuel

'Sweet Mary and Joseph! Samuel, would you look at this!'

Mam pushes a newspaper in my face, the crisp sound of the pages as they crinkle and bend. The inky smell of today's headline mixes with the smell of bacon coming from the kitchen. My fingers grab it. I feel its familiar weight; the fold of the spine is firm and sharp in my hands as it presses the contents at me: read me, read me, read me. But I can't. The fist is almost clenched, the end of the tunnel is almost closed, brick laid upon brick is blocking out the fading light.

My guide dog application is being processed and I'm looking for my own place to live so I can begin my new life, but Sophie's words keep pulling me away and I'm not sure I'm strong enough to do the right thing.

'What is it that I'm supposed to be looking at? I can't see a fecking thing except a headline made up of an N, I, N and a T, oh and is that . . . what is that?' My arms stretch the paper away from me, 'An arse cheek?'

'Arse cheek, I ask you! It's a woman's shoulder, but that's not what I want you to look at.'

'Mam, can you just . . . read it to me? I can't see enough of it.'

'Oh. Right you are. Sorry, I thought . . . never mind.' She takes the paper from me. 'It's in the classifieds:

> *Lost: Six-foot-two Irishman who answers to the name Samuel McLaughlin. Has weak shins and enjoys show tunes. If found, please return to Sophie Williams – phone number below.*

I can't help but smile.

'What have you got to say for yourself now?' She is standing opposite me, the paper rolled up in one hand, the other on her hips. My mind does this sometimes, filling in the parts that I can't see.

'There's nothing to say, Mam, you know why I can't go to her.'

'I know why you *think* you can't go to her – ah shite, the bacon's burning. Hold on, I'm not done with you, not for one moment!' I turn my head and catch a glimpse of her blue cardigan as she marches out of the room. Weak shins and enjoys show tunes. *That's still me, isn't it?* I try to ignore myself. The room is hot, and I need to get out. I shake Michael awake: let's get some air.

It takes me a while to zip up my coat, but I've done it. Mam is thankfully distracted by the smoke alarm going off and I can hear her running up the stairs and waving the tea towel at it. My hand finds the doorknob, turns it and I follow Michael as he rolls over the threshold, taking me along the path towards the park. Drizzle has begun to fill the air, fine misty drops that aren't rain but aren't fog either. I stop to pull up my collar, apologise to the dog that I have just bumped into, and to its owner, who gives me an over-the-top 'not to worry, you're doing a grand job' reply. *Grand job? All I'm doing is walking to the park.* I tell myself off: the guy is only being kind; he doesn't realise that talking to me like a child taking its first steps makes me feel like an idiot.

The past week has been hard. I've had to try and ignore myself constantly and that isn't easy. I mean, you live with yourself, don't you? Michael warns me that there is a rise in the kerb; instinctively, I lift my foot a little higher to avoid falling again. I tell myself to shut up, that she will be better with her new chap. *How do you know he's a decent bloke? He looked like a rock star, for Christ's sake! He could be a rock star for all you know, shooting up heroin and snorting cocaine out of super models' belly buttons. What do you know about her new man?* I trust her; she wouldn't start a life with just anyone.

I stop at the crossing. My hand slides up the damp post, the drizzle cold and wet against my palm, until I find the button and then press it. I wait for the beep. I glance through the gap at the end of the tunnel; I can see there are cars waiting. I turn to see part of a wiper slicing across a windscreen, hear the rumble of the engine and the ticking of an indicator before I step off the kerb. My thoughts of Sophie take a breath as I cross the road. How will I ever do this once my sight completely goes? *Will you get a hold of yourself!* Here I go again. *You'll have a guide dog; you'll have family and friends who will help you; you'll have Sophie. She would help you.* I don't want her to help me; she will have enough to deal with; she'll have a baby. Don't you remember what Sarah was like with William? She was a total nut job – do you remember how crazy she looked? *But you could help each other.* How could I help? I could fall over with the baby in my arms; I could knock boiling water over it.

The path takes me beneath tired trees where the drops of water occasionally slide off the leaves, into my vision, and plop into muddy chocolate-milkshake puddles.

Are you going to let a little disability get in the way of spending the rest of your days with the love of your life? I look up at the trees and down at the milkshake puddle, moving my eyes about so I can make a full picture. You call this a little disability. *Well, not little, but, OK, I get you. I know things will be difficult, but if Sophie loves you the way she says she does?* What's your point? *Well, my point is . . . what are you doing standing in the rain with a face like a slapped arse?*

I have a point.

'And just where have you been?' Mam yells. Michael skulks behind my leg as I take off my coat.

'I went for a walk.'

'On your own?'

'No, I took Michael.'

'Michael! Mr McLaughlin, will you speak to your great eejit of a son and tell him to ring that girl right this minute!'

'Can you just let me take my shoes off first before you start having a go at me?' I groan as I fumble with the laces which have wound themselves into a knot. Sliding my hand down the wall, I lower myself on to the bottom of the stairs and begin to try to loosen the lace.

Do you see what I mean? How the hell could I look after a baby when I can't even undo my shoelaces? *Get Velcro.*

'Right, Sammy, I'm going to pour us both a stiff drink and then we're going to have a chat with your man Bret. He called while you were out in the wild and he says he's got something to speak to you about.'

My damp towel lies on my bedroom floor and I bend to pick it up. It's just another of the many things that I've had to change about the way I act. A damp towel on the floor means I can trip over it; a pair of keys falling out of discarded jeans pockets means instant foot trauma; and a glass placed too close to the bedside cabinet can mean either a face full of cold water halfway through the night or a bleeding sole.

I pull out a pair of black jeans – I can still see that much – but Mam has started to cut out shapes in the labels to help me become familiar with the shapes and colours before the bricks are cemented in. My wardrobe door is mirrored, and I take a step back, so I can look at myself . . . well, small parts of myself. *See? You still look the same*, I say. *She will still love you.* I reach for Michael and tap him against my foot. Not any more, I say, and throw him on to the bed.

Sarah is coming up the stairs. It's strange how I can recognise people's steps, and I wonder if I've always been able to do it – instantly know which member of my family is approaching my door. Her knock is gentle but insistent.

'Yep,' I say as I pull the T-shirt over my head.

'Bret is on Skype.'

'I'm coming.'

'Hey,' I say, sitting down in front of the screen.

'Hey, how's things?' His accent is strong, but his voice is uncharacteristically hesitant.

'Good, man, good . . . you?' I ask. There's a smell lingering in the room, something from my childhood, but I can't quite place it.

'Goooood,' he replies. 'I've, um, buddy, I've got something to tell you and you might want to hear it on your own.'

'On his own! Bret my boy, I thought we had an understanding!' Da leans forward. Sits back. Then leans forward again. Mam is sitting next to me, her knee bouncing up and down.

'It's fine, thin walls in this house anyway.'

'Right. Well. The thing is, well—'

'Spit it out, Bret!' Mam shouts. I jump, and picture Mam frowning at my startled expression.

'Right you are, Mrs McLaughlin. Well, I, I rang Sophie.'

'Feck's sake!' I shout. Other me smiles knowingly. 'I told you to leave it alone. It was my decision.'

'Oh, shut your piehole!' Mam says and hits me with a tea

towel. At least I think it's a tea towel; it could be one of her giant pairs of beige knickers that I've seen hanging over the radiators for all I know.

'I had to let her know that I'd had her email, mate – what kind of man do you take me for?'

'Quite right, Bret, I bet your mother is as proud as punch of you.' I can practically hear her nodding knowingly.

'Just get to the point, will you?' Sarah says. I hear the pop of a bubble; the smell had been eating away at my senses and I couldn't place it until then.

'OK.' He lets out a long stream of breath. 'It's yours, Sam. The baby is yours.'

Mam gasps and claps her hands together. Da clinks his glass against mine which sits untouched on the table. Sarah blows another bubble and I . . . well, I smile. My face smiles in a way that I don't think it ever has before, each muscle happy, each piece of skin tingling with joy. I've never felt this way before. I'm having a child, a child that I might be able to see.

'The dude you saw through the window is called Charlie; she said he's just a friend. Nothing more.'

But it doesn't matter who that other person is any more; what matters is that I get to Sophie, that I see my child before the last brick is set and the tunnel is sealed for ever.

AUTUMN

Week Thirty-Four

Sophie

The midwife extracts a printout from the machine next to the hospital bed and smiles.

'Right, so, you're what? Thirty-four weeks plus six?' I nod as she scribbles this down on the printout. Tomorrow I will be thirty-five weeks pregnant. Already. 'No sign of contractions, Sophie, and you're not dilated at all yet. Just very strong Braxton Hicks, by the sounds of it. I think it's best if you go home and get some rest. Storm Russell is set to hit later, they say, so my advice to you is to make the most of a night in front of the telly. This baby is staying put . . . for the meantime, at least.' She smiles and unbuckles the elastic belts around my tummy, then takes one of the round disks that have been monitoring the tightening across my stomach. Typical. The last few days, Bean has been convincing me that I'm in labour, and then the minute I get to hospital the pains vanish. I've kept the pains to myself. Helen was supposed to be coming over today, but Caitlin has a sickness bug and I didn't want her to worry.

Back at home, I turn off the engine and stare at the house being beaten by the beginnings of a storm. Leaves fly around in angry mobs, taunting and hurling themselves against the windows and the doors; plants huddle in their baskets and cling to each other in tangled fear. I retrieve my case from the boot and struggle towards the front door.

Already, the spilt ink of night is oozing across the sky, its blue-black stain spreading across the pinks and yellows. Charlie left for London yesterday and it seems strange seeing his half of the cottage filled with darkness.

'London?' I had asked when he nonchalantly dropped it into the conversation yesterday.

'Yes.' He added some basil to a bubbling pot of tomato sauce.

'And you've decided now is the time to go?' I pointed to my stomach. He disappeared behind the steam rising as he drained the pasta.

'Your sister is coming tomorrow, isn't she?' I nodded and he placed a bowl of grated Parmesan and some garlic ciabatta on the table. 'Good. And do you promise not to climb any ladders or do any kind of decorating while I'm gone?'

'Promise,' I replied through a mouthful of pasta, but I couldn't ignore the worries that were chasing his decision, snapping at his heels, asking why is he going? What is he going to do there? Is he planning to come back?

'Why are you going to London, Charlie?'

'I've got to visit my mum. Alzheimer's.'

'I'm sorry.'

'It's OK.' He sits down. 'It's a good home and Mum thinks she's in her early twenties most of the time. They think it's a chest infection, so she might have to go into hospital.'

I swallowed down the pasta, praying that she'll be OK, and that Charlie doesn't have anything else to cope with.

I flick on the lights, hang up my keys and run my fingers through my hair.

Receipts from the folder look at me reproachfully and I yawn in response. Tiredness pulls beneath my eyelids and I long for a hot bath and, for the first time in a while, a glass of wine. But the pile frowns and wags its finger, so instead I pour a glass of Diet Coke, flick the TV on and begin to plough through the paper-clipped piles of invoices and room service orders from my newest client. My head shakes at the scribbled-down room reservations, my eyebrows meeting my hairline when my fingers pull out a load of pink carbon-copied receipts. Carbon copies? I didn't even know they still existed. I have a very vague recollection of a strange hand-held machine that you made a backwards and forwards motion with, which copied your card details, but I can't quite believe that this B&B is still using it. I'm going to have to bring them into the right decade if I'm going to be their accountant; this is going to take too much of my time. The TV shouts for my attention: an eighties comedy about a blind man and his deaf friend. I laugh, then sigh as I look at the pile of paper on my table. I push it to one side, grab a packet of popcorn from the cupboard and head into the soft lights of the lounge. A scrape of a lighter, the flicker of a flame and the scented candle releases its vanilla and jasmine into the room as I sink into the sofa. Bean sleeps and I pull the soft fleece throw over us and spend the evening laughing at an eighties double bill before falling asleep.

Week Thirty-Four

Samuel

Sophie's mobile number rings inside my head, the numbers repeating themselves over and over like a jingle for an advert, but I can't call her. The things that need to be said can't be spoken into a microphone, my voice and meaning dampened by the distance across the Irish Sea. I need to tell her these things face-to-face; she needs to see me in all my incapacitated glory before she can make a decision. She needs to meet Michael. Just a few more days and I will be with her; once I've had my guide dog appointment I can go. I would have cancelled it, in fact I tried to, but Mam wouldn't hear of it. I've already been on the waiting list for weeks and to cancel would have jeopardised my chances even further. I'm going to be a father, and I need all the help I can get to be able to cope with that and my diminished sight.

'A golden key can open any door,' Mam told me knowingly.

'What the feck is that supposed to mean?' I asked, throwing my hands in the air.

'Watch your mouth, Samuel!' She clipped me around the back of the head, the same way as she did when I was five. 'It means if you're going to convince Sophie that you can be a father, that you are still the man she fell in love with – even if you're as blind as a bat – then you're going to need a golden key. And for you, it comes in the form of a guide dog.'

I don't have to wait any longer. I've smashed the guide dog appointment – the dogs agree that I'm blind – so I'm going to Wales today.

'Jesus! And I thought your room was bad enough when you were a teenager.' Sarah walks past me; her familiar perfume is stronger today and her hair smells freshly washed.

'Can you see my phone charger? I can't find the bastard anywhere.'

'The sooner you get out of here, the better. You're starting to sound like Da. Here.' She takes my hand and puts the charger inside it. 'Why didn't you ask Mam to help?'

'Are you serious? She'd have me packing for a fortnight in the Alps followed by a trip to the desert, you know what she's like.'

My hand follows the edges of my backpack and I throw the charger inside.

'Have you rung the airport yet? The news says some flights might be delayed because of the storm.'

'I'll ring in a bit; can you see my green V-neck?' I pick up my washbag, feel its contents for deodorant, toothpaste and a toothbrush, and throw it in. I can still see glimpses of these things but I'm starting to rely on my other senses; it's quicker than trying to get myself into the right position to see.

'It's already in your case. Look, you ring the airport and I'll help you sort out this mess. You might be able to find the right clothes, but you couldn't fold things properly even when you could see.'

Sarah puts my phone on speaker and I ask for Belfast airport and the dialling tone connects.

'Hello, I'm just checking on my flight, it's the seventeen thirty-five to Cardiff?'

'I'm sorry, sir, all flights are currently grounded due to the high winds.'

'For how long?'

'We expect things to return to normal by tomorrow, but you should prepare for long delays. I'm sorry.'

'What about flights to England?'

'All flights are grounded for the next six hours. Your ticket will be refunded, of course.'

'Can I book another one for tomorrow?'

'Certainly, sir, just transferring you to ticket sales.'

'Never mind, I'll do it online,' I say and hang up. 'Shit!'

'Calm down, it's only a day. Why don't you ring her? You've got her number.'

'No. I need to see her, if you know what I mean; I need to be able to tell her everything face-to-face. It's not the type of conversation you have over the phone.'

'Fine,' she sighs, 'have it your way.'

'Sammy!' Da shouts.

'I'm blind, not deaf, Da.'

'The flights have been delayed.'

'Yeah, I know, I've just called.'

'Not to worry, eh lad? I've booked us on another flight for tomorrow night. The forecast says Storm Russell should have fecked off by then.

'OK, thanks, Da.'

'Now then, Mrs McLaughlin is off to the chippy, what are you having?'

I try to sleep, but Russell has been dragging wheelie bins down the street and pulling trampolines from gardens. Now he seems to have got bored of our street; he kicks a tin can out of the way, slams a gate and moves on to the next road. I feel along the edges of the braille watch Mam bought me for fake Christmas and 'see' that it is half-three. My hand reaches out for the bedside lamp out of habit rather than need . . . will I still do this once the tunnel is blocked up for good? I speak quietly into my phone and ask Google to connect me to Belfast airport.

'Hello, I was wondering if you could tell me if there are any flights to Cardiff scheduled, or is everything still grounded?'

'I'm afraid all flights to Cardiff are still grounded. The storm is set to hit the west coast in the next few hours.'

'How about England?'

'Most flights to southern parts of England will hopefully resume shortly.'

'Could you tell me if there are any spaces on any flights that are leaving in the next couple of hours?' I ask. I stand up and begin taking off my pyjama bottoms – or lounge pants, as Mam has recently discovered they are called.

'Just one moment while I connect you.'

'Hi, are there any spaces available on any flights to England in the next few hours?' I feel my watch again and reckon I could get to the airport and checked in by breakfast time.

'There are spaces on the EasyJet eight-fifteen flight to London Gatwick, or the—'

'I'll take it.' I give out my card details while stepping into my jeans. I can't risk taking the later flight with Da; the storm might still be raging.

The taxi arrives. I shrug on my jacket and leave a quick note to Da telling him I've got an earlier flight and to wish me luck. At least I'm hoping that's what it says. I'll send him a text when I'm on the way.

The airport is filled with boredom and impatience. Children are crying, couples are arguing, and strangers are snoring on awkward chairs, using bags for pillows.

I book a train ticket from Victoria station to Aberystwyth

while I wait for my flight, and Michael takes me to a fast-food restaurant. I replay the images from last time I was here: the woman in the orange puffer jacket; the tired children swinging from their parents' hands; the garish holiday shirts; the crumpled business suit hanging over the arm of an overweight man. I replay the scene on a loop because all that the end of the tunnel lets me see are flashes of colour passing me by.

The flight is quick, the airport busy and Michael has a hard time guiding me through the sea of disgruntled travellers, their bags on wheels tackling Michael whenever they can, but we make it.

The Gatwick train waits for me with a hiss and a grumble and carries me to Victoria station. My shoulders rock with the motion of the commute as the wheels grind beneath me on the track, but the familiar hum inside the carriage does nothing to cushion the panic that begins to prickle inside. I start tapping my pockets for my phone. I check the seats around me, I ask for help, but nobody can find it. Then I see it: sitting next to the sink where I had washed my hands after the toilet in the airport. I see it flashing with a picture of Da's face as it vibrates off the porcelain and smashes on to the grey-tiled floor.

The train arrives at Victoria, exhaling the doors open while Michael and I wait for the tribe to pass; the surge that smells of sweat and irritation, of perfume and half-eaten sandwiches. The tribe that I once belonged to – the pushers and profanity users, the suits and briefcases and newspapers folded into armpits, their hands clutching designer coffees and twiddling with earphones – pass me and Michael by, and move on as one.

We descend the train, and I lift my bag on to my shoulders. I stumble and apologise my way to the connecting train to Aberystwyth, where Michael demands everyone's attention until people notice him, give him a wide birth and avoid his gaze.

My stomach churns as the journey continues. I've been travelling for what seems like days and the constant movement is making me nauseous. I stare out to where Russell is having his final outburst over the circle of Welsh hills, their summits hidden by the heavy mist and rain that slides down the windows. The man next to me smells of fried onions and something similar to the inside of my gym bag.

'Good afternoon, ladies and gentlemen. Due to local flooding, this train will terminate in Mak-hun-hleth, I repeat, this train will terminate in Mak-hun-hleth. Apologies for the inconvenience and have a good day.'

Machynlleth. Where the feck is Machynlleth?

Week Thirty-Five

Sophie

The nursery calms me as the storm starts to retreat, the empty wind replaced with heavy rain, and I sit in the feeding chair which slides rhythmically on its runners. The lemon walls have taken on a creamy tone from the small night-light that hangs above the changing table; it caresses the soft, oatmeal-coloured carpet, while the mobile above the cot hangs motionless, a smiling crescent moon and a cluster of stars dropping their shadows on to the soft blankets below, blankets that are waiting to enfold a sleeping baby.

Sleep has hidden from me and as the sun tries to lift itself up from beneath the metal-grey sky, my stomach tightens. I lift my maternity nightie and watch my skin harden. Time is running out: I'm thirty-five weeks pregnant today and there is nothing I can do to stop the weeks from passing; they hurtle towards me.

I'm scared. I keep thinking of red-faced women screaming from TV shows, their faces contorted in pain; people in the background shouting for clean towels and hot water. I wish Samuel was here. That he could be with me, that he could be like the men in those shows, rubbing my back, wiping my brow with a cool flannel.

Light from my phone screen flashes and Helen's face grins up at me. The sounds of her kitchen rush into the nursery:

the gurgle of water being added into the sink; the sound of the fridge door being closed; the unloading of the dishwasher. Helen always has me on speaker, always multi-tasking, never still.

'Hi.' My voice betrays me; it is hurt and defeated and broken.

'Soph, are you OK? Is it Bean? Has something happened?'

'No, yes. Oh, it's nothing really, but I'm scared, Helen. I'm scared of going into labour and I can't stop thinking about Samuel. It's stupid, but I keep thinking about silly little things, like how he smiles when he talks about his family in Derry and the chip in his front tooth and . . .' I sniff and blow my nose again; the moon and the stars on the mobile quiver and swing. 'Ignore me. It's just my hormones.'

'Chip in his front tooth?' Greg asks from somewhere in the kitchen.

'Yep,' I answer. 'Illegal tackle from the other team.'

'You'll find him,' Helen puts in.

'And Irish?'

'Yes, Greg, keep up.'

I can imagine Helen rolling her eyes at me, the way she does when Greg says something stupid.

'Tall?'

'Jesus, Greg, what does his height have to do with anything?'

I hear the oven door being opened and I imagine her there with a tea towel in her hands, lifting out a tray of sausages and hash browns; slamming them on to the counter and reaching for her cup of tea while Greg takes a bite out of a sausage, blowing hot steam out of his mouth as he does. I wish I was there right now, with them.

'Well, the thing is,' I hear Greg say, 'there was a tall Irishman with a chipped front tooth here a few months back.'

'What?' Helen and I say in unison.

'Why didn't you say anything, for God's sake?'

'I didn't want to upset you. He said he was a journalist, he was looking for Helen Yates.'

'And what did you tell him?'

I think of the way that Helen had rebuilt her life after Ian had been sentenced. The way she had journalists hounding her, asking for interviews, for quotes . . . did she always know he was a killer? One time they had parked outside one of her friends' houses to take pictures of the killer's daughter. No wonder Greg didn't say anything.

'What do you think I told him? I said I didn't know a Helen Yates. He was—'

'Was he hot?' asks Helen. I'm standing now, walking around the thick carpet, the new smell rippling through freshly laundered bed linen.

'How should I know?' I imagine him throwing his hands up in the air. 'I suppose he was good-looking if, you know, you like that kind of thing?' Greg sounds uncomfortable.

'Helen, hang up the phone. I'm sending you a picture, I'll call you back on my landline.'

I bring up a photo of Samuel from Dropbox, one that I had taken when he wasn't looking: a beer bottle just meeting his lips, his mouth grinning at a Charlie Chaplin film I had made him watch, his hair thick and sticking up on one side. My fingers are trembling as I try to forward it to Helen. I hit send as Samuel leaves my room and lands inside Helen's kitchen. Slow down, Bean tells me with a stretch as I pick up the phone by the side of the bed and call Helen back. Could it be him?

'It's him, Sophie. Samuel was here.'

'Let me speak to Greg.'

'I'm here,' he says.

'Tell me everything, tell me everything about him.'

I smile as Greg tells me that he had been funny, my hand

resting on Bean who has begun to doze. He tells me about how Samuel had fallen, and then he hesitates.

'Sophie . . . the thing is. Well, the thing is, he was . . . well, he was blind.'

'Blind?' I whisper.

'Yep. White cane and everything . . . he said he'd been in an accident.'

'An explosion,' my voice says. I want to put into words this strange sensation that I'm feeling, that makes my skin cold, and steals the saliva from my mouth. My stomach twists and turns as it tries to escape the reality that I'm facing. I think of the way he always noticed small things: a piece of fluff on my shoulder; a drop of mustard that had escaped from the corner of my mouth; the colour of my eyes. He had a way of describing things, almost poetically sometimes. He had laughed when I said that to him: *Don't let my da hear you say that*, he had said as he leant over me, kissing me gently. I close my eyes and concentrate on the darkness that fills the room and it scares me. Images of our time together in Washington pass by like flashes of lightning, splitting the darkness in two: his hand as he took the umbrella from me; the picnic; the cinema; the leaf; the meeting; his expression as he closed the door behind him the day I left him . . . and the taxi ride to the airport without him by my side.

I open my eyes and wipe the tears away: he's going through this without me.

'I can't believe you didn't mention that Hot Irish Samuel was here!' Helen shouts in the background.

'I'm sorry, Sophie, I had no idea,' Greg apologises, his voice muffled by the rub of his beard.

'You weren't to know,' I say, but wishing that he had said something. I wish that he had, because Samuel could have been here, could have shared this pregnancy with me.

'What are you going to do?'

'I'm going to email his friend in DC and I'm going to tell him that I know that Samuel is blind and that if he doesn't give me his address then I'll fly over to Washington and get it from him myself.'

'But Sophie, you're thirty-four weeks pregnant – maybe you should wait?'

'Thirty-five, and I've waited long enough. I'll call you.'

'Wait, Sophie!' But I have put the phone down.

Bret's email drops into my inbox almost immediately, giving me an address in Derry.

I ignore Bean's protests as I find myself on all fours again, reaching for the case that hides beneath my bed and lifting it on to the mattress.

The room is filled with action, with leggings and loose tops, with face cream and deodorant, with make-up and hairspray, with giant knickers and socks and shoes and The Book. It takes moments to pack, moments to book a flight, moments that pass without me noticing the cramps in my stomach have begun to find a rhythm.

I call for a taxi, but the storm has caused flooding. It'll be another hour, the woman says. I glance at my watch: I still have time; I'll still get to the airport in time. Just. I pack my pregnancy notes inside my handbag and tidy around the cottage, picturing his face when I show him my home. My new knowledge of Samuel takes a little time to catch up with me, reminding me that Samuel won't be able to see my new home. This thought distracts me, it stops my hand from wiping down the kitchen counter, it stops me from moving. How will he cope without being able to see? How will he be able to do his job? The new knowledge kicks me into action. I fold up the dishcloth. He will be OK. Billions of people lose their sight; we just have to find a new way of living, that's all.

I smile to myself, pick up my case and reach for the door. But the case is suddenly too heavy in my hand; the room is filled with a sound from my mouth – not my voice, just a breath, a breath that is struggling to find a pitch. The walls sway; the room is off balance; clear lines smudge as my leg muscles surrender, losing their strength. The doorway leans on to its side, the carpet rushes up towards me and everything that surrounds me is swallowed into darkness.

Week Thirty-Five

Samuel

'What in God's name were you thinking, Samuel?' Mam shrieks down the phone. I can almost hear her crossing herself in the name of the Father, the Son and the Holy Ghost.

'I had to get here as soon as I could and—'

'Did it ever occur to you to wake your father? To wake me and tell me what you were up to? Anything could have happened to you, swanning around London. You've got to have eyes in the back of your head when you're in a city like that, and your ones in the front don't even work. I could string you up, so I could!' I put my ear closer to the phone receiver and grimace at the man behind the counter frying fish and chips, hoping he can't hear Mam's voice through the payphone.

'Mam, where's Da now?'

'Where do you think? On his way to find you and your Sophie, that's where! And why haven't you answered your phone? Is it too much to let your mother know you're alive and well?'

'I've lost it.'

'Fecking marvellous!' I wince at the sound of Mam swearing. A sign that I'm well and truly in the doghouse.

'Mam, I've got to go, the taxi is here.'

'Wait! What do I tell your father?'

'I'll call once I've spoken to Sophie, OK? Has his flight landed yet?'

'I've not heard from him, like father like bloody son. And God only knows how he's going to find his way to the train station!'

'He'll be fine, Mam, he's a big boy. Look, I'll be in touch. Tell him to check in to the same B&B as last time and I'll meet him there later. If his flight has only just landed, he'll be at least three hours away. By the time he gets to Wales I'll hopefully be able to introduce him to Soph.' The taxi driver hits his horn.

I slide into the back seat of the taxi and give Sophie's address. It takes me a while to find the seat belt; to hear the click as it locks into place. The driver sighs his impatience. *You think you're in a hurry?* I almost say. I've been stuck in this town for four hours, the roads only now beginning to clear.

'Quite a storm, eh?' His accent lifts and turns. 'Where by you?'

'Sorry?'

'Where do you live? Ireland, is it?

'Yeah, Derry.'

'Storm Russell hit it bad, I heard. Seems to be easing off now, though?' he replies, each sentence sounding like it's a question. He leans forward and looks through the window. 'Are you visiting?'

The word 'visiting' sounds like visit-ten. I smile and shake my head. How did I not recognise Sophie's accent? 'I was wond'ren,' she had said, 'why did you stop playing rugby?'

'I wasn't good enough. I was better lining up numbers than standing in a line-out,' I'd replied as she rolled on to her stomach and traced the bump in my nose with her finger.

A bump in the road brings me back. 'Yes, I'm visiting my girlfriend,' I answer.

'Ah, love, is it?' I notice that the 'it' sounds like 'et'. I laugh and nod.

The rhythmic sounds of the wipers and the heat inside the taxi are lulling me to sleep, my eyelids drifting down, my head leaning back against the headrest.

'Ah, no can do, mate.' My eyes fly open, the darkness filling my vision. The taxi has pulled on to the side of the road. 'The road across is still flooded. Pain in the behind, this dip is, they need to get on and sort it. If you were coming from Aberystwyth way, you'd have made it.'

I look up at the sky and fate shrugs its shoulders. *Really?* I ask it. *Is there anything else you can do to stop me from getting to her?* 'We're not too far away, though, if you fancy a bit of a hike?'

I stare out of the window, the edge of the tunnel, wet and grey, and the pinprick of vision is filled with greens and browns. Michael taps against my leg. *This is a bad idea*, he says. I hear the driver's seat belt unbuckle and the fabric in his denim fold and crease. The air in the taxi changes as he notices Michael.

'I can take you back to town if you want? No extra cost. Best wait it out, I reckon.'

'How far away is it, you know, if I walk?' I ask, ignoring Michael who faces the other way.

'About twenty minutes, give or take. Just follow the path, but it's quite a steep incline through the trees, and the ground—'

'I'll be fine. I've been here before.'

'But—'

'I'm not completely blind, this is just for a bit of help.' I smile my reassurance at him. 'Honestly, I'll be grand.' I don't tell him that I can hear the turn of the cement mixer as another brick has been picked up, slotted into the wall, tapped into place: the tunnel is almost closed. What if I go back, and by the time I return, the last brick has been laid, the tunnel sealed? She's twenty minutes away. I can do this.

'How much do I owe you?'

I sense that he is giving me a discount as he tells me the amount, then waits patiently while I fumble with my wallet and pass him the fare.

'Let me give you a hand up the verge so you're on the right path, eh?'

'That would be great,' I say reaching for the door handle and dragging up a reluctant Michael.

'We'll be fine,' I say to him through gritted teeth and haul him out of the taxi.

Week Thirty-Five
Contractions Forty-Five Minutes Apart

Sophie

It's almost dark. This is the first thought that crosses my mind. Not *I'm alive*, not *Is Bean safe?* But *It's almost dark*. Strange how in the most dramatic of scenes the simplest words come to mind.

The noise from my mouth has disappeared and been replaced with the lilt and dip of my breathing. I take tentative steps into the kitchen, one hand holding Bean, the other holding the counter, my balance still wavering between left and right. I listen to the stillness for a moment, my hand reaching for the light switch, and I blink against the brightness. My legs shake as the tap fills the glass with water, my knuckles white and tense as I hold on to the counter. I drain the glass and glance at the clock. I must have missed the taxi: a car horn, a knock on the door, the door being slammed, edges its way into my subconscious, but it could have been any day, any time. I'm not sure what is real and what I've made up. I can't have been unconscious for long – the sun was already setting when I had picked up my case.

'Bean?' I ask, my eyes filling and overflowing on to my cracked lips. 'Bean?' I ask again. I refill the glass and drink it faster. *This will wake you, come on now, Bean, wake up.* But Bean is tired.

My hand grips the banister and my stomach tightens. My feet wait until the pain has passed until I take the next step.

The bathroom wall is cold beneath my palm; each step feels more difficult than the last. Cold water rushes from the tap into my hands, splashing my face, awakening my senses.

'Bean?' I ask again. But my baby is fast asleep.

The mattress sinks as I sit down and reach for the phone.

'Charlie? It's me.'

'I know. Caller ID.'

'I, I think I've fainted. I'm fine, but . . .' My voice is detached and reassuring; his reaction is not so detached, but it is reassuring.

'Are you OK?'

'Yeah . . . I think so. I'm a bit shook up, I was going to the airport—'

'No. No airports. I'm on my way home, I'll be there as soon as I can. Is Helen with you?'

'No, she couldn't come. Caitlin is poorly.'

'Call the hospital. Now, Sophie. I'm hanging up.' I call the hospital and tell them what has happened, my voice breaking.

Bean hears me: what is all the fuss about? It stretches and turns. Relief cascades down my cheeks and pools beneath my chin.

'Is baby moving?' the midwife asks.

'Yes.' I gasp with relief.

'And how do you feel? Have you lost any blood?'

'No, I think I'm OK. I think I just fainted. I'm still having a few Braxton Hicks, but they have been happening a lot in the last few weeks.'

'I would like you to come in, Sophie, so we can check that everything is as it should be. Some of the roads are still flooded but we could send an ambulance? See if it could get through?'

'Yes, please . . . thank you.'

I pull the duvet over me as my stomach tightens, glancing at the clock before closing my eyes.

Week Thirty-Five
Contractions Forty-Five Minutes Apart

Samuel

My breath is scraping the back of my throat and I stop for a moment. The incline of the hill stretches ahead, and the uneven ground is putting my treadmill training to the test. I'm feeling confident, though. I mean, I've only tripped over five times so far. I take a moment to focus the end of the telescope towards the drop by the side of the road, a road carved out of a forest which has been here for years, deep foliage and trees entwined in a bed of damp and moss. My knees are the colour of shite and I stink to high heaven, not exactly the image I wanted to present to the mother of my child, but, if I remember correctly, the cottage is only a bit further up this hill. Just a bit further.

What will I say to her? I ask myself. 'Hello, sorry it took me so long, but that hill was a fucker'? I'm not sure that will strike the right tone. Michael interrupts my conversation; he taps forwards but there is a dip in the road. He swishes back and forth; there is something else there, something in our way, and he beats against it until he finds the end. It feels like a broken tree trunk. We take our time but manage to climb over it.

How about . . . I resume my conversation . . . 'I'm sorry.

I'm sorry for not trying hard enough to find you, I'm sorry for not telling you how much I love you?' *A bit corny, don't you think? How about asking her why she didn't tell you she is having your baby?* Why don't I wait and see what she says? *Fair enough. What are you going to say about Michael?* Michael stops, and I stand still. I'll say, 'This is Michael, he helps me from falling on my arse.'

My feet are eager, but Michael slows me down: *Watch it, look, there are broken trees all over the place, step this way, not that way, careful, don't rush.* But the cottage is around the corner; I'm almost there. Fate snips away at a piece of thread, and as I step over another tree trunk, my foot misses the tarmac and instead the ground moves, gradually at first, until the whole world shifts. The solid earth from beneath my feet slides away, and for a moment I'm suspended, my arms flailing at my sides, trying to gain some balance. I look up to where the road bends round, to where Sophie is waiting for me and then: I fall.

My feet no longer hold me up; my arms no longer hang at my sides. Instead, as I tumble and roll, my limbs flounder around me: useless, hopeless. North becomes south with a pain in my hip; a scratch across my face. East turns to west as my backpack escapes my shoulders; the thick, dense smell of decay covers my body. Dead leaves – dark and musky – cling to me as brambles pierce through the denim of my jeans, impaling themselves into me, ripping my skin: demanding blood. Up has become down, left has become right, until my foot strikes something hard: a rock? A piece of wood? And I hear my voice scream out.

My body is weightless: there is no gravity pulling me down; there is no light at the end of the tunnel; there is nothing.

I'm lost.

Week Thirty-Five
Contractions Thirty Minutes Apart

Sophie

The wood of my front door is blocking the fists that pound against it. My bedroom curtains remain open, the moon hanging amongst the clouds that hurry past; they have another place to be, another sky to decorate. I'm not sure if I have been asleep: images of Ian, Mum, of Charlie lying in his bed and of Bean suspended in its pink pool – motionless – have danced in front of me, and I can't honestly say if my eyes have been open or closed. Ripples from either side of my stomach clench and twist as I try to stand; my steps towards the stairs are slow and disjointed.

'Miss Williams?' A male voice is shouting. Bang. Bang. Bang. The sound knocks inside my skull. 'Miss Williams?'

I lean forward towards the peephole and focus on the outline of two paramedics, a man and a woman. I draw back the chain and open the door.

'Sorry, I was sleeping,' my mouth says, my words forming normally, just as my body is standing upright in a normal position, and I offer them coffee which they decline as they walk into my home. Normal behaviour for an abnormal day.

They sit in my lounge; they talk about the weather; they

tell me how bad the roads are, but how they are beginning to clear. We would like to take you to hospital and get you checked, they say. Baby is moving; everything is normal.

They carry my case; they usher me through hospital corridors, past curious glances and well-meaning smiles. They scan Bean. My baby is too big now to be seen in one piece; instead I get glimpses of each part and I try to fit them together to make a whole picture: like fixing the parts of a jigsaw. A hand passes across the screen: a little wave – *Hello, I'm here, I'm fine.* The midwife clips the elasticated bands around my stomach.

'Would you like a cup of tea?' she asks me with a kind smile.

'Yes, please.' I close my eyes as she leaves, listening to the rhythm of Bean's heart filling the room. Not the usual thump, thump that you hear in a Disney film or the 'gu-gum' that Patrick Swayze dances with Baby to. This beat gallops, bends and flexes, climbs and descends. She returns with a cup and then pulls the printout towards her.

'No sign of any contractions, so that's good. And your blood pressure is almost back to normal. It was quite low when the paramedics checked you and your bloods show that you're anaemic. So take it easy, OK? We'll give you a prescription for some iron tablets.'

'Thank you,' I say, and rest the bottom of the cup on top of Bean, who kicks it, wobbling the heartbeat. 'Will I be able to go home, then?'

'We'll give it another five minutes. Make sure there are no contractions.'

The consultant strides into the room, his beige mac flying behind him. His tired eyes scour the printout, dart to my chart and smile at me.

'Everything looks good here, Sophie. Have something to eat, take a bath and then get some rest. You're not far off now, and you'll need all of your strength to bring this little one into the world.' He glances at the wavy lines on the green-checked paper, nods and leaves for the night. The midwife yawns behind her hand, squints at the screen and grins.

'All clear.' She releases me from the elastic and turns off the machine. As I leave the room, my stomach constricts, but I'm used to Bean's tricks now.

I'm glad to be home, glad to be back in my bed, but I can't get comfortable; the pain radiating inside my stomach has become more intense. I turn on the light and get out of bed, rubbing my stomach. Trying not to panic, I reach for my phone. It has been almost exactly thirty minutes since the last twinge. They are starting to feel different, as though there is an elastic band stretching around my stomach and somebody is pulling and pulling it towards my spine. I breathe deeply and then, as quickly as the pain came, it is gone, and I feel fine. I feel normal. See, nothing to worry about. But still I reach for my phone.

'Hi, how's the journey?' I ask Charlie in a bright and breezy voice: nothing to see here, everything is perfectly normal.

'Good, the roads are clear. Are you OK? You sound weird.'

'I'm fine, just, you know, a bit shook up.'

We chat for a while, Charlie saying it will help him stay awake, but another twenty-nine minutes passes and the elastic band begins to pull, wrapping its way around my tummy and sinking into my back.

'You should have tasted the scallops, Soph, they were amazing . . . Soph?'

'Mmmmm,' I say, glad to only have to be making a sound rather than a word.

'You sure you're OK?' I exhale as the band begins to slacken and release its grip.

'Mmmhhmmm, just tired. I think I'm going to get some rest. Drive safely, but hurry home . . . I miss you.'

'Right. See you,' Charlie replies.

I hang up, and then look at the clock reproachfully.

'Not yet, Bean. Please.' I run my hand along the crest of my bump just as the door knocks again.

This time at the end of the spyhole is a face that is strangely familiar to me.

'Hello?' I shout, my lips close to the door.

'Ah, hello!' shouts an accent that I recognise, one that stretches and retreats at the end of every sentence. 'Is that you, Sophie?'

'Um, yes,' I reply into the wood and then glance through the looking glass where the man is frowning and leaning towards the door.

'Grand! Would you mind opening the door? Bloody Russell is blowing the hair right off my head!' I unlock the catch. 'Ah, there you are.' He leans forward. 'He was right, you've got weird coloured eyes and no mistake.'

My heart begins punching my ribcage, trying to get out. I push open the door as this tall Irishman enters my home with a clap of the hands, with huge strides and a smile that I've desperately been trying to find.

'Now where is my great eejit of a son?'

Week Thirty-Five
Contractions Thirty Minutes Apart

Samuel

The darkness smells like rotting vegetation and decay. It climbs in through your pores and sticks to your insides.

My foot is stuck, quite literally, between a rock and a hard place and has something wrapped around it which I am trying to untangle. My tongue licks my dry lips and tastes blood, while my ankle scrapes and scratches against the rock every time I try to move it. Time passes. I think time is passing: the moon flashes a smile at me every now and then, things scurry about; vegetation moves and snuffles, heaves and turns. Far, far below me is the main road that leads into town and I occasionally hear the sound of a truck, of a car, of life going on as I lie here in the shadows.

'Help!' I shout again, but my voice is hoarse and shaken as the damp bites into me, teasing the skin along my arms and legs into bumps as though I have an allergy – maybe I'm allergic to the cold. Barbs sink into my palm as I pull and try to manipulate my foot free. I put my chin on my chest and pull as hard as I can to release my ankle. A guttural sound emits from my mouth, my heel pushing against the pain. A crack, a shift, a wave of dirt crashes forward and my foot is free.

My weight is too heavy for my ankle and it buckles as I try to stand, my feet sliding downwards again, but I manage to grab the branches of a tree, stopping myself from falling.

Michael is out here somewhere but I can't find him. He could be anywhere, suffocating under dirt, being crushed beneath the wheel of a truck, snapping and splintering into pieces, his carcass discarded along the roadside like rubbish left to decay and rot. His demise opens a crack in my chest and the security he gave me is now filled with panic. My hand grips on to the branch, one leg crooked and bent as I try to shift my weight on to the other one. My hand follows the branch towards the trunk, and my feet take tentative steps towards it. I follow it down to its base where I begin feeling around for a replacement for Michael. I can't find my way out of here without him. Another car passes; the moon winks – until I see him: Michael the Second. He's broader and made of darker wood and is a bit gnarly around the edges, but he can swish and tap just as well as his older brother.

'So, Michael the Second, where the feck are we?' I lean on him for a minute as we alter the lens at the edge of the telescope, twisting and turning it until we can see some of the terrain. Trees tower above us, their trunks sinking deep into the bracken, their branches waving and pointing to the top of the forest, to where I fell, to where – somewhere up there – Sophie is waiting for me.

'After you, Michael,' I say, trying to keep the fear out of my voice, but it betrays me, and Michael the Second isn't fooled. My leg limps, my mouth grimaces, but the trees keep pointing: *Up there*, they say*, up there. Hold on.*

Week Thirty-Five
Contractions Twenty Minutes Apart

Sophie

There is a giant Irishman sitting on my sofa. A giant Irishman who tells me that Sam is here in Wales, that he should be here in my cottage, that he left hours ago.

'Let me call Mrs McLaughlin,' he says, pulling on a pair of glasses and punching the screen of his mobile phone with slow, deliberate movements. I offer to make us a drink, which he tells me would be grand, my lips smiling at the familiarity of his mannerisms, at the love I already feel towards this loud man. My house is filled with his voice; the depth of it throws its arms around the sofa like long-lost friends, the strength of his presence stretching into every dark nook and cranny, mending cracks and smiling at the creases hidden in the curtains.

I'm almost finished making the tea, when the elastic band begins to wrap itself around me; my focus slides towards the kitchen clock, which frowns and tells me they are coming every twenty minutes. I concentrate on the voice from the lounge: 'Are you sure now, you're sure he was on his way to Sophie this afternoon? And where was he getting a taxi from? Mac-what?' I breathe slowly as the elastic begins to relax. 'Mac-lun-uth?'

'Machynlleth?' I ask, returning to the lounge.

'Our Sophie says Mak-hun-hleth?' he repeats into the phone, my heart quickening. Our Sophie.

'That is not what you said at all, Mrs M, it sounded nothing—'

'That's only half an hour away,' I say quietly as Mr McLaughlin argues with Mrs McLaughlin. He looks up at me from his phone; his eyebrows have the same arch as Samuel's, I notice; thicker, but each familiarity I find comforts me.

'Our Sophie says it's only half an hour away. Of course I've not rung the police yet, I thought he would be busy canoodling, didn't I? Sophie? Yes, she's grand, love, about ready to pop, though!' He smiles at me, his cheeks rising, the skin around his eyes crinkling. 'Of course she doesn't know, do you think I'd be calling you if she did? For the love of God, woman, where are your brains?' He holds the phone away from his ear while long-distance expletives fly across the sea and spray my lounge.

'OK. Right-oh, I'll give the police a bell, ask them if they've seen my stupid son and his friend Michael stumbling around the Welsh hills.' He rolls his eyes at me, and a giggle erupts from my mouth. 'I know, I know . . .' His voice softens. 'He'll be grand, probably got lost and gone into a pub.' He looks away from me and mumbles, 'Love you too, Mrs M.'

'Who, er, who is Michael?' I ask as I pass him his cup.

'Michael? He, well, you'd best ask Sammy about that one.'

'How . . . how is he coping? With the . . . sight loss?' Mr McLaughlin sags with relief.

'You know, do you? About the accident?' I nod as the elastic begins to twist.

'Well, in that case, I can tell you. Michael is his cane, love, helps him get about.'

'Let me, get the taxi numb—' my mouth holds the rest

of the sentence as the elastic thins and begins to drag my insides upwards to an imaginary summit, '—bers,' I finish as the pain slides down the other side of the mountain.

'Are you OK there, Sophie love? You look a bit . . .'

I smile and straighten myself up. 'I'll just get my phone.'

Beethoven plays as I'm put on hold while the taxi firm speak to the driver who picked Sam up from Machynlleth. Beethoven stops in full flow as they explain that Samuel was dropped off by the side of the road.

'Right, and he left him? Your driver left a blind man on the side of the road and encouraged him to *walk* up a hill that has steep banks either side?' I'm walking up and down behind the sofa and Mr McLaughlin is watching me with a mixture of concern and something else. It takes me a moment to place it but the word settles: pride. I feel a blush rise up my neck as I look away from him. 'Well then, I trust your drivers will be the first to help us try to find him. Now tell me exactly where you left him.'

'Right!' I smile as I strap myself into the seat, adjusting the belt below my bump and instructing Mr McLaughlin how to push the seat back so his kneecaps aren't forced up by his shoulders. 'Let's go and find him, shall we?' I take a quick glance at the time, hoping I can get there before the next pain comes. I follow my headlights along the narrow road, rounding bends, and pull up beside the dip, which was flooded, and look up to where Samuel would have had to walk on his own.

The winds argue with the branches of the trees, convincing them to lean to the left, but they resist, their opinions swaying to the right. Darkness tries to hide the snarls, but the wind snaps back.

I follow Mr McLaughlin's torch beam as I step out of the car. I try to tell him that there are hidden trails all along this part of the wood, but the elastic swallows my words and forces me to lean forward; I grip the roof of the car. I close my eyes and breathe out.

'Oh Sam, what were you thinking?' he asks out loud as he shines the torch back up the road we have just driven down.

'Something must have—' My words are swallowed by the pain. I lean my hands on top of the bonnet and concentrate on my breathing. When I open my eyes, Mr McLaughlin is tapping on his phone again.

'I've seen that look a few times in my life, Our Sophie, how long – ah, Mrs M, we've got an emergency on our hands. Me and Our Sophie have just come to where they dropped Sammy off and the stupid eejit has gone off climbing his way up a bloody mountain road, by himself! He must have gotten lost.' I notice the concern that crosses his face as he says these words. They are supposed to sound flippant, but as he looks up at the dense forest that leads up to the road, I can see fear hiding behind his tone. 'But listen, Our Sophie is doing that thing with the face and the breathing and the bending over, just like— mmmhmm, right, grand.' He looks up at me. 'I'm to put you on speaker phone.'

'Sophie?' A soft voice, the same accent, enters the darkness of the roadside.

'Hello?' I answer, breathing out, the trek almost over, the elastic almost slack.

'Ah, it's lovely to hear your voice, so it is, we've heard so much about you.'

'Oh, umm, it's nice to hear you too.'

'Now then, how far gone are you?'

'Thirty-five weeks.'

She takes a sharp intake of breath. 'And how far apart are your contractions?'

'They were every twenty minutes, but I think the last one was only fifteen.'

'Mr McLaughlin? You're to ring an ambulance, do you hear?'

'I don't think I need an ambulance, it's quicker if we drive. The hospital is only—' my breath is taken away, a knot in the elastic holding me still, 'twenty minutes from here.' The pain slides away. 'I'm OK. We need to find Samuel, he could be hurt.'

'Sophie love? Our Sammy was out of me like a bullet from a gun, I went from fifteen minutes to no minutes at all in the time it took Mr McLaughlin to put his shoes on. Now unless you want to risk my daft husband fumbling around in your nether regions . . .' Mr McLaughlin's face loses its colour at this, 'you'll do what I say, love, OK? You get in that car. Better to be safe than sorry.'

'But Samuel—'

'I'll do all that from here, you just take care of my grandchild. Mr M? Give me the number of that taxi firm and I'll start calling the police and the hospitals.'

He does what he is told and passes me a scrunched-up cotton hanky. It has a small horse embroidered into the corner and smells like cough sweets and fabric softener. I take it from his hands and realise that I'm crying. He taps my hand. 'You'll be grand, love, just grand.'

Week Thirty-Five
Contractions Twenty Minutes Apart

Samuel

Our progress is slow. Each step takes time to negotiate and is rewarded by the agony of my ankle; each step could be taking me further away or closer to the end. All I have to guide me is the gradient of the hill, and the odd beam from a headlight. Another car passes, the lights swallowed by shadows and burning through the darkness with each twist and turn of the road, like the warning of a lighthouse. This car banks to the right once it reaches the base of the hill. I call out, but my voice is snatched away by the wind, played with like a game of hot potato. I tear a piece of my shirt off and wrap it around the palm of the hand that is holding on to Michael the Second. Both my hands feel bloody and torn, a far cry from the hand that would sign contracts and tap away on keyboards. Part of me wants to tear off a piece and wrap it around my head like Rambo. *Get a grip*, Michael tells me.

I trip again.

'Fuck's sake, Michael,' I say under my breath as I drop to my knees. *Sorry*, he replies, *I'm new at this.*

The ground beneath me feels like sponge and I sit down, rotating my foot, sharp pains careering through my joints, making my face contort with pain with each rotation. My head feels light; my mouth is dry. I need to get out of here. I'm dehydrated and soon I won't have the energy to drag myself up this hill.

The car below seems to make a U-turn and charges off in another direction. I look up towards the moon that is pushing through the clouds, the beam reaching out towards me like a rope. I grab it, pull myself up, and let it lead me to the summit.

Week Thirty-Five

Contractions Two Minutes Apart

Sophie

'Sophie? Sophie? Listen to me. You need to inhale the gas and air only up until the peak of the contraction, all right?' The midwife tries to take the hose from my hand, but I glare at her. *Just you try it, woman, just you try to take this away from me.*

'If she wants the air, she has the air,' Mr McLaughlin says.

'Pethidine,' I say as I take the mouthpiece away. 'I want pethidine.'

'Ah now, Sophie love . . .' Mrs McLaughlin's voice filters through the speaker phone and the ripples of the waning contraction, 'you don't want that – made Sarah as sick as a dog, didn't it, Sarah?'

'Yeah, Sophie, stay away from that if you can, you're almost there. Da?'

'Yes, Sarah love.'

'Make sure you're not holding her hand, Da.' Mr McLaughlin looks down to where my nails are digging into his palm. 'Worst thing, Sophie, is if you're tensing your muscles. Keep them nice and relaxed, you're doing fine.' I can't believe I have the entirety of Samuel's family as my labour partner.

'Wendy, how's my grandchild doing?' The midwife looks

at the printout and nods happily. Why is she happy? Nothing about this process is making me feel happy.

'Right as rain, Mrs McLaughlin. Heartbeat is nice and steady.'

'Perfect.'

'Mam!' Sarah shouts in the background as the pain in my stomach begins to march towards the summit, dragging me with it. 'The police are on the phone!'

'I'll be back in a minute. Mr McLaughlin? You're doing well, I'm proud of you.'

'Go away with yourself, you mad woman. All I'm doing is sitting here – ow!' He tries to snatch his hand away from me, but I hang on: I'm almost at the top of the hill; I'm almost there.

The contraction ends, and I close my eyes. Mr McLaughlin is stroking my thumb with his thumb. 'You'll be fine, you'll be fine,' he is whispering. I open my eyes and look at him, noticing how grey his skin has started to look and how deeply furrowed the crevices in his forehead have become. He looks away from me and then passes me my phone. Charlie's name is flashing on the screen.

'Where are you?' Charlie asks. I can almost hear the steps he is taking, his hair bouncing up and down as he paces the kitchen.

'I'm in labour.'

'Labour? But—'

'Never mind that, Charlie.' I pull myself further up the bed while I still can. 'Samuel's lost, he's there by the house somewhere. He's blind—' But the cord is pulling me back up the hill; it's steeper than last time and a sound like a scratch leaves my mouth.

'Blind? Sophie?' I hear Charlie's voice, but he is at the bottom of the mountain and I'm being pulled away to the top, the elastic almost cutting me in half. I hear Mr McLaughlin explaining things. I feel the midwife's hand on my stomach, her eyes looking at the monitor and her gentle voice asking Mr McLaughlin if he could leave the room, so she can examine me.

'I think I need to push,' I say. A trolley laden with all things metal is pulled towards her and gloves are put on.

'Let's have a look.' My head turns from side to side. I'm not ready. He's not here. 'Well, you didn't waste any time, baby Williams,' she says.

'McLaughlin,' I correct.

'I can see baby McLaughlin's head . . . plenty of hair there. Have you got any redheads in the family?' She grins, but my feet are being strapped into their walking boots, a rope winched around my waist as I'm pulled away from the ground, the pain tightening around my middle as I'm dragged back up the mountain. 'Shall I get your . . . um, birthing partner in?' I nod as I try to concentrate on my breathing.

'Charlie is out looking for our boy. Nice chap.' He pats my hand and I return to base camp. He sits down.

'I need to push!' I say as primal noises escape my mouth and hang on to the walls, the sensation uncontrollable and all-consuming.

'OK, let's get ready to meet this baby, shall we?' Wendy smiles up at me from between my open legs. 'Good girl, and again.' The pain takes hold of me and I look around for something to concentrate on, anything other than the way my chin is burying into my chest, every muscle in my body tensed. I find Mr McLaughlin's face as a noise, somewhere between a grunt and a growl, leaves my mouth. I concentrate on the tear that is rolling down his cheek, the tiny blood vessels across the tops of his cheeks, the curve of his eyelashes. I concentrate on the way that he is looking at me, the way his rough hand feels in mine.

The same noise, the same urge continues, over and over,

until, with white-light clarity, I feel Bean's head leave the inside of my body.

'Right then, Sophie, now pant when you feel the next contraction . . . nice and slowly does it.'

'Come on, Our Sophie, almost there, almost there.' He smiles at me, his thumb moving backwards and forwards in time with the small rocks he is making in his chair: forwards and backwards, forwards and backwards.

The last push.

Sounds are dulled, like being underwater in a swimming pool. I can hear the noises above, but they are far away: echoes that leak and fade. I know that the lifeguard is pacing around the edges; I can hear my heart pounding inside my ribcage, hear the bubbles leak from my mouth as the last bit of oxygen escapes my lungs. Wendy is telling me I'm nearly there, that I'm doing brilliantly; the urge to push forces me to the surface, my legs tense, as I break through the pain, my baby's head pushing through the surface and gasping its first breath.

'It's a boy,' Wendy says, smiling.

The room stills; time is frozen: the only sound is the beat of my heart and the muffled noises of my son's first cry. My life before this moment is now a thing of the past, a thing that I can never return to. As this tiny creature, with blood still covering his red-haired head, is passed to me, I become a new person. I look down as I feel the weight of him, the warmth of him, filling my open arms. How is it possible to love someone this much when I've only just met him? His fists are clenched, his wide blue eyes, eyes that are the same shape as Samuel's, are looking around the room, trying to find me, trying to see who it is who has been talking to him for the last nine months, trying to see if his dad is here . . . did he make it? Where is he? You said you'd find him.

I look to where Mr McLaughlin is smiling down at his

grandson, his face mimicking mine, a look of pure love, but with the loss of Samuel pulling around the edges.

'Hello,' I say. 'Hello, Bean.'

'Hello, young man,' says Mr McLaughlin, his voice catching in his throat. 'I'm your Grampa.'

Week Thirty-Five
Contractions Two Minutes Apart

Samuel

My body shivers beneath skin covered in sweat but I'm almost there. I lift Michael the Second up and he tells me there is a half-metre gap from where I stand and the edge of the road. I feel around for a loose piece of rock and pull it towards me, stamping and pushing it into the mud to help give me a little extra height before I pull myself up. I throw Michael up and hear him crack his back as he hits the tarmac. Pain screams in my shoulders and inside my biceps as my fingernails dig into the dirt, link their way into the maze of roots that hold the forest together and drag my body upwards. Primal noises escape my mouth and bounce around the forest, as I use every bit of my strength, every last bit of energy that is left in me to climb, to crawl, to get out of this forest and back on to the road. With a final grunt, my hands scratch against the tarmac; they pull my body up and I lie there, rolling on to my back, my breath coming out in shallow, noisy gasps.

'We did it, Michael, we made it.'

I close my eyes and stay slumped by the side of the road, just as I hear the growl of an engine. I open my eyes, sit up and squint towards the sound, where a light is bumping up and down the road towards me. I stand and begin waving my arms as it approaches; the growl slows into a grumble and the driver door opens and closes with a thud.

'Samuel?' a deep voice asks. I focus on the parts of his face that I can make out, the lights from the car showing me that another brick has been added: the circle of light is shrinking faster.

'Yes,' I answer, my voice battered and bruised.

I feel a firm grip on my shoulder. 'You stink of sheep shit.'

'I know,' I reply.

'I'm Charlie, Sophie's neighbour.'

Blue lights flash from beneath the forest, my name being shouted by – three? four? five? – people.

I can't help but think of the irony of screaming for help for hours with nobody around, and then after I've slithered my way through the decay and excrement of the Welsh hills, that there are now four people here looking for me.

'We need to get you to hospital,' Charlie says.

'I don't need to go to the hospital. My ankle is a bit bashed up, but I need to get to Sophie.'

'That's why you need to get to the hospital. She's in labour.'

'Labour? But—'

'They're not going to let you see her smelling like that,' he adds.

I hear the boot opening; feel the wave of a blanket being shaken and then he takes me by the elbow and leads me inside the car. My teeth are chattering and I try to control them. The heater on the car is turned up as he calls the police and explains that I've been found.

'How quickly can I get to her?' I ask. 'I don't want her to go through this by herself.'

'Your dad is with her. She's not alone.' Charlie speaks in strange, blunt sentences; it's hard to amalgamate this with the rock-star image I'd had of him.

'Da?' I say, and I shake my head. If I had just waited for that other flight, I would be with her now. 'Good man,' I say quietly. My da. He always manages to save me. One way or another.

'Yeah. I'll ring him when we get home,' Charlie says. The car bumps and sways up the road and I realise I was still a long way from Sophie. It slows, then the engine cuts out and I'm guided inside. I have no idea where furniture is or if there is mess on the floor. Charlie seems to instinctively know this as he steers me towards the stairs by my elbow; he says nothing as we climb the stairs or as he guides me into the bathroom.

'Sit down,' Charlie instructs, and I feel for the toilet seat. The tap is turned on and I hear a plastic cup being filled. He places it in my hand and I swallow it down in huge gulps. 'Keep still, you've got cuts all over your face.' I flinch as he wipes my skin with antiseptic, his movements slow and gentle. I notice he smells of soap and mints as he picks up my hand, turns it over and repeats the action.

'How is she?' I ask.

'I don't know. I've been away. I shouldn't have left her.' He places my hand on my knee. 'You're done.' I hear him shift and the shower is turned on. 'There's a towel on the hook at the back of the door, opposite the shower,' he adds. 'I'll leave you some clothes on the bed, second door as you come out of here. The trousers will be too small.'

'Thank you,' I say. Tears threaten, and the emotion tightens my chest. I sense rather than hear him give me a nod.

The police have arrived. I take careful steps down the steep stairs. Without Michael, it takes me longer to navigate. A waft of aftershave and a flash of dark hair lets me know that the uniform by my side is a man and he helps me towards the sofa, returning shortly after with a cup of tea and two biscuits. There is too much sugar and not enough milk but it is the best tea I have ever had, and the cup is empty too soon. The police ask me a few questions as I swallow the biscuits and I answer them impatiently.

'Can we go now? I need to get to Sophie.' I stand up, the edges of Charlie's jeans scraping above the socks, and I'm grateful that I can't see the state of myself.

'I've tried to call, but Sophie's phone's not answering,' Charlie says. 'But I'm sure everything is fine.'

'First baby, is it?' The deep voice from the policeman booms into the room, and I wonder if he sings.

'Yes,' I answer.

'Right then.' The policeman claps his hands. 'Looks to me like you need to be blue-lighted to the hospital, then!' His partner groans.

'Can I drive?' the other officer asks.

'No! You're still training.'

'I've been your partner for five years, are you ever going to let me drive?' he moans as he follows his partner towards the door.

I try my winning smile. 'Can I drive?' I ask. They laugh good-naturedly.

'No,' answers Charlie. 'You're blind.'

'Yes, I know,' I reply and any worries about Sophie's relationship with Charlie dissipate. I have nothing to worry about here. Sophie would have laughed at my joke.

'I'll follow,' Charlie says, his voice wavering a little. I think about how he had kissed Sophie's bump, how intense their relationship had looked.

'He can fit in the car, can't he, officer?' I interrupt.

'The more the merrier!' his voice booms as we leave the house and climb into the police car.

Week Thirty-Five

Sophie

'Five pounds eight,' Wendy announces as she looks over her shoulder at me, Bean's scrawny, wrinkled legs kicking and quivering behind her. 'That's a great weight and he's breathing perfectly. We'll need to keep a close eye on him, but for now, there is no need to be incubated. Tough little cookie, this one. OK, Bean, you can go back to Mummy now.' A timid cry fills the room, like the baa of a lamb; it shakes and shivers, then slows as – bundled up in the outfit with a rabbit poking out of the pocket – my son is passed to me. There's a gentle knock at the door.

'Come in!' Wendy says as she scribbles things in her notes. I stare down at Bean; his eyes are looking directly at mine: *Where is he? Is he coming?* I begin humming, 'One, two, three, four five, once I caught a fish alive.' *I'll find him Bean, I promise.* His gaze is pulled away as slow steps advance towards us, but I don't turn to see who it is; I'm too busy looking at every part of my son, the long golden eyelashes, the point of his chin. I lean forward and kiss the softness of his fontanelle, still yielding beneath my lips, and breathe in his smell; it's like nothing I've ever breathed in before.

Week Thirty-Five

Samuel

'There he is,' I say to Charlie who takes my elbow, steering me away from a drinks machine that is hidden in the shadows. 'Da!' The corridor in the hospital is bright; my leg knocks a stray chair out of the way and it skitters and clatters, but at the end of it I can see him. It's been a long time since I've been this far away to be able to see him, all of him, and I commit it to memory, the way he turns as he hears me shout his name, the look of relief that passes across his face, the slow look downwards at my half-mast trousers and the huge smile that lights up his face.

His arms close around me and he holds me tightly, clapping me on the back and kissing the patch of hair just above my ear. He pulls back from me and stretches an arm towards Charlie.

'Charlie, I take it?' His voice smiles. 'Thank you, lad, for taking care of my boy.' His voice rises and falls as he pumps Charlie's hand up and down.

'No thanks needed,' Charlie replies just before Da's hand flicks out of the tunnel wall as he clips me around the back of the head.

'You great big fecking eejit! You've gone and missed it and nearly got yourself killed by the looks of you. Would it have killed you to wait for the next flight?'

'Is Sophie OK?' Charlie interrupts. 'Are they OK?' I can hear the worry in his voice and I'm glad that Sophie has had him with her.

'They're grand, Charlie boy, just grand.'

'Missed it?' I ask. Da's eyes fill with tears.

'Yep, gone and missed the birth of your . . .' he hesitates, then slaps me on the back, 'first-born child.' He nods towards a door. I turn towards it and scan it until I see a few letters that make up 'labour room'. 'They're in there,' he says quietly, pride edging in.

The door stands in front of me, but my feet won't move. My life will never be as it was if I open that door. I will never be able to leave her; I will never be able to save her from this new person I have become if I take another step. What if she doesn't want me and my new life, the life that will come with Michael and a guide dog and a person who needs to be guided across a busy road? I will never be able to recover from that. If she doesn't want me, how will I live? My thoughts stop: they disintegrate like sand through my fingers, because a noise, which resembles a goat, is leaking out from behind the door.

My feet move, my hand forms a fist and the fist knocks on the door.

'Come in!'

The fist opens, my fingers spreading wide and pushing open the door.

My legs are shaking beneath me as I limp into the room; for a horrid moment I think I might pass out. The room is low-lit, and it takes me a second to scan the interior, to put together the small glimpses that the tunnel is gifting me. A midwife is sitting at the foot of the bed, her back to me. From the arch of her shoulders I conclude she must be writing something down. There is a bed in the middle of the room, and at the end of the bed I can make out the bump of feet. I can hear the snuffle of a baby and then the melody of a nursery rhyme from a voice that reaches out to me. I take a deep breath and close my eyes. The notes break down the bricks at the end of the tunnel; they smash them down, and for a split second I can see: I can see my whole life ahead of me. I open my eyes and follow the tiny light, the tiny images that are as precious to me as every breath that I'm taking. I stand still; without Michael, I don't know what is in front of me. I bend my head and try to check the floor, but I'm petrified I might fall.

'Sophie?' I ask, her name falling from my lips, the same way the leaf fell from the tree all those months ago. My voice stretches towards the bed, turning the head of the midwife. From out of the darkness comes a hand; it reaches towards me, it links its fingers in mine and brings me forward until Sophie is there. I can only see part of her eye at first, but it is filled with love. I lean forward, her hand holding mine tightly, and rest my head against hers.

'I'm sorry,' I try to say but the words are lost in a gulp, in a sob caught somewhere inside my chest, as I look down. I see a tiny mouth, the lips pouting and parting into a perfect 'O' as it shakes with a yawn. Fingers tipped with pale, minuscule fingernails, the colour of sea-shells, bat in front of the mouth and I reach for them, sliding my finger inside the palm. The tiny hand grips my finger. *There you are*, it says. I wipe the tears away from my face – they're blurring the end of the tunnel – but I blink and drink in every part of the puzzle pieces in front of me. I look into the baby's eyes and smile when I see parts of hair – the same colour as my sister's – pushing their way into my sight. I feel Sophie's breath in my ear. 'It's a boy, Samuel,' she says. I reach for his head and stroke his skin. My son. I can see my son. I turn to Sophie, my hand shaking as it follows the curve of his head.

'Thank you,' I say.

'What took you so long?' she asks.

'I got lost.'

Week Thirty-Six

Sophie

'Hot Irish Samuel, we meet at last!' Helen stands on her tip-toes and throws her arms around his neck. 'Mmm, you smell good.' She takes a deep sniff.

'Hello? I'm standing right behind you,' Greg grumbles as Helen releases Samuel.

'I smell like baby-puke,' I add, as I reach for Helen, giving her a squeeze. I pull away as she looks past me into the cottage. Bean shouts from his play-gym that he wants some attention and her feet follow the sound, a deep breath exhaled and a smile on her lips.

'Good to see you again.' Greg slaps Samuel on the back, then realises what he has said and does a weird 'sorry' expression at me.

'You too,' Samuel replies and steps forward to shake his hand but stands on Greg's toes instead. 'Shite, sorry, mate.'

'Oh! He's ginger!' Helen laughs from the lounge as we follow her. 'He didn't look that ginger on the photo, he's properly orange, like he's . . .' but she's grinning and reaching down for him.

'Strawberry blond,' I say with a yawn.

'Ginger,' Samuel insists as Helen sways back and forth, looking around the lounge, tapping Bean's back.

'Greg, give them the present,' Helen commands. I carry a

tray and put it on the sideboard, noticing, not for the first time, how different my body feels without Bean's bump. Greg passes a blue gift-wrapped parcel to Samuel, who continues to sit in the same position; he hasn't noticed that the present has been passed to him and a lump rises in my throat.

'Samuel, can you open it while I sort out the drinks?'

He jumps slightly and reaches out to where Greg places it into his palm. He unwraps it carefully and I can see in the set of his mouth that he is worried he is going to do something wrong. Samuel drops the paper and gift tag to the floor and lifts the lid off the box.

'Sophie, it might be best if you—'

'It's more for you, Samuel, to be honest. Go on, take it out.'

His eyebrows dip in a V shape as he tries to use the last of his sight to help him. Helen smiles at me and shifts Bean further up her shoulder.

Samuel's fingers flutter over a square-shaped piece of plastic. I raise my eyebrows at Helen as Samuel begins to smile.

'It's a 3D print of Bean's scan, so Samuel can see what it looked like. We wanted to give him back a bit of what he missed.'

'Thank you,' he says, grinning. His fingers slowly run over each contour, eyebrows creasing in concentration, as he gets back part of the time we lost.

'So, have we decided on a name yet?' Samuel strokes the picture. I watch as his hand follows the edge of the sofa, trailing along the arm until he finds the table next to it, carefully placing the photo down. I shake my head, trying to keep control of the emotion lodged in my chest. Samuel stares at the floor for a moment and then nods.

'What are you nodding at, Samuel? There isn't one name that we both agree on . . .'

He reaches down, runs his fingers against the carpet until he grabs the wrapping paper and the tag with Helen's handwriting on. 'Bean' is written across the front but the card is folded in the middle, the 'a' hidden from view, lurking deep within the crease.

'Ben,' he reads.

'Ben?' I repeat. 'It's perfect!'

'Did you just fist-bump each other?' Helen interrupts. I slide myself under his arm.

'We did . . . it's taken us a while to perfect that and no mistake.' Samuel kisses the top of my head.

I watch Samuel as he sleeps. I watch every movement beneath the paper-thin eyelids with their map of tiny veins. I watch as the crease by the side of his mouth deepens when he turns towards me, his arm throwing itself around my waist, pulling me towards him.

'I will be blind soon,' he had said, kissing my shoulder as I fed Ben, his tiny, wrinkled fingers clenching and unclenching the duvet as his chin worked up and down, little notes of contentment escaping between gulps.

'How soon?' I'd asked, even though I knew it wouldn't be long. I'd already noticed the things Samuel was missing: a corner of a wall; the handle of a cup; the edge of the sofa as he stands up; a step up to the lawn.

'Soon.' He reached for Ben's head and stroked his flame-red hair.

'I love you,' were the only words that I could think of to say.

'Thank you.' He laughed.

'You're welcome.'

'Ben loves you too.'

Samuel pulls me closer, bringing me back to the here and now. 'It's considered rude to watch people while they sleep, you know,' he murmurs into my hair. 'It's punishable by flogging in some countries.'

'Stop talking nonsense,' I reply, but I'm smiling as I lie in his arms, listening as his breathing becomes slower.

My life is unrecognisable from the one that I used to have. When Ben was passed into my arms, the love I felt for him scared me: to love something this much, must surely be impossible. But then Samuel had walked in. And for a split second, I worried that my heart wouldn't be able to contain any more love, but then love found new places to explore, places that I didn't even know existed: new places to hide, new places to fill and grow. It exploded into every part of me: every cell, every drop of blood, every tear, every moment of laughter and every moment of sadness. It consumed me.

How do our bodies contain it? How does it stay wrapped up inside us? It should glow; it should radiate from the tips of our fingers, from our skin; with every breath it should leave our mouths in tiny golden whispers. I think of Mum and how she must have been filled with this too, this light, and I wonder if her last breath was touched with gold. Did it bounce around this house, waiting for me to come home and catch it?

Think of all the good in the world. Imagine if we could see it glimmering, this golden mist: the helping hand that reaches out to steady an elderly lady as she tries to stand on the bus, the warm drink that we pass to the homeless, the kind words we say to someone who is having a bad day.

Love surrounds us.

Just because we can't see . . . it doesn't mean it's not there.

Week Thirty-Six

Samuel

I'm lucky. I know this because I'm sharing my life with a woman who I know loves me as much as I love her. I'm lucky because we are alive and are able to hold our son. I'm lucky because I have been given this gift, this gift of sight for another day.

I'm trying to remember that I'm lucky as I spill boiling water on to my hand, attempting to make Sophie a cup of coffee: it's half-four in the morning.

'Feck!' I say quietly as I fumble my way towards the tap and blast the cold water on to my hand. Ben hasn't settled all night, and no matter how many times Sophie has tried to feed him, he has cried and fought against her. A creak of a floorboard upstairs draws my attention as I dry my hand on a tea towel: third drawer down, directly beneath the toaster.

I'm beginning to learn the sounds of this house that is now my home – for the time being at least. Sophie and I have decided that we will 'survive' the next six months. We know we need to make plans about our future, about my life and family in Ireland, the guide dog that I will need, the career I will begin, but we have decided it can all wait.

The McLaughlins are all coming back over in a couple of weeks to see us, even though Mr and Mrs McLaughlin's faces seem to permanently fill Sophie's screen, Mam giving feeding advice, Da telling her to let us find it out for ourselves, Sarah telling Sophie the best way to tame the wild hair that my son has inherited. I'm not sure why they need to visit at all, but it will be good to see them in the flesh, so to speak.

The floorboard creaks to the rhythm of Sophie's sways; Ben is quiet. I reach for the coffee, my fingers gripping the cup, the tiny block of light guiding my way: two steps past the door, turn left, thirteen stairs to the top, the eleventh slightly higher than the others. I reach the top and Ben begins to whimper, a sound that brings his knees tight into his chest and turns his cheeks red, makes his fists clench and his back arch away from whoever is trying to comfort him.

I place the cup on the changing table – two steps forward, three steps to the left – and then follow Sophie's hushes. My hands reach for her, for the warmth of Ben, and she responds by guiding my hands around his back. My body seems to know where to position my other hand; I see a flash of red hair, a flash of white clothing, the red palate of his mouth. I take over the shushes as Sophie gulps her coffee and sits down in the feeding chair. I re-position him on to my shoulder and rub his back. Who teaches us these things? How do we know to do this? How do I know – a man who cannot see, who knows nothing about babies – how do I know to rock on my heels, to stroke his hair, to kiss his head?

I know every crease of his face, every arc of his eyelashes. Each puzzle piece I know by heart: the meandering line of his hairline, hair that sticks up in a blaze of shock, the arch of his eyelids, the splattering of tiny veins that hide just beneath the surface. I know the exact shade of the deep pink of his lips – lips that are full and that quiver and shake before they stretch and explode in a frustrated cry. I can tell you the shapes of the tracks and grooves of his ears, ears that are pointed at the top, like an elf. I can tell you that his nose is exactly the same length as the top section of my little finger and how the curve of his cheeks almost meets the puffy bags beneath his eyes which are a deep blue, the same shade as Mam's. I can put each piece of this puzzle in its correct place; I can build a perfect picture of my son.

'Maybe he needs some fresh air? Do you think your mam is awake? I could ask her?'

'Mam used to send Da out in the car with me. She said she was convinced I'd end up being a racing driver.'

'Shall we try it?'

Ben arches his back again and lets out a cry that rattles and shakes his body.

'It's worth a shot. Probably best if you drive, though,' I grin at her.

Sophie drives through her yawns, opening the window a fraction to let the cool October air in; to keep her senses alert. I turn my head, the pinprick of vision rewarding me with a glimpse of Ben's sleeping head. The car takes us through the sleeping town and further into the hills before rising over a crest of road, flanked by the sea stretching out towards home on the left and the roll of the sleeping green giants to our right.

'Mum used to bring us here when town got too busy.' She begins to describe the small town of Borth as we approach it. The roads are quiet, and the shops that line the narrow street are closed: the ice-cream parlour that boasts fig and honey flavours; the crooked art gallery; the vintage clothes shop. The people in the houses that stand sentry are fast asleep inside, duvets pulled up to chins, soft night-lights wading off nightmares as children sleep. The movement of the car is too fast for me to track one thing along the small street, but soon the road stretches forward towards a beach. High sand dunes extend towards the sea, the dune grass waving in the morning breeze. The car slows as the tyre tracks sink into the brine-kissed sand. Sophie rolls us forward, then brings the car to a stop. She leaves the engine running as Ben sleeps, taking my hand and pointing to where, across the glittering bank of water, the sun is beginning to rise. The gentle waves of the estuary reach out towards the sunrise, towards the beginning of another day.

Sophie unbuckles her seat belt, leans over the hand brake and rests her head on my shoulders. The sun sweeps its arms across the horizon as Ben stirs, a bleat escaping his mouth, his eyes opening and trying to focus.

We climb out of the car; the pale indigo of the sky dips into the rising yellows and golds while the waves gently lap against the shore. The air is thick with the smell of the sea, but the wind is gentle, barely lifting my hair as Sophie unclips Ben from his seat and changes his nappy. The sand cushions our frames as we sit at the base of a dune. Sophie shifts as Ben drinks hungrily, and I can feel the tension in Sophie's shoulders relaxing. Seagulls flap and glide above us as the sun pushes the stars back: it's my time to shine.

Sophie stands as Ben begins to fuss, little snuffles of breath, his head frantically turning from side to side. She begins to walk, but instead of getting up, I stay seated, surrounded by the golden wheat of the dune grasses, the sand running between my fingers, and the image of Sophie and my son walking towards the water's edge. Because I know. The tunnel is about to close.

I can hear the cement being mixed; the scrape of the trowel as the last brick is picked up. I concentrate on everything that I can see: the curve of Sophie's waist, the way she is walking, half walk, half dance; the way her hair is being lifted at the ends and the dimples in her cheeks. She turns and smiles with our son in her arms, his hair catching the golds of the sun. The sky behind them is filled with a kaleidoscope of colour; the circle of light dazzles through the tunnel, making the shadows cringe and shy away as the darkness frames them. I smile because I know that I could go my whole life with my sight, but I doubt I would ever see anything more beautiful than the scene that is shining through the end of the tube, the scene that is about to be obscured. I ask for just one more minute: one more minute of capturing the vision in front of me as I hear the brick being picked up.

My breath is even; my heart is steady: my time is up.

The points are set, and the final brick slides into place, but I'm still smiling. My world in the shadows is over, and as the tunnel is finally closed, I get up, and walk towards my family, towards my life filled with light.

The beginning.

Epilogue
Four Years Later

Charlie

Dear Sophie,

I wake every morning with my wife lying beside me, with my son walking into the bedroom holding his toy rabbit by the arm. Every morning I wake to the pain that I feel when I know that they are not there.

My body is a machine. It functions, it walks and talks, it breathes, it sleeps, it goes about living a half-life. Like reading the end of a book without reading the beginning.

For the last four years, I have lived my life through you, have made your family mine, have begun to fill my half-life with your full one. Even my pet is yours. I sometimes wish I could have a dog that could guide me through this half-life with half a family, with half a purpose, that it could guide me to the right side of the road, could take me to the right place, because I can't seem to find my way.

I'm glad that my last few years here have accomplished something good, something which has given me a purpose for hanging on, for staying and living with the destruction I feel every morning, when their images disintegrate no matter how hard I try to hang on to them.

I'm going to miss Ben the most. In the spare bedroom, I have left him the Thomas the Tank Engine set that he wants. There is plenty of track to build and I have boxed away new engines for the days when he begins to miss me, for the days when he asks where his 'Chunkle' is.

I want to thank you, Soph, for giving me a reason to live, for letting me be part of your family and most of all, for being my friend, but I know now that it's not enough. You have stayed here because of me. I know that the mad McLaughlins want you to go to Derry every summer, how you don't go over for Christmas because you don't like to think of me alone, but I know how much you want it too, to be surrounded by them. For Ben to be surrounded by cousins and second cousins, by aunties and uncles, and be spoilt every day by Nanny and Grampa, especially once your new baby girl, Alice, is born.

I watch the three of you together, the way you look at your boys when they play in the garden, the way you hold on to Sam as if you're the one that's blind, and it fills me with grief.

I've been selfish, I know I have, but not any more. It's time to let you have your family without me hanging about on the sidelines.

By the time you get this, I will be gone. No mistakes this time.

It's time for me to start living again, to fill the other half of my life.

I'll send you the address once I'm settled. The restaurant I've found needs work – just like me, and I will need time to fix us both.

See you on the other side,

Charlie.

x

Acknowledgements

The First Time I Saw You began as a very different book. It has been shaped and moulded, loved and championed by so many that I don't honestly know where to begin thanking people, so I'll start as before, with the woman who made my life as a writer possible: my wonderful agent, Amanda Preston. When you learn about literary agents as a newbie writer, you learn about the contracts they negotiate, the doors they open and the advice they give you . . . what you don't hear about is the voice at the end of the phone talking you off the ledge when you're having a meltdown, the ideas and inspiration they pass on to you when trying to karate chop writer's block and the endless hours they work behind the scenes. Thank you Amanda, for everything.

My next words of gratitude go to my wonderful editor Jennifer Doyle. Jen is there at every stage, always answering my stupid questions even when she's on her way home, always speaking sense – yep . . . there was *way* too much sick in this book! And always cheering me along. She is Mr McLaughlin Senior's biggest fan and am I hers.

To Katie Sunley, who has been a wonderful support through the whole editorial process, even going so far as to send me a Google map so I could find my way from my hotel to the RNA Awards, I'd be lost (literally) without you.

And Phoebe Swinburn, who has now gone on to pastures new. I will miss working with you so much, you have been an absolute dream to share this journey with; there at every turn with a smile and a tweet. You're an absolute goddess and will continue to take the world by storm.

Huge thanks go to all at ILA who work tirelessly on my behalf, giving my words sexy accents all over the world.

The biggest of thankyous go to the writing community. This job can be an incredibly lonely process but thankfully I'm part of some amazingly supportive Facebook writing and reading groups. The Fiction Café admin staff who work so very hard to make it such a wonderful, safe environment to be part of, I'm so incredibly grateful for everything you all do. Your support over the last year is something that I continue to cherish. Wendy Clarke, I count my lucky stars every day that you created this group, thank you. A special mention to the following members who are often the ones I turn to when I'm having a rough day or when I've had some exciting news: Jenny Kennedy, Kate Baker, Julie Morris, Natali Drake and Kiltie Jackson . . . you're all rock stars.

I'd be nowhere near as savvy about the publishing industry if it wasn't for the Savvy Authors' Snug! Ahoy to all the members, thank you for helping me, laughing with/at me and for your constant support. We might all be slightly mad but at least we're in the very best of company!

To the RNA for their support and guidance, I'm hoping to see you all again very soon.

I have some very dear friends who I left behind when I changed my career but who never leave me behind. They are my shoulders to cry on, my openers of prosecco and the most focused of focus groups. Thank you to Emma Jackson, Claire Ashley, Julie Henry and Louise Brindley-Jones.

This book wouldn't have been finished at all if I didn't have my very special writing buddy Nicki Smith working alongside me. She is the kindest, most generous person I know. She listens as I babble on about my ideas, my worries, my hopes, my waist size, my bladder control and my word count. You are my rock.

The greatest of thanks to my mad family, both close and extended, and without whom there would be no fodder for my books!

And last in my acknowledgements but always first in my heart: Russ, Ethan, Ally, Max and Bean, without you all, I wouldn't be able to find my way.

Read more by Emma Cooper!

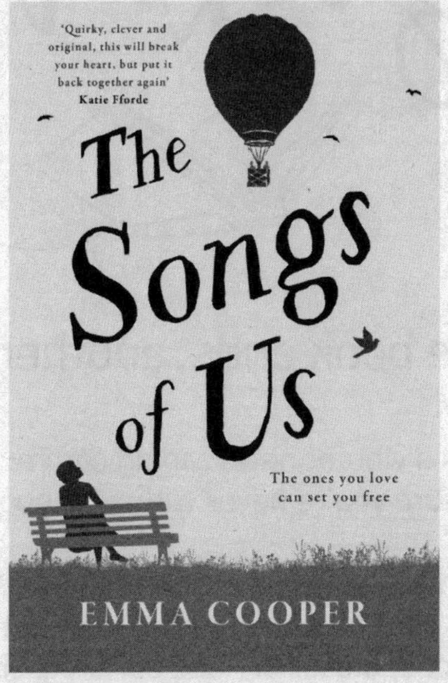

'Our life – no matter what happens in between – starts and ends with a heartbeat: our own personal rhythm, our own song'

Available now